THE
HIGH PRIEST'S DAUGHTER

THE NETWORK SERIES
by Katie Cross

Mildred's Resistance

Miss Mabel's School for Girls

The Isadora Interviews

Antebellum Awakening

The High Priest's Daughter

War of the Networks

THE
HIGH PRIEST'S DAUGHTER

Katie Cross

KW

The High Priest's Daughter

Young Adult Fantasy

Text copyright ©2015 by Katie Cross

Cover designed by Jenny Zemanek with Seedlings Online at www.seedlingsonline.com
Typesetting by Chris Bell, Atthis Arts at www.atthisarts.com
Ebook formatting by Kella Campbell with Ebooks Done Right at www.ebooksdoneright.com

Published by KCWriting.
Visit www.kcrosswriting.com for more information.

ISBN (paperback)   978-0-9915319-9-8
(ebook)   978-0-9915319-8-1

Visit the author at www.kcrosswriting.com

To Ta-rah, Beaner, and Scholes-woman.

Forever.

The Southern Network

Going to the Southern Network made me more nervous than opening a bag of hissing cats.

Southern Network witches were known to be hostile, behave brutishly, and hate women anywhere outside the kitchen. Three things that didn't particularly endear me, a seventeen-year-old female witch who never left home without my sword, to their way of life.

"Well, Bianca, are you ready to meet High Priest Mikhail?" Marten asked me with a half-grin. The sun sank in the horizon, as useless as a paperweight, giving light but no warmth. Marten wouldn't allow me to use magic to transport to our meeting in the Southern Network because I'd never been there before. "Too great a risk," he'd said with a little *tsk* of his teeth. "Transporting without ever having been to a place, or at least near it, is just asking for trouble." So we'd been riding in the cold carriage for over an hour, watching the glacial landscape glide past. Marten didn't have to ride with me, of course, but he was thoughtful in that regard.

"I think the more appropriate question is whether Mikhail is ready to meet me," I said, irritable after jostling over the terrible, icy roads.

Marten chuckled, but it didn't quite reach his eyes. Nothing made him truly laugh anymore, not since the love of his life, our previous High Priestess Mildred, died eight months before, in the summer.

"I won't be the first Assistant to ever cross borders with an Ambassador," I said, pushing thoughts of Mildred aside. "But I may be the first female Assistant brave enough to venture into the Southern Network. Don't you think?"

"You're not breaking any laws," Marten replied as if convincing both of us. "The Mansfeld Pact between the four Networks allows for Assistants to accompany the Ambassador outside their Network on official business, it's just that not many have. Certainly not to the cold tundras of the Southern Network, anyway."

"Now seems as good a time as ever to break tradition. A war is about to start, isn't it? Let's add more chaos into the mix. It's a habit of witches in my family."

Marten laughed again—much louder this time—but I'd been serious.

Through the forest of thick evergreens I caught occasional glimpses of Mikhail's looming ice castle. The second month of winter gripped the Southern Network with relentless strength, forcing me to use a flame incantation to generate heat so my fingers didn't freeze. A little ball of flame hovered between my cupped hands, sparking and warm.

Even the castle seemed to feel the bitter effects of its southern residence. Frost clung to the outer facade of stone, sparkling in crystalline shades of blue and white. Narrow turrets poked the charcoal sky. Unlike Chatham Castle in the Central Network, which was made of warm gray stones, boasted ten turrets, and sprawled out like a tall, lazy mountain, the Southern Network palace was skinny and narrow. What it lacked in girth it made up for in height, breaking apart in only five or six pieces with the shortest turrets towering at least fifteen stories. Snow capped most of the evergreen trees here, which pressed right up to the castle.

"Prepare yourself," Marten said under his breath, shooting me a sharp glance. His hazel eyes remained warm despite his severity. "And let me do all the speaking."

"I strive only to be an obedient female in the eyes of the South," I quipped. The carriage moved from a bouncing dirt road onto paved cobblestones. "Isn't your head cold?"

He ran a hand over his bare head. "Being cold builds character," he said. Before Mildred died, he'd looked like a man in the prime of his life. Middle thirties, lithe shoulders, an occasional smile in a serious bearing. But her death had taken its toll on him, and he no longer used magic to transform his looks the way many older witches did. Marten was somewhere in his seventies, perhaps older if the wrinkles around his face and the way his skin sagged off his bones meant anything. I'd worked as his Assistant for the last eight months, and he'd taken me under his wing in a grandfatherly kind of way.

"If being cold builds character, then I'm the most well-rounded witch in Antebellum," I muttered, and my breath fogged out in billows. I stared out the window, memorizing the landscape. We didn't have trees like this in Letum Wood, the forest that spanned most of the Central Network. Ours were massive and thick, hiding dangerous secrets. The forests here seemed distant and sharp, more indifferent than treacherous. I tightened my grip on my sword, Viveet. She glowed a bright blue in her sheath under my touch, comforting me. We'd arrive soon, and I didn't intend to leave her in the carriage. They'd have to pry her from my frozen hands before I went anywhere unknown and hostile without her. A little burst of magic stirred in my chest at my agitation, the way it always did, but settled with a sigh.

The carriage halted ten minutes later. A long, slim stairway led to a single wooden door. Southern Guardians lined the walkway, hovering so close I could have touched the shiny gold buttons on their gray wool jackets. Frost covered their swords and turned their cheeks bright pink.

"Well, the castle is simple," I said, climbing out of the carriage and studying the straight facade of the building. I could appreciate the intimidation factor of their forbidding, silent welcome.

"Functional," Marten said. "Let's get inside."

We moved quickly up the stairs, stopping at the top when a male witch with sweeping light hair and dark eyes moved into our path. He had a small, scrunched face, as if he wrinkled it in surprise all the time. Just like the Southern Guardians, his intense expression made me feel like a dirty pot.

"Dmitri," Marten called jovially. "It's good to see you again. Bianca, this is Dmitri, the Ambassador for the Southern Network. He and I have worked together for almost twenty years. Dmitri, this is Bianca, my Assistant."

Dmitri's small eyes slid over to me in question. I held his gaze, but couldn't suppress a shiver down my spine. His frigid stare rivaled the freezing temperature.

"Velcome, Miss Bianca," Dmitri finally said, pronouncing his words with the exaggerated, crisp accent of the Southern Network. "You are daughter to the great High Priest Derek, are you not?"

"I am."

"Hmm. Vat are you here for?"

"To meet with Mikhail," I said before Marten could answer for me.

Dmitri's lips puckered into a sour frown. "This is an . . . unexpected surprise." He lifted an eyebrow in accusation, his eyes falling to Viveet beneath my heavy, fur-lined cape. "His Highness does not like surprises."

"She'll be no problem, Dmitri," Marten said. "She's here to learn, not negotiate."

The rounded, wooden door behind Dmitri swung open with the heavy *thud* of a falling lock. A wave of heat flooded over us. "Vatever you say," Dmitri drawled, indicating for us to follow him into the main corridor.

We stepped into a long hall filled with white and blue banners depicting a snarling polar bear—the Southern Network flag. A fire roared in a great hearth to the left, and a sweeping staircase led up a pair of unlit steps to the right. Unlike Chatham Castle, which never stopped moving and breathing and living, this castle sat in austere quiet. Not a worker or a Guardian or a politician broke the unnerving silence. How could the center of a Network, the very heart of a vast land, be so calm?

"Come," Dmitri said. "Ve von't keep him vaiting. He vill entertain you in the throne room."

The narrow hallway led us deeper into the castle. We stopped at a set of broad double doors decorated with sparkling gems on the hinges and the doorknob. The citizens of the Southern Network had never been known for their humility. Or their height.

"His Highness vaits inside," Dmitri announced with one lingering, uncertain look at me. He grasped both golden handles and pushed the doors open wide, spreading them into a dim room of war.

Paintings of battle scenes filled every nook and cranny of the room, leaving little wall space. A detailed tapestry displaying a particularly gory fight spread across the back wall. Chipped axes. Broken swords. A shield encrusted with diamonds. I could barely take in the sparkling, deadly glamour. Greatest of all the many decorations was Mikhail himself, the High Priest of the Southern Network.

"Your Highness," Dmitri declared. "You have . . . visitors."

Dmitri left us on a furry white rug of polar bear fur, standing before the terrible glare of Mikhail's calculating eyes. What I could see of his eyes, anyway, which were almost lost in the folds of his face, so small as to be mostly slits. Mikhail, a squat man, boasted the same compressed face shared by most of the witches I'd already seen here. His legs weren't long enough to touch the ground from where he sat, so they dangled freely, like a child's. A shaggy mane of reddish-brown hair stood straight out from his head. Dangling gems swayed on his red beard, where they'd been braided in. A bright opal the size of my fist hung from the longest braid of all, nearly touching his barrel chest.

"Velcome, Marten," Mikhail boomed. His eyes disappeared into his face when his forehead ruffled. "You have brought a voman. Vy vould you do this thing?"

The malice in his voice reverberated through his chamber. I put my hand on Viveet under my cloak. Dmitri had vanished. No Assistant, servant, or other stirring of life attended to Mikhail except for a scantily clad woman wearing gold fabric and an apron of gems. She lingered behind his left shoulder with haughty disregard, her face half-hidden behind a veil drawn across everything but her eyes.

"My Assistant, Bianca," Marten said without apology. "Bianca, this is His Highness Mikhail of the Southern Network."

I inclined my head and curtsied, but didn't say a word. Mikhail continued to glare at me. I tightened my grip on Viveet.

"I don't care who she is! Get her out of my castle. The only vomen I allow are my vife and concubines."

"She stays with me."

Marten's firm, stubborn tone made me wonder if he had *other* reasons for bringing me. Putting up a strong front in the face of Mikhail's demands, for one. Or setting Mikhail on edge for another. A display of fearlessness, perhaps? Marten's prowess with both magic and politics couldn't be understated, which was only one of the reasons Papa considered Marten one of his most trusted advisors. No doubt he had some angle behind bringing me.

Mikhail glowered from his throne of gold. His wealth—or perhaps obsession with it—came from extensive mining in the summer months. The Mansfeld Pact forbade trade and travel between Networks, which meant that all the precious stones they harvested remained within the Southern Network. They used to have metals in abundance, but either they'd mined them all or couldn't reach them anymore. Their desperate need for new metal for swords had likely pushed them into a forbidden alliance with the Western Network, something Marten wanted to get to the bottom of today. If Mikhail's desperation ran deep enough to form an illegal alliance with the Western Network, war would follow.

"It's good to see you again, Mikhail," Marten said, bowing at the waist. "I trust you're willing to discuss Derek's concerns with us."

Mikhail scowled, but must have sensed that he wouldn't get his way. "Begin. Vat do you vant?"

"We've come to ensure that the Mansfeld Pact still stands. Rumors have surfaced lately that you are forming an alliance with the Western Network. That, of course, cannot be true."

"Rumors from vhere?" Mikhail demanded, planting his hands on the side of his throne and leaning forward. The opal in his beard swung back and forth. "Vhere do you hear this?"

"Everywhere."

Mikhail leaned back. "They lie."

"Is talk of your shortage of metals a lie also? Without metal, one cannot make a trustworthy sword."

"A lie! Ve are fine!"

"I didn't ask how you were doing," Marten countered. "I asked whether you needed metals to forge weaponry for your Guardians."

Mikhail flung his hand in the air. "You ask too much questions. Ve have broken no laws. The Southern Network is stronger than all Networks!"

My eyes fell on a smaller seat, one carved of wood, looking painfully bland next to the sparkling opulence of Mikhail's gold and ruby chair. I stared at the two words in the *Yazika* language of the Southern Network inscribed across the top of the chair. I'd seen the writings of the South before but only knew a few words. The inscription on the chair said, *Second Greatest.* Likely the less-than-impressive throne of Mikhail's *voman.*

Mikhail watched me take in the details of his war room with the same insolent expression Dmitri had given me. Too annoyed to be frightened, I stared back until he looked away with a mutter.

"Derek simply wants your reassurance that you won't turn to Dane in the Western Network for metals to forge more weapons. Doing so would break the century-long agreement that's existed between the Central, Eastern, Western, and Southern Networks. It would also bring a war upon you from our Network that you could never prepare for."

Marten's tone had dropped, sounding not just confident, but certain.

"You insult me!" Mikhail said, throwing his hand in a rude gesture. "Vhy vould I need anyone else? No! Ve need no one. Ve are strong and healthy. Tell Derek to leave us alone, and take this voman out of my house! She's not allowed. You insult me!"

The concubine behind Mikhail shifted, causing tiny bells along the bottom of her pants to tinkle. Marten didn't respond, so neither did I, although my fingers itched to show Mikhail exactly how powerful a woman *could* be. I'd chop the opal right out of his beard and take it home to show Merrick.

"It's always good to have your reassurance," Marten said. "For we are always watching, and always aware of all borders."

Mikhail shifted in his seat. "Go. My time is precious and not to be vasted on you. I can't stand the voman. She's smug and annoying. You insult me!"

I winked.

"Leave!" Mikhail screamed, leaping to his feet. "Leave my house! You are not velcome back! Leave the voman next time. If I see her again, I kill her!"

Dmitri appeared at our side.

"We trust in your continued goodwill toward the Mansfeld Pact,"

Marten said with a steely tone that startled Mikhail into silence. "Breaking such a powerful oath would shatter you. Not a witch in your Network could do magic for the rest of his life. Not even Dane and the West Guards can protect you from Derek's wrath if you combine forces with the West and try to wage war on the Central Network. That much I can promise you. Derek will not be bullied."

Mikhail swallowed and seemed to think over what Marten said for the briefest moment before he exploded again.

"You think I don't know?" he screamed. "I know the Pact! Now go! Leave! You've insulted me by bringing a voman, and now you insult me by assuming I have no brains. LEAVE!"

"Go now," Dmitri said under his breath. "Or he'll curse you beyond recognition."

"He'll die if he tries," Marten said, and Dmitri shrunk away. While I wanted to give Mikhail the opportunity to try to hurt me—if I didn't get my own revenge, Papa would kill Mikhail with his bare hands—Marten didn't seem inclined to be hostile in another Network. He grabbed my arm.

"Come, *voman*," he said quietly. "Let's go home."

A Unique Position

The next day I faced a far more formidable foe: My old teacher Miss Scarlett and a one-on-one private etiquette lesson. I preferred Mikhail's less-than-cordial hospitality to Miss Scarlett's love affair with rules, but I went because Marten had asked—even insisted—that I perfect my manners.

Miss Scarlett eyed me with disapproval when I eased into the room with thirty seconds left to spare. Had I been late by even ten seconds, she would have locked me out and forced me to reschedule. I knew by experience. Explaining to Marten that I'd missed my first class because of a ten-second fluke had been downright embarrassing.

She wore her dark hair in a severe bun, smelled like cumin, and enjoyed watching witches squirm in her presence. She maintained the tightest, straightest spine I'd ever seen. I'd only caught her smiling once, and even that had been debatable. Despite her rigid personality, she'd given me a charm bracelet last summer that had saved my life in a fight against the vilest witch of all: Miss Mabel. When I tried to return it later she refused, telling me to keep it in case I needed it later.

Miss Scarlett had taught at Miss Mabel's School for Girls when I attended, before Papa raised her to Head of Education over the entire Central Network after Mildred died. Head of Education was a stressful position, especially with all the schools that Mildred established. Education, and consequently the Network, had flourished under Mildred's reign. Unfortunately, Miss Scarlett's workload lent itself to a militaristic schedule when she taught.

"The Eastern Network is a place of art, sophistication, and refinement," Miss Scarlett began without preamble. "They respect creativity, live from the sea, and seek peace. For the last century, the ruling family of Aldana have maintained a tradition of hosting Ambassadors overnight. Your trip to the Southern Network was short, no doubt. But it would be an insult to Eastern Network culture to come and go the same day. Consequently, you shall spend the night, dine with the High Priest and High Priestess, and then meet with them to discuss business before you return."

"Why?" I blurted out. "It seems like a waste of time."

Or just another chance to mess up somehow. She shot me a severe glare. Exasperated, I raised my hand and waited for her to acknowledge me.

"Bianca, you may now speak."

"Why do I have to stay the night?"

"Because it's custom. Something I'm hoping we can cram into your stubborn head before you leave in two days."

I fought back a sigh. She certainly wasn't wrong that I lacked etiquette and social skills. Determining which fork to use out of ten choices didn't appeal to me much, not when a forest with running trails awaited me outside. Still, it *was* my job, and though I was occasionally locked in a castle all day, working as Assistant to the Ambassador had definite perks. Traveling all over Antebellum was just one of them.

"When you eat with a crowd of witches, it's not polite to put your elbows or arms on the table." Miss Scarlett stood at the end of a long table in the formal Dining Room. I stifled a yawn. "You also shouldn't yawn or slurp your soup."

She walked behind me and grabbed my shoulders, straightening my posture. I grimaced but didn't complain. She'd tackle me to the ground before she'd let me get away with poor form.

"Keep your back straight."

"Yes, Miss Scarlett."

Although I was going on eighteen years old and had graduated from an intense foray into the Network educational system with my life intact—no mean feat when Miss Mabel was my teacher—I still lived under Miss Scarlett's dutiful thumb. I wondered, as I dipped a silver spoon into a bowl of creamy soup, if Miss Scarlett felt as annoyed by it as I did.

"What is the appropriate way to address another Network's High Priest?" she asked.

"By his chosen title."

I spoke before I ate and made certain not to slurp the soup from the spoon. She nodded in approval and continued her original course of pacing back and forth. I dipped the spoon carefully back into the bowl, unnerved when she stopped and stared at me. I froze. What could I have done wrong in five seconds? Something big, undoubtedly. I glanced up from underneath my eyelashes, the spoonful of soup hovering above the bowl.

"Do I have something on my face, Miss Scarlett?" I asked. Last time I'd shown up for her etiquette class I'd had a stick in my hair.

"What do you want out of your life now that your Inheritance Curse is gone, Bianca?"

What did I want from life? What kind of question was that? I was only seventeen. Seventeen-year-olds didn't have life figured out.

Unless you're Leda, I thought, considering my best friend. *But she's planned her life out since she was three.* Considering how painful the last year of my life had been, I was doing exactly what I wanted. Living free.

I opted for the safest route: innocence. "What do you mean?"

Last summer, I won a magical fight against Miss Mabel on the night she murdered the High Priestess. Thanks to Leda, I also survived a curse and a binding that should have killed me when I turned seventeen. Staying alive despite my rampant magical powers proved difficult enough—every time I became agitated or emotional, magic flared with a little burst of life inside me. While mourning Mama's death, the powers had spiraled out of control; I proved dangerous to myself and others. The powers were mostly tolerable now, as long as I gave them an outlet by running through my old home, Letum Wood.

"You know what I mean," Miss Scarlett said, pulling me from my reverie. I never could get away with feigning innocence around her, so I gave up trying and set the spoon back down. "Do you want to be a Council Member?"

I recoiled, nose scrunched. Council Member? Live in an office surrounded by paperwork, scrolls, and messages? Never.

"That's what I thought," she replied drily, studying my horrified grimace. "How about Ambassador? Your current job puts you in line for that perfectly. Marten is certainly training you well. He's an attentive mentor."

My thoughts skimmed over Marten's job. We traveled around the Central Network often and would soon venture to the Eastern Network. All things that no one else could do, according to the Mansfeld Pact. Although we stayed more active than Council Members, we spent just as many hours in the office as out. Did I enjoy my job? It wasn't bad. Certainly wasn't the worst.

Did I want to dedicate my life to it? I didn't know yet. I'd already heard word that a few girls I went to school with were engaged, but marriage wasn't a route I'd considered much.

"Being an Ambassador isn't the worst," I said.

"You're in a unique position," she said in an almost word-for-word intonation of something that both Marten and Leda had already said. "You can get an early start on your future. By the time most girls your age start to make these decisions, you'll be well established."

Defying all etiquette, I propped my elbows on the table and leaned forward.

"What if there isn't much of a future for me to plan for?" I retorted. Miss Scarlett's eyebrows rose—the only indication that I'd taken her by surprise.

"You mean because we may be at war soon."

"Yes."

Something lurked inside her annoyance with me. A flash of compassion, perhaps? Living in the castle meant I'd come to know Miss Scarlett much better in the past year. While she was unyielding on rules, I occasionally sensed a rarely-seen soft side. Miss Scarlett had a story, and I was determined to figure it out one day.

"Set aside the war," she said, shoving my elbows off the table with a spell. I pitched forward, nearly smacking my nose on the polished wood. "If there was something you could do every day that would make you happy, what would it be?"

I reared back in surprise. No one had asked me that question. "Anything?" I asked, testing the waters. She nodded, her lips pursed.

"What brings you joy?"

"Joy?"

What did happiness and joy have to do with planning my future? Weren't adults supposed to suffer through their careers?

"Yes, joy. Don't you want a career that brings you joy?"

"I've never thought of my career making me happy."

Miss Scarlett lifted one eyebrow. "If you don't like what you do every day, you'll live a pretty miserable existence."

I couldn't fault her logic. "But I don't know what I want."

A little smile crossed her face, as if she fondly remembered such aimless, youthful days. "Then I would recommend finding something that you're passionate about so you aren't ornery for the rest of your career."

My whole life up until last summer had centered on survival, not passion. I wasn't sure I knew how to plan ahead. Finishing a Network school like Miss Mabel's School for Girls vaulted students from the protective bubble of school straight into adulthood. Considering that I'd finished two and a half years early, I'd embraced my freedom with open arms, but now had no idea what to do with myself.

"How did you decide what career you wanted, Miss Scarlett?" I asked. A thoughtful look crossed her face, and for a moment I lost her to a memory.

"A very dear witch encouraged me to discover what I wanted to do the rest of my life, to find out what brought me the most joy and to pursue it. That's what I did. That's what I'm trying to do for you today."

"Teaching? You wanted to teach for the rest of your life?"

She smiled at my wide eyes. "Yes," she said. "I wanted to teach."

"Where did you grow up?" I asked.

"I grew up in an orphanage in the Northern Covens, near Newberry."

My eyes widened again in surprise. I'd been to Newberry before with Mama and Papa. It lay near the border of the Eastern Network and not too far from the border of the Northern Network.

"You were an orphan?" I whispered, following up with a lame, "Oh! I'm sorry. I-I didn't mean it like that."

"It's quite all right," she said, straightening her jacket. "You had no way of knowing. My mother died giving birth to my younger sister. My father followed soon after."

My mind launched back to the afternoon my grandmother died while I was in school at Miss Mabel's. Miss Scarlett had been at my side, helping me get through those first few moments of shock. And when I climbed into the carriage to go home, she had a look in her eyes that told me she'd known sorrow. Instead of saying something else insensitive, I waited to see if she would say more. When she didn't, I turned the conversation.

"And teaching was what you wanted to do for the rest of your life," I repeated with a lingering touch of astonishment. I couldn't imagine putting up with a bunch of teenage girls that, like me, really didn't want to learn the things she had to teach us.

"Yes. I've never regretted it. But we aren't talking about me, are we? We're talking about you, and you still haven't answered my question, though you've done an admirable job of avoiding it."

I smiled sheepishly.

If I could do anything that would make me happy, I'd run through Letum Wood every day. Plant a garden. Live under the thick canopy of trees that, while dangerous, felt far more like home to me than the walls of Chatham Castle did. But that could never happen. Papa was here at the castle as High Priest for the rest of his life, and my home and heart belonged to Papa. Besides, running wild under the trees would never move my life forward. I'd begin to despise the routine, knowing that I never really did anything important.

"I don't know," I admitted. "I honestly don't."

She nodded once, looking as if she'd expected that answer all along. "It doesn't have to be decided today, but it would be wise to attempt to figure it out before you turn forty."

She walked behind me, the skirt of her dress swaying, her back straight and perfect.

"Now, let's continue with your soup."

The soup had turned cold, so I warmed it with an incantation, my mind whirring with questions. The rest of the lesson passed in a blur of books on my head, straight spines, and constant shoulder correction. Once finished, I stopped in the doorway and glanced at her over my shoulder.

"Thank you, Miss Scarlett. I'll think over what you said."

She paused, seeming surprised, then nodded. Her tight lips softened. "You're welcome, Bianca. Let me know what you decide."

Winter cloaked Letum Wood in a shroud of gray and white early the next morning. Even though most leaves had fallen months before, I still couldn't see the sky through the canopy of branches and icicles. A low fog crawled across the ground and wrapped around my feet while I stared, waiting to begin my morning run.

"Contemplating the mysteries of life?" asked a droll voice from just behind me. I whirled around, coming face to face with Merrick. He stood only a pace away from me, so close that I could feel the flush of his breath on my cheek. His proximity seemed to create new gravity, and for a moment my balance felt off.

"Just looking at the forest," I said, hating myself for sounding breathless. My mind told me to take a step back, put some space between us, but I didn't. "It's beautiful even in the winter."

He lifted an eyebrow. "Sometimes," he said, glancing past me with his emerald green eyes. "Most of the time it just looks dead."

His blonde-streaked brown hair, worn to the shoulders, had been pulled back in a neat queue, leaving his stubbled jaw glimmering in sandy tones. A protective leather vest lined with pieces of metal along the edges hid his broad, strong shoulders. The fluid confidence of his movements made him more striking, if possible. His unfortunate attractiveness often flustered me. Even *I* would admit that. Although not out loud, of course. He'd proven to be a surprising friend that understood more of my strange, wild-child ways than most.

Disconcertingly understanding, in fact.

His eyes suddenly seemed to laugh at me, and I realized with a blush that I'd been staring at him. Heat flooded my cheeks. "Well," I said, turning back to face Letum Wood and regain my equilibrium. "Shall we get going?"

"I have a busy day today," he said, adjusting his half-armor, which he always wore these days while out in Letum Wood. "So let's just run for an hour."

I started onto the trail, my feet clad in a protective pair of leather shoes and my braid bouncing between my shoulder blades. Merrick didn't care that I wore pants—something that most witches gawked at. But running in a skirt rarely ended well.

We didn't usually speak much while running; sometimes we went the entire hour without exchanging a word. So when he interrupted the silence halfway into the run, I knew something had to be on his mind.

"I spoke with Sanna today," he said as he ducked a tree branch. "She says they've found a few more poachers in Letum Wood trying to kill the dragons."

"Seriously? They didn't learn from the last poachers?"

Last summer I'd caught two poachers trying to kill the blue dragon. Through a series of lucky events, and the first explosion of my rampant magical powers, I saved the blue. The poachers were executed for treason.

"Don't worry," he said, barely out of breath although we'd been running for thirty minutes. "The dragons ate them."

His nonchalance in the face of such terrible deaths nearly made me laugh. Then I remembered the glisten of saliva over the dragon's pearly white teeth and thought better of it. Poacher or not, death by dragon would be a horrid ending.

"Angelina must be sending witches to kill the dragons," I said, catching myself before I fell on a slippery patch of snow. "Miss Mabel certainly isn't."

"Getting rid of the dragons would cripple Chatham Castle. Sanna thinks most of the poachers are associated with the Factios."

"Good," I muttered. "One less gang member to worry about."

The idea of our castle in danger made me more uneasy than I'd admit. Chatham Castle stood as more than just a symbol of our Network—it housed nearly all of our leadership. A majority of Council Members kept houses in the Covens they oversaw, but most of the time all ten Council Members stayed at the castle. And, of course, other important figures like Papa, High Priestess Stella, the Head of Guardians, and the Head of Protectors dwelt within the castle's walls. If the castle fell, so would the Central Network. I imagined this was only part of the reason that the dragons were under a blood oath to protect it.

"Can I ask you a question?" I risked a peek over my shoulder on a straight stretch of trail. A flush had crept over Merrick's skin, and his face looked more rugged than ever. I quickly turned back around, but not for fear of tripping.

"Of course," he said.

I leapt a boulder and swung left when the trail forked. It would loop toward the castle, giving us another thirty-minute trail back.

"If the Western and Southern Networks form an alliance the way we suspect, and the Eastern Network does nothing, we'll have to face two Networks alone. Can we do that? Do we have the strength?"

Merrick didn't respond right away. "We may not have a choice," he said, as if he'd realized it long before. Knowing Merrick, he probably had.

"You didn't answer my question."

"Yes, I did."

I shot him a brief glare. "Well, I don't think we're strong enough to hold back two Networks. No matter how much Papa prepares."

"We could hold them off."

"But not win. Miss Mabel attacked us with Clavas when she killed Mildred. That means she's had access to at least some Almorran magic. Maybe the lesser scrolls? If not the *Book of Spells* itself," I added grudgingly. The idea that Miss Mabel or Angelina might have already found the magic sent a little ripple of fear through me. The lesser Almorran scrolls were just rumors, but so was the *Book of Spells* until Miss Mabel showed up with Clavas. The nasty creatures originated from Almorran magic, which meant someone had the scrolls, the *Book of Spells*, or both.

"Miss Mabel is in the dungeons, B. She can't hurt you."

"But her mother, Angelina, is not."

He didn't try to counter my statement. "My point is this," I said, "we're going to need some outside help. What if we sent two or three Protectors up to the Northern Network to see if they'd help us? Maybe they'll join the war."

I monitored his reaction—despite the fact that we were running—to see what he thought. His eyebrows shot up. He skirted a large root sticking up into the path and landed hard in a pile of slush, spraying the back of my pants.

"The Northern Network isolated themselves from the other Networks almost three hundred years ago," he said with a dismissive wave of his hand. "They won't want anything to do with us now. Why enter a war that isn't their own? Besides, some witches think that no one even lives up there anymore."

I rolled my eyes. "I'm sure they're still there. Entire populations don't just disappear because we haven't heard from them. Besides, who knows? It's worth a shot, isn't it?"

"The Northern mountains are treacherous, B. There are so many peaks and crevasses and ravines that transporting there blind is a death wish. Anyone who went to search it out would have to travel on foot, and it could take the messenger half a year to reach any civilization. Assuming they didn't get lost, of course."

I dropped back on a wider stretch of trail. "How do you know?" I asked, eyeing him.

"History," he said. "I actually enjoy learning from it, unlike some witches."

I ignored the direct jab. "What of history?"

"The Northern Network cities and villages lie so far north that trade routes were risky, even fatal. It's part of the reason they decided to close the routes and block us out. They could self-sustain and grew tired of the wars breaking out between Networks."

Despite his misgivings with my plan, I felt more convinced than ever that the Northern Network might be an untapped resource. At least Merrick wasn't one of the witches lulled back into a sense of security. After the High Priestess died and Miss Mabel was locked away, the Southern Network pulled its Guardians back from the wall separating our Networks, and the Western Network abandoned its quest to block our river, leaving the Borderlands like a dog with its tail between its legs.

Merrick shrugged the conversation off. "Let the idea of scouting out the Northern Network go, B. It's not worth pursuing. Look, I'm going to take the lead because time is running out, and I need to get back. We have a late mission tonight I need to plan."

"But—"

"No complaining. You need to work on your speed anyway, slow poke."

He sped off ahead of me, setting a more grueling pace. I'd be able to maintain it, but it would cost most of my energy and half of my patience. With a sigh, I took off after him. No matter how fast he ran, I *would* keep up with him.

I couldn't seem to help myself.

The esteemed Butler Reeves had shown up with a tray of tea and a plate of my favorite raspberry scones one bright morning the previous summer. After serving us—which felt so awkward that I'd finally taken the tea pot from him and told him I preferred to pour—he'd busied himself with alphabetizing our books and dusting the parlor, letting us know that he wasn't going to leave. Eight months had passed, and he still puttered around.

Despite his odd entrance into our life, Reeves said little, kept the apartment cozy, waged a war on the dust motes that cropped up, and glared when I left mud behind. Finally accepting the inevitable, Papa gave Reeves an adjacent room that connected to our apartment and effectively integrated the old man into the daily routine and fabric of our lives.

A warm fire crackled in the hearth when I stepped out of my room the next morning, greeting me with the homey scent of burning pine.

"Would you like breakfast, Miss Bianca?" Reeves asked, sending me a look that suggested I daren't refuse my daily porridge. Papa had been siphoning food into storage to prepare for possible war, which limited availability of the best breakfast items, like bacon. Fresh food was difficult to find in the winter anyway, so an already limited plate rapidly shrunk down to a mealy bowl of porridge for breakfast.

"Of course, Reeves," I said, brushing a few strands of wet hair off my shoulders, my cheeks still flushed from the morning run. "Thank you."

His piercing gaze deepened at my quick acquiescence. I snatched a piece of buttered bread next to the bowl of paste and hurried to the door.

"Thanks Reeves!" I called over my shoulder, and the door slammed behind me. Celebrating my porridge-free departure with a grin, I slipped around the corner and collided with a skinny body. My piece of bread smeared butter onto the rich velvet of a black cape.

"Hey!" a nasally voice called out, whirling around and taking my breakfast with it. "Watch it!"

"I'm sorry! I didn't—"

My hasty apology ended when I saw a familiar pair of wide ears and a pointy nose. Clive, the Coven Leader over Chatham City, glared at me down his long nose. He'd tried to remove Papa from his position as Head of Protectors last year by staging protests, one of which I accidentally attended. My uncontrolled magic had blown out of control, injuring ten witches. Clive had taken his complaint all the way to Mildred, the High Priestess, and I'd been restricted to the castle grounds. Just seeing Clive stirred a flutter of magic in my chest again, but I forced it down.

Clive's lips morphed into a sneer. "Bianca Monroe," he said. "What a delightful surprise."

"Coven Leader Clive."

"You should watch where you're going. It's not polite to run into your superiors in such a violent fashion. It could be construed in the eyes of the public as a hostile attack."

Clive's rat-like face drifted to another witch just behind him. He carried a small purple quill and a long scroll. The circular badge on his jacket identified him as a writer for the newsscroll, the *Chatham Chatterer*.

"Lovely," I muttered. Papa's reputation had suffered enough thanks to Clive, who continued to stage protests over Papa's *obsessive preparation for a war that clearly won't happen*. The last thing we needed was Clive telling all of the Central Network I had tried to attack him in the castle halls.

"If you'll excuse me," I said, clearing my throat. "I need to go to work."

"I was just interviewing for an article in the *Chatterer* on your father's decision to use Network funds to buy and store grain in case we go to war." Clive sidestepped into my path. "I think getting your opinion on the subject would be a . . . wonderful addition."

The reporter stepped forward eagerly, quill in hand. Papa didn't allow the *Chatterer* to interview me because of stupid questions like this, so I shot him a warning glare. He stumbled back again, swallowing.

"I don't think you want my opinion on this subject," I said.

"Oh," Clive whispered, his eyes alight. "But we very much do. You see, your father is blowing this supposed war out of proportion and it's costing witches currency. Witches don't like to part with their hard won currency. But I'm not sure that's something you understand since you live a charmed life in a castle and want for nothing."

Charmed life? My mother died in my arms, the High Priestess sacrificed her life for me, and up until last summer, I expected to die at age seventeen because of a curse. I bit back my retort and replaced it with a saccharine smile.

"Or some witches just like to be contrary because they're bored with their own lives. I hardly see how preparing for something that is entirely plausible hurts our Network at all."

Clive smiled with thin lips. I expected a forked tongue to flicker out. "We've seen no activity from the Western Network to indicate they may be hostile—hardly any activity from them at all since Mabel's attack, really—and the Southern Network allowed you to cross their borders a few days ago, am I right? Surely that's not a sign of a hostile Network."

"Perhaps Mikhail is smarter than that," I replied coolly. "Not allowing us in would be a blatantly hostile move. Any good leader planning a war would hide his plan for as long as possible by cooperating with every other Network. And any good leader like my father would prepare for the worst from the beginning. Don't you think?"

Clive's nostrils flared. "Your father is costing this Network currency and making fools of us!"

"Calm down," I said, stepping away from him. "You've made enough of a fool of yourself the past six years as Coven Leader that he doesn't need to help."

"Why I never—"

"Merry part, Clive." I pushed past him with a wave. "Enjoy your breakfast."

He fumed in my wake, unaware of the buttered piece of bread stuck to the back of his expensive cape.

Marten's office wouldn't have been a bad place to work had I been Leda and enjoyed being indoors, sitting in a stone cage while staring at a beautiful day passing by without regard for my imprisonment.

Unfortunately, I wasn't Leda. Not even close.

We traveled often enough that working for Marten had been mostly educational and exciting, but letters had to be answered and meetings attended. Unfortunately, today promised to be one of those dull office days. He normally tried to warn me in advance so I could mentally prepare. A long morning run usually helped, though my run-in with Clive left me in a foul mood.

"Marten, I just ran into—oh, merry meet, Papa."

I halted in my tracks in the doorway, startled to find Papa lounging in a chair across from Marten's desk, his brow furrowed. I'd just interrupted another of their chats. Marten had mentored Papa ever since he started as a Guardian, so Papa often turned to him for advice now that Mildred was gone and he ruled as Highest Witch.

"Come in, Bianca." Marten waved me in. "Derek and I were just discussing a few things. Nothing you can't hear."

Papa whacked me affectionately on the leg as I passed by him. "Marten's giving me advice on how to deal with a spunky teenage daughter with a mind of her own. What do you think we should do? Tie her up by her thumbs?"

"Build her a cottage in Letum Wood and force her to live in the trees," I said blithely. "That'll show her."

Papa balled up a piece of paper and threw it at me before standing. I stopped it mid-flight and turned it into a snowball that smacked him on the arm.

"Thank you, Marten," Papa said. "As always, your advice and support is much appreciated. I'll try your suggestions and let you know."

"It's my pleasure, High Priest," he replied cordially. Papa and Marten clasped forearms before Papa winked at me and disappeared out the door. I glanced ruefully at two stacks of envelopes that had accumulated overnight. How I loathed replying to messages. Most correspondences came from Border Guards or Coven Leaders who complained that their tomatoes weren't growing right because the Eastern Network was hexing them.

"I have good news," Marten said, settling back into his chair. "Once you finish those letters, I've found a few more libraries I want to search for the *Book of Spells*."

The bright sunlight, which reflected off a blanket of white snow outside, made the top of his bald head as shiny as a porcelain bowl. The fire crackled in the hearth, and a fresh cup of tea awaited me. Marten always had tea for me in the morning in his rigidly clean workspace that testified to his background as a Captain of the Guards before he became Ambassador. Paintings filled the blank spaces on the wall, and two padded chairs stood across from his desk. Other than my little desk in the corner, there wasn't much there.

"Oh?" I asked. "Where?"

"The Western Covens. I don't see any reason for the *Book of Spells* to be hidden there, but one never knows. We're getting desperate. We've searched every other Coven for the past eight months. These are the last of them."

The likelihood of finding the ancient grimoire of Almorran magic hidden in a random library wasn't good, but we had to try. We'd scoured every library and bookshop in the Central Network, hoping to find it before Angelina, Miss Mabel's mother. Most of the Central

Network thought Miss Mabel's imprisonment meant the end of the war, but I suspected differently. Angelina could be rallying her forces, trying to succeed where her daughter failed.

"I'll finish the letters soon." I slipped the first three off the top. "Then we can get out of here."

My motivation to finish the boring paperwork didn't change the fact that office business took time. After several hours of work, the scratch of quill against paper still droned on with endless disregard for my suffering. My eyes flickered up to the clock, and I stifled a low groan. It wasn't even ten o'clock yet. My stomach growled. Stupid Clive stole my good mood *and* my toast.

"You've only been here for two hours," Marten said in a droll voice. "Surely paperwork can't be *that* bad."

"Torture, really. I'd rather be strung up by my thumbs."

Marten chuckled. His calm, gentle exterior hid a quiet intensity. Only through working with him for the past eight months had I come to realize the degree of his magical skill and talent. When it came down to raw power, he rivaled Papa.

"I forgot to tell you," he said. "I sent a message to Newberry to order your carriage. You leave tomorrow morning for the Eastern Network. Very early tomorrow morning, so you'll want to transport to Newberry by five."

"Oh, right. A carriage ride." I'd forgotten that my first trip to the Eastern Network would require a carriage, just like our journey to the Southern Network. Despite my pleas that I'd rather transport—I'd transported to unknown places before—Marten wouldn't allow me to take any risks.

"It'll be a very educational ride for you," he said, interrupting my thoughts as if he'd read their direction. "There's more to a Network than just the diplomats, you know. Seeing the landscape and country-side is a rare privilege. I hope you can enjoy it."

According to the Mansfeld Pact, only a High Priest, High Priestess, Ambassador, Ambassador's Assistant, or a Protector or Guardian could cross the borders for these diplomatic meetings. I silenced the urge to complain; so few witches received such an opportunity. A two-day carriage ride wouldn't kill me.

"I'll make the best of it."

Marten continued. "Newberry is on the border of the Eastern Coven, which will cut down your riding time. I'll meet you at Magnolia Castle the next evening. You'll travel nonstop, under the protection of the white flag of the Ambassador."

A book slid off the top shelf of a bookcase behind him and landed on my desk with a heavy *thud*.

The History of Antebellum.

"Take that with you," he said. "Every Ambassador, and Assistant, needs to have a thorough understanding of history in order to do the job well."

"I'm not sure the horses will be able to carry me and such a massive tome," I said with a rueful grin. He returned it, and I settled back into the rhythm of responding to letters with a sigh.

False Confidence

The door to our private apartments slammed open that evening, admitting Papa with an ungracious belch of armor, leather, and blood. Reeves had just set out a simple dinner of beef stew.

"Grief, Papa," I said, rising to my feet. Dirt and sweat streaked down one side of his face, which was slowly morphing back into its regular form. Papa always transformed his appearance when working with the Protectors. "What happened?"

"Factios attack in Chatham City again."

Papa strode over to the water basin and splashed his face and hands, peering out the window with a quiet murmur. I followed his gaze to see plumes of smoke rising from Chatham City, a burning testament to the ongoing war between the Factios—a group of violent gang members—and the gypsies.

"Same kind of attack as last time?"

"They painted a bright red *A* on the road," he said. "Yes, I think it's safe to assume that it originated with Angelina, just like all the others."

A shiver ran through me. The Factios had stirred up trouble for months, but only when winter hit had their devastating attacks increased exponentially. A bright red *A* emerged during most of their vicious acts, leaving no doubt about where the Factios gained their power and resources. But their fearless leader had yet to make an appearance. Most of the Factios members that were caught and interrogated had never met Angelina. She worked through letters and word-of-mouth.

"So Angelina is still fighting through the Factios."

"Yes."

He ruffled my hair as he walked behind me and headed to his room to change. When he returned, hair wet and body scrubbed clean, he sat down and dove right into his stew without a word.

"Do you have to go back to work tonight?" I asked. He nodded. I hid my disappointment by picking up my bowl and drinking from the lip.

"I need to review Tiberius's plan for training Guardians for an attack in the Southern Covens," he said. "After that, Stella and I have a meeting with the Head of Highways that I've put off too many times."

Stella was the new High Priestess, empowered a month after Mildred died. At first, Coven Leader Clive had protested Papa's choice. According to tradition established by the first High Priestess, Esmelda, High Priests, High Priestesses, Heads of Guardians, and Heads of Protectors were not allowed to marry, so they would put all their focus into their careers. Stella had been married once, and had even had a young son, but both had died during the Dark Days. She served as Council Member over the Southern Covens and never remarried. Most of the Network shrugged Stella's history off. She had been a beloved leader for so long that it seemed only natural to appoint her. Clive hadn't gained much traction fighting against Stella, so he eventually gave up.

"Forgive me, Your Highness, but your arm is bleeding." Reeves stood just behind Papa, studying the skin above Papa's right elbow. Papa inspected it with a grunt.

"The Factios used something," he said, forehead ruffling. "It was a kind of weak burning potion. They put it in bottles that they threw into a fire. The bottles exploded and sent the potion flying everywhere. It burned everything it touched. Some of it must have rubbed off on my skin."

I walked to his chest of healing tinctures and rifled through it until I found the bottle marked *remoulade*. Grandmother's favorite.

"Here," I said, grabbing a napkin. "I'll put remoulade on."

The wound looked normal enough—open tissue, blood, and swelling—but something about it smelled different.

"Your wound smells like . . . mustard."

"I don't know what it is," Papa said, plowing through his meal with his good arm. "But I've never seen it before."

"That's odd."

If it had caused this much damage to Papa after minor exposure, I wondered what it had done to the gypsies it hit directly.

Two drops of remoulade fell from the edge of the vial and dripped down the offended skin. It sizzled and smoked bright green until the skin absorbed it. By the time I put the cap back on, the wound had already formed new growth. I replaced the remoulade and settled back in my chair. Papa leaned back, drinking the last of his mug.

"You're leaving for the East in the morning, right?" he asked.

"Early, yes."

He cleared his throat, leaned forward to rest his elbows on his knees, and said, "I need to talk to you about that."

I rolled my eyes. "I'm not twelve, Papa. I promise I will be on my best behavior and—"

"No, no." He waved his hand. "Not *that*. I trust you to act appropriately. I'm going to send Merrick over with Marten so you have a Protector there in case anything happens."

"All right."

He paused. "I want . . . I want you to act as if Merrick's not there."

The intensity of Papa's gaze didn't make sense, and I struggled to grasp what he meant.

"I don't understand."

He dragged a hand through his dark brown hair. "I was going to send Anthony, but his wife went into labor. Merrick is the only Protector left that doesn't have an assignment for that evening and the next day. I have to send him."

"What's wrong with Merrick going?"

"He's Merrick," Papa muttered. "That's what's wrong."

"Why is that—"

"Merrick is a man, B. And you're still a child. That's why it's a problem."

I groaned and covered my face with my hands. "Papa, don't do this! It's . . . weird. And I'm not a child."

He stood up and started pacing back and forth like an agitated panther.

"I see a lot of myself in Merrick, B. I've been that age before, and you're a very pretty girl, and Merrick is a talented young man and—"

Mortified, I leapt to my feet. "Stop!" I cried. "Please stop. Jikes, Papa. This is . . . just stop. Merrick and I are friends. Just friends! That's . . . that's all we've ever been."

The way Merrick had stepped so close to me on our run that morning replayed through my mind with a little flutter, but I shoved it away. Were we just friends? I'd never felt such nervous butterflies in my stomach with *friends* before.

Just friends.

"I still don't like it. You deserve better than Merrick can give you."

"Give me? Papa, I'm only seventeen. I'm not looking to get married. Grief. I just barely started to really live."

"Boyfriends happen fast, B. One minute you're flirting, and the next you're kissing, and then—"

"Whoa! Papa!" I threw my hands over my ears and closed my eyes to shut the awkwardness out. "I know what happens! Mama taught me all about that stuff. You don't have to explain it to me."

He continued on with dogged determination. "Your mother is gone now. Someone has to have this talk with you."

"Then make it Stella! If I have any questions, I'll go to her. But don't . . . no, this is too much."

"All your friends are starting to court Guardians, which means that you'll probably start courting as well. Look, I'm fine with you courting but . . . just . . . not Merrick, all right? Anyone but him."

He stopped pacing and stared at the fire, his hands clasped behind his back. The firelight glinted off his tight jaw, illuminating his eyes with a warm orange glow. Wrapped underneath all the protective layers that Papa kept himself cocooned in, I saw a glint of fear. I put my hand on his arm.

"Papa? What's this really about?"

He turned to me with a burdened sigh. "I don't want you to get even more mixed up in the world that Merrick and I live in, B. He's talented and strong and will have a wonderful career as a Protector."

29

Something recoiled inside me at the thought, but I kept it locked away lest it stir up my magic and cue Papa in to how I really felt. "What's wrong with courting a witch with a wonderful career?" I asked. His eyes moved back and forth between mine.

"Because I want you to have a better life than your mother. She spent our entire marriage waiting for me to come home, worrying that I wouldn't, and raising a wonderful, beautiful, feisty daughter without her father. I want better for you."

The pain in his voice made my heart ache.

"She loved you, Papa," I whispered. "She would never have wanted it any other way. She was happy."

He turned away, back to the fire. "Maybe," he said, jaw flexing. "But I won't let the same happen to you. Stay away from Merrick, all right?"

"What about our morning runs?" I asked with a flash of panic. "Who will run with me in Letum Wood?"

His eyes narrowed. "You still run with him every morning?"

"Yes, of course. It keeps my powers under control. I have to run."

His expression darkened like a brewing storm. "Just leave Merrick alone, B. That's an order. We'll find someone else to run with you. Got it?"

"But—"

"This isn't just about you and your future, you know. Merrick needs to focus on his career. Just because he made it into the Protectors last summer doesn't mean Zane will allow him to stay if he doesn't meet expectations. Don't be the distraction that prevents him from achieving his full potential."

Something inside me withered away, like a candle snuffed out. Not run with Merrick? Who would train me? Who would laugh at my radical opinions on running barefoot? Would I really ruin Merrick's chance? Serving as a Protector had always been his dream.

But Merrick is my best friend, came the traitorous thought, accompanied by a bright flash of laughing green eyes. *And maybe . . . maybe there's more to it than that.*

"I'm the parent, remember?" Papa said, and I realized that I'd spaced out while he was speaking. "I know what's best for you, B, and

"I'm meeting Brecken's family," she said, lighting up. "We're having dinner. He has five brothers, but I'll only get to meet three of them. His mother always wanted a girl, but never got one. I have a wonderful feeling that she and I will be best friends! Maybe I'll even have a mother again."

I sighed. Camille had been madly in love with the mysterious, dark-haired Guardian Brecken for almost a year now. Why couldn't she just put it off one more weekend to play games like we always did?

"Michelle?" I asked desperately. "Are you leaving too?"

A guilty smile lifted the corners of her lips. "Nicolas and I are going to work with the dragons tonight. Sanna is finally letting him meet the red, and I don't want to miss it. The red's been brutally ornery since laying her eggs."

Nicolas, Michelle's boyfriend, had worked with the persnickety Dragonmaster Sanna since last summer. Blind old Sanna lived alone in the woods as the only Dragonmaster in all of Antebellum. The race of pure-blood Dragonmasters had been nearly exterminated over a hundred years earlier, but Nicolas's family line intersected with Sanna's somewhere in the past, and he possessed enough Dragonmaster blood for the dragons to accept him. It certainly explained his obsession with the scaly creatures.

"Oh," I said, deflating. "So all of you have dates tonight."

"It's not a date!" Leda cried.

I preferred Leda's scorn to the pity coming from Camille.

"I suppose so," Camille said, but trailed off when I shot her a glare. Michelle buried herself back in her cookbook and didn't say another word, avoiding my bad mood, as she did any conflict.

"When will you be back?" I asked, hoping to finagle at least one game of *Networks* or even a risky trip to the kitchen to filch a rare dessert from Fina, the Head Cook. Papa's ration on food extended to sugar, so Fina didn't make nearly as many treats as she used to, which only made the mission more risky.

"I won't be back until late," Leda said. Camille smiled hesitantly. "Me too."

"I'll be back tomorrow," Michelle whispered, cringing.

A call from the bottom of the turret prevented my reply. I immediately recognized Rupert's high, nasally voice. I'd enchanted the doorway to our tower so no one, High Priest and Priestess aside, could come into the Witchery without my permission. Every time Rupert came by, I felt grateful for the restriction.

"Ugh," I moaned, throwing a hand across my eyes. "Not *Rupert*, Leda."

"Leda?" Rupert's voice wound up the spiral stairs. "Are ya ready?"

"She's busy!" I called back. "Go away!"

Leda threw an empty ink jar at me, which I caught before it gave me a black eye. "Coming!" she sang, pulling her cloak off an odd coat rack made of gnarled wood.

"Wait!" I said, scrambling forward. "Leda, I need your help! I leave for the Eastern Network in the morning and need to know the history. Can't you stay and teach it to me?"

She paused in the doorway. "Go to the library."

"Can't you just give me the highlights?"

She rolled her eyes. "Fine. Here are the highlights. The East is the only Network that appoints their High Priests and Priestesses according to lineage, like the mortals used to do with kings. The ruling family of Aldana loves swords. They've been in power for over three centuries after brutally murdering the last royal family by burning them alive, children and all. Diego is known to be a pacifist obsessed with the Mansfeld Pact. Anything else?"

"Ugh." I recoiled, but Leda's serious expression never faltered. "Really? They burned them alive?"

"I never joke about history. Merry part, Bianca."

She flounced away with an unapologetic huff, leaving me in her wake. Although I knew she was right, I couldn't help my annoyance. Why were they so okay with everything changing? Didn't they want to stay in the security of our friendship in the Witchery, playing games and giggling all night?

"Rupert is a nice guy, Bianca," Camille said, pulling a fur-lined cloak of rich red over her shoulders. "And he wants to be with Leda, which is more than most witches will tolerate. I think you should cut him some slack."

"I still don't think he's good enough for Leda," I muttered, glancing back out over the sparkling white landscape below.

"Why not?"

"He's . . . boring."

"So is Leda."

"He's old."

"He's in his mid-twenties. Not *that* old. Merrick is twenty-three, and you like him."

"Merrick is just my friend. He's my teacher, not . . . not—"

Camille rolled her eyes. "Sure. A friend. Go easy on Leda. She eats prunes every day to aid digestion. She's the oldest soul I've ever met in my life. She needs a witch like Rupert. She'd run most witches over."

I didn't answer because I didn't want to admit that Camille was right. An envelope fluttered into the room, landing on Michelle's book. She read it, stood, and glanced at me apologetically.

"Nicolas is waiting for me," she mumbled. "Merry part, Bianca."

Camille checked herself in the mirror for the twentieth time after Michelle transported away. I glanced around the Witchery, at a loss for what to do with myself for the night. My eyes fell on Marten's book, and I sighed.

Pathetic.

I was going to study, just like Leda. My thoughts drifted to Merrick, but he'd mentioned a new mission on the run that morning. Besides, after the awkward discussion with Papa, I needed some space from boys.

"Don't worry, Bianca," Camille said with a warm smile, setting a hand on my shoulder. "You'll have fun in the East, and we'll all look forward to hearing what you thought."

She departed, disappearing down the turret stairs in the graceful shuffle of her dress. I stared at the empty Witchery, which felt cold in the aftermath of their familiar storm, and pulled my knees into my chest.

Why did everything have to start changing just when it was finally going well? My friends and I had fallen into a lovely routine of time together ever since my birthday last summer, but lately everything seemed to be up in the air. Miss Scarlett made me question my future, Papa didn't even have time to finish dinner, and my friends were too busy for me. I couldn't stop it from happening. It seemed the future would come whether I wanted it to or not.

Heartless, cruel fate.

My eyes fell to Marten's thick book. "Fine," I muttered, calling it to me with an incantation. "I'll study."

Attack

og clung to the carriage on the highway outside Newberry the next morning, right where the Central Network met the boundary of the Eastern Network. A chilly mist crept through Letum Wood in haunting fingers of vapor and smoke. Everything dripped gray in the dark morning, including my hood. The thick cloud felt like snow gliding past my face. No real signs of life existed beyond the carriage driver waiting for me on top, hunched over like a gargoyle.

"Ready to go?" Marten appeared from the mist, a cloud of white swirling behind him. "The driver was sent from the Eastern Network, so he knows the best roads to take. Should cut down some driving time."

I glanced to where the road disappeared into a two-track lane somewhere in the distance. The road had decayed over time from disuse. Perhaps I could convince the driver to let me sit with him on top. One more glance at his bulky, droll figure, and I thought better of it.

"Sure," I said. "Two days stuck in a bouncing box will be great."

Marten smirked and opened the door, motioning me inside. I climbed in, running my fingers along the crushed red velvet seat. Holes had worn through the floor, and the stingy drapes lay in shreds. It had only enough room for one witch to sit with outstretched legs, which meant the horses could pull it for a longer stretch of time. The door closed behind me with a creak.

"It'll be a bumpy ride the first hour or two," Marten said, draping an arm along the open window. "Your driver will have to work through this old road to reach a functional highway."

He hovered just outside the door with a hesitant expression.

"Keep an eye out," he said, the corners of his lips tugged down in worry. "You should be safe enough, but the Eastern Network is restless. Scared, even. They don't want any strangers. I don't think they'll be hostile to a carriage bearing the white flag, but . . . just keep an eye out. Oh, and Reeves sent this to me to give to you."

His eyes twinkled as he tossed the massive tome, the *History of Antebellum*, on the seat next to me.

"Ah," I said. "That would have been a shame to forget."

With that, Marten disappeared with a wry grin, leaving a spiral of mist in his wake. The carriage lurched forward. I wrapped my hand around Viveet's hilt. The sound of the horses' clopping hooves echoed in my box as we moved into the white blur of cloud. I forced myself to relax against the seat and glanced at the *History of Antebellum*.

It would be a long ride.

Bianca. Bianca . . .

I jerked awake with a gasp the moment my head slammed into the side of the carriage with a *whack*.

My heart calmed when I realized that the voice I'd heard was only another disorganized nightmare. The strange vision of fire began to fade in the way that dreams do: slowly, like the dissolving of bubbles. I sought for it again, but felt only an impression of heavy darkness, like emerging from a long depression. It faded when I leaned forward and opened the window, drawing in a breath of crisp air.

The hours had long since blurred into each other as we rolled past the Eastern Network's lush farms, clear lakes, and occasional low, green forest crawling with bracken. It was the second evening of our journey. My jumpy driver insisted on riding through the night. The jarring on my bones and joints grew almost excruciating, despite our break to change horses every six hours. I jogged as much as I could whenever we stopped, hoping to stretch my aching muscles, but in the end it didn't help.

Coated with a light sheen of cold sweat, I wiped a hand over my face and peered out the window. Beyond the flattened vistas stood a white, glowing structure in the distance. Magnolia Castle. I lurched from side to side as the box settled over a bump in the road.

"Just a nightmare," I whispered, shoving a hand through my hair. "Just a nightmare. We're almost there."

Despite many layers of clothing, my fingers felt stiff from the chill. I used an incantation to warm them and leaned forward to study the landscape, my breath fogging out in front of me. A dull *thud* interrupted my thoughts, followed by an agonized scream from the driver. A second *thud* and a flash of light came next.

"Are you all right?" I yelled.

The driver bellowed incoherently in response. A third and fourth *thud* rocked the carriage, and I saw a bright flame flare out of the corner of my eye. The shaft of a flaming arrow had struck the carriage a few inches from where I peered out the window.

"Whoa!" I cried, leaning out the half-open window to douse the blaze with a spell. The old drapes caught fire, but I yanked them off and threw them to the road.

"I've been shot!" the driver screamed.

I hesitated, knowing Papa would want me to stay in the carriage, but I wasn't willing to let the driver shriek in agony. If he was that hurt, he wouldn't be able to drive anyway. I snapped off one of the smoking arrows, shoved it in my cloak, shucked off my boots, and climbed out of the box using the remaining arrow shafts as steps.

"I'm coming," I called.

Panicked, the horse had bolted at a gallop, sending the box jumping and careening down the road at a reckless speed. I grabbed the luggage bar and pulled myself up the side, gripping the edge of the window with my toes. The driver clutched his left shoulder where an arrow stuck out at a right angle. Blood oozed between his fingers, dripping down his dirty shirt.

"Hey! Help me, and I'll take the reins," I yelled, but the driver continued to thrash around. I ducked out of the path of an oncoming branch. Transporting around the branches was out of the question, as I'd have to accurately gauge the speed the carriage was moving at.

Seeing a stretch of open space without low hanging branches, I carefully scrambled forward and lifted my leg over the driver's seat.

"Give me the reins!" I cried over the thundering of hooves.

Magnolia Castle appeared through flashes of trees, growing brighter every moment. The driver's flailing arm slammed into my nose, sending me backward. My stubborn grip on the back of the seat barely kept me from flying off the carriage and smacking the ground below. My eyes watered. I could feel hot blood seeping down my nose and over my lips.

The driver suddenly sat down, his face as pale as cotton. Taking advantage of the momentary lull, I vaulted myself over the back.

"Give me those," I muttered, jerking the reins from his shaking hand, my eyes still stinging.

"Get it out of me!" the driver screeched, reaching for the arrow. "Get it out!"

"No! It'll bleed, just leave it in!"

But he grabbed for it anyway, so I cast a sleeping incantation on him. He blinked several times and then slumped forward, his head hitting the forward dash. The horses, still frantic, thundered down the road.

"Fine," I said, bracing myself. "Run yourselves out. We're almost there."

The pockmarked dirt road turned into smooth cobblestone. As if they knew where to go, the horses veered to the left at an intersection, despite my attempts to slow them, and kept running. Two East Guards standing at a sweeping gate made of twisted iron waved their arms to get me to stop.

"I can't!" I shouted as we roared past. I was just about to transport off the carriage and let the horses run themselves out when the end of the driveway appeared ahead. It circled into itself, leading around a majestic, flowing fountain spewing into the sky. A sweeping set of stairs, funneling up to the entrance of the infamous Magnolia Castle, stood just off the circle. My eyes widened, temporarily blinded by the blazing torchlight after the dim byways.

The horses slowed themselves and came to a stop by the stairs, as if that had been their intent all along.

"Bloody fool." I glanced down at the driver and secured the reins. "You almost killed both of us."

No turrets cluttered Magnolia Castle like they did Chatham and the Southern Network. White stones, a surprising bleached color that looked like bones in a desert, comprised most of the sprawling structure. Despite the winter season, the clusters of magnolia trees cluttering the gardens off to the left bloomed in full splendor, emitting a delicious fragrance. Legend said that the magnolia trees never stopped blooming, giving the castle its name. Marten waited for me at the bottom of the steps.

"What happened?" he asked calmly, though I sensed panic beneath the facade. "Are you all right? Do you need the apothecary?"

"Oh, I just decided to stir things up a bit because I was bored, so I asked them to shoot us with flaming arrows."

Seeing that I wasn't on the verge of death, he seemed to relax for a moment. "Sleeping incantation?" he asked with a raise of an eyebrow, studying the driver.

"He was panicking and almost killed me."

"Well chosen," Marten murmured. "But by the look of your face, whoever fought you almost won."

I reached to feel blood on my upper lip and chin. I'd already forgotten about it. Now that I remembered, it started to pound. I'd have a lovely black eye in the morning.

"Sure you're all right, Bianca?" His eyebrows dropped low and his lips puckered. "Looks like a nasty blow to the face."

"Fine."

"What happened?"

"The driver and I had a moment of confusion, that's all."

"If I had known that this would happen I would have—"

"It's not your fault, Marten." I waved it off with a careless hand, as if my face weren't pulsing with pain. "Really. It all ended well enough."

He gave me a reluctant grin. "Didn't Merrick teach you to watch your opponent's hands?"

"The *driver* wasn't supposed to be my opponent."

I clenched my hands to hide a slight tremor. Holding the rampaging horses had fatigued my grip. East Guards swarmed the carriage in uniforms of green and ivory. Three went immediately to the horses and three trained their bows on me. The Captain strode up to Marten.

"What's the meaning of this?"

Marten calmly gestured at the arrows still embedded in the side of the carriage, and then at the driver. "I have the same question for you. It appears that someone in your Network shot at a peaceful delegation. Or, I should say, at the High Priest's daughter."

"Lower your arrows," I said. "I don't want another round."

The Captain paled at Marten's words and barked orders, but his men had already moved into action. Two East Guards pulled the driver from the carriage box, and a third joined them to carry him away to an apothecary. Two others reached for me, but I batted them away.

"I'm fine."

The sound of a crisp pair of shoes tapped down the staircase leading to the castle.

"Marten, is everything all right?" A concerned, musical voice floated from the shadows, so quiet it was almost a whisper.

A male witch wearing colors of ivory and deep green, just like the East Guards, strode toward us with a small flock of witches behind him. He boasted dark skin and features, a smooth face, and strong jaw. His eyes, however, were dark pools of black and brown. He couldn't have been much older than Merrick, maybe twenty-six.

"You must be Derek's daughter, Bianca," he said, bowing. He over-enunciated the *i* in my name so it sounded like *Beeanca*. "My name is Niko Aldana. I'm the oldest grandson to the High Priest, Diego Aldana. What has happened to you?"

A quick glance at my wrinkled, bloodstained dress made me grimace.

Great first impression, Bianca.

Although I probably looked a shade worse than death, I dipped into a light curtsy anyway. If I hadn't, Miss Scarlett would have found out and forced me into another lecture. She'd know somehow.

"It's an honor to meet you, Niko. I'm sorry it's under these circumstances."

"Not as sorry as I," he replied, his voice quiet with concern. "Do you need me to call the apothecary? I didn't realize you'd been injured. Is your nose broken?"

"Good question." I gently probed the skin. "I think it's okay."

"I'm outraged that you would be subjected to such a thing in our Network," he said in a voice that trembled with fury. "Once you get the chance to clean up, I will have my East Guards get all the details from you and launch an immediate investigation. Grandfather will hear about this from me as soon as I see to your comfort. My personal servant Celio will carry you to your room."

Niko gestured to a set of stairs that disappeared into a lush array of gardens with torches lighting the way. A thick, muscled man in black breeches and a white shirt stepped forward, arms folded across his chest.

"Oh, no!" I cried, mortified. "That's very appreciated, but I can walk. Really."

Niko's forehead ruffled. "Are you sure? You've had a great shock. I can't imagine how you kept up your strength, being a delicate young lady."

Marten snorted.

"I'm fine," I said. Niko hesitated, but finally acquiesced with a nod. His eyes fell to Viveet, who peeked out from the folds of my skirt. He turned away, forehead ruffled and lips pressed.

"Let's get you both inside," he concluded. "We can speak regarding formalities later, after you are more comfortable."

Magnolia Castle

Whether they felt guilty over my less-than-welcoming arrival to the Eastern Network or they feared the wrath of my father, the Eastern Network wrapped me in hospitality and comfort. They assigned me a maid named Ariana, a soft-spoken girl of about fifteen, with beautifully dark eyes, voluminous hair, and skin the color of milk.

"Do you receive many guests, Ariana?" I asked, following her up the twisting stairs along the outside of the castle. Unlike everyone else, she hadn't given my bloody face a second glance, as if she saw this kind of thing every day.

"You're the only foreign visitor we've had outside of an Ambassador for a long time, Miss."

"Call me Bianca."

"Miss Bianca."

"Or just Bianca."

"Yes, Miss Bianca."

"Close enough."

She led me into a hallway dimly lit by wall sconces and torchlight. Fronds of deep emerald green filled the sidewalls, and ivy grew along the golden frames of oil paintings that littered the hall. The calm corridor soothed me.

"For you, Miss Bianca," Ariana said, opening the third door on the right. Like Niko, she softly pronounced her *i*'s with the sound of an *e*, so it sounded like she said, *Mees Beeanca*.

"Just for me?" I asked, stepping in. A large chamber of polished white stone awaited me. The fire crackled high and hot with tempting warmth. I wanted to lie down in front of it and go right to sleep. A new set of clothes, just about my size, lay near a steaming bath.

"Can I get you anything else?" Ariana asked.

"Thank you, no. This looks like everything."

She disappeared without a sound, leaving me alone. I ripped my clothes off and melted into the bath without a moment's hesitation, lingering until all the chill slipped out of my bones. Once finished, I scrubbed the grime of travel off myself, gingerly cleaned the blood from my face, worked through my hair with a sweet-smelling bar of soap, and finished by wrapping my body in a fluffy towel.

I'd just donned a long-sleeved muslin dress, combed my hair, and started for a platter of food on the table when someone knocked at the door.

"Bianca?" The thick wood of the door muffled Marten's voice.

"Come in."

He stepped inside with Merrick in tow. The door closed behind them with a quiet *snick*. Marten whispered under his breath and a slight shimmer ran down the door. A sealing incantation. If anyone from the Eastern Network was trying to listen in, they wouldn't hear a word.

My stomach flipped at Merrick's entrance. I'd forgotten he would come with Marten.

"Merry meet, Marten," I said and turned to Merrick. "What are you staring at?"

Merrick's gaze had focused on the slight bruising around my eyes. Luckily I'd scrubbed all the blood off my face, though it wouldn't have been the first time he'd seen me with a bloody nose.

"Marten said they shot at you with a couple flaming arrows," Merrick said, his tone coiled and angry. "He didn't say they hit you in the face."

"That was an accident," I said. "The driver was panicking, and I somehow found myself in the path of his flailing arm. That's all."

"Should have kept your hands up," he muttered, seeming to accept the explanation, but his scowl remained.

I threw a wet towel at him. "Want me to give you a black eye to match?"

He grinned and deflected the towel with a spell. I didn't move fast enough to block it, and it hit me in the torso with a wet *slap*.

"See?" he replied with a smug grin. "Keep your hands up."

Marten eyed me with fatherly concern. "How are you feeling, Bianca? I know you told Niko you didn't need an apothecary for your nose, but it wouldn't be a problem to get you one. Maybe we should."

I shook my head and instantly regretted it. The jarring movement sent a deep ache through my nose. I grimaced, which also hurt.

"A bit sore," I said with a pained smile, "but I've had worse."

"How's the driver?" Merrick asked, looking at Marten.

"Fine. Ariana stopped in to say that the driver is doing well, and the shoulder wound will heal nicely."

"At least *some* of my training has gotten through all that hair of yours," Merrick said with a wink. A sarcastic retort hovered on the tip of my tongue when Marten interrupted.

"As much as you two enjoy flirting, let's not waste time. I want to talk about what happened." Marten settled into a chair at the table and helped himself to a few dried grapes. "I want to discuss it before you speak with Diego's Guardians, who are ready at your convenience."

I plopped onto a chair and ignored Marten's reference to Merrick and I *flirting*. The very idea of Merrick flirting the way Camille and Brecken did almost made me snort. Merrick and I didn't flirt. I didn't even know how to flirt. We bickered.

Big difference.

"What do you want to know?" I asked, grabbing a small puff pastry. Hot cheese and something that looked like spinach spilled out when I pulled it open. My stomach growled, so I popped the whole thing in my mouth.

"What happened?" Marten asked.

After chewing through the melted cheese, I recounted the events with detailed precision. Merrick stood back a few paces, arms folded over his chest, wearing a brow-furrowed expression of concentration that meant he'd slipped back into Protector mode. Likely he didn't appreciate the flirting insinuation either.

"So nothing too suspicious happened," Marten concluded when I finished. "The Guardians have confiscated the carriage, so I can't have you look at the arrows, Merrick."

With silent magic I called the arrow I'd broken off the carriage to me. It popped into the air from where my cloak lay on the bed and zipped to my palm.

"Here," I said, tossing it to Merrick. "I took the liberty of stealing one of them."

"Impressive," Marten said, his eyes alight. "You're well-trained, my girl."

I looked at Merrick to make sure he'd heard the compliment after his insistence that I didn't know what to do with my hands in a fight, but he'd turned his full concentration on the feather, which had barely survived the flames.

"The flanges are the right color of green," Merrick said, running his finger over the end. "The East Guards use a very specific feather, with a certain pattern, that makes them identifiable. This is an imitation, but not a bad one."

He handed the feather back to Marten. "The anti-war rebels wouldn't try to imitate the East Guards' arrows," Marten said.

Marten and Merrick locked concerned gazes for a moment. Something in their expressions clued me in. Shooting at a peaceful delegation, imitation arrows, all in a bid to strain relations between the Central and Eastern Networks.

"You think it was West Guards shooting, don't you?" I asked.

"I know it," Merrick said. His low retort and the confidence in his gaze sent chills down my spine.

"Diego will never admit that there are West Guards prowling around his Network unknown. Likely he'll be embarrassed, at least," Marten said, stroking his jaw with the tips of his fingers in deep thought.

"What other excuse could he give?" I asked.

"East Guard training gone wrong, likely," Marten said. "He won't say anything concrete, I'm sure."

Merrick scowled. "That's because Diego is a fool."

"We'll see what the East Guards conclude," Marten said with a sigh. "I wrote to Derek to inform him of what happened."

"What?" I screeched. "You told him?"

"I certainly wasn't going to tell him in person."

"Ah. Maybe that was a smart move." When it came to me, Papa had a protective streak the size of the Central Network. "How did he take it?"

"Tolerably," he said in a dry tone. "He wrote back, *Keep your hands up*."

Merrick tilted his head back and laughed. I set a sneezing hex on him.

"He's not angry then?"

"Furious. But not so angry that he wants to pull you back. Besides, he thinks your . . . *diplomacy* could use some work."

I thought over his explanation with little reaction. My diplomacy was fine. My patience with other witches was not. In truth, I felt too tired to sort out the details. I didn't want to think about any Network shooting at me, let alone the one I was currently sleeping in.

"Well, they didn't hit me, so let's stop talking about it and go to bed. I haven't slept in days."

"I'll do some research early tomorrow morning before the meeting," Merrick said to Marten. "See if I can find anything."

"Get some rest, Bianca," Marten said kindly. "Do you need a potion to help you sleep?"

"No, thank you."

Marten nodded and patted me on the shoulder. "Good night then."

Merrick followed him out, but paused in the doorway. "I'll be sleeping in the hall," he said, glancing at me from over his shoulder. "Marten's room is directly across from yours, so let me know if you need something. I'll send the East Guards in to get your story after you've eaten."

"The hall?" I asked, standing. "Why the—"

The door closed on my question, and it dissolved into the night.

Nightmare

A nightmare gripped me tight that night, seeming to hold me by the neck. No matter how hard I tried, I couldn't wake up. Darkness assaulted me from all sides, coming with such force that it ripped the air from my lungs. No matter where I turned, nothing but a vast emptiness stretched around me. I couldn't see, couldn't breathe. A voice spoke through the thick, dim blackness.

Bianca.

A pulse waved through the darkness in long, undulating motions.

Bianca.

The voice sounded familiar, like looking at someone I'd never seen before but recognized.

Let her go.

The thick smoke grew heavier until a moving shape in the distance caught my eye. Miss Mabel stepped into my nightmare with her usual coy smile. Her blonde hair fluttered around her shoulders, glowing in lines of white-hot fire, and her ruby-red lips smoldered like coals when she smiled at me.

Merry meet, Bianca darling, she whispered. *I do miss you.*

Let my daughter go.

I shot straight up in bed, panting. Viveet glowed bright blue, clenched so tightly in my hand she nearly caught fire. I blinked, taking in my unfamiliar surroundings until I remembered traveling to the Eastern Network.

"Ugh," I whispered, pressing a trembling hand to my face. The voice in my dream slipped through my mind one last time.

Let my daughter go.

"What happened?" a deep voice asked, and I jumped into an instant crouch on the bed. A hand slapped over my mouth before I could yell. "Don't make a sound," Merrick whispered. "You'll wake the East Guards, and the last thing you need is more attention."

He removed his invisibility incantation and materialized as a dark, broad shape next to my bed. His sword gleamed a deep, burning purple. I relaxed and dropped to my knees on the fluffy mattress. Viveet calmed, settling into a hazy sapphire glow. But the dream remained, replaying itself in flashes of black oppression and Miss Mabel's bright blue eyes.

"What were you screaming about?" he asked, sitting on the edge of the bed next to me.

"Was I screaming?"

"Once or twice."

"Bad dream," I said, dismissing it. "That's all."

"You going to be okay?"

"Yes. I'll be fine."

"Can I do anything?"

Don't leave, or I'll dream again, I wanted to plead, but Papa's admonition to leave Merrick alone held me back. I pressed my fingertips to my lips, which burned after the touch of his hand.

"No," I said. "But thank you."

Slivers of moonlight reflected in his eyes as he stood. "I'm outside if you need me."

He left in silence. I ran a hand over my face and through my still-damp hair, and fell onto my back with a heavy sigh.

"I'm going mad," I muttered.

The door closed behind him while I stared at the heavy canopy above the four-poster bed, wondering why my heart was still pounding.

Let my daughter go.

Another weak wave of darkness washed over me, and I shuddered. Her daughter? That could only mean Angelina had been in my dream. But why would I dream of her? I'd only caught glimpses of her last summer. Angelina was a ghost, a rumor. No one even knew her face.

Was it a dream? Could Angelina have been trying to communicate with me? I snorted. "Impossible," I said aloud, hoping the sound of my own voice would comfort me. No magic in our world allowed a witch to invade the mind of another. Thoroughly unnerved at the idea, I scrambled into the linen dress I'd worn before bed and slipped into the hallway. Papa didn't have to know.

Merrick glanced up when the gentle croak of the door announced my presence. I sat on the stone floor next to him. Unlike my room, which stayed warm from the banked fire, the hallway was chilly from a gentle draft.

"I can't sleep," I said without meeting his eyes. I leaned back against the wall. "I thought I'd keep you company."

"Here," he said, lifting his cape and spreading it around my shoulders. "It's cold out here, and your hair is still wet."

"Don't you need it?"

"No. It's fine."

A musky scent of evergreen clung to the cape, and I wondered where he'd been. A comfortable silence swelled in the air until he broke it with a quiet admission. "I used to have nightmares after my father died. My mother would wake me up because I'd scream and scare my sisters."

I glanced at him in surprise. I knew about as much about Merrick as I did political history. He was unusually close-lipped about his family, and I realized then that I didn't even know he had siblings. A torch above us highlighted strands of blond in his hair.

Did you dream that your most frightening enemy wanted you to free her daughter, the woman who killed your mother? I wanted to ask, but said instead, "What were your nightmares about?"

"The night my father died. I was always lying in a storm, my leg broken. Sometimes I could even feel the pain again, and I'd wake up with my leg throbbing. The mind has a funny way of dealing with stressful events. It may seem like you're all right when you're awake, but when you sleep you realize that you're not okay at all."

He spoke with a quiet, even tone, but his eyes were far-gone. I studied his profile. The handsome chin, the stubborn jaw, the dusting of facial hair that shimmered gold in the faint light. I looked away before he caught me, surprised to feel a knot in my stomach.

"Do you still have dreams?" I asked.

"Yes, but not about him."

I didn't ask him what they were about. His life as a Protector lent itself to far more barbarous, nightmarish situations than he ever would or could speak of. Our dreams might have been different, but I felt a moment of kinship with him all the same.

"Papa has dreams too," I said, though I'd never told another witch. "I hear him talk in his sleep. I can't really understand what he says," I clarified when Merrick looked at me with a sharp gaze of concern. "He doesn't reveal any secrets or speak about his work. He mostly calls out for Mama, or says something to me."

"You're his life," he said, bending one knee to rest a forearm on it. "I doubt your father will ever be able to really give you up."

I wondered at the odd pitch in his tone, but it faded so quickly and seemed so strange that I shook it off.

"Tell me about your mother."

"You want to know about my mother?" he asked with an amused crook of his lips.

"I'm curious about the woman who dealt with you for so many years," I said with a playful grin. "She must be extremely patient."

The unreleased laugh in his eyes faded back into strict solemnity. "Not my whole life. But a good portion of it."

A question hovered on the tip of my tongue, but I held it in, afraid that I'd lose him if I asked.

"I haven't really been home to stay in a long time," he said, propping his head against the wall. "I couldn't handle my father's death and . . . Mother sent me away. Said I'd always suffer under his ghost if I didn't find my own life."

Though he'd still left much unsaid, I let it slide without questioning him further.

"How old were you?"

"Seventeen."

My eyes widened. "But you're twenty-three now."

He grinned with very little amusement. "Yes. Six years is a long time."

"You haven't been back even once?"

"I've seen them a few times, but I have my job here."

I noticed that he said *job* and not *life* and wondered if they were one and the same for him. Papa's admonition crept through my head again.

"Do you miss them?" I asked, shaking the thoughts off.

"Every day."

The finality in his tone suggested that he wouldn't speak of them again, whoever they were. I didn't press it, and stared at the other side of the hallway in deep thought. The castle moved quietly in the background. A soft murmur of voices passed in the stairs at the end of the hall, and if I listened hard, I could hear the quiet hiss of the ocean outside. The Eastern Network, while not without her perils, calmed me.

"So," he drawled, drawing my attention from the deepening thoughts of my dream about Angelina. "I spoke with Nicolas the other day. It sounds like things between him and Michelle are getting more serious than you'd like."

My attention popped to alert like a Guardian to the bugle. "What?"

"Told me all about . . . his plans."

"Tell me!" I demanded in a low whisper, grabbing his arm. "You must tell me! Is he going to propose? Is he going to take Michelle away from me?"

Merrick laughed, but didn't shake my hand off. The feel of his skin against mine was so foreign and startling that I let go. We normally lived under an unspoken no-touch policy. To feel him so close made me dizzy.

"Nicolas and Michelle's relationship is not your business," he said with a chuckle. "Why do you care, anyway? Shouldn't you be happy for your friend? She's living the dream. Graduated from school, lived at the castle for a while, now she can get married and live her life."

I scowled and folded my arms across my chest when a chilly breeze whispered past me. "Yes, of course I'm happy for her. I'm just not happy for me."

"Oh, there it is. A nice, friendly attitude."

"It's not like that!" I cried in frustration. "It's just . . . I just wish things wouldn't keep changing so fast. I've never lived without the weight of a curse on me. I'm used to surviving. For the past few months I've been able to just live and be normal, and it's been—"

"Irresponsible?"

"Freeing," I countered. "I don't want to let that go yet."

"Life is never the same from day to day, Bianca. You're going to have to accept that eventually. Leda, Camille, and Michelle will live their own lives, which means you should too."

I said nothing, but let out a long sigh. He was right, but I didn't want to admit it.

"Let's talk about something else," I said, perking up when a new idea came to me. "How about you teach me a few more words from the Guardian language? I'm dying to know what Tiberius is saying when he yells at the recruits. He's swearing, I just know it."

Merrick tilted his head back in a full laugh, and, finally realizing I meant it, gave in with a shake of his head.

"All right, all right. You're right. He most definitely is swearing. This is what he's saying."

Spunky

I woke to the sound of gulls.

When I scrambled out of bed—though I didn't remember climbing back into it after my conversation with Merrick regarding the advantages of a bow and arrow extended into the earliest hours of morning—I glanced out a circular window. An eternal, massive line of blue stretched across the horizon. White-tipped waves rolled and crashed on a golden, sandy shore in front of the castle, breaking on rock cliffs that rose a short distance to the left.

"Blessed be," I whispered. "This is beautiful."

I'd never seen the ocean before, so I was eager to get a full view. I was pleased to find I still wore the linen dress I'd slipped into the night before.

"Perfect. Now I won't have to change."

After running my hand through my hair to get rid of the tangles and checking to make sure I didn't have any dried drool on my face, I brushed my palm down the dress to smooth out any wrinkles and headed for the door.

The halls of Magnolia Castle were white and flat, with the rough texture of a smooth, softly gritty stone. Because I'd arrived after dark, I hadn't appreciated how much light echoed through the corridor. The morning sunshine pushed out the night, making everything feel bright. Elegant crystal sconces lined with gold led the way to a little nook with light blue divans at the end of the hall. A nearby hallway admitted sunshine through open skylights, which allowed the bracing sea breeze to pour in. It felt silky and smooth, carrying the scent of salt.

"Did you get lost already?"

Merrick's voice startled me. I paused, whirling around to find him leaning against the wall outside Marten's room. My heart hammered.

"No. Just . . . exploring."

"Right. Well, Marten wants to talk to you." He jerked his head to the side. "In his room."

I sighed. "Of course."

Marten eyed me with a critical gaze when I walked in. "Rough night?"

"Something like that," I said through a yawn. Merrick moved to the other side of the room, looking well rested for having stayed up half the night.

"Diego has invited us to breakfast with himself and Niko before we move on to negotiations. Tradition is very important to him, so although I'd rather talk and get it over with, we'll eat breakfast first."

"Sounds riveting. What would you like me to do?"

"Pay attention," he said, tapping the side of his head. "The Aldanas won't allow us to take notes during the meeting. They are very careful about things like that, so remember everything you can."

"No notes?" I asked, my eyebrows furrowing. "That sounds ridiculous."

"Welcome to the East," Merrick muttered.

Marten hesitated. "Diego is careful, which is why he doesn't employ an Ambassador but handles all negotiations himself. He's a man of rules and tradition. The Aldanas usually take breakfast in the Sword Room, which you, of all witches, will find interesting, I think."

"Redemptive," I admitted, catching a glimpse of myself in the mirror. Despite my finger-brush straightening session, my hair remained a wild mane. I used an incantation to calm the worst of the fuzz, glad to see it straightened into less of a nest. My hair didn't curl like Camille's, but neither was it stick-straight like Leda's. I lived in hair limbo, which would have been annoying if I cared more about it.

A light tap sounded at the door, and Ariana's voice followed.

"Ambassador and Miss Bianca, the Aldanas have sent me to escort you to breakfast."

Marten looked at me.

"Here we go," I said, motioning for him to go first. "Take me to the infamous Diego Aldana himself."

Ariana, Marten, Merrick, and I didn't speak as we walked down the sparkling hall.

"Here is the Sword Room, Ambassador, Miss Bianca, Protector." Ariana curtsied and stepped to the side, motioning with a sweep of her thin arm into a room with a whitewashed door.

The brilliance of hundreds of glittering swords stopped me in my tracks. Niko, who stood just inside the room, grinned at me.

"Good morning, Miss Monroe."

"Merry meet, Niko."

"You have heard of the Sword Room, I imagine?" Niko asked after I moved in behind Marten, eyes wide.

"Once or twice," I said. Hundreds of swords lined every wall, gleaming in golden and silver radiance. The weapons remained open to the air, hanging and twisting slowly in place, reflecting the rising sunlight. It felt like standing inside a massive chandelier.

"Does it fulfill your expectations, Miss Monroe?" Niko asked, smiling as if he already knew the answer.

"Exceeds them. And please, call me Bianca."

Niko pressed his lips together in a way that surely meant I'd amused him, but he was too kind to say it. No doubt I'd committed some faux pas that would have appalled Miss Scarlett.

"I noticed your own sword last night," Niko said, his eyes straying to my empty hip. Of course, I wouldn't openly wear Viveet to a diplomatic meeting. She lay underneath my skirt, strapped to my thigh with a special sheath. Since Viveet was shorter than a broadsword, her tip extended just beyond my knee when I stood, which made her easy to hide. Thanks to her own magic, when I sat down she shrank just enough that she wouldn't stick out. "I will admit I was surprised to see a female witch with a sword. But then, the Central

Network is not as traditional as the East, I think, for you were also barefoot last night."

He finished with a kind smile. A slight blush rose to my cheeks. I'd forgotten that I'd removed my shoes to climb on top of the carriage.

"Yes," I drawled. "Well, I suppose I'm not your typical Central Network female."

"You are Derek's daughter; I can imagine that you wouldn't be. You slept well, I hope?" Niko asked. I managed to tear my eyes away from the glittering swords to respond with a smile.

"Yes," I said, suppressing the urge to touch every blade. Some of them looked distinctly smaller, like Viveet. Definitely made for women. "I slept very well. Thank you for your hospitality."

Niko's slender, graceful form, like that of a dancer, was so different from Papa's brazen strength that I couldn't help but stare. He wore a crisp black coat with a golden watch chain dangling from his breast pocket. I thought of Papa, who, even as High Priest, typically strode around Chatham Castle in half-armor or a pair of dirty leather breeches and a white shirt. I imagined Papa imitating Diego's formal air of propriety and almost scoffed at the thought.

"I'm glad your accommodations were pleasing. I think we owe you at least that much after your trip here. Your chamber is our second-best room, and we save it for our traveling guests," he said, brushing the hospitality off as if he'd only loaned me a cup of sugar. "Come, I would be honored to introduce you to my grandfather, His Greatness, Diego Aldana."

Merrick stepped back, standing unobtrusively against the wall, his eyes roving over the whole room. Marten had already found his way over to Diego, who stood in a beam of sunshine near the window. For a man in his nineties, Diego didn't look a day over fifty-five. He reminded me of a silk ribbon in the wind, and his voice rippled up and down in smooth motions. He had dark hair and olive skin that made the stunning darkness of his chocolate eyes even deeper. Attractive streaks of gray spread through his hair, which filled his head in a thick ebony mop.

"Bianca Monroe, secret daughter to the great Derek Black," Diego said with a perfect bow and warm expression. He held out his hand and took mine in his. His skin felt warm and soft, like a worn piece of leather. "It's a pleasure to meet you."

"Not as great as my pleasure, Your Greatness," I said, dipping into an impressive curtsy. Marten sent me an approving wink, and I breathed a little easier.

"Are you hungry?" Diego asked. "I have ordered a breakfast feast just for you."

"Ravenous."

Diego laughed from deep in his belly. "Oh ho! She's spunky."

I managed a smile. He thought I was spunky because I admitted to ravenous hunger? I hoped he didn't get a real view of my sarcasm.

"My sweet wife Isobel will not be joining us today," Diego said in a tone full of regret. "She is ill and does not come down for meals anymore. We try not to strain her health because the Apothecaries aren't sure what ails her."

Old age? I thought, but pasted a sympathetic smile on my face instead, averting my eyes to the floor out of respect. The Eastern Network High Priestess, Isobel, was at least as old as Diego, though I didn't know her exact age.

"I'm sorry to hear that," Marten murmured. "Please tell Isobel that we'll bear the loss of her company as best we can. She's a lively conversationalist."

Diego smiled like a young boy in love. "That she is. But no more of this delay! Let us eat!" He waved his hands in the air. "Miss Monroe is ravenous, and I simply won't have it in my house!"

Breakfast outdid my expectations. It wasn't a meal so much as an extravagant display of art. Diego made it out of the ordinary, no doubt, to either impress us or intimidate us. We didn't dish the food up from the table, as we did in the Central Network; instead, four butlers circled the table with rotating dishes from the sideboard.

"Would you like an eel, Miss Monroe?"

I maintained a smooth facade, though the muscles of my nose twitched. "Yes," I said, leaning back to give the butler access to my plate. The formality made me itch. A rubbery black ball landed on my plate. I hadn't really wanted it, of course, but Miss Scarlett hadn't covered how to politely refuse a chewy morsel of unwanted food.

Trays continued to rotate through the table—platters of clams, smoked fish, salmon, and skewers of shrimp coated with coconut. Baskets of fresh bread sat in the middle of the table, flat and thin. They tasted like crackers sprinkled with seeds. It seemed more like a militaristic show of force than breakfast.

See what we have? Diego seemed to be saying. *All the food from the ocean we could ever want. We don't need the Central Network. We don't need anyone.*

I speared a second bite of crab cake, unable to argue with the logic. They had great food.

"Bianca, I hear you like sword fighting," Diego said, motioning toward the swords twirling in eternal splendor. "You must be curious about our collection."

"Yes, of course," I said, following his gaze to the wall. "It's impressive to say the least."

"The strength of the Eastern Network lies in our history," Diego said with pride. "The Aldanas alone have maintained an unbroken line of High Priests and High Priestesses for three hundred years now. The continuation of tradition makes us strong."

Merrick's words from months earlier filtered through my mind. *Traditions make us weak, predictable.*

"We abide by the rules, and the rules are good to us," Diego continued quietly, with a reverential tone. His eyes flickered to Marten. "And we will always continue to do so."

"Do the witches of the Eastern Network agree to a familial line of rule?" I asked.

If I startled him with the question, he gave no sign. Marten sent me a warning glance.

"Why wouldn't they?" Diego asked with a shrug, stirring a heaping pile of sugar into a glass of warmed milk. "They've never known anything different. And all we have to do is look back to—well, let's just say that the Aldanas have never experienced any kind of violent political uprising."

Marten took a sip of his drink but said nothing. I clenched my hand into a fist around the cloth napkin on my lap. Diego had just made a direct jab at Mildred, who organized a Resistance to take over as High Priestess and save the Network from destruction at Evelyn's hand.

Niko's eyes had widened, but I cut him off before he could soften the blow.

"Except for three hundred years ago," I replied with a saccharine smile, unable to help myself. "When the Aldana family slew the entire Castaneda regime by setting them on fire and stuffing them into a cave to die."

Diego's smile twitched, but he never faltered, like a true politician. I kept my calm gaze on him and waited while he studied me. Everyone, the butlers included, seemed to hold their breaths until Diego smiled.

"It appears Miss Monroe knows her history and does not like to be bested." He tapped the side of his nose. "Like I said: spunky."

A noise at the door prevented me from searching for a response. A letter floated into the room to Diego. Once he finished reading it, he waved it into the fire.

"I must apologize," he said, setting his napkin on the table and gaining his feet. "I've been summoned to an urgent meeting."

"Not at all," Marten said, standing. "We understand that you must take care of business."

I hurried to my feet as well, knocking a snail off my plate with the prongs of my fork. I caught it mid-flight and tossed it back, accidentally sending it into a small fruit drink above my utensils. My eyes widened in horror, but neither Diego nor Niko seemed to notice. The butler across from me lifted a hand to his face and cleared his throat. Merrick rolled his eyes.

"My grandson will see you through the meal, and I will meet you at eleven thirty." Diego clicked his heels together and bowed. "It's been an honor to dine with both of you this morning. And please, accept my apologies for your unfortunate accident last night." He gestured to my face, which showed further signs of bruising around my left eye. "We are looking into it now, but it appears it may have been a training accident gone awry."

I smiled. "Thank you, Your Greatness."

Niko, Marten, and I finished the rest of the lavish breakfast with light conversation and the pointless prattle of witches asking questions they didn't really care about.

Isobel

"Miss Bianca?"

A knock on the door startled me from my perusal of notes written by a previous Ambassador after a meeting with the Eastern Network. I lay on my stomach across the bed in my room, waiting for the hour to pass until our meeting with Diego began. While they hadn't exactly condemned us to our rooms, Ariana made it clear enough that we weren't supposed to wander out of our little hall.

"Just a second," I called through the wood.

"No rush," Niko replied. "I will wait as long as needed."

Merrick transported into my room, no doubt having heard my visitor. He put a hand on the hilt of his sword. I rolled my eyes.

"Seriously? It's just Niko."

Merrick ignored me, and I shot him a warning glance. His erect posture seemed to stiffen even more.

"Merry meet, Niko," I said after pulling the door open, purposefully blocking Merrick from sight.

"Good day," he said with a smile. "As a gesture of goodwill to make up for yesterday, I have come to see if you'd like a tour of the castle."

"Of course!" I said, delighted at the idea of getting away from paperwork for a small adventure. "I'd love to."

"Let's begin now," he said, inviting me into the hall by extending a bent arm. I slipped mine through his. "That will give us time to finish before the meeting."

Even Ambassadors had few opportunities to glimpse the world

of another Network, as most only met once every two or three years, which meant I'd take another carriage of flaming arrows if I could see more of the inner workings here. Small details like the number of servants, the type of decor, and background noises could hint at greater things. I followed Niko several steps down the hall before noticing a twinkle in his eye.

"Is something amusing you?" I asked.

"The way you speak," he said. "*Merry meet,* I mean. I've only heard that phrase in books. With your accent, it's quite charming."

It was the first time I'd ever been in a position to have an accent, but I realized here in his world, I was an oddity.

"You have one too, you know," I said. "You speak very smoothly. Central Network witches, especially in Chatham City, often sound like they're choking on a hairball."

He tipped his head back and laughed.

"Tell me more about the Aldanas," I said, assuming he'd appreciate the topic and hoping I could glean enough history to avoid having to read about it.

"What?" he asked with a sparkle in his eye. "Don't you already know so much about it?"

I smiled sheepishly. "Ah, that. Yes, sorry if that was out of line."

"No, no. No apologies expected. Grandfather is very proud of our heritage. So proud that sometimes he forgets himself and his manners. He is an old man, after all. As you know, my family has held power for three centuries," Niko said as we walked down a long hallway lit by skylights. "The Aldana line is the strongest in the history of Antebellum."

We walked slowly so I could take in the ornate decorations of Magnolia Castle. We moved up and down in level, but never beyond the wing they'd sequestered us in. I had little doubt that this small portion of the palace—while grand—held little importance. I couldn't fault them for not taking me further into the heart of the castle. The idea of Niko and Diego wandering around Chatham Castle and learning who-knows-what about us sent a shudder through my body.

The bleached white walls often gave way to ocean views, and the salty air brought in a cool breeze that kissed my cheek at every window. Despite the winter season, I didn't feel the cold deep in my bones, the way I did at home.

"You are next in line to High Priest, aren't you?" I asked, looking up at him.

He nodded in a solemn way that made him look like his grandfather. "Yes. My father died in a carriage accident when I was young, so I take his rightful place of honor."

Niko had been groomed to take over as High Priest from the day he was born in much the same way I'd been raised to fight for my life. Although our worlds were on very different paths, I suspected Niko and I weren't all that different.

"And your wife?" I asked, recalling the Aldana tradition of marrying a peasant from the villages to ensure a connection with their witches. "Have you found her strolling along the beach yet?"

Niko's grin came after a flush of his cheeks.

"To my mother's disappointment, no. But I will eventually. It's very difficult because she has to be the right kind of person to win Grandfather's approval."

"What about your mother?" I asked. "Is she as hard to please?"

"No." He laughed softly, shaking his head back and forth. His tone was affectionate and filled with love. "My mother is much more patient because she, too, was once a peasant. Like my grandmother, Isobel, Mother recognizes that people can change and learn. Grandfather expects witches to fill their roles immediately, instead of learning how over time."

My forehead wrinkled. "Even a poor village girl that's never been in the castle?"

"Even then."

"Sounds like a nightmare."

"It can be difficult at times, but Grandfather has been running this Network for almost sixty years now. I am happy to defer to his wisdom. May I show you the ocean?" he asked. "It is the pride and joy of our Network. Everything in our lives depends on it."

"Yes!" I said, excited by the prospect. "I'd like that very much. I'd never seen it before this morning."

I followed him to a doorway and stepped onto an open porch

with a dusting of sand scattered across the top of the white stones. Although I'd caught glimpses of it from the window this morning, nothing compared to a full view of the majestic band of water. Cliffs on the left plummeted straight into the ocean, where waves splashed and bubbled in frothy white bursts.

"Oh," I breathed, my eyes widening. "It's beautiful."

The expansiveness of the ocean overwhelmed me. How did Niko not feel as if he would be swallowed by so much nothing? The comforting trees and vivid green canopy of Letum Wood felt like a hug compared to all this sky. I couldn't help but feel a little frightened of just how big it was, and how small I felt next to it, with no greenery or forest to keep me from feeling exposed.

Niko leaned into the breeze and closed his eyes.

"The ocean is our lifeblood," he said, his accent more pronounced. "Ever since we signed the Mansfeld Pact, we have depended on it for everything. Because of the ocean, we have unlimited resources to provide food and trade for our people. If you look to the right, you can see the port. Some fishermen have come back in. They must have filled their nets rather quickly this morning."

I followed his direction, surprised to see two vessels, their white sails furled, moving toward us. Rope, canvas, and wood clogged their masts. Sailors scattered around the port to prepare the ships for docking.

"It's more beautiful than I imagined," I said, setting my arms on the wall. "The ocean seems very . . . powerful."

"Perhaps you can go swimming on a later visit," he said. "That is one experience I wouldn't want you to miss while you are here, but other things take priority on this trip."

"Oh?" I asked with an arched eyebrow. "Like what?"

"My grandmother Isobel would like to have tea with you before the meeting. Would you agree to that?"

I reared back in surprise. "The High Priestess wants to meet with me?"

He smiled. "Yes."

"But . . . why?"

"Because you are our visitor and the High Priest's daughter. Impressive, if you ask anyone that knows of Derek's talent and power.

Besides," he said, eyes twinkling in a way that made me feel self-conscious, "Grandmother says that any young woman who carries her own sword into another Network sounds like a witch she would want to meet."

I wondered how Isobel and Diego seemed to know my father, but reserved the question to ask her instead. Having tea with the High Priestess was an unexpected honor I wouldn't refuse.

"I'd love to have tea with your grandmother."

"Wonderful," he said, his shoulders relaxing. "Allow me to take you there now. She's waiting for you."

We finished the rest of our tour in silence, winding out of what I imagined to be the east wing and into another. Niko came to a stop before a set of double doors decorated with a pair of ornate gold handles shaped like coral. He knocked with one knuckle, and a maid immediately opened it. She looked at him and me, gave a nod, and pulled the door open.

"Enjoy tea with my grandmother, Bianca," he said with a smile. "Ariana will escort you back to the meeting when you've finished."

He bowed and departed with easy grace. I watched him go, hesitant, until a quiet voice called from inside.

"Bianca Monroe? Please do come in."

I took in a deep breath. The maid cast me an odd glance, but I smiled and slipped inside, preparing myself to meet one of the most powerful witches in all of Antebellum.

The room I walked into sparkled in tones of cream and baby blue, with gold-lined walls. Light from outside bounced through the satin drapes, glinting off the framework of a floor-to-ceiling mirror. It smelled like sea spray.

I tucked my hands behind my back, feeling out of place in such an opulent chamber. Papa and I were minimalists, forced into Chatham Castle by situation, not preference. A room of militaristic design, with swords and armor instead of silk, chiffon, and lace would have intimidated me less. I longed for the Sword Room again, where a simple linen dress didn't seem so out of place.

Oh well, I thought, eyeing a painting of an elegant woman in a white dress on the wall. I crept forward despite my sudden insecurity, vaguely aware of my presence in a massive mirror on the wall.

"You must be Bianca. I'm delighted to have you for tea."

I twirled to the side to see a striking woman sitting in a chair by the window. Her black hair shone in the bright daylight, swooped into an elegant bun at the back of her head. She was pale, with dark circles under her luminous eyes, but looked no older than fifty. In politics, one never knew the true age of another witch; the older generation often transformed their appearance.

"Your Greatness," I said, dropping into a curtsy. "I'm honored to meet you."

Isobel's deep brown eyes, set in a slender face, seemed to twinkle. I couldn't help but feel at ease. I imagined she would have floated if she could have walked, but she remained on a chair with a white blanket pulled over her lap. She held out both hands for me.

"It's wonderful to meet you. Come, take my hand and have a seat next to me. We have much to discuss!"

I took her hand without knowing what I would do with it afterward, and managed to dip into a curtsy a moment before it would have been too late.

"I've been looking forward to meeting you ever since Diego told me you were coming with our friend, Marten. It sounds like you've had quite an adventure. I am so sorry about the violent attack on your carriage."

"I'm honored to come, High Priestess. I'm not much of a guest. I fear I've stirred up trouble just by arriving."

She laughed. "You let me be the judge of that. How do you like Magnolia Castle? I told Niko to give you a special tour so you could see the view."

I smiled and sat down in the chair next to her. "Of course. You have a very obedient grandson."

"He is wonderful, isn't he? Niko is just like his father and his grandfather, though that may not be a good thing."

"He's very kind."

"Tell me, how is your father doing? He used to come with Marten as his Protector. After a while I got to know him pretty well."

"He's doing well."

"You're the first High Priest's daughter, aren't you?"

"Yes."

"Has that been difficult?"

I hesitated, peering into her curious dark eyes. Yes, it had been very difficult, but I never admitted it, and no one had asked.

"It's been a challenge," I said, searching for the diplomatic answer Marten would have suggested.

She smiled quietly as if she understood. "Ah, I see. Derek must worry about you every day. Does he allow you to leave the castle?"

"Yes, of course."

Her eyebrows shot up. "By yourself?"

"Why wouldn't he?"

She recoiled. "Because you make him more vulnerable, do you not? I assume that's why your Network traditionally does not allow High Leadership to marry or have children."

"I suppose it is," I said, startled that I hadn't thought of it myself. "I travel with Marten to the border towns often, so it's mostly safe when I do leave," I added, lest she think me unprotected and Papa irresponsible.

Lines of concern formed on her brow. "Hmm . . . I must admit I was surprised he allowed you to come so far away. I would never have let my children travel to other Networks. They aren't allowed to go into the markets without Guards either."

"We have dragons at Chatham Castle now. There aren't many witches that would attack me on castle grounds with dragons overhead."

She laughed. "No, I suppose not. Well, that makes me feel a little better about your safety. At least you're not wandering the Network unprotected. Except for on a carriage ride to here, I suppose."

She sent me a sly grin. Her concern and warm prattle reminded me of a grandmother.

"I'm very safe here with Marten and our Protector," I said with a reassuring smile. "And Papa is quite protective, but he's taught me defensive magic ever since I was a child. I've learned to take care of myself."

Isobel grinned. "Which is just why I think I shall like you, Bianca Monroe. An independent girl after my own heart. Now tell me, what do you think of the ocean and our castle?"

"Both are very lovely."

A maid in a starched white uniform set out silver cups and plates on a table that moved to sit in front of us.

"Niko insisted that I take this as my personal chambers when I fell ill," Isobel said, glancing around us. "It's the nicest room in the entire castle, and used to be reserved for Ambassadors. That means I spend a lot of time alone while Diego works, but . . . it's a nice place. Diego comes in for dinner every night, and Niko visits every morning."

Two younger boys ran around the sandy beach outside, shrieking and laughing as they dashed through the surf bare-chested in old pants cut off just below the knee. The High Priestess watched them with a warm smile.

"Those are my great-grandsons," she said with a fond chuckle. "Sometimes I wish I could bottle their energy and take it for myself. I apologize that I can't more properly receive you." She smoothed out the lines of her blanket over her skinny legs. "I'm not well, you see, and standing tires me. My youngest son, Tomas, designed this clever chair for me. Do you like it?"

She moved the blanket to reveal a set of wheels attached to each post of the chair.

"My maids wheel me through the castle as I need it. There's a handle along the back. It helps immensely in preserving my strength."

"He's very clever," I said. "I've never seen that before."

"My children are all very smart. Even those that aren't with us anymore," she finished with a pained expression.

"Niko mentioned that you lost a son a few years ago. I'm very sorry."

"I've lost more than that," she said with a sigh. "One son died just after he was born. The Apothecaries think he had a heart problem, for he only lived a few hours. He died in my arms, poor boy."

My heart went out to her. Surely the grief of losing a child rivaled—if not exceeded—the heartbreak of losing a parent. "I'm very sorry."

"Oh, don't apologize. Such is the way of life." Isobel's face narrowed in sudden question. "Do you mind if I'm completely honest with you, Bianca?"

"Of course not."

She pressed her lips to one side of her face in obvious distress. "I hate pouring tea. I always spill, or mix in the wrong amount of sugar, or steep it for so long it tastes bitter. Since I have a feeling you hate formality as much as I, let's skip it, shall we?"

I released my first genuine smile, relieved that I wouldn't have to pour either. "Yes!"

Isobel smiled and rang a little bell on a table next to her chair. "Gabriella, please return this tray of tea and bring us two mugs of our best hot chocolate, with cookies. Thank you, dear girl."

Gabriella glided from the doorway, nodded, and removed the tray. Once she left, Isobel leaned back in her chair, rested her hands on her lap, and slouched in a most unbecoming way. I laughed.

"I'm too old to put on airs," she said. "Sitting up so straight exhausts me. I'm glad to see you are someone I may relax with. Are you comfortable?"

"Not as comfortable as I am without shoes, but yes, I'm quite comfortable, thank you."

"Oh!" she cried with a laugh. "How lovely. We are kindred spirits. I simply can't stand shoes. My feet are so old these days, it causes me pain to entrap them. Let's both remove our shoes!"

"Gladly," I said, releasing my feet into freedom. Isobel removed hers with an incantation and soon we were talking about all the formal customs we loathed—curtsying among them. I quickly forgot that I'd ever been afraid to meet her. Gabriella brought a plate of cookies and we sipped at the soothing hot chocolate and enjoyed the breeze lingering in the air.

"You have a lovely rug there, High Priestess." I gestured to an elaborate tapestry as long as me. It lay on the floor close to her chair, appearing out of place.

"That rug was a very special gift from Diego when we first married. It's a magical rug called a Volare. Have you heard of them?"

A Volare! Who hadn't heard of them? They were exquisitely rare rugs, crafted over a thousand years before, with magic woven into their ornate tapestries. The special magic the weavers used had long since died away. A Volare was more than just a floor decoration; it could fly. They also held strict obedience to their owners.

"No!" I gasped. "You have a Volare?"

Her eyes sparkled. "I do. I cherish it deeply. Except for my children and my position as High Priestess, it's my most prized possession. I don't know how Diego came across it, but that doesn't really matter. It's as loyal as they say and follows me everywhere."

To demonstrate, the chair with wheels moved forward, and the Volare followed close behind.

"How wonderful!" I cried, clapping.

"Now, I want to tell you the real reason I invited you here today. Aside from the excitement of hearing a new accent, of course."

Intrigued, I straightened up. A solemn shadow had fallen over her face. "Is something wrong, High Priestess? May I do something for you?"

"Perhaps."

Her eyes flickered to the doorway, and she waved the doors to her chambers shut. She sealed them with an incantation. Gabriella had left the room, leaving us alone.

"I love my husband with all my heart," she said, pressing a palm to her bosom, "but he is so protective. He's pulled Niko in with him, so the two of them hardly tell me anything of what's happening in Antebellum anymore. They fear worrying will tire me out, but it's just the opposite. I worry more not knowing what's going on."

Desperation surfaced in her eyes, and her fingers reached out to curl around mine with surprising strength.

"They haven't told you anything of what's going on?" I asked, my voice lifting in surprise. She pressed her lips together and shook her head.

"Not within the past few months, no. I know that Derek is High Priest and that's all."

She leaned back, as if the display of emotion had tired her, and her warm fingers slipped away from mine. Her soft touch reminded me of Grandmother, and I missed it when it left.

"The maids were placed under orders not to speak to me about it either. Before I became ill with . . . well, whatever this is," she motioned to her body with a wave, "I ruled at Diego's side. We made decisions together. And now . . ."

Her voice trailed off. She stared into the distance, then shook her head. When she met my eyes again, she gave me a tired smile.

"Don't think Diego heartless, dear child. He's a wonderful witch who is only trying to protect me. When I heard Marten was coming, I hoped I could plead for his help, but now I have you, my new friend. Do you think I'm a wretched wife?"

"A wretched wife? Goodness, no! I'd love to tell you everything I know. But . . . if Diego finds out—"

"He won't," she said, cutting me off. "I'll not let on at all, I promise. I'm so disconnected from a world I once loved very much. I'm not ready to die yet, though my body ages on." She smiled weakly. "It's terrible to lose one's health."

I didn't have the heart to deny such a mournful tone.

"Of course I'll tell you."

"Oh, Bianca, thank you!" she breathed. Her shoulders sagged. "I shall be in your debt, and I never forget a debt. I'll do anything you need. All you have to do is ask."

"I don't know everything, of course," I said, "but I'm happy to tell you what I do know."

Captivated by her hungry expression, I launched into a summary of the building war between the Networks, starting with the Western Network's incursion into the Borderlands and Miss Mabel's attempted overthrow.

" . . . And now Miss Mabel is in the dungeons," I said, minutes later. "Her mother, a witch named Angelina, has increased her attacks on our Network lately. She set fire to Chatham City."

"Oh dear," she murmured, leaning back in her seat. "It sounds very frightening. Does Angelina scare you?"

"Angelina? No."

"Of course not." Isobel smiled, though it appeared faint. "I doubt she scares Derek either, which is how it should be. A Network needs a strong leader."

"Papa isn't afraid of anything."

She smiled softly. "All of us fear something, Bianca. All of us. Your father wouldn't release such an odious woman from the dungeons, would he? There's no way she can break free? Surely she'd leave your Network, and try to find refuge in another. Maybe even come here."

"No," I said firmly. "He will never let her go."

She heaved a breath of relief. "Good. I imagine all of us are in danger if that Miss Marple—"

"Mabel."

"Oh, right, Mabel. If that Miss Mabel character were to be freed, we would have a great reason to fear. Have you seen any signs of the Southern Network planning to act?"

"Not necessarily. But they will, I'm sure of it."

"I'm inclined to agree with you, though I doubt my husband does. It's frightening, isn't it?" Her fingers fiddled with a bunch in her skirt, and when she looked out the window, her pale lips had pulled down. I feared that I'd said too much. After a few moments of deep thought, Isobel seemed to rally herself. She straightened. The color came back to her cheeks, and when she smiled, the last of my reservations faded away.

"Thank you, Bianca. I truly am in your debt, for now I know what to expect, and I won't be so frightened. I will sleep better tonight than I have in months thanks to you."

Deciding that I'd already pressed my luck by telling her what her husband wouldn't, I decided I might as well push the boundary a bit further.

"May I ask you something now?"

"Of course. Anything."

I licked my lips, then launched into the question before I lost my nerve. "Would Diego join sides with us in a war, or would he want to protect only the Eastern Network?"

Niko's insistence on the Eastern Network's stability, the display of Guardians around the castle ever since my arrival, the lavish breakfast

Katie Cross

that testified of wealth all led to two conclusions: Diego was making himself appear stronger than he was, or the East was truly ready to care for themselves and *only* themselves.

"I can't predict what my husband will do," she said carefully, "but I don't feel that he would care for any interests outside of our own."

"You think he'll focus on just protecting your borders."

She nodded. "Yes. Diego is a wonderful ruler, but he's very, very stubborn."

The news sank in my chest like a weighted stone, but I smiled, not wanting her to see how disheartened I felt. The Central Network would have to fight on her own.

"Thank you, High Priestess. I appreciate your candor."

"And I appreciate yours," she said with an affectionate squeeze of my hand. "I think the two of us shall be good friends, don't you?"

I grinned and held my cooled chocolate drink in a toast to her. "Yes. Very good friends."

Battle of Wills

"Let's begin," Diego declared thirty minutes later. "Although I love seeing you again, my old friend Marten, it's good to get business over with, eh?"

We congregated at the broad table in the Sword Room, sunlight slanting through the open windows. Niko sat across from me and Merrick stood not far behind, arms folded in front of him.

"Isobel is wonderful," Marten had said once Ariana escorted me back to his chambers. "I've always been impressed with her social manners and etiquette. Yes, I'm glad you were able to meet her. She has more patience than any witch I've ever met, having dealt with such a stubborn husband for so many years."

I had wanted to point out that Marten had secretly loved Mildred all his life, so if anyone had experience with stubborn partners, it was he. A butler walked up to my side, offering a plate of refreshments, but I waved him away with a smile, still feeling full from the hot chocolate and cookies.

"I'll get right to the point," Marten said, sitting on the edge of his seat but still appearing casual and at ease. "The Southern and Western Networks are concerning us, and Derek wants to know what you'll do if they break the Mansfeld Pact."

There was no active correspondence between the leaders of the Networks, although the Mansfeld Pact permitted the High Priest, High Priestess, or Ambassador to converse as needed. Most news from other Networks came from their spies or our Protectors infiltrating the castles or listening at the borders. On the rare occasion that a Protector or a spy was caught, his own Network denounced him as a rogue and forced him to fend for himself at the hands of the offended Network. Or, in some cases, the Networks worked out a deal to swap the captured. The Mansfeld Pact had been created to stop war and corruption, but I wasn't sure it had really done much.

Diego ran his tongue over his teeth, making his lip puff out as if a mole lay under his skin.

"I shall be honest with you. I think the Central Network is scared. I think there is no war." Diego leaned forward. "You have a new High Priest, a new High Priestess. You were threatened by one of your own last year."

Marten smiled. "Do you remember Derek? He escorted me here years ago."

Diego's furry caterpillar eyebrows narrowed. "Yes."

"So you no doubt remember that he's not afraid of anything."

Take that! I thought, but schooled my expression into neutral indifference, grateful for Marten's deeper understanding of the political game. While I wanted to roll my eyes, Marten kept his cool. Both Diego and Niko straightened their backs.

"You're imagining problems that aren't real," Diego said. "The South protects themselves. The West does nothing. Derek may not be afraid, but he is overreacting."

"May I be frank about one thing?" Marten asked. Diego nodded once, sharp and punctuated. "As you know, one of our own witches recently murdered our High Priestess. Mabel lost and Derek won, of course, but our greatest concern was the army of Clavas she brought."

"Clavas?" Diego echoed. "Surely you imagined it."

"One doesn't imagine Clavas," I said before I could stop myself. Their screeches, their wraithlike bodies, the hot black blood that spilled from their barely living corpses still haunted my mind.

"No Clava has been seen since the Mortal Wars," Marten continued. "We wouldn't be so worried about the Western and Southern Networks if we hadn't seen what Mabel was capable of."

"She's in your dungeons," Diego said. "What can she do?"

"She doesn't work alone."

Diego rolled his eyes. "You've had her locked up for the last eight months and nothing has happened! You are jumping to conclusions, my friend. The Eastern Network would not join your fight, even if it came to that, which it won't."

Marten stared at Diego for several long moments, seeming at a complete loss. I didn't blame him. What could be said? Diego was choosing to remain blind, just as we had expected.

"I see," Marten finally said. "Well, I also came to warn you. Mabel and her mother, a witch named Angelina, are not forces we are ignoring, and neither should you. If there are any signs of dark magic in your Network or along your borders, or rebellions among your witches, please do not dismiss the possibility that someone from your Network could be involved."

Diego's eyes flickered. "When I have plausible reasons to believe that Antebellum is in true danger, we may talk again," he said, drawing in a deep breath. "Until that time, I shall react in the way that will best serve my own Network."

Marten nodded and reached his arm across the table to grip Diego's forearm with a forced grin of congeniality. "I would expect nothing less. Thank you for your hospitality, Diego."

All of us rose. Diego nodded, his eyes slipping to mine. A definite note of suspicion lingered in the glance. I couldn't wait to leave. Everything had begun to feel entirely too close and stuffy.

"Ariana will show you out so you may transport home. Be safe," Niko said at the door. I met his drawn eyes, wondering about the odd look in their depths, and nodded as I passed. Merrick fell into line behind us without a word.

The smell of the ocean brushed against my cheek with cool draughts of air as Ariana led us down the hall, the breeze ruffling my hair when we stepped onto the balcony. "Your belongings have been transported back to the Central Network already, Miss Bianca," she said.

"Thank you, Ariana."

"Merrick, you transport last," Marten ordered. "I'll go first. Bianca, meet me in my office after lunch. We have an appointment with your father this afternoon."

Marten disappeared. Feeling a pair of eyes on me, I spun around and glanced down. Isobel waved from her sprawling balcony. I smiled but didn't dare wave back. With a sigh, I closed my eyes and whispered the transportation spell, grateful to leave the salty sea air behind.

I'd Give My Life

I transported back to my bedroom from the Eastern Network, changed my clothes and stared out at Letum Wood for a few minutes. After the daunting expanse of the ocean, I longed to run beneath the icy trails of the forest, held by branch and root in a safe little cocoon.

"Later," I promised myself, glancing at the clock. 12:15. The meeting with Diego hadn't taken very long. Camille and Leda would be meeting up in the dining room for lunch soon. My bedroom door stood ajar, admitting two deep voices from the main part of the apartment. I froze.

"If Dane and Mikhail attack the Central Network and we can't hold them off, I'm worried the only way to stop them will be for me to get rid of Dane myself," Papa said. "The West Guards are strong, but they're also leader-centric. The chaos of losing Dane would buy us time to gain the upper hand."

"Does Zane agree?" The deep, rolling voice of Tiberius, Head of the Guardians, swept through my room. He was a massive, stocky man, with arms the size of tree trunks and a beard that could have used a trim ten years earlier. He was the perfect antithesis to quiet Zane, the Head of Protectors, who had taken over the Brotherhood of Protectors when Papa became High Priest.

"Zane agrees that getting rid of Dane is a good option," Papa replied, "but he doesn't like it. He knows he couldn't defeat Dane on his own."

"Can you?" Tiberius asked.

"I hope so."

"Dane is a Watcher, Derek. He may not have sight as powerful as Isadora's, but he sees many things. You can't sneak up on a Watcher."

The blood in my veins turned to ice. Papa try to kill Dane, the High Priest of the Western Network? A suicide mission, certainly. Even more stunning was the revelation that Dane was a Watcher, a witch with exceptional skills in deducing future events and sensing personality traits. Our most powerful Watcher was Isadora, an old woman that lived in Letum Wood and loved tea. Knowing Dane also carried that gift sickened me.

"I've been discussing the war with Isadora for weeks," Papa said. "We're working out a plan for if things go the way she thinks they could. It's all preliminary now, as no glimpse into the future is certain. I may not have to do anything as drastic as going after Dane on my own, but I wanted you to know that I've thought of it. It may come down to desperate measures, so I wouldn't be able to tell you in person. I value our friendship, Tiberius. More than you know."

The ringing *crack* of Tiberius slapping my father's shoulder came next.

"If anything ever happened to you, or if you weren't here to protect Bianca, you know I'd give my life for her, don't you?" Tiberius asked in a gruff tone. "So would any of the Protectors or Captains of the Guard."

A long pause stretched in the room. "I thank you for that," Papa said. "I shall not fear for my daughter should the worst happen."

Tiberius snorted. "Yes you will."

Papa laughed. "Well, if you're in charge of her then yes, I would. I'd fear for everyone at that point. But thank you, my friend. While I worry about many things, it's Bianca I fear for the most. She means everything to me."

"We're all family, Derek. You lost Marie, and we lost part of you. All of us mourn. Bianca's a rotten child, but at least she can handle a sword better than most of my Guardians."

My heart squeezed into a tight fist, making it difficult to breathe. The idea of Papa being fallible, like the rest of us, haunted me daily. While he was powerful, perhaps one of the most powerful witches in the world, he wasn't impenetrable. It scared me more than anything.

I thought of telling Papa about Angelina's voice in my nightmare but decided against it. It had only been one dream, and he clearly had too much on his mind already.

And now so did I.

"Merry meet, girls!" Camille chirped from behind my left shoulder the next day. The crowded dining hall moved around us in the organized chaos of crashing plates, talking witches, and crackling fire. "Look who came to lunch with me! Miss Scarlett set me up with a new tutor because I'm failing transformation."

Leda, who sat across from me, stared past my shoulders with narrowed eyes. Her suddenly pale face—which now resembled driven snow instead of a pasty sheet of paper—gave her surprise away. Michelle stopped eating, fork halfway to her mouth, eyes wide.

"Merry meet," drawled a languid voice. "I suppose I shouldn't be surprised to see all of you here at Chatham Castle since Bianca *is* the High Priest's daughter after all."

My heart did a double *whomp* and landed right in my throat.

Priscilla.

I set down my fork, stood up, and whirled around with a beaming smile and my metaphorical hackles raised.

"Merry meet, Priscilla. It's . . . a real surprise to see you again."

Standing like a blemish-free goddess was our old school mate, the infamous and impossibly talented Priscilla. Like Michelle, she'd been a third-year student when I was a first-year. The Competition to be Miss Mabel's pupil had come down to me and the fiery, graceful redhead in front of me. In a test of weaknesses, Priscilla had given into vanity, and I had won the Competition. If the guarded intensity of her eyes meant anything, Priscilla hadn't forgiven me for living yet.

Priscilla smiled with a particular shade of condescension known only to those who know they're beautiful. She wore an elegant, simple gown of deep green, which highlighted the flecks in her wide eyes. Her lashes, so long and full they nearly touched her eyebrows, batted innocently.

"It's always good to see you, Bianca," she said with casual sweetness.

Michelle's face had gone bright red. She ducked down, pretending to eat. Leda looked away, acting indifferent and aloof, although the back of her neck had flared crimson.

"Why are you at Chatham Castle, Priscilla?" I asked, keeping my smile pasted on with determined will. Priscilla had run most of the social circles at Miss Mabel's School for Girls, instilling fear and respect into those frightened by her. Which, in retrospect, was everyone except me. But she would have no power to do so here.

"I'm surprised you haven't heard," she cooed, a pink tinge coloring her cheeks. "The news has been spreading everywhere. Miss Scarlett hired me as her Assistant."

Traitorous Miss Scarlett!

"Congratulations."

"I'm teaching a few classes on transformation and potions every morning to the children of castle workers as a personal favor to Miss Scarlett," she said with a smile. "It's a program Mildred instituted during her reign."

It happened before her reign, actually, I wanted to say, but smiled instead. "Lovely."

"Yes, and during the rest of the day I'll be Miss Scarlett's Assistant," she continued quickly, no doubt worried I'd think less of her for working as a lowly teacher. "She has such a high position and such a busy job, I'm sure I'll be swamped with loads of things to do all the time."

"One could only hope," I said between the clenched teeth of my smile.

"Merry meet, Leda," Priscilla murmured, inclining her head. Her hair moved like warm firelight. "How are the kitchens, Michelle?"

"Fine," she whispered, eyes averted.

"I hear you're working on your third-year marks early, Leda," Priscilla said with a cordial tone that I didn't trust. "How are they going?"

Leda had cracked open a book and purposefully covered her face with it. She didn't respond. A hint of uncertainty whipped through Priscilla's eyes before disappearing into her cool hauteur.

"Leda's quite busy studying," Camille said with an awkward smile while she elbowed Leda sharply in the ribs. "All the time. Not that that's surprising; she always did love to study. She's finished two marks already and is working on her third."

"Congratulations. That means you'll graduate early. Which marks did you choose?"

An awkward pause filled the air while we waited for Leda to respond, but she continued to ignore us. Michelle looked between Camille, Priscilla, and I in confusion.

"Her first was Advanced Political History," I said, clearing my throat. Leda turned a page. "She just passed Public Speaking and is now working on the Esbat mark."

"Er, have a seat, Priscilla," Camille mumbled, setting her tray next to Leda. "Might as well eat before our food gets cold. Will that fill you up? You hardly have anything on there."

"It will be fine. I . . . I think I'd rather sit down there," Priscilla said, motioning to the empty end of the table. "Merry part, girls."

She sashayed away, settling her half-filled plate of food in front of her with the stiff, regal movements of a High Priestess. Camille glared at me and then at Leda, who had set her book aside once Priscilla departed.

"Way to go," Camille snapped. "You scared her off."

"She deserves to sit alone for once in her life," Leda said with a low growl. "She was horrible to me at school, and you know it. She started a rumor that I like girls and not boys." The back of Leda's neck brightened further. "And she transformed the sugar into salt when I poured it on my porridge one morning."

"She won't be alone for very long," Michelle whispered, motioning to a table across from us with a nod. "Those Guardians have had their eye on her ever since she walked up."

Camille wouldn't be cowed, though she did hesitate. "I know Priscilla isn't perfect, but this is her first day here. It's awful to be new and friendless."

"It's also awful to *be* awful," Leda retorted. "She's horrid and you know it!"

Camille chewed her bottom lip in indecision. "Maybe she's changed," she said weakly.

"Are you crazy?" Leda hissed. "She called you mushroom head when your hair was frizzy."

Michelle nodded. "I went to school with her for three years, Camille. She wasn't kind, not even as a first-year."

"She wasn't kind tonight," Leda said. "You heard her tone."

"Yes, but she was no doubt hesitant to talk to all four of us without any friends on her side. Anyway, just because she's a bit stuffy doesn't mean that *I* have to be like her," she concluded. "I'm at least going to sit with her. If she's kind to me then great, I'll be her friend. If not . . . well, at least I tried."

She picked up her plate and moved away, looking less certain with every step. Priscilla wore a guarded look of question when Camille sat down across from her but, seeing Camille's kind smile, shrugged with an expression that looked like relief. Camille fell into a happy jabber, and I turned back to my food.

"Camille was the first person to be nice to me at school," I said, feeling a twinge of guilt, however subtle.

Leda scoffed. "Camille can get sucked into Priscilla's controlling gravity if she wants, but she better not expect me to chum up with her."

I echoed the same sentiments. I'd had enough dealings with conniving, beautiful witches for the rest of my life. But I couldn't deny that I watched the two of them from the corner of my eye. Perhaps Priscilla had changed but felt scared to approach all of us on her own.

The rest of us finished our meal in an awkward silence.

We'll See

"How did the Eastern Network visit go?" Leda asked that weekend. "Sorry we never had a chance to discuss it when you returned. I've been so busy between work and school I've hardly been in the Witchery at all."

"That wouldn't have anything to do with Priscilla being around the Witchery now, would it?" I asked with a knowing grin. Leda ignored me. Although Priscilla didn't speak much to any of us except Camille, she'd been lurking around the turret, helping Camille study or talking about the latest fashion trend from the Ashleigh Covens. Leda's presence there had been almost nonexistent.

Leda and I sat on two thick stumps deep in the heart of Letum Wood. Lounging beneath the winter deadfall relaxed me. While beautiful, the charms of the Eastern Network held no sway over my heart. My soul belonged to the forest.

"The Eastern Network was . . . interesting."

Leda cocked an eyebrow. I rarely had anything to say that Leda found engaging or intelligent. "Do explain," she said.

"Hey girls," Camille said, arriving breathless and apple-cheeked, wearing a long red cloak with white and black fur around the hood. "Sorry I'm late. Did I miss anything?"

"No," Leda said, motioning to a vast field before us. "Sanna hasn't introduced Nicolas to the gray dragon yet. It's still lurking in the trees." She cast me an offhand glance. "I think it's just annoyed by Bianca and won't come out."

"Good!" Camille cried. "I didn't want to miss it."

A dragon circled lazily in a silvery gray sky, the familiar scales blending in with the clouds. We sat far away near the woods because the dragons had a special wariness of my presence. Last winter my volatile magic made me both unpredictable and powerful. Dragons, I learned, did not like unpredictable, powerful things. Although my powers flared up less frequently now—they hadn't abated completely, as I still mourned Mama—the dragons remained uneasy about me. Some wouldn't come near me.

Camille sat on the third stump next to us, wrapped her arms around her knees, and hummed under her breath.

"As you were saying?" Leda asked, motioning for me to continue with a twirl of her hand.

"Diego is pompous and arrogant," I said, catching Camille's attention. They listened to me recount the visit, and I told them the entirety of my discussion with the High Priestess Isobel.

"What did your father say about Diego when you reported back?" Leda asked, thinking, as ever, about politics. I shrugged.

"He wasn't surprised. We'll keep moving forward with our plan. You don't think Diego was right, do you?" I asked, relying on Leda's strange knack for understanding the political world in a way I never would. "We aren't overreacting by preparing for war?"

"I think there's a chance Diego's right," she said. "Derek is a new High Priest, after all, and there's pressure for him to prove himself to the Network. He may be overly cautious."

"But Miss Mabel used Almorran magic. She had Clavas. There's no disputing that."

Leda shrugged. "Maybe she just found lesser scrolls and not the *Book of Spells*."

"Seriously?"

She rolled her eyes. "I'm just stating what others have said."

"Others meaning Clive."

"Others meaning educated scholars and politicians," she retorted. "Diego's opinion was just an opinion. Which means it's not necessarily right or wrong. It's nothing for you to take personally. It's politics. Something you may want to learn for future meetings."

I shrugged it off. "I doubt I'll be invited back to any meetings."

Leda snorted. "Not after taking your shoes off with the High Priestess *and* going against the wishes of the High Priest."

"Hey!" I cried. "She took her shoes off too!"

"Doesn't matter. That was a clear breach of etiquette."

"Thanks, Miss Scarlett."

"You shouldn't have told Isobel about Miss Mabel," Leda said, chewing on her bottom lip. "Clearly Diego didn't want her to know for a reason. Her lack of knowledge was an advantage for us that you just removed."

I bit my bottom lip, refraining from telling Leda that I'd sent Isobel a *Chatham Chatterer* newsscroll so she could read the news herself.

"I'm glad you told Isobel and became her friend," Camille piped up, joining the conversation for the first time. "She sounds lovely. I'd like to meet her."

"Diego didn't want her to know because she's sick, that's all. I liked Isobel."

"I want to ride her Volare!" Camille cried, eyes shining. "Can you imagine? It would be romantic, don't you think?"

The gray-toned dragon swooped into the field, landing softly next to Michelle. His black and silver scales glinted in the winter sunlight and his breath puffed out in great clouds of steam. Michelle laughed when it nudged her back with its massive head.

"How did it go with Brecken's family, Camille?" I asked, hoping to turn the subject away from Isobel. For whatever reason, I didn't want to share her. It felt like I had a grandmother again. Since I'd already lost mine, I wanted to hold Isobel selfishly close to my heart.

"Wonderful!" Camille said, lighting up like a new torch. "Tabby and I got along so well, you just wouldn't believe it. I think she likes me better than her daughters-in-law. His father didn't say much, but then again, I didn't really stop talking with Tabby long enough to speak with him."

I tilted my head back and laughed. Camille would be the one to talk another witch into silence.

"Quiet!" Sanna bellowed from the other side of the field. A necklace of black dragon scales bounced on her chest as she waved a fist at me. "You're distracting the dragons."

The gray, apparently agitated by the sound of my voice, pranced uneasily, dancing back toward the forest. I shut my mouth lest Sanna send me away or set a hex on me, like last time.

Sorry, I mouthed.

Sanna's eyes had gone dark long ago, but she was spry for being over one hundred and twenty years old, and willing to wallop any young witch over the head if she felt it needed. I'd found myself underneath her cane several times.

"Don't make another noise or I'll set the boils hex on you!" Sanna waved a knobby fist at me. I grimaced. The boils hex had lasted for a miserable three days.

"I hope I die before I get that old," Leda muttered, her nose wrinkled. "What if my mind disintegrated and I couldn't think? I wouldn't want to live."

I smirked. Who would Leda be if she couldn't be self-righteously smarter than everyone else?

Nicolas, a sweet, tall, round fellow with giant hands as gentle as a kitten reached out to the gray dragon and calmed it with a touch.

"Brecken's mother is younger than I thought," Camille continued idly. "She married Brecken's father when he was in his early thirties. Can you imagine? Anyway, she started having babies at seventeen and had them every other year until she just couldn't stand it anymore. Brecken is the youngest."

"She sounds like the mother you never had," I said, crossing my ankles.

"It felt like having a mother again, and that was wonderful. Oh, it's been so long since I've felt like I was part of a family! Wouldn't it be just wonderful to marry Brecken, have babies, and see her every day? What a dream!"

I nearly choked on my own surprise, so Leda pounded my back with a heavy hand while I sputtered for air. Camille often daydreamed about how handsome Brecken was or pondered what he would wear on their next date. We were used to her prattling excitement over *that.* But marriage and babies?

"What?" I finally gasped. "Babies?"

Camille let out a sigh. "Oh, I don't know. It's just a dream. I'd love to get married and settle into a family. I don't care about a career like you and Leda."

I reached over Leda to grab Camille's arm. "Camille, have you spoken with him about—"

"Bianca, hands off," Leda said, plucking my arm off Camille. "Jikes. Your emotions are as hot as a burned potato some days. You better calm down before your magic flares and Sanna curses you. Listen, Camille, if you want to marry Brecken and have his babies, great. I think you should. But you need to understand what it's like to be the wife of a Guardian. You won't live in one place all your life. Brecken works here, right? That means you'll have to live in Chatham City."

Camille's eyes widened in a moment of horror, then she calmed. "Brecken can just transport to work every day," she said. "Or I can transport to see his mother during the day whenever I want if he insists on living here."

"I don't think he really has a choice," I muttered, thinking of Tiberius's strict rules over his Guardians, even Captains like Brecken who enjoyed a little more freedom. Sanna barked orders in the background while Leda lectured Camille on the difficulties of Guardian life that she, herself, knew nothing about by experience.

"I don't really think it's Camille you're going to have to worry about getting married and moving away," Leda said, nudging me out of my reverie. Her eyes rested on Michelle. "Looks like Michelle may beat her to it."

I glanced away, not wanting to entertain the thought of my friends getting married. I'd always have Leda—who had no desire to get married and give up her career—though the thought wasn't all that comforting.

"We'll see," I said, remembering Merrick's mention of Nicolas and Michelle. "We'll see."

The Darkness Has Come

Let my daughter go.

A gaping black monster of flame and brewing evil loomed over me, growing with every breath I took. Fire spurted around its feet, which stood on a familiar cobblestone road. Miss Mabel stepped out from the midst of the great beast wearing a dress of bright red that pooled around her like a puddle of blood.

You took what is mine. I want her back.

The monster dissolved into a thousand pieces, scattering on the air. When the dream progressed, I was standing on top of Chatham Castle, looking down on Chatham City. Bits of the monster fell over the city and burst into flame.

Let my daughter go.

I jerked out of the nightmare, sweaty and panting, to find nothing but the darkness of my canopied bed around me. My chest heaved.

Light from outside filtered through my bedroom window. I'd fallen asleep on top of my bed without a blanket. My fingers felt stiff from the cold when I pressed my palm to my eyes. Instead of dispersing into uncertain vapors in my mind, the dream replayed itself with frightening clarity.

Explosions. Fire. A wall of heat. Screaming and darkness. Chaos. The close streets and buildings of Chatham City filled with smoke. In the strange quality most dreams possessed, everything had been elongated. The stretched shadows had come alive, screaming. Witches streamed past, their hair smoking, their bright clothes on fire.

Angelina's voice whispered through my room on a sudden breeze.

Now I take from you.

Bright clothes, I thought with a grip of fear. *The gypsies.*

"Papa!" I screamed, shooting to my feet. "Papa, wake up!"

Papa came running out of his bedroom, half awake, sword in hand, and shirtless. Seconds later a massive *boom* ricocheted from Chatham City and rolled outward in a cloud of gray smoke. I pressed my palms to the cool glass of the window. Flames were already visible, even from this distance, blooming into an *A* on the city landscape.

"The gypsies," I whispered. He took the scene in with calculating eyes, standing next to me with his dark hair sticking up on end.

"Stay here," he said, pressing a heavy hand on my shoulder. "Don't leave."

He murmured something under his breath, and his eyes changed to a light hazel. His hair shortened, then disappeared as if he had sucked it all inside, leaving a bald, shiny head in its wake. His shoulders shrank, and his hands grew small, and suddenly a witch I didn't know at all stood before me.

"I'm serious, Bianca," he said, holding up a stubby, hairy finger in warning. "Stay here."

"Papa, no!" I cried, grabbing his arm. "You can't go out there! It's Angelina! She's doing all this. What if she's waiting for you? Maybe she orchestrated this just to draw you out!"

"Go wake up Stella, explain what happened, and tell her I'll come back within an hour to check in. If I don't, let Zane know."

"But Papa—"

He had already transported away, so my cry echoed in my bedroom. I hesitated, glanced down to find I still wore the dress I'd worn all day, then transported to Stella's personal chambers.

Stella kept her calm as usual, but switched into High Priestess mode the moment I sputtered out the last of Papa's message. Despite the midnight hour—she was clad in a nightgown with her hair in a silvery braid down her back—she was still as graceful as ever. Within minutes, she'd roused most of the Council, summoned Tiberius and Marten to her office, and sent two contingents of Guardians to the scene.

Marten arrived with a grim face. "Bianca," he said, acknowledging me with a nod. "Glad to see you're already here and ready to help."

I didn't tell him that my promptness for work had nothing to do with an active choice. Drawing attention to myself wasn't my plan for the evening. Finding my friend Jackie—a beautiful gypsy girl that had attended Miss Mabel's with me as a first-year—was my priority.

Stella murmured something in Marten's ear and he disappeared, which gave me great relief. It would be easier to slip away without him around. Sensing that Stella had forgotten I was there, and knowing they wouldn't let me do anything anyway, I left the room without a sound, then transported away.

While I wasn't at all gifted with precise transporting, I could get close to where I wanted to go, and tonight was no exception. I landed several blocks away from where Jackie lived with her father to find an exact replica of my dream.

Witches ran past me, screaming. The smell of burned flesh and silk hung heavy in the air. Several gypsies sprinted by, hands flailing, wailing in the odd way unique to the gypsies. Smoke clung thick and fast to the buildings, and I could barely breathe. A palpable darkness, stronger than the cloying smoke, threatened to suffocate the breath from my lungs.

Burying my nose in my elbow, I squinted and rushed into the smog. Gypsies struggled into the street, trying to get out before their own homes caught fire. An older woman stumbled and fell before I could catch her. I rushed to her side and gently pulled her to her feet. I stifled a gasp when our eyes met. How well I knew those old eyes.

Nan, Jackie's grandmother.

Behind her came Jackie, appearing from the depths of a darkened house. She skidded to a stop when she saw me.

"Bianca," she said, breathing heavily. "What are you doing here?"

"I'm here to find you!" I said, transferring Nan to Jackie's waiting arm. "What can I do?"

"Go home!" she replied, her dark skin flickering in the light of the flames that moved down the street. "It's not safe! The fire is moving too fast."

Most of the wood on the gypsy side of town had been rotting for ages, so it burned with wild abandon. Buildings fell in plumes of smoke and ash.

"Is your family safe?" I asked, flinching when an explosion of sparks burst from a house across the street. She hesitated.

"Leave!" Nan screeched, pointing to the sky. "The darkness! It has come."

Through the haze I could barely make out the wings of five dragons flying over Chatham City. My brow wrinkled. *Dragons.* At least one had flown around Chatham Castle at all times since Miss Mabel's attack, but so many? Surely the fire wasn't drawing them, for they were forest dragons. The only thing that would draw them with such surprising thickness was Almorran magic.

"My father," Jackie said, fear in her chocolate eyes. "I had to leave my father while he went after my two baby brothers. Can you make sure they get out of our house?"

"Yes. I'll go find them."

"His name is Ijet. My brothers were staying three doors down from our home, in the house with the green shutters. They're just small boys! I-I can't go myself. Nan is our only elder. I must make sure she's safe or we'll have no one."

"The darkness!" Nan cried again, trembling.

Whatever Nan saw was not of our world, for the streets burned bright and hot in the inferno. I put a hand on Jackie's shoulder.

"I'll run back and make sure they're safe," I said. "Get Nan out of here."

I didn't waste another moment. The hungry fire had moved so close I could feel the heat on the backs of my arms. Guardians moved toward us, pulling witches from their houses, carrying small children, and supporting the elderly, but they hadn't moved in as far as Jackie and I yet. It would be too late to check on Ijet soon.

Following her directions, I ran to the end of the street. Beads of sweat formed between my shoulder blades as I approached a dilapidated house with green shutters on the left. Flames shot out of the upper window of the small hovel next door.

"Ijet!" I yelled. The smoke was so thick I could barely see. "Ijet? Are you here?"

No call answered me, so I ripped part of my skirt free, wrapped it around my face and plunged into the smoky room. In the poor light I could just make out a few pieces of furniture against the wall. Smoke poured down a staircase at the rear of the house.

"Ijet?"

The back door was open, allowing a current of air to fan the flames. Ijet must have escaped that way. Relieved, I whirled around, prepared to transport away when a pitiful cry came from the stairwell. I stumbled forward to find a small foot peeking out of the smoke on the fourth stair. A small boy, no older than four, stirred, coughing pitifully when I pulled on his leg and brought him into my arms.

"Hang on!" I cried, blinking against the sting of the smoke in my eyes. "Hang on!"

I slung him half over my shoulder, grateful for all the stones Merrick had made me carry during training, and hurried into the street. I set the little boy down and tapped the side of his face.

"Come on!" I muttered. "Wake up little one!"

He revived with a shuddering gasp. "Where's Da!" He rubbed his bloodshot eyes with his fists, choking on the smoke. "Da!"

My heart clenched. So Ijet was still there. Not wanting the little boy to wander the streets toward the fire, I grabbed a nearby stick and handed it to him.

"Hold this, will you? Don't let it go until I come back and tell you it's safe. This is very important. I need you to hold it and give it to your father when I come back. Do you understand?"

He hesitated, lip blubbering, throat rasping, before finally taking the stick. I dashed back into the building, ignoring the open flames shooting through the windows one floor above. I wouldn't have much time before the house collapsed.

Halfway up, about two stairs beyond where the little boy had lain was another foot. I grabbed it and felt the calves of a boy of six or seven. After slinging his limp body over my shoulders, I struggled blind to the front door under his weight. The four-year-old started to sob when I appeared with his brother.

"Bianca!" a voice called. "Bianca!"

Just as I set the second boy down, a familiar head of dark curly hair and bright eyes appeared. Brecken!

"Help me!" I grabbed his arm when he jogged up to me. "Help me save a witch inside. Quickly!"

"Let's make it fast. This building is going to fall."

Tears poured down my face from the sting of the smoke, which had thickened as the houses around us caught fire. I took Brecken's hand, and we plunged into the hazy room together. A crash from above shook the rafters when I scrambled up the stairs on my hands and knees, eyes slitted nearly shut. We made it all the way to the top of the stairs before I saw the flames. In their dancing yellow light I could just make out a lumpy form on the ground. *Ijet.* Above us, a hole showed a glimpse of night sky, billowing smoke in great plumes. A burning board lay across Ijet's back. I scrambled the rest of the way, trying to kick the board free with my bare foot.

"Use a spell!" I cried, but no matter how hard we tried to lift the board off Ijet with magic, it didn't budge. Together we kicked, pulled, prodded, and pushed until it rolled off, nearly burning the bottoms of my feet.

"I'll take his shoulders," Brecken shouted, his voice muffled by a scarf I recognized as Camille's. "You take his legs. Magic isn't working!"

Coughing and sputtering, my chest constricting from whatever oppressive weight lay on the world, I grabbed Ijet's ankles, and together we worked him down the stairs. The ceiling on our right collapsed, sending a spray of ash onto the backs of my arms.

We struggled into the street to find Jackie had returned and held her smallest brother in her long, caramel arms. She let out a piercing shriek when she saw us bearing Ijet between us. Three other Guardians appeared out of the vapors.

"We've got to go!" they shouted, taking Ijet from us. "This whole area is in flame!"

A streak of blood ran down Jackie's trembling face. Her hemline was singed all the way to her knees. Red, bubbling blisters covered her legs.

"Jackie," I whispered in disbelief. "Can you walk to the castle?"

She nodded, pressing her full lips together. Her usual feline grace didn't fail her, even under extreme stress and pain. The two Guardians gathered Ijet, Brecken picked up the seven-year-old, and I took the smaller boy from Jackie.

"Come on," I said, cradling him. "Let's take you to safety."

A rush of air from above startled me, and I glanced up to see a red dragon soar past. Sanna rode atop it as it flew, maintaining an even speed without flapping her wings and aggravating the flames further. A mist appeared in their wake, and the fire targeted by the glowing spray calmed, settling into the small lick of a campfire. Sanna disappeared from sight as the dragon flew up to change its direction. In the distance, I thought I saw Nicolas riding the blue, a Protector at his back, no doubt trying to use similar magic to subdue the fire. I pressed my palm to the little boy's chest and whispered a healing blessing as I jogged behind Brecken and Jackie. His ragged breathing calmed, easing into the wispy breath of a sleeping child.

My heart pumped with fright, giving me strength to wade through Chatham City, one arm under Jackie, the other holding her brother, until we made it down the long road to the castle. The shadows of circling dragons swooped over us every so often. Despite my poor history with them, their presence comforted me.

Stella had already set up cots, medical stations, and food in the lower bailey, and Apothecaries from all over the Network transported in to help. Servants, called from their homes or rooms, bustled around in organized pandemonium with Mrs. L at the head. It was too cold outside to allow witches to sleep in the baileys, even though the fire felt as if it would never leave my skin.

"Bianca!" a shrill voice called. I glanced up to see Leda waving her pale arms frantically in the torchlight. Jansson stood just behind her, assisting a gypsy with burns on her face.

"Look, Jackie, there's Leda," I said. "She'll help."

Jackie blinked, glancing at where I pointed, but didn't seem to understand. Blood continued to fall from a swelling knot on her head.

Leda rushed forward. Clearly she'd been roused from sleep as well—her hair was loosely bound and she wore an old dress—but she barked out commands like a Captain.

"Put Jackie there. Brecken, put the little boy . . . there." Leda used magic to summon another cot small enough for the four-year-old. A second bed for the older child popped up next to Jackie's. "Put her brothers by her."

Jackie lay back on the mattress and stared at the sky, mute. The stars shone a bright, mocking white. Apothecary Assistants rushed forward, pulling packets of herbs from their inner pockets before swarming the children. The witch examining Jackie murmured under his breath while grinding greenish herbs in his palm, then held his cupped hand in front of her face. The herbs rose in a cloud, swirled around her nostrils, and slipped inside her with every breath she pulled in. Finally her muscles relaxed. I backed away, grateful to see her still alive.

"I'm going to go help with others," I told Leda, giving her a questioning glance. "See anything to avoid?" She paused, blinking, then shook her head to clear my future possibilities.

"You'll help many," she said, rendering me grateful again for her curse of foresight. While nowhere near as strong as Isadora's ability as a Watcher, she still came in handy often. "Just stay away from Gilly Street."

Brecken and I transported back to Chatham City. A dark weight hung in the air where the smoke continued to spread, filtering through houses and alleys with a haunting presence. We supported old women, carried young babies, and helped injured witches back to the lower bailey to receive care. The night slipped away, lost in wailing and looks of stunned disbelief. The terrible smell of burned hair clung to my nostrils.

The gradual dawn of morning signaled the end of the hellacious night. The fire had settled for the most part. It burned on but destroyed only those homes it had already touched. I stood alone on the stairs leading from the high bailey to the castle's main doors, watching the medical interventions below, replaying and analyzing each moment of the night one at a time, the way Papa taught me.

You have to deal with frightening experiences right after they happen, B, he'd always said. *You might shake or get sick, but that's okay. It means your body is dealing with it. Deal with it. Don't put it off.*

My hair hung limp on my shoulders. The cloth I'd torn from my skirt hung around my neck, stained gray. Smoke had saturated my clothes to the degree that I knew it would never come out, not even under Reeves's talented ministrations. I'd have to throw the dress away or finish the deed and burn it.

"You were a mad woman out there tonight," Merrick said, walking up behind me. "I saw you helping Brecken and the Guardians."

I glanced at him in fear. "Don't tell—"

"Don't worry, I won't tell your father, but you know he's going to find out somehow."

"Papa's going to kill me," I replied woodenly, and because I felt so close to cracking, I smiled. Merrick mirrored my own sordid amusement, and seeing him made my throat tighten. The sick hollow in my stomach grew and nausea overtook me in one long wave.

"Come on," Merrick said, grabbing my shoulder. "You need to vomit. You'll feel better."

He hauled me to my feet and shoved me toward the stairs leading to the top of the Wall. I couldn't speak because I would have emptied my stomach right there, so I kept my mouth clenched and breathed through my nostrils, trying to huff off the scent of the dying, who lay under white sheets in the corner of the high bailey.

Once I arrived at the edge of the Wall, I leaned over it and vomited, retching until my ribs hurt. Then I pressed my burning cheek against the cold stone and closed my eyes, swallowing back the taste of acid in my mouth. Merrick stood next to me, a steady hand splayed between my shoulder blades.

"Better?"

"Yes," I whispered. "Thanks."

I straightened and met his gaze. Smoke blackened his face, highlighting his reddened eyes. Bloodstains marred his shirt and torn breeches.

"Reeves sent you this," Merrick said, and a small slip of paper appeared between two of his fingers. "I went to the apartment to find Derek, and Reeves asked me to pass this on."

"Papa's all right?" I asked eagerly, feeling a weight lift off my chest. Merrick rolled his eyes.

"Jikes, B. He's only the most talented and powerful witch in the Central Network. A little Almorran fire isn't going to frighten him."

"It is Almorran?"

"*I* think so," he replied, looking out past the castle. "I've never felt anything like it, not since Mabel attacked with the Clavas."

I unfolded the paper with relief. Talented and powerful or not, Papa wasn't indestructible.

Sustenance awaits, read Reeves's note.

The idea of eating breakfast, engaging in something so normal and unassuming in such a nightmarish haze, sounded wonderful. The usual tremors of shock that normally moved through my body after enduring something so harrowing had already started to subside. Watching Mama die and fighting Miss Mabel twice must have trained me well.

I glanced up at Merrick. "Hungry?" I asked.

"Starving," he said, keeping a hand on my shoulder and steering me toward the castle. "Let's go, little fire girl. I want to hear all about your night."

I'll Fight

"I'm not sad to see it gone," Jackie admitted a week later, staring at the charred remains of the gypsy community in Chatham City. Fifty witches had died, forty of them gypsies. "It was just slums, really. What did we lose?"

"Your home," I said.

Her full, dark lips pressed together in silence.

The day was thick with low pearly clouds and the threat of snow, heralding the third and final month of winter. The tips of my fingers had nearly turned numb. Winter in the Central Network felt like icicles driving into the marrow of the bone. I wore a heavy cloak, but it afforded me little warmth.

The breath of frigid winter air had cooled the rubble over the past week, so I kicked aside a few boards, searching for something. I didn't know what I expected to find, but hoped for tokens of the life that had once thrived here. If it had been so easy for the Factios to destroy so many lives, why couldn't it happen elsewhere? Was the rest of the Central Network in as much danger? And the dream I'd had before the fire. Had that been premonitory, or just a strange coincidence?

Let my daughter go.

I shuddered and turned my thoughts.

Marten, who had worked with the gypsies ever since Mildred's reign began, and Papa were meeting with Nana and Ijet, amongst the other gypsy leaders. Although Jackie and I weren't allowed in the meeting, I already knew what they'd be talking about: the departure of the gypsies from Chatham City. While I hoped Marten could use his diplomatic powers of persuasion to convince them to stay, I doubted it.

Papa was still livid with me—clearly not resigned to the inevitability that I'd always make dangerous decisions—for leaving the room against his orders, which is why he'd banned me from the meeting. So Jackie and I meandered restlessly through the wreckage together.

"It was a horrible place ta live, really," Jackie said, and we started moving through the rubble again. Unlike the rest of the gypsies, Jackie paid careful attention to her accent because she wanted to present a professional demeanor. But blips of her Chatham City gypsy accent slipped through every now and then. "Burning it probably did Chatham City a favor, getting rid of disease. At least now we could rebuild."

"Will you?" I asked, peering inside a darkened house.

"No," she said. "We won't."

Our feet left tracks in a layer of snow mixed with soot.

"Are all of you going to leave?"

"Not yet. Nan and I will go back north, to the land we received in the Mansfeld Pact. Many of our witches still live there. It's safe. It's home."

I stopped to look her in the eye. "If all of you leave, the Factios will take over Chatham City. Chatham Castle is vulnerable to attack."

Jackie shot me an acerbic look that stung. "*If* they attack the castle," she retorted with an edge of bitterness in her voice. "Only your father thinks they will. Their vendetta seems to be against the gypsies."

"He's not the only one," I replied, managing to keep the snap out of my tone by sheer willpower. "Tiberius, Marten, Zane, myself, Stella, the list of those who agree goes on and on."

"And all of them are politicians," she said. "All witches with a reason to profit from a war."

I clenched my fists. *Profit from war?* Hadn't the Factios just burned down her home? Hadn't she seen the red *A* marked in the sky? And yet she quoted something Clive had said in the article the *Chatterer* published. Profiting from war sounded so ludicrous I nearly laughed.

"What about Angelina?" I asked. "At the very least, we know she's leading the Factios. Maybe she has something to do with all the other Networks as well. Maybe Angelina is the one pulling them together against us."

Jackie scoffed. "I think Angelina is a myth, a front for someone else."

"What?"

"No one has ever seen her, not even the Factios members that work for her. She supposedly burns red *A*'s into storefronts—"

"Or cities," I muttered.

"Or cities," she conceded reluctantly, "and stirs up violence and trouble here in the Central Network, but only takes credit for her deeds through her reputation. I think she's fake. Made up. Just like your father's predictions regarding war."

I sucked in a deep breath, wounded. Why would Papa make up such a thing? Did they really believe he *wanted* a war?

"Look, I didn't mean it like that," Jackie said with a frustrated sigh. "I'm sorry. That wasn't nice ta say. I just . . . I don't get it, ya know?"

My hands relaxed. Jackie had just lost her home. For her, the fire wasn't just a harrowing experience—it uprooted her whole life. Although I didn't understand it, I at least knew that her anger didn't really have anything to do with Papa: She was scared. Papa was an easy target to blame for all she'd lost. I forced myself not to take offense at her blatant honesty. Besides, so many witches disagreed with Papa now; I was part of a small minority of believers.

"What don't you get?" I asked, forcing an even tone. She relaxed, and her sharp, worried gaze softened. We started walking again, to my relief. My energy felt less pent up that way.

"Why should the gypsies stay in Chatham City and give our lives to protect *your* castle? Mildred's dead. She's the only one that's been good to us, and even she let us wallow in that poverty-ridden mess without help these past years."

"Do you still see Chatham City as something that doesn't belong to you?" I asked in surprise. "Is Chatham not your castle and your city as well?"

Jackie shook her head. "No. It never has been, despite how much Mildred tried to work us into the culture. We'll never belong here, Bianca. We're freaks. We've tried for over sixty years now, and witches still fear us. It would be better if we went back to the north where we know we're safe."

This girl bore no resemblance to the fearless Jackie who had once wanted to represent the gypsies in the Network. This was a shell of a girl, a scared young woman. A witch needing courage again.

"What about your dream to be the first gypsy in politics?" I asked, annoyed that she would give up on a goal that had been her whole focus less than two years earlier. Wouldn't Angelina really win the war if witches started giving up and going away? Expelling the gypsies from Chatham City wouldn't start or end anything, but it would represent one more chink in our armor, one more weak spot to exploit.

"That was never going to happen," she said. I hated Angelina. I hated what she'd done to my friend. The lives she'd taken. The hopelessness she'd sown without even showing her face. How powerful must she be to cause such chaos?

Jackie faced forward without looking at me. Her forehead still had a swollen bump on top, marked by stitches keeping her skin together. The scar would be an eternal reminder of the horror of that night.

"There is still so much to fight for, Jackie," I whispered. "Don't give up just because things have become scary. They're about to get much worse."

"I'm going north with Nan," she said again, as if convincing herself. "Da too, although he plans to come back. Not all the gypsies want to leave yet, but Nan is determined, and we have to keep her safe."

"There will be no safe place when the West attacks." I turned away, staring out at the sea of burned rubble. An abandoned doll lay in the wreckage, her porcelain face half-burned. "Not anywhere."

"Our home is much safer than here," she insisted, her jaw set. "What about you?"

"What about me?"

"What are you going to do if there is a war?"

I glanced at the burned remains of the streets of Chatham City and wondered the same thing.

"I'll fight."

We continued down the street without another word.

The Chatterer Archives

"We've convinced most of the gypsies to stay for now," Marten said when I stumbled, bleary-eyed, into his office the next morning. "Barely. One more event and I can't say we'll be able to hold onto them. An entire contingent of Guardians and two Protectors will live amongst them in plain clothing for the time being, and two more Protectors have been assigned to find Angelina. Somehow she continues to evade us."

The firm, dubious expression that had been on Jackie's face replayed itself in my mind. "Will it be enough to keep them here?"

"Let's hope."

"Do you think the Factios attacks are linked to the Western or Southern Networks?" I asked, recalling vapid moments of my dream when I'd seen the fire descend on the city and heard Angelina's voice. Marten's forehead furrowed in thought.

"What do you mean?"

I swallowed. "Angelina. What if Angelina is controlling more than just the Factios?"

Marten seemed to think it over. "It would make sense. If she truly wants a war, the way she seems to, just focusing on the Central Network would be short-sighted."

No, I wanted to say. *I'm worried she's focusing on me also.*

"The fire was strange, wasn't it?" I asked. "It wasn't just fire. It was oppressive and . . . dark. We couldn't do any magic near it, like the fire just absorbed our attempts. I've never heard of that before."

He eyed me with a strange gaze, but the trickle of curiosity behind it spurred me on. "What are you getting at?"

"What if . . . what if all this strange magic that's happening, the oppressive fire, the explosive potion bottles the Factios threw at the gypsies . . . what if it's Almorran magic given to them by Angelina? What if we are too late and Angelina already has the *Book of Spells*?"

A moment of panic whipped through Marten's eyes, but he calmed immediately. "I suppose it's possible. But none of those things can be proven to be Almorran, let alone from the *Book of Spells*. There are many ancient magics that any witch could draw from to harm us."

"But not Clavas."

"No, Clavas are Almorran, but Mabel used those, not Angelina. The magic she's using could be anything."

"How would we know it's *not* Almorran if we don't know Almorran magic at all?"

"It's something to think about," Marten conceded. "Although we don't know that the *Book of Spells* has been found."

"We don't know it hasn't."

"True. But until it's confirmed, we must keep looking. We can at least assume that Miss Mabel didn't have the book last summer when you heard her and Angelina discussing the need to find it."

"Assuming the book they spoke of was the *Book of Spells*."

He fell into deeper thought. "You make several good points, Bianca. Well done. Spoken like a true Ambassador."

I think Angelina is giving me dreams, I wanted to add, but bit my bottom lip. That addition would surely degrade any credibility my theory had garnered, and I didn't want him to lose the surge of pride in his tone.

"Thanks."

"Regardless," Marten said, "I had an idea the other day regarding the *Book of Spells*, so I wanted to follow up on it. We don't have a lot of time to search as we have a meeting with Border Guards in the Eastern Covens at noon, but we'll take a look. Transport to the *Chatterer* archives. I'll meet you there."

I obeyed, grateful to leave the subject of Angelina behind for a while, even if it meant turning to the bleaker prospect of the seemingly fruitless search for the *Book of Spells*.

The witches that worked in the *Chatham Chatterer* archives rustled in the background of the old building with as much enthusiasm as a listless tree. Judging by the sheer amount of dust moving around the place, not very many witches came through anymore. Except for the two workers, I observed no other signs of life.

The *Chatham Chatterer* newsscroll updated itself every day, or sometimes every hour or two, leaving no trace of previous articles—a vexing issue in itself when you really liked one but then couldn't find it ten minutes later. Fortunately, the article didn't disappear entirely. An archive existed in a small town outside of the Chatham City limits, protected from fire, theft, or water by complex incantations. The archives housed every article ever published in the *Chatterer*.

"These are the shelves of articles written during the Dark Days," Marten said, motioning to an entire row of journals as we walked past. "This is where I want to look."

Any mention of the Dark Days piqued my interest. A lack of finger marks in the thick layer of dust indicated witches showed little interest in these particularly thick journals.

"What are we looking for?" I asked when he pulled a collection off the shelf.

"I remember rumors about the *Book of Spells* circulating when I was just a Captain of the Guards, around the time I met Mildred. I wanted to look into it again."

He flipped the book open, skimming slowly enough for me to catch a few of the headlines. *Riots in Newberry. Disease in Chatham City.*

"It certainly was a frightening time, wasn't it?" I murmured, tracking the horrid details through the articles. Grandmother had spoken of it with the same token of reverent fear. My stomach clenched just thinking about it. Weren't we on the verge of something just as horrific? Perhaps more so.

"It was a frightening time," Marten said, "but Mildred brought it out of the ashes beautifully. She gave the Central Network new life."

He replaced the tome and ran his hand along the spines of the others as if he knew them by feel. Finding the one he wanted, he pulled it from the shelves. It was as hefty as the first. He handed it to me and shuffled to the side, seeking another. Once he found it, he balanced it in the crook of his arm and left the stacks.

One lone witch sat at a circular table on the other side of the room, sipping something from a silver teacup and poring over a book. We moved to a larger table where both of us could clutter the space.

"Start skimming," he said. "Look for anything on the *Book of Spells*."

Not only did the *Chatterer* archives include every article ever published, it included the ads as well. In my perusal, I passed notices for new caramels at Miss Holly's Candy Shop, a potion to treat nail fungus, and a new style of wool capes. Glimpses of history waited in the archives for someone to care about them again.

"Here's a report," Marten said thirty minutes later, tapping on his book. "But it only claims an Almorran spell was used, not the book itself, and it looks like the witch was drunk."

"Sounds like another dead end," I murmured, skimming past hair potion ads when a familiar word caught my eye.

Almorran.

I stopped and read back.

Almorran Book of Spells in the Southern Covens?

"Here's one," I said, turning the book so both of us could read.

The Almorran Book of Spells, reputed to still exist thousands of years after the evil Almorran race of witches was completely wiped out, has reputedly been stolen from a poor farmer in the Southern Covens.

Willard Stacey, an illiterate witch in the farming village of Ellsworth, stirred up a ruckus two years ago when he first claimed he'd found the book of dark magic in the floor of his kitchen. Willard recently came forward again this week saying that someone had bewitched him and stolen it months ago. He states he's very "concerned that it's back out in the world with no one to stop whoever stole it," though he can't recall the thief, nor when exactly it was stolen. His nine-year-old son, a witness to the event, confirms his father's testimony but refuses to speak on the details of the matter.

Dougall McKenzie, Coven Leader over Ellsworth in the Southern Covens where Stacey resides, states, "Willard is occasionally delusional and prone to drink. The only thing that's been stolen is precious time from the witches of this community."

The Network authorities have no comment.

I glanced at Marten in disbelief. "Is this it?" I asked. "The one you remember?"

He nodded. "That's the one," he said, his shoulders slouching in disappointment. "I remember reading it when it first came out. Poor Willard Stacey was ruined for the rest of his life."

I skimmed the article again. Something in the words rang a bell in my head. I stopped reading to stare at a blank spot on the page.

Southern Covens.

"Marten," I said, my voice sounding distant and strange. "I don't think he was lying. In *Mildred's Resistance*, Mabel's grandmother May said in a letter that she went to the Southern Covens on a business trip once. What if the timing coincides? What if May took the book?"

"I'm sure May had a lot of business meetings throughout the Network. She ran the most prosperous Network school."

"She ran a school, not a thrift store. Why would she travel to the Southern Covens?"

"Meet with a prospective student?"

"So far south?"

"May stealing the *Book of Spells* from this random witch is a big stretch. Not to mention a poor farmer finding the most powerful book of black magic in his floorboards?"

"Let's just say that it *was* the *Book of Spells*," I said patiently. "Wouldn't it make sense that May would go after every rumor in the hopes of finding it, just like we are? May was trying to take over Antebellum, wasn't she? Even Mildred suspected the *Book of Spells* back then and before she died."

"Perhaps," he said. "It may be a lead. At the very least, we can check it out and see if it is."

The pages of the book whirred under his thumb and finally stopped.

"Look," he said, pointing to a new article. "Willard Stacey died shortly after all this mess. Says it was from a deranged mind."

He slid his book over the top of the table to me, his finger on a small article at the bottom.

Famed Farmer Willard Stacey Dies from Madness.

A suspicious feeling in my gut told me that Willard had been telling the truth—at least as far as he knew it to be true—and that the witch who had taken the *Book of Spells* from him was none other than May, the vile grandmother of my teacher. If true, that meant Angelina or Miss Mabel could have inherited the book on May's death. Which meant that Marten and I had wasted eight months searching for something that had already been found.

And a powerful book of magic lay in the hands of a witch who sought to destroy the Central Network.

"Have any serious rumors of it popped up since then?" I asked.

"Not that I've heard." He shrugged. "But that doesn't mean anything."

Oh, it meant something, all right. But I'd need proof to convince Papa and the others. "The article mentions a son. Can I see if his son is still there? I'll feel better about it if I could just talk to him."

Marten hesitated. "I suppose we have to follow every rumor to the end, don't we? I don't see any inherent danger that your father would disapprove of . . . it's fine," he said with a nod. "Go tomorrow morning and report back before lunch. No longer. We need to check the Borderlands tomorrow to make sure the West Guards aren't sneaking up on us."

Bartie Stacey

I left for the Southern Covens as soon as I finished scarfing down breakfast the next morning. After a quick kiss for Papa, who'd been studying a map of the Network borders all morning, I transported to Ellsworth at the heart of the Southern Covens.

The slow-moving Southern Covens were full of heart. The residents cut and stored ice in the winter, packing it in thick sheds of sawdust to send north. Chatham Castle would buy the ice throughout the year for parties, balls, and medicinal use. The richest witches in Ashleigh City bought it for ice sculptures and cooling down in the summer. For the rest of the year, when the freshwater lakes weren't two feet thick in ice, the Southern Covens' witches chopped wood and lived off of small family farms in the midst of Letum Wood.

When I arrived, wearing a heavy cloak lined with velvet and fur, Ellsworth seemed to have been forgotten. Only half the stores were open, and piles of snow littered the road. No doubt most witches were out on the ice. Unfortunately, my presence hadn't gone unnoticed. In a world where everyone knew everyone, an unknown witch in leather shoes strolling down the dirt road drew too much attention. I ignored the eyes that watched my every step and approached a blacksmith. He was a scrawny man, wiry from years of hard work, but strong through the shoulders, with massive forearms. He regarded me through lidded eyes, a tuft of brown hair wafting from underneath his hat.

"What?" he barked.

"I'm looking for the son of Willard Stacey," I called, hovering in the doorway. "Do you know him?"

The blacksmith pulled a white-hot iron from the heart of the fire and dipped it into a cauldron of water. It hissed and sizzled, small droplets bouncing off the top of the water around it.

"So what if I do?"

"I'd like to speak with him."

"What if he doesn't want to speak with you?" he replied, going about his business as if I wasn't there.

"I'd say that's a conclusion he should come to himself."

The blacksmith glanced up, studied me, and snorted. Not without some amusement, to my relief.

"His name is Bartie. If you want to speak with him, he's an hour walk down the road. His farmhouse is on the right. Small wooden building with a barn in back."

"Thank you," I said gratefully. He nodded, sifting through a gamut of black tools that lay before him, not seeming to notice when I slipped away. Once out of sight of the sad little town, I began to run. The movement warmed me as I headed down the snow-packed road, noting every house I passed. Very few children played outside, making it seem stark and barren.

Bartie Stacey's farmhouse appeared before half an hour had passed, thanks to my quick pace. It had been far too long since I'd pushed myself for speed. Running on trails meant I sacrificed speed for safety so I didn't trip over rocks or roots. At the farmhouse, failing shutters hung from the windows, and chipped red paint peeled like dry skin from the walls. A few chickens scattered when I walked up the dirt path from the road. I stopped when a dog growled at me.

"Bartie?" I called. The dog stood up, nose in the air, chest rumbling. "Mr. Stacey?"

A flash in an upper window caught my eye. Within moments, a spiny figure appeared in the door.

"What?"

"Are you Willard Stacey's son, Bartie?"

He hesitated, lingering in the dark shadows so I couldn't make him out. "So what if I am?"

"I'd like to talk to you about your father and the *Book of Spells.*"

"Do you now?" he asked in a low drawl.

"Yes."

He stuffed his hands into his pockets and rocked back on his heels. "It's been a while since we've heard from the likes of you."

My forehead wrinkled over my eyes. "The likes of me?"

"Witches wanting to come poke fun at Pops. Destroying the good name of Stacey. Pops wasn't crazy. He didn't lose a shred of sanity in all his short days."

"On the contrary," I said, wondering if this had been the best idea. "I think your father was telling the truth."

Bartie hesitated before shuffling forward, moving closer to the light. I caught a glimpse of deep-set eyes in a stubborn face. *Definitely a farmer,* I thought. It seemed like farmers all had the same earthy look, as if the soil had become part of their personalities.

"Searching for the book yourself?" he asked.

My "yes" faltered on my lips. He was testing me; I could tell from the gleam in his calm face. No doubt others, with more sinister intent than I, had come to find the truth behind the rumors. I sensed he'd turn me away in a heartbeat if he suspected I wanted the book—regardless of the purity of my intent—and I'd lose my chance.

"Not exactly," I said, honestly. "I came to ask more about the witch who took it from your father."

He tilted his head back, as if that helped him judge my character. A long silence stretched between us, broken only by the cluck of the chickens. I waited for him to proceed.

"Come in," he finally said, evaporating into the darkness. The dog followed him, and so did I.

I sat with Bartie at a table barely big enough for both of us, in a house filled with useless trinkets and moths. Most of the wooden walls, some of which suffered the growth of a dark mold along the top, remained bare. Bartie brought an old iron kettle over from the fire and poured me a cup of hot water.

"I don't have any tea," he said without apology. "But hot water is as good as cold water on a chilly day like this."

I managed a polite nod. I'd drink bitter herbs if he'd give me information about Mabel's grandmother, May. Bartie was a lean man, with elbows sticking out of knobby arms, large knuckles, and defined cheekbones. He sported an unkempt mop of grayish brown hair that hadn't been cut in a few months.

"Will you tell me about your father?" I asked.

Bartie sipped his water, his Adam's apple bobbing in his throat. "He was a quiet man that lived his life and minded his own business. He certainly didn't like all the attention that the *Book of Spells* gave him."

Finding the temperature of the water to his liking, Bartie tilted his head back and drained the whole cup in a heavy swallow. My own steamed in my hand. Just to be polite, I took a sip.

"Then why did he tell the world that he'd found the *Book of Spells*?" I asked. "He must have known it would draw unwanted attention."

"Because he was also a man of the truth," he replied with reverence in his voice. "He worried that such a powerful book could fall into the wrong hands. If he just let it go, it could mean the end of everything."

I watched Bartie carefully, and in just the few minutes we'd been conversing, I could tell that he really believed the *Book of Spells* had been in his father's possession. My eyes darted around the little alcove. But why would the *Book of Spells* have been here of all places? Surely this house couldn't be older than a hundred years, while the *Book of Spells* had existed for millennia.

"Can you tell me everything you remember?" I asked.

He hesitated again. "You must have some idea of who has the book or else you wouldn't be here asking all these questions."

I set aside the hot, flavorless water.

"Yes," I admitted, wondering how open I could afford to be. Seeing the burning intensity in his eyes, I decided to be as honest with him as I wanted him to be with me. "I do believe I know, but I need a few details to confirm it. If it is the woman I believe it to be, we have a real problem on our hands."

"How old are you?" he asked, reaching out to pour himself another cup of hot water. I noticed his lack of magic and wondered.

"I'll be eighteen this summer."

"I never said it was a woman," he said, taking me by surprise. "The witch who took the book, I mean."

"Pardon?"

"You said you thought a woman took the book from my father," Bartie replied, blowing on the water but keeping his eyes on me. "I never said it was a woman."

"If it's not a woman, that muddles my suspicions," I retorted with a wry grin that seemed to set him at ease. "Was it?"

Instead of replying, Bartie downed the nearly boiling water again, wiped the back of his hand across his lips, and leaned back in his chair.

"I was seven years old, and had just finished milking the cows."

Bartie was an only child. His mother had just died of sickness, and his father could barely handle the day-to-day work on the farm in his grief. The two of them managed to keep the farm running, but the house fell into disrepair. One day a spark from the stove fell onto the floor, igniting a dry patch of wood. They stamped it out, but not before several boards burned. Willard pulled the boards up to find an old book with a moldering leather cover and cracked binding.

"Father couldn't read," Bartie admitted, blinking rapidly, "but I could. Mother taught me. He showed me the book, but I didn't recognize any of the words. I don't remember any of them now, either, but I do remember. . ."

He trailed off, appearing uncertain, maybe even shaken. I raised my eyebrows in what I hoped he would interpret as an encouraging gesture.

"This may have been a figment of my imagination because I was quite young at the time, but when I read a few of the words out loud, I felt . . . heavy. Darkness seemed to surround the words."

I sucked in a breath. He'd just described, word for word, the way I felt during the fire in Chatham City, and most frightening of all, in my dreams.

Bartie stopped speaking and studied my face with concern. "What?" he asked. "What is it? What did I say?"

"I know what you're describing," I said, remembering my determination to be honest with him. "I've felt it myself. At least I think I have."

He seemed skeptical but continued. "Father tried to burn it, but it wouldn't burn. We set it in the middle of a bed of coals and nothing ever happened. That's when he knew it was something bad. Really bad."

"Did he suspect it to be the *Book of Spells* then?"

"Not until later."

After their botched attempts to destroy it, Willard confided in a trusted friend that turned out to be not so trustworthy after all. Despite his refusal to show his friend the book, word spread like wildfire through the town, catching the ear of a visitor who took news back to Chatham City, telling the story along the way.

"Nothing happened for a while," Bartie said with a shrug. "Father's friend advised him to just get rid of it, to throw it into the woods or the lake and forget about it, but Father couldn't. Someone else would find it then, and who knew what could happen? He went to the High Witch, the Coven Leader, and the Council Member, but they just laughed at him or ignored him."

Bartie sucked on his front teeth for a second. "To be fair, it did seem outrageous that the *Book of Spells* would appear in the floorboards of a poor, illiterate farmer, but Father had never lied. I'd never seen him so uncomfortable. He couldn't sleep at night, could barely focus during the day. We put the book in the floor of the corner room and never went back for it."

"When did she come?" I asked. "The witch who took it?"

"A year or so after we found it. The rumor had circulated through the Network by then, and the *Chatterer* had already written its first article about it. They kicked me out of the common school after it was published, saying we were mad."

My heart sped up. "What was she like?"

He grimaced. "Quiet. Intense. Cold as ice. Just showed up on the porch one day. Not even the dogs detected her until she spoke. They slunk away and wouldn't even look at her. I was sitting at the top of a tree. It was afternoon, and I'd just finished my chores. When she transported onto the porch, I looked down on her from a bird's eye view.

Her hair was dark as pitch, with wide curls. She wore the finest dress I'd ever seen. She frightened my father, I could tell. She never went inside the house either. Never strayed a single step off the porch."

Bartie spoke as if he were in a trance, reciting it verbatim from the depths of his memory.

"I didn't make a sound because I was too scared to move," he continued. "She put some kind of incantation on my father. He disappeared into the house, then returned with the book and handed it right to her. After that, she evaporated into thin air."

When young Bartie scrambled down from his perch in the tree, his father had a dazed expression on his face, and his eyes were foggy, like they'd been filled with mist.

"He was like that for several days," Bartie said, shaking his head. A few drops of water lingering on his beard scattered on the table. "When the fog disappeared and he stopped walking into walls, he didn't remember the book. Every time I brought it up it gave him a headache. That's when I got really scared. I asked him about the book every day. Sometimes I'd talk about it so many times he'd box my ears. But in the end, it seemed to wear the magic down. By my ninth birthday, two years after he found the book, he began to remember it again. He remembered the lady, though not much more than her dark hair, and started squawking about it in fear. The *Chatterer* came back down for another interview, and Father told them the book was stolen."

My heart hammered. The details, the circumstances were all too perfect. "I read that article," I said. "That's what brought me here."

He snorted. "Everyone read that article."

"Did you ever see her again?" I asked, taking care to control my eager tone. He shook his head. "If I showed you a painting of her, would you remember?"

He shrugged. "I only saw the top of her. Not her face. Father was murdered shortly after that article was published anyway, so he's no help."

My heart caught in my throat. "What?"

"Witches hated us after Papa brought it up again."

"So they killed him?"

Darkness flittered across his eyes. "I think that witch came back in the night and killed him when he started making a racket again. Luckily I wasn't there at the time. I slept in the barn because it was cooler. One day I woke up, went in the house, and he was dead."

"My mother was murdered when I was sixteen," I said with a pang of sympathy. "It rots."

He managed a brief smile. "Yes," he said. "It does."

I glanced outside to see where the sun had moved, for I saw no clocks in his house, and judged myself to have been there at least an hour, if not more.

"Thank you, Bartie, for answering my questions. You've been extremely helpful."

He nodded, his lips pursed. I stood, thanked him again for the hot water, and started to the front door.

"Think you can get her?" he asked. "Whoever it is that you're looking for?"

I hesitated. "The witch that I believe took your book is dead already, but she has a daughter."

"Passed it on?"

"I think so, but I don't know."

"I hope you do find her," he said, pouring another glass of cooling water. "She was a nasty witch. Never seen anyone like her in my life."

You have no idea, I thought, transporting away before the dog could growl at me again.

"So?" Marten asked, glancing up from his desk when I strolled in. "How did it go with Willard's son?"

I had stopped by my bedroom to sift through *Mildred's Resistance* before returning to Marten's office, troubled by all Bartie had told me. I couldn't prove the reliability of Bartie Stacey's story—perhaps he'd been a frightened little boy stricken with grief and a strong imagination—but I couldn't deny the correlations between his story and what I knew of history.

"It went . . ." I trailed off, not sure how to articulate my grim thoughts as I sat on a chair and rested *Mildred's Resistance* on my lap. "Well, let's just say I didn't quite expect it."

I recounted everything. Marten listened intently, and when I finished, fell into a silence similar to mine.

"It *is* interesting," he murmured, and I felt a wash of relief. He motioned to the book. "Correlations?"

"Yes," I said, sending the book to him with a floating incantation. I had dog-eared the two pages in which May spoke of the Southern Covens. He sent me a chastising look, and I blushed, mumbling *sorry* under my breath. He straightened the corners and perused the pages, staring at them, unblinking. I let him drift in his thoughts.

"I'm glad you pursued it," he said. "We may not have concrete proof, but it's as solid as a story as I believe we'll ever really find. You believe Bartie?"

"I have no reason not to," I replied, grateful that Marten didn't seem skeptical. "What does he stand to gain by lying about his deceased father? Why would he lie? Besides, he described it in a way that I couldn't help but believe."

Marten hummed under his breath, eyes tapering in thought. "Why would the most powerful book of dark magic in all of Antebellum rot in the floorboards of a farmhouse, do you think?"

"Why not?" I countered, answering the same question that had haunted me. "Who is to say that it hasn't bounced around across all these years? It could have been hidden, lost, or found its own way there. The possibilities are limitless."

He nodded absently. The idea that a single book threatened to destroy all I loved was nearly too much to comprehend. How did one fight something that wasn't supposed to exist?

"If this story *is* true," Marten mused, head tilted back to stare at the ceiling, "and May did steal the *Book of Spells* all those years ago, then we . . ."

His thought lingered, unfinished. *We've been wasting our time.*

"We're in big trouble," I whispered, my voice hoarse. "But how do we find out for sure? I don't want to panic until I have to."

Marten set the book aside and straightened. "We ask the one witch—aside from Angelina—who would know."

"Who?"

"Mabel."

My stomach clenched. *Miss Mabel.* I hid my irrational explosion of fear at the thought of seeing her again.

"Talk to Miss Mabel? Papa won't allow it."

"I think I can convince him. We need to explore this story more, and she's our best shot."

"You know how careful he is about anything to do with her ever since those two West Guards snuck through the dungeons to set her free two months ago. Not to mention the latest attempt to break her free with the servant."

"You let me convince your father. Working with strong personalities is part of my job. Derek trusts me and will understand. If the *Book of Spells* has already been found—if it even exists—it changes everything."

Miss Mabel

That evening, after Marten left to convince my father, I escaped to the Witchery, grateful to set aside all thoughts of Miss Mabel, Bartie Stacey, and the *Book of Spells*. Camille and Leda were climbing the Witchery steps when I jogged up behind them.

"Merry meet, Bianca," Camille chirped, her hair bouncing as she ascended the stairs. "How were things at work?"

"Fine," I said, planning to tell them everything later once I'd sorted through my thoughts on Bartie and Angelina and May. "How was your day?"

"Wonderful!" Camille cried. "Thanks to Priscilla I finished my classes early and went to see Brecken's mother. She needed help with a baby quilt."

"How is Tabby doing?" I asked to steer Camille away from the dangerous topics of family and marriage. Once she started, she never stopped.

"She's good," Camille said with a warm smile, pulling her cloak closer around her to ward off the chill. "It's so easy to spend time with her. She's nothing like my old aunts Bettina and Angie. She's very . . . soft."

She prattled about the quilt until we reached the top of the turret. A bright winter sun sparkled off the thin windowpanes. Despite the sunshine, the air felt frigid. Leda commanded a fire the moment she stepped into the circular room and drifted over to a stack of books waiting on the table. She read a note on top of the stack, then smiled and stuffed it into the book on top.

"A present for you?" I asked, my breath fogging out in front of me as I dropped onto our old divan and closed my eyes.

"Yes."

Though she tried to hide it, I heard a sudden guardedness in her tone. My eyes popped open as she opened a lovely blue leather book covered in gold trim.

"Rupert sent them to me," she said with the slightest hint of a smile, as if she were revolving through emotions too quickly to decide on just one. "He thought I might enjoy a book on the scholarly dissertations of Sybil that I haven't been able to locate."

I groaned at Rupert's name. Camille and Michelle were already too far gone into their romances for me to save them, but Leda? I could try to keep her with me for a few years.

"Sybil?" Camille asked. "Wasn't she driven mad or fell in love with a horse or something?"

"Neither," Leda snapped. "She was one of the most brilliant witches that has ever lived. She was taken before her time."

Sybil had been an eccentric witch. She loved education, books, and anything to do with herbology, and scholars considered her to be one of the most intelligent witches in the history of the Central Network. Like all the greats, she died in a tragic accident: drowned in a pond while conducting an experiment. Leda idolized all the essays Sybil left behind.

The divan felt cold and hard as a rock behind me, but I didn't mind. All I needed was a place to close my eyes and think for a while. The added bonus of Camille's chatter in the background—"Do you think Tabby would like this light pink dress? I'm going back tomorrow evening for dinner."—helped me focus my thoughts on nothing.

I drifted into a pleasant half-sleep, aware of the warmth of the fire on my face and the cold nip of the air above me. Camille's voice faded into a pleasant breeze, and suddenly I lay in the warm grass outside Grandmother's cottage. The smell of honeysuckle and fresh soil floated on the wind. Grandmother hummed as she hung the laundry on the line with her arthritic hands. Mama stood in the house, staring at me from the window with her queer gray eyes and wild black hair. I smiled.

Bianca! Mama called, leaning out the window and laughing. *Bianca, can you hear me?*

I pushed onto my elbow in the grass, confused. Mama's lips were moving, but the voice wasn't hers. The warm kiss of the sun faded, darkened by a bank of broiling clouds.

Bianca, sang the now-cold voice. *We need to talk.*

I shot to my feet. Grandmother disappeared, the cottage grew dark, and a terrible storm swept overhead, dimming the sunshine. Mama's gray eyes faded. Her hair grew, blowing off her neck in the wind, until a narrow nose and an attractive, superior face emerged from the distance. I didn't know her by sight, but as the darkness fell over my mind, I had no doubt.

Angelina.

She stared at me with chill, unnerving eyes of the brightest blue. *Bianca, let my daughter go.*

A crash of thunder shook the air. The cottage began to rip apart in the wind, blowing away in chunks. The storm brought an unusual darkness: a palpable one. It weighed so heavy on my chest that I felt as if I could stroke it.

Let my daughter go.

I jerked awake with a cry.

Leda and Camille were staring at me, wide-eyed and frightened, from the other side of the room. The banging in my dream had been real; someone thumped on the Witchery door far below.

"Sorry," I panted. "S-sorry."

Grateful for an escape so I didn't have to explain, I leapt off the divan and rushed down the stairs, fleeing the horrific nightmare. When I yanked the door open, Merrick stood outside.

"Derek needs you," he said, tilting his face to one side in concern. "You all right? You look like—"

"Yes, I'm fine. What's wrong?"

"Another dream?"

My mouth dropped open. "How'd you know?"

"I know more than you think," he retorted. His hand twitched as if he wanted to reach for me but didn't dare. "Come on, I'll walk you there so you can pull yourself together. He wants to see you now."

Papa and Marten waited for me in the High Priest's office, which looked like a personal military fortress. Crossed swords hung on the wall above the fireplace across from three glimmering shields arranged in a triangle. A sprawling tapestry featuring a roaring dragon decorated the back wall, where a secret entrance had been filled in decades before. His office was simple and to the point, just like Papa.

A new injury crossed Papa's cheek, stitched together with dark pieces of string, so he only greeted me with a warm half-smile. He didn't say anything until Merrick closed the door and stood against it to prevent anyone from wandering in. A flurry of light zipped around the edges, sealing the sound of our conversation from listening ears.

"We have a problem," Papa said, motioning to Marten with a nod. "Mabel refuses to talk to Marten. She says she'll only speak with one witch."

I glanced between their grim expressions in suspicion. The hair on the back of my arms rose.

"Me."

Papa's nostrils flared. The skin on his face was taut, but bags hung off his eyes, a testament to the weariness of his endless job.

"Yes." Marten said quietly.

Silence filled the air, as oppressive and expansive as the dark magic in my wild dreams. Was it a coincidence that I'd dreamt of Angelina moments before I went to see her daughter?

No. Coincidences weren't repetitive.

"I see," I whispered, buying time.

"Are you sufficiently concerned that Mabel already has the *Book of Spells*?" Papa asked Marten in a clipped tone. Marten met Papa's intense gaze without flinching.

"I believe a discussion between Mabel and Bianca is necessary, yes."

"Meaning that the downfall of the Network could hinge on this decision? This conversation could prevent a war?" Papa demanded. "I won't have Bianca exposed to her for any reason except to prevent the possibility of total annihilation of the Network."

I stepped forward and put a hand on Papa's arm. The tension in his body seemed to unwind.

"I'll do it gladly, Papa," I said, forcing a clear voice. "We need to know if May already found the *Book of Spells*. It really could change the fate of the Network."

Despite my bravado, a tight vise had constricted in my chest. Speak with the witch who murdered my mother and the High Priestess? What would I say? Would I be able to control my magic? Just thinking of Miss Mabel stirred the dark dragon that lived in the innermost parts of my heart. Papa studied me, as if seeking to understand whether or not I was lying to sound brave.

"She can't hurt me in there, anyway," I added. "You'd never let her."

"Not physically."

"Or mentally," I said. "I'm stronger than she is."

Papa ran a hand through his hair. "Fine," he muttered. "But you only have five minutes."

"Ten," I said. "At least."

He glared but gave in with a nod. "Ten and not a second more. Merrick, transport to the dungeons and let them know we're coming."

The dungeons felt damp and bleak.

Light flickered over the walls in weak licks of flame. Papa led the way, and Marten followed just behind me. No one said a word, and I was glad. Really, what could have been said? I was about to face Mama's murderer. Angelina's voice rang through my head.

Let my daughter go.

Papa stopped outside a heavy iron door and turned to me with an unreadable expression of steel and ice.

"She's in a cell. You'll be in the room alone with her, but she can't touch you or curse you. She can't do any magic whatsoever here. This cell is under my power alone. Not a living soul can do anything to it. Any changes to the magic controlling her imprisonment would require my blood. The only thing she'll be able to do is talk to you. Understand?"

"It's fine, Papa. I'm not afraid." I hoped the lie would comfort him.

He tugged on the door, but hesitated. "She's . . . different. Just be prepared."

I wasn't sure what he meant and didn't have the time to ask. He whispered an incantation that I'd never heard before but committed to memory to study later. When I stepped inside, the door closed behind me with a firm *thud*. Papa and Marten wouldn't be able to overhear the conversation, which gave me a bit more courage. My eyes accommodated gradually to the dim light of the claustrophobic room.

I peered into the shadows, seeing nothing but the glint of light off iron bars on the left. Two torches illuminated the wall to my right, casting a gleam onto the floor where I could walk up to the bars that separated me from my worst enemy.

"Bianca, darling. How good it is to see you again."

Her voice came from the darkness, setting my hair on edge. Such an alluring, silky voice for such a maniacal devil.

"Miss Mabel," I said, gritting my teeth. "You asked to see me."

A fine layer of straw muffled the rattle of manacles on the stone floor. She shuffled into the light. Had I not known with certainty it was her, I would never have recognized her. Unable to transform her appearance with magic, Miss Mabel had become her true self: a wrinkled old witch.

By all accounts she should be in her sixties or seventies, though she used to transform herself every day to look as if she were twenty-four. But now bags hung off her high cheekbones underneath the hollows of her eye sockets. Her eyes were the same electric blue, and her body slender. Perhaps *too* slender. Heavy wrinkles pulled her face into a perpetual grimace. Underneath the layers of age, I began to recognize my old teacher. A wan smile, perpetual mocking, the hooded gaze of indifference.

"I did so want to see you," Miss Mabel said. "It's been a long time since I've spoken with my favorite pupil."

"We never liked each other."

A coy smile bloomed on her thin lips. So familiar, so icy. So trapped behind bars.

"That's what I liked about you, Bianca. You've got spunk. Tell me, how are things out there? Are they just as lovely as you thought they'd be once I was subdued in prison?"

"You know very well what it's like," I retorted, stepping further into the room but keeping myself at arm's distance.

"No, actually, I don't," she said, and I could tell she meant it. "Derek does a fabulous job keeping me locked up in here. I know that you're having a problem or twelve, but that's all. You might not believe it, but I'm quite isolated in my cozy little hole."

A hungry gleam emanated from her eyes. Six months without sunshine had left her skin nearly translucent.

"Let's get to the point, shall we?" *Let her wallow in ignorance.* "How long have you had the *Book of Spells*?"

Her chest bucked, as if she were suppressing a cough.

"Who says I have the *Book of Spells*?" she asked, palms up at her side in an innocent gesture. "I haven't even got a pot to call my own here."

I hesitated. Marten had taught me that diplomatic conversations were struggles for information. The more you had, and the less you revealed, the greater the power you retained. I wasn't sure what I should tell Miss Mabel and what I should conceal.

"I stumbled onto some Almorran magic the other day," I said.

She *tutted* under her breath and shook her head reprovingly. For a moment, I was swept back to the year she taught me in the attic of Miss Mabel's School for Girls.

"You show your ignorance with such a stupid remark," she said, lifting her chin. "Don't you know there are lesser Almorran scrolls floating around?"

The idea curled my gut. Was she lying? "You're trying to tell me that a couple of scrolls have survived thousands of years? It seems far-fetched that even a book would last that long."

She chuckled. "You underestimate the power of the dark Almorran magic, Bianca. Evil doesn't just last, silly fool. Evil thrives. It protects itself, don't you know? It's the most purely selfish thing in all of Antebellum. It exists because it likes to exist. You may not give it credit for being an entity unto itself, but it is. Just try fighting it, and see how you feel."

Her eyes lit up in a sudden flash, as if a bolt of lightning moved through the room. I didn't move as I watched her.

"Besides," she said, "one doesn't just stumble across Almorran magic, does one? No. Almorran magic finds those that will give it the greatest opportunity for power. Selfish, remember? Mother dearest must be giving you real problems if Derek allowed you in here to speak with me, eh?" Her eyes sparkled. "Dreams, perhaps? Fire? Death and destruction? All kinds of icky, scary spells that haven't been seen before?"

I clenched my fists, striving for control as magic flared hot in my chest. *Dreams, perhaps?* So my suspicions must have been correct. My nightmares weren't idle dreams; Angelina gave them to me. My chest felt cold.

"Goodness," she cried, leaning back in surprise so that the shadows nearly cloaked her face again. She rubbed her fingertips over her lips, her eyes alight with some internal flame. "Did I guess correctly? Is sweet Mother dear trying to get me back? Yes, she must, or else you wouldn't have gone so pale. I'm going to guess she's giving you dreams. It's her favorite method of communication, you know. She does love a sleeping, vulnerable mind to toy with. It feels terrible, doesn't it? Being trapped and unable to get free?"

I turned away.

"Perhaps it's not me you should fear, Bianca," she said. "For Angelina is infinitely more powerful than you could ever imagine. One could even say she's a master at what she does."

Her cloying tone told me she meant something else, something important, but I couldn't decipher the implications of her words. *Don't let her do this,* I told myself. *Don't let her win by unnerving you. Get back to the point, Bianca. What was the point?*

"Did May find the *Book of Spells?*" I asked, regaining my composure. "Is that why Angelina is so powerful?"

Miss Mabel smiled. "Ask whatever you want, Bianca. No matter what I tell you today, you'll learn—or face—the truth soon enough. Angelina always gets what she wants."

"What truth is that? That you'll rot to death before you ever see the light of day again? Papa will never let you go."

"The truth is that you need me," she hissed, gripping the cold iron bars in her hands and shoving her face against them. I stepped back, startled. "And when you realize it, you'll come back and set me free."

"I'd rather die," I snarled. She studied me with distant annoyance.

"Yes," she said. "I believe you. You would rather die than let me see freedom again. But your life isn't the one you should worry about bargaining for, is it? Angelina is already in your mind, silly child. Even I can see that. Don't you think she knows how to get what she wants?" Her voice grew low. "Or, more importantly, don't you think she's willing to do whatever she must to get what she wants?"

"And what does she want?"

"Me. She wants me. Mother always was a bit more sentimental than May, you know. Far more sentimental than I would ever be. She has a bit of a soft spot for her daughter." She grinned. "And don't *you* know how weaknesses can be exploited?"

The feel of Mama's lifeless body falling into my arms replayed itself in my mind. I folded my hands behind me and cleared my throat.

"Why did you want to talk to me?" I asked. "What do you want?"

She smiled. "Information, of course. And you've just given all of it to me, Bianca darling. Thank you for the lovely chat. Give my regards to Isadora, will you?"

Miss Mabel smiled and faded back into the darkness from which she'd come. I searched for her in the empty air, but seeing only the dim glow of her bright eyes, left the chamber without another word.

Before the Storm

arten took the next couple of days to think over what had happened with Mabel and decide what we should do about the *Book of Spells*. I'd given up on finding it, convinced that Angelina had it. We focused on Network business and didn't speak of Miss Mabel again.

The snow and winds swirled in bitter winter wrath through the Central Network, a late blizzard lasting nearly two days. I worked with Marten, stayed up late trying to avoid sleep, and ran with Merrick in the snowy mornings to keep my agitated powers at bay despite Papa's request that I run with someone else.

When I stepped into the Witchery after a full day of visiting border towns and checking event logs—which were always *un*eventful—I stopped in my tracks. Priscilla sat in front of the fire reading a book. The rest of the Witchery lay quiet and empty. As soon as she saw me, she started and closed the book.

"Oh, sorry. Camille said I could stay here and—"

"It's fine," I said, motioning her back down when she made a move to stand. "I don't care if you sit in front of the fire."

She hesitated and finally relaxed again. I wondered where her old friends Jade and Stephany were. Priscilla had spent most of her free time with Camille, and I'd noticed she seemed to have no other ties. Why didn't Jade visit her here? Why didn't I ever see her with letters from Stephany or her parents? Perhaps their friendship hadn't been deep enough to span the gap that comes with growing up. I thought of my own friends, grateful we'd found a way to pull together so far.

"I'm just glad you weren't Leda. She'd kick me out," Priscilla mumbled under breath, and I laughed. Her forehead ruffled in surprise, as if she'd expected me to pounce her instead of agreeing.

"You should be glad I'm not Leda," I said. "She can hold a very long grudge."

"So I'm learning."

"She's just loyal," I said, setting my bag on the table, grateful that the room was already warm. "Once she finds a friend, she takes them in like a family member, though she'd never admit it. Try to tell her that and she'd probably hex you and say you're a sentimental sap. But in the end she's ornery out of love."

Priscilla snorted and looked at the fire, a dubious expression on her face. I moved closer to the hearth, hands outstretched, surprised by the lack of tension in the air. It had been well over a year since Priscilla and I had spent any time one-on-one, and it hadn't ever gone this smoothly.

My fingers started to thaw—I'd been outside during a long dispute with a Border Guard who had nearly crossed into the Eastern Network trying to hunt a squirrel.

"How was work?" Priscilla asked, though her voice sounded rigid and formal. She glanced at me from the corner of her eye, and kept her neck so tall I thought she'd snap.

"Ridiculous," I muttered. "Some witches don't think."

"What exactly do you do again?"

"Whatever Marten wants me to do. Mostly Assistant stuff, I guess, though I don't really know what other Assistants do. Being the Ambassador's Assistant isn't the same as a Council Member's Assistant."

"Do you like it?"

I stared at the fire, forcing myself to think about the answer. "It's not the worst job," I said. She peered at me in surprise.

"You're kidding, right?"

"No."

Priscilla leaned back. "Some witches work their whole lives to become an Assistant to . . . anyone. You're not even eighteen, and you've already become the Assistant to the Ambassador. You've traveled to

Networks that no one else will ever see. This job should be the best thing that ever happened to you."

I squirmed, thinking about Miss Scarlett's lecture during our last etiquette lesson last month about how *work should bring joy.*

"I didn't say it was the worst job, did I? It's just not . . . I never planned for a career. I never planned for a future, so now that I have to face it, I don't know what I want to do."

Her eyebrow lifted, and she seemed so much like her former self that I felt more comfortable. High-handed Priscilla I could take. But this quiet, polite girl that had taken her place recently flummoxed me. Without her followers from school to dote on her she seemed a bit . . . lost.

"What does enjoyment have to do with anything?" she asked, though I wasn't convinced she'd said it to me. "Seems like a dream job to me."

I stared at her, wondering how honest I should be.

"When I went to the Eastern Network, angry witches shot flaming arrows at my carriage and hit my driver," I said, meeting her astonished gaze. "The horse bolted. I had to climb out of the back of the carriage, put the driver under a spell, and take the reins. When I went to the Southern Network, Mikhail forbade me from ever returning because, as a female, I dared to carry a sword. Today, five witches yelled at me because their logbook, which I have nothing to do with, was wrong. A dream job?"

She had the presence of mind to appear sheepish. "Oh. I didn't realize it was so dangerous."

I scoffed lightly and sat down. "Neither did I."

She studied me in the ambient light of the fire. "But that's perfect for a witch like you. You're brave. You can handle situations like that because you're in them so often."

Her words annoyed me. I wasn't brave. Most of the time I was just desperate, doing what had to be done to save my family. I craved a normal life. Consistency. Things to remain happy and solid for more than a year at a time.

"Can . . . can I ask you about your mother?" she ventured quietly. "You can say no. It's just that there are all these rumors about what really happened and . . ."

Surprised that Priscilla would broach such an intimate subject without sounding catty or imperious, I simply nodded.

"I've asked Camille so I wouldn't bother you, but she said it wasn't her story to tell. What really happened?" she asked. "Rumors swirled that Miss Mabel killed your mama, but all we ever officially heard was that an accident happened in the attic. We heard you screaming, and someone running through the school. Witches from the Network swarmed the school for days afterward, and then you were living at the castle, Leda and Camille left, the school closed, and no one heard anything else until Miss Mabel killed the High Priestess."

Her voice went a bit distant. My heart began to pound in my chest, though not as hard as it used to. Mama had been gone for over a year now. The pain had faded, I supposed. Instead of fresh, hot, and stinging, it felt dulled, like the low, constant pulse of a heart. Always present but not as frantic. I met Priscilla's guarded eyes.

"Miss Mabel killed Mama to make me angry," I said. "Or to weaken my father. Or because she's cruel and vile. I don't know her real reason, but she murdered her with magic."

Priscilla's eyes widened. "And you saw?"

I nodded, feeling the familiar tug in my chest that meant my powers were awakening again. "Mama fell into my arms."

A long silence filled the room, and I realized that Priscilla didn't know what to say.

"My powers spiraled out of control last year," I said, filling the strange vacuum with words, hoping it would somehow lead out of this conversation. "Miss Mabel came back and wanted me to kill my father, so I learned sword fighting to help me control my emotions."

"Then you fought Miss Mabel at the Ball," Priscilla said. "I remember reading about that in the *Chatterer*."

"And won," I added with a crooked grin to break the sudden strain in the air. To my surprise, she returned it. Perhaps Priscilla wasn't so bad. A bit stiff and circumspect, but not nearly as haughty as she used to be.

"Was Miss Mabel terrible as a teacher?" Priscilla asked. "She must have been frightening."

I thought of the day Miss Mabel cursed me for hours on end, the look in her eyes when she forced me to sign an unknown binding, the moment she attacked and murdered the High Priestess, and the expression on her face when she refused to remove the curse from my grandmother.

"She wasn't the worst teacher," I whispered. "When she wasn't being sadistic and crazy. In fact, I learned a lot from her. A lot more than I care to admit."

"So many witches hate your father now that he's High Priest," Priscilla said, her forehead furrowing. "Even I've thought he's a bit overzealous in his preparations for war because nothing has happened since Miss Mabel's attack. The Western Network has been perfectly quiet. The Southern Network never does anything. But now that I'm at the castle, I can't . . . I can't help but wonder if he's right. If we're just in the calm before the storm."

"It is," I said, thinking of Mikhail's refusal to answer our questions and Diego's stubborn blindness to the truth. The beginnings of a perfect storm were already brewing. "Trust me."

Priscilla stared into my eyes for so long that the edges of my vision began to blur.

"I think I do."

"Where are Jade and Stephany?" I asked. "I'm surprised your friends never come to visit."

Priscilla pressed her lips together. Her nostrils flared. "I don't know," she said. "We haven't spoken since school closed."

"Really?"

"Jade and Stephany weren't really my friends. I didn't realize it until after school ended." She looked down at her lap, where her fingers fidgeted with a wrinkle in her dress. "Now that I've seen you and Leda and Camille and Michelle together, I'm beginning to wonder if I ever really had friends. Jade or Stephany wouldn't have been nice to me the way Camille was, or made my favorite cake like Michelle did last week."

I didn't know what to say at first. "I suppose Leda isn't making the best impression then," I said with a wry smile. Priscilla didn't return it.

"Actually, I don't blame Leda," she said with a furrow of her porcelain brow. "I wasn't very nice to her at school. I guess I was a little jealous because she didn't seem to care what other witches thought, and I did." Her eyes met mine. "That's what I learned the night I lost the Competition to you."

"That you cared about what other witches thought?"

"Yes. Too much. At school I was so afraid of losing my *friends* that I did anything to keep them. I acted rudely to others to get a laugh. In the end, they deserted me anyway."

She ended with a bitter sigh.

"Then they weren't really your friends after all," I said, feeling a rush of gratitude that Camille had been more welcoming than I. "We're your friends now. Camille adores you, you know."

Priscilla seemed skeptical, but I didn't give her the chance to voice any doubts.

"Speaking of Camille, why aren't you out on a double date with her and Brecken and some other Guardian they've rustled up? Sounds like she's been determined to set you up with a Guardian that will ride you off into the sunset on a white horse just like her."

Priscilla snorted, but seemed relieved at the change in topics. "I hate horses."

Delighted with her sudden cheek, I tilted my head back and laughed. The muscles in her stiff shoulders seemed to unwind, and she cracked the smallest smile.

"You mean you don't love courting Guardians?" I asked in fake shock.

"I hate it."

I sobered. "Really?"

She nodded and let out a sigh, absently brushing her silky red hair over her shoulder. "The only reason I agree to go is because Camille gets so excited. Don't get me wrong—I have fun with Camille, but most of the Guardians are just so . . ."

"Rough around the edges?"

She smiled a little. "Yes. I suppose so. Anyway, I don't have the heart to tell Camille that I don't intend to find a boyfriend."

My eyebrows shot sky high. "Really? But you're so pretty."

Priscilla scowled. "There's more to life than beauty, Bianca."

"Right," I said, retreating sheepishly. "I know, it's just that . . ."

"You thought that because I'm pretty I would naturally want to court hundreds of witches and get married and have babies?"

"I didn't mean to—"

"Well I don't want any of that! I want a life. I want to make my own decisions. I want a career. No marriage is going to weigh me down, make me so miserable that I weep into my pillow every night because my husband never pays attention to me!"

Her voice rose to an almost hysterical pitch, and her cheeks flushed a bright red. I blinked.

"Priscilla, I didn't mean to insinuate that you had to get married or—"

"I'm sorry," she said, clipping me off again and turning away. Her fists clenched into white knuckles on her lap. "I'm sorry. I shouldn't have reacted like that. It's just . . . my parents are . . . they want to marry me off. My mother wants me to live the same life she's living, only she's miserable and unhappy and my father is a lech. I hate both of them. I won't be like either one."

Her passionate outburst made my heart pound. "Is that why you're here at the castle as Miss Scarlett's Assistant?"

"Yes. I hate teaching and Miss Scarlett frightens me. But it was my best opportunity to get as far away from Ashleigh as I could." Her zeal began to fade. Her shoulders slumped, though I doubted Priscilla could really slouch the way I did. "And now I'm making my own life, even if it's not what my parents wanted, or really what I wanted either."

"Good for you," I said. "I think you should do whatever makes you happy."

Priscilla smiled with the edges of her lips. "Happy. Right."

"What do you want if this isn't it?" I asked, motioning around us as if the Witchery encompassed all of her deepest desires.

"Something more," she said. "Something far from here. Something grand and exciting and . . . impossible. Anyway, thanks Bianca. And please don't tell Camille that I . . . well . . . you know."

I laughed. "I'm not going to tell her or else she'll try to drag me along instead. Sorry, you're stuck. By the way, what are you reading?"

I motioned to the old book on her lap.

"A book on transformation I found in the library. It's pretty boring though."

"Care to teach me a few tricks?"

She lifted an eyebrow. "You want to learn transformation? Don't you already know everything? You earned your marks as a first-year. What could I teach you?"

"Ha!" Did Priscilla feel intimidated by me? Beautiful, regal, intelligent Priscilla? The idea seemed absurd. "I only learned what I needed to survive. Besides, my papa taught me a lot of magic my whole life. That's why I passed the marks."

"Do you know transformation?" she asked, warming to the idea.

"I'm not terrible," I said, demonstrating by turning a nearby book into a box of chocolates.

"You're not good at it either," she said. "You didn't speak clearly, which is why the details of the transformation aren't fully formed. See how half the box of chocolates is black and half is white? That's because you didn't really know what you were going to do."

She set a sharp eye on me. I wondered if Miss Scarlett had started to rub off on her.

"Uh, no. I didn't," I admitted, reversing the spell. If Leda caught me messing with her volumes of knowledge, she'd pull my hair out. Priscilla watched me do a few more incantations to show the extent of my skill.

She closed her book. "You need help, Bianca. I could show you a few tips so your objects appear more authentic if you want."

"Sure," I said. "I'll even transform you a box of chocolates to show my appreciation."

"Don't bother. Anyway, with a job as dangerous as yours, you could use it. Maybe it'll save a life one day. Let's get to work."

I woke up a few days later in a cold sweat. No nightmare from Angelina had plagued me in the night, but dreams of Miss Mabel had.

They didn't terrorize me like the ones with Angelina's voice did, so I knew my own mind was tormenting me this time.

I'm going to guess she's giving you dreams, Miss Mabel had said. *It's her favorite method of communication, you know. She does love a sleeping, vulnerable mind to toy with. It feels terrible, doesn't it? Being trapped and unable to get free.*

I didn't have the heart to tell Papa, who hadn't even come back to the apartment to sleep the previous night. I hadn't spoken with him in days thanks to all his meetings, though he'd sent me a few hasty notes with corny jokes scrawled on them. Since Papa was busy, and so was Stella, and my friends didn't know the extent of my troubles, I knew of only one witch I could tell my secrets to.

I shot out of bed and changed, eager to get the burden off my chest, grabbing *Mildred's Resistance* before transporting away.

Isadora lived in Letum Wood, on the edge of the tract of land that housed Miss Mabel's School for Girls. While I harbored ill memories of the school, I couldn't deny that good things had happened there as well. Without it, I would never have met Leda, Camille, and Michelle, nor lived past my seventeenth birthday. I forced aside the insistent thought that I wouldn't have lost my mother either.

I arrived to find Isadora and Sanna standing on the porch, staring into the trees with distant expressions on their faces. The wintry air was thick with cold, and my breaths billowed out in gusts, so I was surprised to see the two aged sisters outside. They didn't acknowledge me at first, so I waited on the path, my cloak heavy about my shoulders.

"It's not very pretty out there, is it?" Isadora asked me.

By the tone of her voice, I knew she didn't mean Letum Wood. Letum Wood had never been pretty in the winter. Though it thrived, lush and thick, in the summer, all traces of life deserted it in the cold months, leaving brown ivy strands and empty trees behind. I still thought it beautiful, in a strange, haunted kind of way.

"No, it's not," I said.

Isadora shifted her eyes to mine, and for the first time since I'd known her, she appeared very tired. Papa had mentioned before in idle conversation that he'd been working with Isadora often, seeking out future possibilities to plan ahead, and I wondered if all the talk of war was getting to her too.

"I like to stand in the cold sometimes," she said with a sheepish smile that wrinkled her skin. "It helps me focus without distraction."

"Strange," Sanna muttered. "Very strange."

"I'll discuss our conversation with you later, Sanna," Isadora said with the perfect manners she prized. "Thank you for coming."

Sanna moved off the porch with a surly glare in my direction. I exhaled in relief when she hobbled into the woods, followed by a slinking shadow I couldn't make out but knew to be a dragon.

"Come inside, Bianca," Isadora said, whirling around. "We have much to talk about."

Isadora sat down on a creaky rocking chair. "I've been expecting you for days now."

I told her everything about the *Book of Spells* that had been bothering me: my visit to the Southern Covens, the article in the *Chatterer* archives that seemed to coincide with events in *Mildred's Resistance*, and my suspicion that May concocted it all. Isadora listened with vague interest, mostly thinking, her lips pushed to one side.

"You brought *Mildred's Resistance*? May I hold it? I've never actually read it myself, as Mildred didn't want a lot of witches knowing the details. She held her privacy—what little she had—very close to her heart. Lavinia insisted on writing the book, however, so that future generations would know the whole story. She interviewed me after all the events died down, strange girl. Anyway, let's see what you have."

She skimmed the marked pages of *Mildred's Resistance*. Once finished, she glanced at me over the top of the book with foggy eyes.

"It's hardly proof, but it's not entirely innocent either. Nothing with May was an accident."

"Did you work with her very much?"

Isadora sucked in a deep breath. "A few times. She was a very intent witch, and her loyalties were clear to everyone but Evelyn, it seemed. She cared for no one, not even her daughter or granddaughter, more than she cared for herself. She displayed remarkable selfishness."

"Sounds familiar. I was hoping you'd find more of a connection. It may not make much sense, but it seems so right to me."

Isadora eyed me studiously. "This business about the *Book of Spells* isn't all that's on your mind, is it?"

My face flushed. I didn't want to tell her about my nightmares, about my fear that Angelina really had connected with my mind, but I desperately wanted to at the same time. How could I explain the dreams without sounding mad?

"No," I said. Hiding information from Isadora would be pointless. "It's not the only reason I'm here. I need someone to confide in."

Isadora stared at me with the most frank gaze I'd ever seen. Her eyes went distant, the way Leda's occasionally did, and moments later she shook her head and seemed to come back to herself.

"Tell me," she said with firm resolve, and relief made me weak. I spilled everything about the dreams I could remember. Their timing, the way I felt, the voice that spoke to me outside the dreams, and Miss Mabel's troubling suggestion. Isadora faded in and out but listened without interruption.

"Oh my," she whispered once I finished. "This trouble of yours extends far deeper than I thought."

My stomach flipped. "What do you mean?"

"How often are you dreaming?"

"Infrequently. I can't predict it."

Isadora's forehead wrinkled into deep lines. "I can see how they make you feel, though I can't really see the details. There's much . . . darkness associated with them in your mind. But I don't think it's all of your doing. Some of the darkness is your own fault, of course, but not all."

"Angelina is causing the dreams, isn't she? Just like Miss Mabel said."

Isadora seemed to share my sentiment, or perhaps my thought, for she grimaced. "Yes, it certainly seems that way. It would have to be through Almorran magic, if the darkness means anything."

"The darkness in my mind?"

"Yes, and no. There is darkness in your mind, but there's also much darkness in the dreams you've had and . . . will have."

Will have. So my time dreaming with Angelina wasn't over, and by the apprehension in Isadora's eyes, I feared it wouldn't be for some time.

"I thought that none of our magic allows a witch to influence the mind of another," I said. "That alone means it's likely Almorran, doesn't it? Which means May found the *Book of Spells* in the Southern Covens, and it's likely Angelina received it once May was executed."

"It makes a likely case. Historically, some witches have proven themselves able to insert thoughts into others' minds but not to control them the way Angelina does yours when you sleep. For example, I can perceive your feelings and personality traits and see possibilities for your future, but I can't decipher your direct thoughts. The fact that she communicates with you in these dreams and influences you to not wake up means that she wields power over your mind, like Mabel suggested."

"Will this change me in some way?" I asked, my breath escalating. "Angelina's use of Almorran magic to influence my mind?"

"Change you? Not unless you allow it. Mark you, perhaps. Almorran magic is difficult to foresee and predict because it's so unknown to us and because its power lies in the Almorran Master. The nuances of the magic change from Master to Master, though its fundamental elements remain the same."

"The Almorran Master?"

"The most powerful witch within the sphere of Almorran magic," she said, seeming awkward without a cup of tea in her hands. The cups lined the walls, as they always did, but she offered me no refreshment. "There has only been one Master at any given time. The aspirants to the position ascended through seven levels of skill, each of which required some horrible sacrifice to attain, to eventually become the Almorran Master through the spilling of familial blood."

I swallowed. "I see." *Blood sacrifice. Seven levels of skill. Almorran Master. Familial blood.*

"Almorran magic takes a long time to perfect because it draws on the magic of other witches. In order to do that, the practitioner must exercise remarkable power. Almorran magic influences, even gives power to, other witches that allow its control. But in the end, it always takes more from them than they receive. It's selfish and evil. I believe that Angelina has, through time, ascended the seven levels and become the new Almorran Master."

I thought of the Factios and their fighting tactics, wondering if Angelina controlled them through Almorran magic.

"Let's say Angelina does have the *Book of Spells*. Why would she have waited so long to use it?"

"Mildred," Isadora said. "Mabel has long feared Mildred, so I'm guessing Angelina felt the same way. I may be wrong, of course. Only time will tell the whats and whys. Angelina's main request is for you to set her daughter free?"

"Yes. It's her only request. She basically repeats the same thing every time."

"Sounds like she's trying to be careful not to reveal too much about herself through the connection. Have you ever spoken back to her in the dreams?"

"Spoken back?" I asked in surprise. "No."

"Any magic that invades the mind is not one-directional. For her to have any sort of control over your mind, she had to form a connection. If she's talking to you, you can talk to her. Push back. Try to get information from her."

I blinked. "Push back," I whispered. "I never thought of that."

"Try it next time. It may help lead us to her."

"How do you know all this?" I asked, my forehead furrowing. "If Almorran magic is so unknown, I mean."

"I'm very old, Bianca. I've seen and studied much in my life. Those who do not learn history are doomed to repeat it. Besides, I see into witches' minds all the time." She smiled softly. "While it's not the same as the Almorran way, it works along similar lines. Paths and emotions are somewhat betraying in themselves, you know."

I didn't know, but I pretended like I had. "Can I ask you one more question?"

"Of course."

I hesitated. "Should I tell Papa about the dreams? I've thought about it, but he's so busy, and I don't even know . . . it doesn't even make sense, does it?"

Isadora paused in thought. "The choice is yours," she concluded, which really didn't help me at all. "But no matter what happens, your father will not release Mabel. His knowing about the dreams may not change anything. Perhaps make him worry for you more."

"That's what I thought," I said, relieved. Perhaps my logic wasn't poor after all. "Thanks."

Isadora's eyes narrowed. "Pay attention, Bianca. Dark days are coming again, and there's nothing we can do to stop them."

"Nothing?" I asked desperately. "Almorran magic can't be unstoppable, can it? How did Esmelda defeat it?"

"Those are days long past. Magic was different then than it is now."

"But it still means that Almorran magic isn't unstoppable. There must be a way."

She looked at me with a queer expression. "Perhaps there's something," she whispered, turning to peer into Letum Wood for a long span of time. "Let me look into it. There just may be something."

Night came with a bitter chill later that week. Leda and I sat together at the table, huddled over a textbook on the Declan language, while Camille hummed and read a romance novel, her ankle bobbing up and down. It promised to be a cozy, calm night with my friends, the kind that I cherished and never wanted to lose.

"Move the divan back, Camille," Leda growled, readjusting her heavy cloak over her shoulders. Her nose had turned bright red at the tip. "You're hogging all the heat again. It's cold in here!"

"Sorry," Camille said, using a spell to move the couch back without tearing her eyes from the book. It would only take her half an hour to slowly scoot it back. Priscilla sat on a chair in a warmer spot of the Witchery, but by no means hogged any part of the fire.

"Just repeat the words in Declan after me," I told Leda with a breezy voice, hoping to distract her from her wrath. "It's the easiest of all the languages to pronounce. Just wait until you get to the Almorran language. It's ridiculous."

Leda mumbled an idle threat under her breath, but my intervention worked because she turned away from Camille with a *humph*.

"Fine," she muttered. While it did seem backward for me to tutor Leda, I wasn't about to relinquish the tiny morsel of power it had given me. The days I could claim any intellectual advantage over Leda were galloping to a rapid close. Once she finished the Esbat mark, I wouldn't have any real know-how over her except for applied magical power, which she cared little about compared to knowledge.

"I don't like learning languages," she said, surveying the words on the page. I stared at her in surprise. The concept of Leda not enjoying learning in any form floored me; it seemed more likely that the sun wouldn't rise in the morning.

"What?"

"It's just not as interesting as history," she said, quickly adding, "I'm good at it, and I'll do it, I just don't enjoy it as much."

"But you'll memorize political books?" I asked, motioning toward several thick volumes stacked on the floor near her bed. None of them even applied to her current lessons.

"I'm not memorizing," she mumbled through clenched teeth. "I'm reading them to stay informed. I need to know all of those policies before I can become a good Assistant."

I glanced at the circlus on her wrist. The marks for Advanced Political History and Public Speaking left one empty space for the Esbat. Although I'd expected Leda to clam up in front of an audience, she'd actually conducted herself very well. Miss Scarlett had asked Leda to speak in front of the entire kitchen staff, and then in front of two contingents of Guardians, and to teach a class to the servants on political history. The final test happened at a rally in Chatham City. No one booed—I sent a silencing spell in the direction of anyone who tried—so Leda never grew flustered, although her neck had blazed bright red.

I had just started conjugating the verb *to run* when the Witchery door burst open and Michelle flew in.

"Guess what?" she cried, breathless and red-faced. "Guess what just happened?"

Camille sat up. "Is everything all right?"

Michelle dropped her bag to the floor. Her mouth opened and closed wordlessly several times, and she lifted her left arm to reveal a braided blue and silver cord sparkling with subtle jewels.

"*What!*" Camille screamed, leaping off the old couch. "What is that? Is that a cord of engagement?"

Michelle blushed so deeply I thought her face would catch fire. Leda and I stared at her, mutually dumbstruck, mouths open. Priscilla was the first to smile.

"I'm engaged!" Michelle whispered. "I'm engaged!"

Camille started screaming and jumping up and down, curls bouncing. Michelle caught on to her fervor and hopped with her. Leda and I exchanged disbelieving glances until Leda finally stood up.

"Wow, Michelle!" she said, eyes wide. "I . . . congratulations!"

Camille hugged Michelle again, still awkwardly bouncing in Michelle's thick arms.

"Congratulations, Michelle," Priscilla said quietly, her hands folded in front of her. Michelle nodded but didn't meet her eyes.

"Where is the hand fasting ceremony?" Camille asked, eyes bright. "When is the date? How did he ask? Are you going to do it here? Can I help you pick out your dress? Is Fina going to cater? Will you do it in the gardens?"

"Sit down, Camille!" Leda called. "Give Michelle a second to breathe. Jikes."

Michelle glanced shyly at me, and my breath stilled when I realized I hadn't moved. Her cord of engagement was simple but beautiful. It wasn't that her engagement at age twenty came as much of a surprise—plenty of young female witches married before nineteen, even. But it meant all of us were growing up and moving on, and I felt paralyzed.

There wasn't a thing I could do about it.

Leda shot me a sharp look, which roused me from my stupor. I stood and offered a stunned half-smile.

"Congratulations, Michelle. That's wonderful."

My words sounded as enthusiastic as a wooden board, but she didn't seem to notice. Leda's glare deepened, so I ignored her. Camille had been set loose again and bounded over to the table.

"You can have Henrietta do the dress! Oh, a *wedding* dress! With lace and tulle and fabric and ribbon. You're going to be beautiful, Michelle!"

Michelle fidgeted with the ends of her sleeves. "Will you help me plan a few things, Camille? I have no idea what to do."

"I'd love to!" Camille cried, beaming. "It just so happens I have a few bridal scrolls around here somewhere."

Leda and I returned to our seats, staring at the fire in shock, while Michelle, Camille, and Priscilla congregated around the table.

"Wow," Leda whispered. "Good for her."

I turned my eyes back to the book so it looked like one of us had resumed our previous activities, but I wasn't sure my fixed gaze would convince anyone.

"Why do we have to grow up?" I asked in a rush of bitter complaint. "Why can't things just stay the same? Wasn't this night perfect? Isn't it wonderful to be together and not worry about splitting up? You work with Rupert, Camille dates Brecken, Michelle works in the kitchens, Priscilla is suddenly friendly, and we all meet here at the Witchery every night. Why does such a good thing have to end?"

"Things are always changing, Bianca. And Priscilla is not friendly."

"Not *always* changing," I countered. "They've been wonderful for the past six or seven months, haven't they?"

"No!" she cried with a laugh. "We've been preparing for war for six months. I've studied so hard my brains are oozing out of my head. You started a difficult job and have to learn etiquette. The last six months have been anything but perfect."

I turned away with a scowl. "They were perfect for me. And yes, Priscilla is nice now," I said, just to be contrary.

"Coming to the castle was a change and good things came of it," Leda said.

"But that was different."

"How?" she asked, folding her arms across her chest and adopting that look that said, *I'm-going-to-win*. I chided myself too late. Debating Leda over something like this was just asking to lose.

"Because . . . because things were bad then. And now they're good. We shouldn't change a good thing."

"Things were bad for you, maybe," Leda said. "They were okay for us at school. You think I looked forward to moving into a busy castle?"

"Yes! You took advantage of it right away and got a job, didn't you?"

She rolled her eyes. "Fine. Bad example. All I'm trying to say is that life changes all the time, Bianca. We can't stop it, so why fight it?"

My eyes drifted to Camille, Priscilla, and Michelle seated at the table, pouring over a scroll of dress designs. Michelle glowed from the grin on her lips to the light in her eyes.

"Besides," Leda continued, reading my mind. "Look at how happy Michelle is. Would you deny her happiness just because you want to keep things the same?"

"No," I muttered, but it sounded petulant. I wanted to be happy for Michelle, but I couldn't really feel it. Michelle's departure would be just the beginning. Camille would go next, and then Leda, and I'd be left behind in a cold castle with a father so determined to save the world I'd hardly ever see him.

I thought I had finally found comfort and happiness.

"Let's finish the Declan lesson," Leda said, but I couldn't focus on the correct pronunciation of verbs, and my eyes kept straying to the scene laid out at the table.

Would you deny her happiness just because you want to keep things the same?

No, of course I wouldn't. But I didn't have to like all the changes. Leda pulled me back to reality with a question about the language, and I immersed myself in something apart from my depressing thoughts.

The Southern Covens

I want what is mine, Bianca.

Although I knew I dreamt, I found myself sitting in Marten's office on a particularly glum winter day. Half-frozen slush descended outside, a product of the end of the third month of winter and the slow approach of spring, but I remembered the office had been stuffy, lulling me to sleep with its quiet and warmth.

I shall take it if you don't give it to me.

Darkness plumed out of the fireplace in a black mist, infiltrating every nook and cranny of the room as if it sought something. The usual rush of fear assaulted me, but instead of trying to escape or wake up, I forced myself to calm down. This was the first dream I'd had since Isadora suggested I communicate with Angelina a week earlier.

We all want what we want, I responded, standing. *That doesn't mean you should have it.* My own voice sounded distant, somewhat muffled, for I didn't vocalize the words but thought them instead. Speaking back to her felt surprisingly easy, and I wondered why I hadn't tried it before.

The strange mist surrounded my feet now. Swirls of it appeared as fluid as water, moving in silky grandeur over the floor, while the rest bubbled like foam around the fireplace. It ebbed and flowed, rocking me back and forth.

But I will have it, Angelina replied. *For I always get what I want.*

Always? I challenged, heart thumping. If I could just learn a little more about Angelina, a little more about her past, perhaps we could find her and the *Book of Spells*.

Always.

A barrage of confusion overtook me. Screams. Grunts. Yells. The foul smell of burned flesh. No fire, but that same oppressive weight pressed on my shoulders. I saw blood and smoke and death and blank eyes peering out of drifts of deep snow. The eyes became bodies, and the bodies became fields of dying Guardians. In the distance loomed a giant wall shrouded in a white storm.

You have been warned.

I jerked awake at my desk in Marten's office, just as I had imagined in the dream, and remained frozen to the spot. My eyes darted to the fireplace, expecting to see the pitiless darkness, but nothing came.

"Bianca?"

Marten peered at me from behind his desk, his forehead ruffled. I sat up, blinking rapidly to clear my thoughts.

"Sorry," I murmured, rubbing a hand over my face. "Sorry. Just a bad dream."

He stared at me for a long pause. "It's time for us to go," he said, glancing at the clock. "We have a meeting in the Southern Covens. Diego sent me a letter saying there's a section of the Eastern Coven border near the Southern Network wall that witches have been using to conduct black market trades. They stand on either side of the boundary and toss goods back and forth. We need to go check on it."

I stood when he did, grateful to escape the close office. The door shut behind me, and I followed Marten out, leaving the darkness of the dreams in my wake. A whisper trailed in the air.

Let my daughter go.

The Southern Covens in the winter weren't much to brag about.

A wall of stone five stories high stood on the border between the Southern Network and the Central Network. The Southern Network built it in the tempestuous war years that led up to the formation of the Mansfeld Pact. It effectively blocked them off from every other Network. Not far beyond it stood the ice castle, not quite visible in the distance, where the paranoid High Priests could keep an eye on the Eastern and Central Networks from the highest turrets.

Today the Southern Covens bustled with their annual market, celebrating the onset of spring. Despite a lack of crops to sell, many witches that had been cooped up for hours in their cabins kept themselves busy creating crafts that would prove useful during the more productive summer months. Woven baskets, goat milk soap, rugs, a few simple tapestries, and smoked meat hardened into long, thin strips hung from the stalls. The market hosted at least two hundred booths and stretched along the Southern Wall as far as the eye could see.

"The whole Southern Covens come out for this," Marten said when a witch with boots covered in cow manure transported in a few paces away. "They only hold it once at the end of winter, right before spring, if the weather is good."

I peered up at the bright, cloudless sky. The air felt so bitterly cold that the sunshine seemed to pinch my cheeks instead of warm me. I pulled my fur-lined cloak closer around my shoulders.

"It's cold," I said with a shiver, wondering, not for the first time, how Marten tolerated such chill with no hair. He didn't seem bothered, glancing about with assessing, sharp eyes.

"Keep your eyes open," he murmured. "Something doesn't feel right."

"What do you mean?"

He shrugged it off. "Let's start walking toward the Eastern Network. We need to talk with a few Border Guards about the problem."

As we filtered through the happy crowd, Marten's brow creased. I'd just wandered close to a stall offering rose petal perfume when the skin on the back of my neck prickled. Marten was right. Something felt off.

A startled cry rose over the crowded marketplace. I whipped around, pulling Viveet from her sheath. My gut clenched. Sprawled on top of the wall, spread out in an unnerving display of force, stood a long train of Southern Guardians leading all the way to the turn of the wall into the Eastern Network. In the middle, Mikhail looked down on us, his golden armor glinting with rubies and sapphires. Next to him stood a witch I'd never seen before but recognized even from so far away. He wore the loose linen pants and arrogant bare chest of the West Guards. His hair hung down his back in a long braid. Only a West Guard leader would prance half-naked in such a bitter cold, trying to prove his strength.

It had to be Dane, the High Priest of the Western Network and a powerful Watcher. His presence could not be a good thing, even if no West Guards stood behind him.

"On the wall!" someone screeched, pointing. "Look on the wall!"

Dane and Mikhail stood angled toward each other, clearly in discussion. They stared down on the Southern Covens with imperturbable faces and hardened eyes. I searched frantically for Marten but lost him in the melee of the crowd. Angelina's voice whispered through my mind with such intensity that I stumbled.

You have been warned.

As quickly as it came, it left. I shot back to my feet. "Marten!" I cried. "Sorry. Let me pass. Excuse me. Marten!"

"Look on the wall!" another witch cried in a shrill voice. "They're going to attack. Run!"

Panic gripped the market, and witches began to flee, grabbing whatever they could carry. Never, in the hundreds of years since the passage of the Mansfeld Pact, had the High Priests of two Networks stood together with an army of Guardians behind them. It allowed only one awful conclusion.

War.

"Marten! Jikes, old man," I muttered. "Where did you go?"

He transported into sight several steps away, nearly colliding with a witch who had picked up her small cart of trinkets and was attempting to run away with it. I stopped in relief.

"Bianca," he called, waving to me. "Over here. I just spoke with Tiberius."

"It's happening, isn't it? They're going to attack just like we thought?"

When I looked back at the wall, I saw only Mikhail and his army of Guardians. Had I imagined Dane?

"Get out of here," Marten said, not bothering to answer my question. "Send any witches you see to Letum Wood and tell them to hide or run for their lives. Tell anyone who can transport to do so. But above all, get home. Report to Stella. And do not, I repeat, *do not* try to be a hero today." He grabbed my shoulders and shook me to drive home the point. "Do you understand? You must be safe. I don't want anything happening to you."

"Yes, I understand. Where's Papa? Does he know?" I asked, breathless. Witches ran past us, screaming. The happy lull of the market had given way to the strangled cries of stunned panic. The ice blue flags of the Southern Network flapped behind us, sounding as loud as the crack of a whip.

"Derek is already aware."

My thudding heart slowed for just a second. If Papa knew, we had a chance. My eyes strayed back to the intimidating ranks awaiting us. A very small chance.

"And Tiberius?"

"Just arrived. Guardians are transporting into Letum Wood and the other villages as we speak. They've already trained for this. Go now, Bianca. Go! I'm going to help protect and evacuate the children and witches who can't transport while Derek deals with the fighting."

He shoved me away from the wall and transported away. A full panic had overtaken the market, drowning out the strange quiet that had fallen when Mikhail first appeared. Fleeing witches knocked a torch into a wooden stand, setting the dry boards on fire. A vat of fresh ipsum fell, spilling sticky liquid and making the air smell like smoke and yeast. Only a desperate few witches remained behind to collect goods, but even they began to give up, retreating with empty hands.

I climbed on top of a bale of hay. There, in the distance, near the road leading into the Southern Network, stood Papa. He stared at Mikhail with a fearless, calculating expression that made me shudder.

"Be safe, Papa," I whispered and turned away.

I jumped down to transport back to Chatham but stopped when I heard the shrill scream of a little girl behind me. My cape twirled with me when I spun around to find a lone child.

"Mama!" she cried, standing alone in the midst of the pandemonium. "Mama!"

She had soft blue eyes and blonde hair and wore a cheap dress of gray wool. She stood alone, fingers in her mouth, face streaming with snot and tears. I glanced around but saw no one that seemed to belong to her.

"Mama!"

"Run!" a witch bellowed, arms flailing as he ran past me. "They're about to attack!"

One glance confirmed it. The South Guards had disappeared off the wall, leaving it strangely empty save Mikhail and his Ambassador, Dmitri. I dodged the panicked witches and grabbed the little girl. A roaring *boom* shook the ground. A plume of black smoke exploded from the entrance to the wall, not far from where Papa had been.

"Where's your mama?" I asked, but the little girl continued to sob. Her arms and feet felt ice cold. Another explosion rippled through the air, closer this time. Wagon wheels and bits of hay flew through the air in the gray cloud that followed. Bright red ash rained from the billowing plumes of smoke. Witches underneath the falling ash dropped to their knees, screaming in agony. Instead of being extinguished, the ash flared white-hot when it touched their skin, burning through it in moments.

"The good gods." I pulled off my cloak, wrapped the child in it, picked her back up, and started to run. Only the most powerful of witches could transport others, which meant I had to escape on foot to save both of us.

By the time I dodged the stalls and broke free from the market, four more explosions had sounded, each closer than the last. The final *boom* sent me to my knees. I clutched the girl closer to my body as I stumbled but caught myself before I fell on top of her. Shards of rock hit the backs of my arms and legs, drawing blood. When I looked back, my heart nearly stopped. South Guards poured through the wall on ropes, using holes blown in the stone and the main entrance. They ran with murder in their eyes, swords raised, headed straight for us.

"No!" I yelled. "I will not die this way!"

All the witches in the Southern Network would lose their magic for the rest of their lives for breaking the Mansfeld Pact, which meant they'd have to fight like mortals. Even though we had magic on our side and could surely defeat them, I still felt a heady rush of fear.

The little girl screamed until she gagged. I put a sleeping incantation on her while struggling back to my feet. She went limp in my arms seconds later. Although she was nothing more than dead weight now, at least I could focus. My eyes widened when an ax flew through the air at my side, striking a witch running ahead of me in the spine. He fell to the ground, his face skidding in the dirt. Flashes of my last dream resurrected in my mind. Blood. Bodies. Death.

Let my daughter go.

The familiar half-armor of the Central Network Guardians streamed out of Letum Wood to meet the oncoming South Guards when I started running again. A young Central Guard with blonde hair and a goatee slowed when he passed me.

"Get into the woods!" he yelled, pulling an arrow from his quiver and firing it. The slam of a falling body sounded too close behind me for comfort. "Go now!"

Spurred to great speed, I sprinted past him, dodging the torrent of Guardians roaring by. Letum Wood engulfed me. Once ensconced in the safety of the dark canopy, my legs seemed to gain strength. I moved faster, with more certainty, carrying the quiet child in my tiring arms. Central Guards popped up from time to time, usually in pairs, but they paid me no mind as I fled. It was clear by their determined, knowledgeable movements that they had practiced this before.

Although I didn't know any trails in this part of Letum Wood, I followed a path that seemed to appear the moment I needed it. Branches and leaves parted steps ahead of me, showing me the way.

I plunged deeper into the brittle branches of the forest, panting, but even the canopy I loved so well couldn't entirely protect me. Two minutes later, I heard the telltale sound of running feet behind me. I surrounded myself with a protective incantation to keep spells as well as physical objects away, making a mental note to thank Merrick later for teaching it to me. One glimpse over my shoulder took my breath away. It wasn't South Guards who pursued me.

"West Guards," I whispered.

Why were West Guards in Letum Wood?

I pushed myself harder. The West Guards could follow the impression of my magic, but I still didn't feel comfortable removing it. My chest heaved in panic as I wove through the trees, my legs taking me as fast as I could go.

Just when my body threatened to give out, several branches rattled off to my right. My eyes caught a large rock formation with a small cleft. A cave! I veered that direction abruptly, sliding through a thick copse of trees. I slipped inside the cave, glancing behind me just long enough to notice that my footprints hadn't remained in the snow. I removed the protective spell and threw myself and the child into the dark space.

The West Guards stopped just short of the cave. With determined effort, I slowed my breathing. The two of them hissed back and forth in a foreign tongue. I swallowed, my heart pounding. The little girl stirred but didn't move. The West Guards chattered on, their hasty words sounding livid. I waited for them to burst through the trees, to grab me and the little girl, but they never did. It was as if they didn't even see the cave.

Was it possible that something else protected me? That some other magic had caused the appearing path, the rattle of branches, the lack of footprints in the snow?

I set the girl on the ground and crouched low, peering around the rock near the ground. As soon as the West Guards turned their backs, I put a paralyzing incantation on both of them. They fell to the ground, faces pressed to the snow, and didn't move.

"Well done."

I whirled around, protecting the child with my own body. A group of ten witches emerged from the darkness of the cave.

"Who are you?" I asked.

"The same as you, likely, considering you speak our language and just paralyzed two West Guards," said a middle-aged man with a thick black beard. "We sought shelter here as you did. How did you know about this hiding place?"

"I didn't. I just kind of . . . found it."

He stared at me with questioning eyes. "I know you. I know your face."

I ripped my cloak off the little girl. "Who I am doesn't matter now. Do you know this child?"

A woman in the back stepped forward. "That's my cousin's daughter," she cried, rushing forward. "What happened? Where's her mother, Merna?"

"I don't know. I found her alone in the market. She's fine. I put a sleeping spell on her so she'd calm down. Can I trust you to get her back to her family?"

The woman scooped her out of my arms. "I *am* her family."

"Thanks."

The bearded man stopped my departure by stepping forward.

"You're the High Priest's daughter, Bianca," he said. I hesitated. Not many witches wholeheartedly supported my father these days. Or, by extension, me. Normally I just transported away before their opinions grew too heated.

"Yes."

His eyes softened with despair. "I guess he's been right all along, hasn't he?"

"He normally is. It's annoying."

"If Derek is leading this fight, he has our support."

I found a semblance of a smile. The woman tried to offer me my cape back, but I waved it off.

"Keep it," I said, glancing around. "You'll need it more than I will. I'll use a levitation spell to take these two back to the Central Guards just outside of Letum Wood before I head back to the castle," I said, motioning to the West Guards. "You stay here and be safe."

"This is war," said someone in the back. "It has to be. They wanted to kill us."

"The Mansfeld Pact is broken now, isn't it?" the bearded man asked.

"Yes," I murmured, glancing at the two massive men lying face-down on the ground. "So it would seem."

Do Not Come

"**M**ichelle?" I yelled, taking the stairs to the Witchery two at a time. After leaving the Southern Covens, I'd transported to the kitchens to find Michelle, but she wasn't there. I went to Sanna's cottage, but Michelle was nowhere to be found, which left one more spot.

The Witchery door slammed open ahead of me, hitting the wall with a *smack*. I skidded to a halt. Michelle sat at the table, face pale. A crinkled letter sat in her trembling hand. She looked up at me with horror-stricken eyes.

"My family is under attack," she whispered.

I rushed to her side and read the letter over her shoulder. It was hastily written and barely legible.

Meesh,

The Southern Network is here. They set fire to the village. We'll write more later. Papa said DO NOT COME.

There was no signature. I put my cold hands on her shoulder. "The Southern Covens are under attack," I said. "I was just there. The Southern Network broke the Mansfeld Pact. Marten is trying to evacuate all the residents as we speak. Central Guards are already there, fighting back."

"Bianca," she said. "That's my family. Next to Nicolas they are—" She swallowed. "They're my whole world."

I knew her glazed look of helpless shock. After living through more than fifteen years of Papa serving as the Head of Protectors, and now as High Priest, I understood the horror of living through questions like *Will he die? What did I say to him last? Will I see him again?* So I knew exactly how to help her out of the sludge of those darkest thoughts.

She needed a task, a mission.

"I know how much your family means to you," I replied, tightening my grip on her thick shoulders. "But we can't do anything for them here in the Witchery. And your brother is right: We can't go down to help right now. We wouldn't even know where to find them, and we'll just put ourselves in greater danger anyway. Let's go see Stella. She'll know what we can do."

Michelle glanced up, blinked twice, and seemed to move back into herself. I watched her gather her inner strength.

"Yes," she said distantly. "I'll follow you."

After I reported to Stella, who embraced me with a quiet breath of relief, she put us to work immediately. I didn't even ask for updates; I could see in her eyes that no good news came from the Southern Covens.

"Later," she said, squeezing my hand and reading the unspoken question in my eyes. "I'll tell you everything I know later."

Michelle and I found work in the formal Dining Room, where Camille and Leda were already cutting bandages and preparing medical supplies. The wounded Guardians who were still able to transport were already returning to the castle for care, then transporting back to the fight. Women, attacked by South Guards, showed up, their faces pale with shock. Three had been raped. Two beaten. The hushed, whispered reports painted a bleak picture of chaos and fire. No one seemed to know what was going on, and we had to be satisfied with conflicting rumors and reports. I watched all their faces for Merrick, but he never appeared.

Hours later, when evening came in full strength and spare rooms overflowed with cots and moans of pain, a hand gently grabbed my arm as I offered a Guardian a fresh drink of water. When I turned around, Stella pressed a finger to her lips and motioned for me to follow. I passed the water to Leda, who sent me a questioning glance as I left.

"Transport to my chambers," Stella said in the hall, and we both disappeared from the corridor. Once safe in the calming air of her rooms—which smelled like lemongrass—she faced me with weary eyes.

"I thought you, of all witches, deserved the truth since your father is leading the fight and you know more than most. It goes without saying that I trust you, probably too much."

The reminder thickened my throat. "What's going on, Stella?" I asked quietly, swallowing. "What do you know?"

She let out a long breath and sank to a chair. With Papa on the front lines, she bore the burden of carrying the Central Network forward without allowing it to panic, and I marveled at her strength.

"I haven't told anyone how extensive and detailed the reports have been from Zane, Tiberius, and your father, but suffice it to say that the entirety of the Southern Network is pouring into ours to fight. And now, within the last two hours, West Guards have started attacking at random."

I didn't want to explain that I'd already seen them. "West Guards?" I asked. "What?"

"The Southern Network broke the Mansfeld Pact," Stella said. "They have borne the consequences. Now that the Pact is broken and the battle well on its way, the West Guards move freely about our Network. They seem to have retained their power, which means they aren't officially in league with the Southern Network."

"But they can't help the Southern Network, can they? Surely that wouldn't be allowed—"

"They aren't helping the South. They're just attacking us."

The truth halted a dizzying breath in my chest. It was all coming to pass just as we had feared.

"Surely Mikhail can't expect to win against us without magic."

"No, but winning may not be his agenda. Distracting us, crippling us, hurting us, any of those may be the goal. They may not have magic, but they still have hands and legs, don't they? They can fight and burn and rape and pillage. And they are. Obviously with some success based on what we're seeing come back to the castle. We're only seeing the healthiest of the wounded, you realize. The rest of them are dying on the battlefield or stuck in the Southern Covens."

I sucked in a deep breath. Too fast. All this was happening too fast. Hadn't I just been at a market festival that morning? Hadn't everything been so happy?

"That's ridiculous!" I retorted. "Fighting without magic is . . . it's insane! They may as well be mortals. Surely not even Mikhail is so mad as to fight against my father, against the Central Network, when all they can do is throw axes."

"You're almost right," Stella said with a sudden note of steel in her voice. "But the West Guards are bringing a magic to the battlefield that we've never seen before. We have to spare Protectors and Guardians to fight them, which leaves us stretched a bit thin."

I felt the color drain from my face, already seeing the answer in her eyes.

"Almorran," I whispered. "The unknown magic is Almorran, isn't it?"

She closed her eyes and ran a hand over her face with a humorless chuckle. "I have no other explanation."

"Is there any way we can stop this before it becomes a full war? Can't this just end in one battle? What about the East?"

"Diego will not come," she said. "You know that as well as I."

I cursed under my breath.

"The north!" I cried. "What of the Northern Network?"

"What of them?" she asked with a sad little laugh. "If there are still witches living in those treacherous mountains, they want nothing to do with us. It's been hundreds of years since we've had any communication with the Northern Network. They shall not swoop in to save us. No, Bianca. This is our war. We must fight it."

"Where's Isadora?" I asked, unwilling to give in to the grim reality that this was war, and not just a horrid battle. "She'll know! She was going to look into something for me and—"

"Isadora is with your father and has been since early this morning. She must have seen the inevitable because she appeared in the middle of a meeting and demanded to speak with him in private."

It brought me little comfort. If anything, it made everything so much more bleak. No witch possessed more powerful foresight than Isadora. Leda's ability to see possibilities for the future looked like a child's toy compared to the things that Isadora saw and understood. If she had seen this coming and hadn't offered an escape, it meant there was no way out but through the fight.

"We're really under attack from two Networks, then," I said, sinking into a chair.

"One of which is using a magic we're having a hard time countering," she added with a shake of her head. "I don't know everything that's happening there, and I'm not sure Derek or Tiberius or Zane do either, but I can assume that Mikhail isn't at the disadvantage we would have expected for a Network that broke such a powerful agreement."

"What about Papa?" I asked, sounding hoarse. "When did you last hear from him? Is he all right?"

A flash of concern flickered across her face. She drew in a deep breath, and it faded. "An hour ago."

I felt some relief. A pounding knock sounded at her door, and Coven Leader Clive called through the wood, "High Priestess! A word, please!"

"Worm," I muttered.

"Chatham Castle is safe from foreign invaders for now," she said under her breath. "But that doesn't speak much to snakes nearby, does it? No doubt Clive wants to stir up all kinds of ugly protests now."

I managed a smile, and she returned it. When she stood, some of the mettle that reminded me of Mildred had come back to her expression.

"Go help the effort here however you can, Bianca. But stay in Chatham. The last thing your father needs is you acting like a hero in the Southern Covens. Do you understand?"

I nodded. The familiar command wounded my pride. It's not like I *sought* opportunities to jump into dangerous circumstances. It seemed they found me. Recalling the brutal hatred in the eyes of the South Guards as they ran at me, screaming, made me never want to go back.

"I won't."

She paused. "Make me a promise?"

"Sure."

"Don't go into Letum Wood alone."

I blinked in disbelief. "Ever?"

She nodded. "Don't go running by yourself or venture into the forest for now. It's not going to be safe for some time. Derek couldn't handle anything happening to you right now."

My chest seized with pain at the idea. "But Stella—"

"You can do your runs around the gardens or practice sword fighting with the Guardians stationed here, but I must demand that you not run alone in Letum Wood. Besides, we're at war now. As the High Priest's daughter, you'd be quite a prize for either the Southern or the Western Networks."

I swallowed, thinking of Isobel's concern for me. How could I make such a promise? Letum Wood was the only home I had left. Chatham Castle was simply my residence; Letum Wood was where I belonged. Running there kept my magic under control.

"Promise me now," Stella said firmly. "I need to hear you say the words. I trust you enough that I won't make you take a vow."

Clive banged on the door in the background. "High Priestess!"

"What . . . I . . . I promise I won't run in Letum Wood alone," I whispered faintly, unable to deny her request. My heart trembled.

I must demand that you not go into Letum Wood alone.

She let out a relieved sigh. "Thank you. That means a lot to both me and your father. Go help your friends again," she said. "I'm calling all Coven Leaders tonight with the bugle, and I have a handful of frightened Council Members to deal with." A third round of heavy banging shook the front door. "And Clive on top of it," she muttered with a bitter roll of her eyes.

I transported away while watching Stella walk to the door, her shoulders back and her bearing as calm as I'd ever seen.

The Witchery became a prison.

Katie Cross

Three days into the fighting, Brecken's mother, Tabby, received a notice that he'd been injured. He remained alive but stuck in a wounded area. Due to the danger, family members still weren't allowed to transport to the Southern Covens. Camille had come back to the Witchery that night pale and terrified. Seeing the stark fear on her face had brought it home for all of us. I thought of Merrick and Papa every night when I went to bed, afraid of what I'd dream.

Would Stella tell me the same news about Papa or Merrick one day?

"I'm too worried to eat," Camille said early one morning when Leda set a tray in front of her. "I can't stop thinking about Brecken."

It was the last day of the last month of winter. Hints of spring lingered on the air despite the battle over the Southern Covens that had raged for four full days. Surrounding Covens had started preparing the moment they heard of the attack: blocking roads, setting up sentries, hiding witches who would set spells on the South or West Guards before they could set flame to unsuspecting villages. The defenses kept the South Guardians in the Southern Covens, but just barely.

The West Guards, on the other hand, were terrorizing the entirety of the Central Network. We couldn't guess where they'd show up next. Three West Guards had set a library on fire in the Northern Covens, while three others killed an entire field of cattle in the Western Covens. They weren't always genocidal, but they struck fear deep in the hearts of all our witches.

"You won't be much use to Brecken when he returns if you don't have any energy or health yourself," Leda said to Camille, but she'd already used that line of reasoning at dinner the night before, so Camille shook it off.

"I'll be so relieved it won't matter. I'll just throw myself into his strong arms and . . . and . . ." Camille's eyes welled up with tears when she stumbled. "K-kiss his face until he passes out!"

In a move so unlike her that it testified to our desperate times, Leda forced a patient tone and said, "Fine, Camille. Don't eat for Brecken's sake. Eat so that you keep his mother from worrying about you. Tabby doesn't need to stress over you while she's worried about

Brecken. Once you've eaten, you can go visit her. That always cheers you up."

That did the trick. Camille sucked in a breath, composed herself, stared at the bowl of porridge, and picked up the spoon with a little sigh. Leda gathered her books and stuffed them into her shoulder bag.

"Are you leaving now?" I asked.

"Yes. Jansson sent Rupert to organize the relief in the Letum Wood Covens, so I've taken over as Assistant for a while. I'll be back tonight." She cast a wary eye on Camille, then looked at me in silent command to watch over her.

Dealing with the panic along the Eastern Network borders had sapped nearly all my energy. Marten returned every morning with enough time for me to report the location of the worst of the hysteria, the steps I'd taken to fix it, and any other emergencies that had to be dealt with before he returned to the Southern Covens to help Papa. Thanks to his power and magical ability, Marten had stopped an entire contingent of South Guards from attacking one of our makeshift hospitals where Apothecaries worked frantically to keep up with the dying and injured. Unfortunately, we needed Marten's influence and quick mind in the battle, leaving me to deal with the Ambassador's role alone. To my surprise, I didn't mind it so much. It passed the time.

Though my days felt hectic—visiting towns along the eastern borders, worrying over Camille, trying to coax Michelle out of her anxious silence, and stalking Stella for updates—I itched with restless uncertainty. It seemed as if the rest of the Network felt the same way. We had been at peace with our neighbors for so long that none of us knew how to cope with this strange new reality. Guardians dying. An increased production of caskets. Families displaced. It was both surreal and all too real.

As soon as Leda left, Camille gave up on eating and shoved the porridge away. "I'm going to see Tabby," she declared, standing. "You can have my porridge, Bianca."

But I couldn't even stomach the thought of eating my own. "Of course, Camille," I said. "Be safe."

"That's it? You aren't going to try to stop me?"

"No. Do you want me to?"

"No! Of course not." She swallowed back her sudden rush of emotion, and in a calmer tone said, "Thank you, Bianca, for understanding and not trying to babysit me. I just can't bear the thought of Tabby getting word about Brecken and me not being there."

I smiled crookedly for a moment. "I would do the same. Has Miss Scarlett canceled your classes?"

She nodded. "For the time being. Not that I'd be able to study anyway. Michelle is with Nicolas because the dragons' agitation is boiling over. It's requiring Sanna, Nicolas, and sometimes Michelle, even though she's not a Dragonmaster, just to keep them restrained."

A shadow moved across the Witchery. I glanced up to see the blue soar smoothly past the tower, one of three dragons spiraling through the air. He shot fire out of his nose, then flew into it, scattering the smoke like a ghost.

"Where's Priscilla?"

"She and Miss Scarlett are making sure all the students get home safely from the Network Schools. Are you sure you're okay if I leave? You'll be here alone."

I gestured to a pile of envelopes that had arrived for me that morning. *Urgent* and *Must Read Immediately* covered all of them in red ink.

"I'll be plenty busy," I said. "Diego is livid that witches keep crossing the Eastern Network border now that the Pact is broken and is threatening death to any Central Network witch they catch. I have to deal with that on Marten's behalf. Go see Tabby."

She gave me a wobbly smile and left. I sighed. Just when I was about to haunt Stella for an update for the second time that morning, an envelope materialized in front of me.

Bianca Monroe.

I didn't recognize the neat handwriting. When I touched the envelope, the paper unfolded itself, revealing an elegant script inside.

Dearest Bianca,

I hope this letter isn't too indulgent of me to send, but I am quite worried about you. I feel we became good friends on your visit to

*Magnolia Castle a few weeks ago, and I so appreciate you sending
me the newsscroll from your Network to keep me informed. I keep
it hidden in my room and think of you every time I go barefoot.*

Despite the bleak circumstances, I smiled at Isobel's sweet words.
They felt like a soothing balm, an anchor, in such a scary time.

*Dear girl, are you all right? Is your father in the middle of the
fighting as I suspect? Do you hear from him much, and is he well?
I imagine Derek must already have plans in place to defeat this
new horror and atrocity. Can the Eastern Network help him with
his plans somehow? I'm hoping that you aren't going into Chatham
City or the forest alone still. Are you? I suppose you already know
how I feel about that. Stay safe, Bianca. It seems the whole world
has changed.*

*Please let me know if I may lend assistance. So far the attacks
have not included our Network, but I'm bracing myself for the
inevitable.*

*My main purpose in writing is to tell you not to fear regarding
Diego's threats on the borders. (No one must know I have
sent this letter undermining his authority.) I know he says he
will react with swift justice if you cannot stop your witches
from coming into the East, but he will not. All our efforts are
concentrated on protecting ourselves from the Southern Network.
In all your stress, I didn't want you to fret over one more
unnecessary worry heaped on your shoulders. Do what you must,
but do not fear his wrath.*

*Forgive me if this letter finds you at a bad time, and don't feel
obligated to respond. Imparting my worry is enough for now.*

Stay safe as best you can.

*Yours,
Isobel*

I folded the letter back together. "What a wonderful lady," I murmured, and indeed, felt better about Diego's threats. With a quick

glance at the clock, I started a response to Isobel, setting aside all the frantic needs of the Network for just ten more minutes.

The war in the Southern Covens raged for another week without change, heralding the first month of spring and the freezing sleet that came with it.

We continued to wait. For news. For casualty lists. For letters. Camille received no further word on Brecken, and the Southern Covens still weren't allowing family to visit.

Marten checked in every morning with surprising regularity, which meant I always had a sense of what was happening. Every day he looked more haggard, and every day I felt as if this misery, which had lasted ten days, would never end. It seemed like nothing had existed before the war, and nothing would happen after. I half-wondered if we'd been locked in a strange new reality for the rest of our lives—or perhaps we'd always been here. Pacing the Witchery every night, I itched to do *something* beyond my poor attempts to control the borders diplomatically.

Late in the evening after a weary day training new Border Guards, I found Michelle sitting at the table in the Witchery, her head in her hands. Streaks stained her face, though I saw no tears. She straightened as soon as I walked in, sniffling.

"You all right, Michelle?" I asked, feeling a sudden rush of prickling cold. "What's happened?"

She looked down at her hands. "I still haven't heard from my family, and it's almost been two weeks," she whispered, and the words caught in her throat. "Papa had problems breathing before the attack. Even walking tires him, makes him short of breath. I can't imagine that they . . . they could have left the farm quickly. He doesn't know how to transport. He doesn't care . . . care much for magic. They haven't written back! I'm so . . . so scared!"

Deep sobs tore from her chest, wracking her broad shoulders. "Oh, Michelle," I said, sinking onto the chair next to her. "I'm so sorry. I bet they can't get any sort of paper wherever they are. Witches are hoarding messenger paper, trying to send it to the Guardians to update their families."

Of the five of us, Michelle had remained the quietest. Camille fretted constantly, Leda worked without stopping, Priscilla almost never showed up except for in the late evenings, and I paced with restless, frantic energy. We'd tried to get Michelle to talk, but she'd withdrawn into a stubborn, weary silence. Seeing her crack brought me relief.

"What if something happened to Papa?" she asked, looking at me through bloodshot eyes. They welled up with tears. "I couldn't handle it! I miss my family, Bianca. I want to see them again!"

I put a hand on her arm and swallowed back tears of my own. How deeply I understood! Her desperate, childlike cries tore at my heart. I had to do something.

"Then let's go," I said, latching onto the crazy thought as soon as it entered my mind. "Let's go find them."

The shock of my statement stopped her emotions. "What?" she asked, recoiling. "What do you mean?"

"I just heard updates from the Southern Covens. All the refugees are out of the war zone now. They moved them north to the border between the Letum Woods Covens and the Southern Covens, in the village of Perth. The fighting hasn't reached that far yet. Papa just requested more Apothecaries, which means it can't be too dangerous, right?"

"Did Stella say it's safe for witches to travel there?"

"Uh, no. She probably won't for a long time either," I said. "But that's just to keep curious onlookers and the general populace out of the way. You have a legitimate reason for going. Your entire family is there. Besides, no one has to know we're going."

A flicker of hope illuminated her eyes. "My dad's cousin, Luke, lives just outside Perth. I bet they went there." Her expression darkened. "Or he may not be anywhere at all."

"Don't think it."

She glanced away. "I don't know, Bianca. What will Camille and Leda say?"

"Nothing, because they won't know."

It wasn't something we should do at all, really, but Chatham Castle was driving me mad. Most of the Guardians usually said, *I don't really know what's going on everywhere, I just know about my contingent. Anyway, it was all so confusing. The magic is so strange, so deadly. I've never . . . never seen it. I never want to again.*

When pressed, they all described the same suffocating feeling I'd known in my dreams, the feeling that oppressed Bartie Stacey when he read from the *Book of Spells.*

"Isn't it dangerous?" Michelle asked, moving me back into the present.

"Yes, but not as dangerous as it would have been a few days ago. Papa lit some kind of fire that burns through snow and spread it across the Southern Covens farmlands. The Southern Network couldn't put it out or break through it, so they've been stuck behind it, closer to the Southern Network wall. We could just go long enough to find your family and come right back. An hour, tops."

The idea started to sound so good in my mind that I shifted in my seat, impatient to leave right away. Michelle perked up a little.

"An hour isn't that long."

"Not compared to waiting ten days."

"It's mad," she said, staring at me with an expression I couldn't interpret. "But you're right. It's better than sitting around here worrying."

"Infinitely better. At least, I think so. But I'm not the most trustworthy witch when it comes to dangerous ideas."

Michelle cracked her knuckles and stared out the window. A slushy mixture of rain and sleet fell from slate skies in what should have been a peaceful day. If our Guardians—and possibly our loved ones—weren't dying, perhaps I could have enjoyed the quiet weather.

"What if we're caught?" she asked, eyeing me. "Your father would be furious."

"Nah." I waved it off. "If anything he'd get angry at me, not you. It's not like he's even around to notice, right? He has bigger things on his mind. Anyway, we could transport into Letum Wood, right next to Perth. Both of us have been there, haven't we?"

She nodded. "I used to go as a little girl to visit Cousin Luke."

"Perfect. Both of us will be able to transport. I've gone to Perth several times with Marten. From there we can just follow the road using invisibility incantations."

"It could work," she said softly. "If we were gone no more than an hour or two. No one would even know."

"And if anything happens, we'll just leave. Both of us know how. Think it over," I said, setting a hand on her shoulder. "I know how worried you are about your father. Maybe this will give you some peace of mind."

Camille too, I wanted to add. I'd already decided that I would try to find Brecken while Michelle talked to her family. Perth held the hospital now, and it allowed a few visitors from families in the area. Brecken could be there. I didn't even entertain the hope that I might run into Papa or Merrick. They'd be behind enemy lines, likely, or right in the middle of a battle. Knowing that I'd find out right away through Stella if one of the Protectors was lost gave me some consolation. So far none of them had died, though Tobias received extensive injuries while sparring with a West Guard. He'd continued to fight until he collapsed from blood loss and Nathaniel, another Protector, pulled him away.

"Let's do it," Michelle whispered. "Tomorrow morning. It's the only time I have off, and I don't want to draw any suspicion by going tonight. Nicolas will know something is up."

"Are you sure?"

She set her jaw. "Yes, then I'll be able to recognize Cousin Luke's house. Let's go find my family."

The Wounded

W e didn't tell anyone else when we left the next morning. Chatham Castle seemed to be going about business as usual; it was the perfect time to slip away.

"Are you sure?" Michelle asked, and I nodded. "What if we let Leda—"

"We can't tell Leda or Camille. Leda will tell Stella, who will restrict me to the castle by magic until I'm thirty. It's bad enough that I haven't gone into Letum Wood for almost two weeks. If I'm restricted to the castle walls, I'll destroy you."

Michelle sighed. "You're right. So you didn't tell Camille that you're going to look for Brecken?"

I shook my head emphatically. I'd let Michelle in on my plan last night when Camille had come back with swollen eyes and a courageous but faltering smile. She still hadn't received word on Brecken's condition.

"Definitely not. Then she'd really worry."

Besides, I didn't want to be the one to deliver any bad news.

"Ready?" I asked, forcing an easy smile even though a pile of butterflies lived in my stomach. Perth was a secure area—more than anywhere else in the Southern Covens, anyway—but I still didn't know what to expect. Viveet hid underneath my heavy winter cloak, and I kept one hand near her.

Michelle swallowed, looking a bit green around the cheeks. "Yes," she murmured. "I'm ready."

We disappeared from the Witchery with separate spells. The heavy pressure of transportation took my breath away, lasting just long enough to start my lungs burning before it dropped me. The discomfort faded into a moment of panic. Instead of the comforting closeness of Letum Wood, I faced the middle of Perth in broad daylight.

"Wonderful," I muttered, wondering if the unlucky placement had something to do with poor concentration because of nerves.

At first, I only saw chaos on the streets of Perth. I couldn't find Michelle, and I concluded she must have transported herself more accurately. The main Central Highway cut through the middle of Perth so most witches from the Southern Covens had come here before scattering to whatever Covens or villages would take them. Witches chattered in the streets, bustling with a low, defined intensity. A handful slept in the cold sunlight in alleys or hunkered over pitiful fires to keep their hands warm. Most of them hurried, flinching at every distant sound. Luckily, not a single one paid any attention to me, a stranger in their midst that shouldn't, by any means, be there.

A stench hovered on the air, like sewer water and cow dung, the result of so many witches packed into one place. One elderly woman cradled a chicken on her lap and stared at the street without comprehension. Most of the witches in the Southern Covens were brawny, like Michelle, and lived simple lives. This war had more than uprooted their routine; it changed their very perception of life.

I slipped through the crowd unheeded, heading toward Letum Wood, worried that I'd draw more attention to myself by disappearing behind an invisibility incantation. When I passed a girl who couldn't have been older than twelve, shoeless and shivering in the sunlight while clutching her little sister, I stopped.

"Here," I said, twirling my cloak off my shoulders and settling it around both of them. I slipped off my winter boots, feeling a shiver when the cold earth met the bottoms of my feet. "You need these more than I do."

The eldest girl ran her hand along the fur in shock, but the little girl wasted no time burrowing in.

"But, Miss—"

"Put the shoes on," I coaxed. "Go ahead."

She hesitated, wide-eyed, and finally obeyed. Once her feet touched the inside, she sighed with relief.

"Keep warm," I said, squeezing their shoulders, wondering if Henrietta would clobber me for losing my two best winter cloaks. "Help is coming."

By the time I'd made it to the spot in Letum Wood where I was supposed to transport, Michelle was pacing back and forth. "What happened?" she cried. "We didn't plan for anything going wrong! I almost left without you. Where are your shoes?"

"Let's just say my transportation skills haven't improved. I'm sorry."

"You lost your shoes transporting?"

"Don't worry about it."

"Fine, let's just go."

Michelle took charge by pushing through the brush, keeping inside the forest where we could follow the road but not be seen. I followed behind, startled to see a new, authoritative side of my friend. Despite the need to walk quickly, I couldn't help but touch every tree we passed, soaking in the feel of the forest as if I'd been starved. Although small, a part of my heart seemed to knit back together. It had been far too long since I'd breathed in Letum's air.

"I haven't been to Cousin Luke's in a while," she said, plowing through the forest and the occasional pile of snow that numbed my feet. "But I think I know where it's at . . . if he still lives there, of course. We haven't heard from him in years."

I jogged to keep up with her long, determined stride. We walked on the edge of the forest until the traffic on the road diminished, and the houses stretched farther and farther apart. The only witches we saw stayed close to their homes, eyes on the southern horizon.

"That's it! Up there on the right," she said, motioning to a house of red bricks covered with peeling white paint. She burst out of the trees and ran across the road, panting from her strenuous efforts.

"Cousin Luke!" She shoved through a gate and into a small yard, which housed at least fifteen witches. "Cousin Luke!"

A shaggy head of white hair popped out of the upper window. "Meesh?" came a high-pitched voice. "What are you doing here?"

Michelle stopped under the window. Her voice shook. "Is . . . is Papa here? Mace? Ted?"

"Course your papa is here," Cousin Luke said. "Where else would he go? Rian is out fighting with the Guardians, but Mace is here. Ted too. Your father took a little injury to his leg and isn't feeling well lately, so he can't come down. But you're welcome to come up."

Michelle let out a relieved, stuttering laugh. "Course," she said, tears filling her small eyes. "Course he is. I'll be right up!"

I grabbed her elbow before she hurried inside.

"I'm going to go back to Perth to see if I can find Brecken. I'll transport back here in an hour, all right?"

She smiled, wiped at the corners of her eyes, and disappeared inside without another word.

When I transported back to Perth—landing exactly where I wanted, thankfully—I followed the muddy street the other direction in search of the wounded. After walking for almost fifteen minutes, a familiar glint of sunlight on a set of half-armor caught my eye.

"Excuse me," I called, running to catch up with the Guardian. "I'm looking for a possibly wounded Captain. I'm . . . his sister. Where is the wounded area?"

A young male witch with a mop of bright orange hair turned around. He must have been a new recruit because he couldn't have been much older than sixteen. His shaggy brows lowered over his eyes.

"Who is it?"

"Brecken Jameson. He's a Captain and—"

The boy jerked his head to the far end of the street. "Brecken's down there, with the other seriously wounded. Just keep going."

My mouth dropped open. "You know him?"

"After what he did, everyone knows him."

"What happened?"

"He caught something in the leg saving a group of young recruits during an unexpected ambush. If he hadn't jumped in the way to stop it, all ten of them would have died. Don't know what it was. Something from that weird magic the West Guards are using." He shook his head. "Brutal."

The young Guardian clenched his fists and jaw. I swallowed the sudden rise of nervous fear that told me I shouldn't be in the Southern Covens. With his obsession about protecting me, Papa would be livid if he found out.

"Thank you!" I cried. "You've been very helpful."

"Be careful," he called when I stepped away. "The Apothecaries still aren't letting many witches in to see the wounded. They want to prevent sickness from spreading. You'll have to wait for a couple of days, I think. If he lives that long."

After winding through the dense street for another ten minutes, I stumbled on the makeshift hospital. My heart leapt in my throat as I peered over a hastily constructed fence to see hundreds of cots lined up in an empty field. Three Guardians manned a rickety gate at the front, holding back a line of at least fifty witches that stretched along the fence.

"Jikes," I whispered. "He wasn't kidding."

Two or three Apothecary Assistants spoke with those in line one at a time. From what I could tell, they only allowed two family members into the wounded area at a time. An Apothecary Assistant would speak with the family members, jot down a few notes, and another would walk with them through the crowd of beds. At that rate, it would take days to get to Brecken.

I glanced up at the sun, which appeared hazy through the smoke from the southern border. *No time.* After taking careful note of the outfits the Assistants wore, I disappeared into a back alley between buildings nearby.

"Well, Priscilla," I muttered from the shadows. "Time to put your transformation lesson to the test."

After working a few magical spells, I slipped out of the alley, my dress transformed into an Apothecary Assistant's uniform and my hair in a short blonde bob. Priscilla would be gratified to see how perfectly the spell had come out thanks to her tutelage. I headed for the gate with a confident stride. Instead of waiting in line, I walked right to the gate, heart hammering in my chest, and stood there until one of the Guardians acknowledged me.

The closest Guardian opened his mouth to call out and stopped. He blinked, studying my face and my clothes, lingering on my feet. I felt a rush of horror when I realized I'd given my shoes away and hadn't replaced them.

"Can I go in?" I asked. He returned his studious gaze to my face.

"You don't have shoes on."

"I gave them to a little girl and her sister on my way here."

His brow furrowed, and it wasn't until I saw the intense expression on his face that I recognized him as the blonde Guardian that had saved my life during the invasion, shooting a Southern Guardian with his bow and arrow.

"Who are you?" he asked. "I've seen you before."

"I'm going to be late," I said, slowing my voice to match the un-hurried tone of the Southern Covens. It wouldn't be long before he re-ally recognized me, even if I had changed my hair color. Word would move through the Guardian ranks until Papa found out. And then I'd never leave the castle again.

"What's your name?" he asked, his eyes narrowing. "I *know* I've seen you before."

"Jane. Let me through. I've been working here for days now."

"It hasn't been open for days. We just opened it yesterday."

My nostrils flared. "Well, I was working to get it ready, all right? Let me through, or I'll get in trouble."

"Seems weird that I recognize you but haven't ever seen you here at work before. Did you cut your hair?"

"Oh, and you keep track of every Assistant?" I snapped. "Let me in!"

He hesitated. My breath stilled in my chest. No doubt he recog-nized some kind of magic at work, though he hadn't identified what it was yet. These newer recruits remained behind the real action for this very reason; their immature judgment could allow anything to leak through.

"Fine," he muttered with a jerk of his head. "Go to work." He turned back to a hysterical mother wailing about her only son but watched me from the corner of his eye.

I found no pattern to the hundreds of cots laid out. Apothecaries, Assistants, Guardians, and cooks all rushed back and forth from table to cot, trying to save as many as they could. Several Guardians carried the bodies of the deceased away. A sick feeling rose in my chest.

So much death.

I sped through the rows at a half-jog. My hour here would be up soon; we'd already been away from Chatham for at least that long. An apothecary headed my direction at one point, arm raised and mouth open to ask me something, but I snatched a couple of herb packets from a table and pretended to be occupied. He moved past me with a growl. I picked up a water pitcher and moved on, seeking a familiar head of curly brown hair.

"Jikes, Brecken," I muttered. "Where are you?"

Another ten minutes passed with no luck. I almost gave up hope when a stray brown curl on a pale forehead caught my eye. I rushed to the cot, breath held.

"Brecken?" I asked, crouching in the dirt. His eyes fluttered open, latching onto mine in confusion. A sheen of sweat covered his face.

"Bianca? Is that you? What are you doing here?" he whispered.

"I came to find you," I said, putting a hand on his shoulder. His skin felt hot to the touch, even through the fabric. "Camille's sick with worry."

The pained, rigid lines of his face softened. "I've begged for paper and a quill," he said, "but there's none here. There's nothing here but death."

The stench of antiseptic potions and the metallic smell of blood nearly made me vomit, but I swallowed through it. Sheets dotted with dried bloodstains covered Brecken's lower body.

"What happened?" I asked. "I heard you saved some other Guardians."

He hesitated, then grabbed the top of his blanket and whipped it back. I sucked in a breath. His right leg was cut off just below the knee. Long white strips saturated with blood encircled the end of the stump.

"Oh, Brecken. I . . . I didn't . . . what happened?"

He shook his head. "Not sure. A black object moved toward my

179

new recruits, so I jumped in the way. Something smashed into my leg. I fell, blacked out from the pain, and woke up here a few days later. The West Guards are using some kind of potion or spell that burrows into the flesh and never stops. If they hadn't cut my leg off, it would have moved through my body and killed me."

His voice sounded wooden.

"Bloody mess," he muttered, yanking the covers back up. "I'm next to worthless now! Witches dying at the hands of the lecherous West Guards, and I'm lying on a cot!"

I leaned forward and pressed the back of my hand to his bright red cheek. "You're feverish, Brecken. You're burning up."

He hugged his arms closer to his body. Beneath the blanket, he trembled. His eyes closed in exhaustion. "I'm fine."

"We have to get you out of here," I said, more to myself than him. "Now."

Despite the fires clustered between every four beds for warmth, the heat didn't reach this far. He'd die of exposure before the infection claimed him.

"There's nowhere else to go. The convoys back to Chatham City are full, and so are the houses of those who live here. I might be sick, but a little fever and pain isn't much compared to what others are going through."

He squeezed his eyes shut, tilted his head back, and gritted his teeth. I rolled my eyes. Fine time to be self-sacrificing. If I let him die, Camille would perish of a broken heart, and then who would calm Leda down when she went on a tirade? There had to be something I could do. Walking back to Chatham was clearly out of the question, and Brecken couldn't transport in this condition.

"I won't accept that. There has to be something."

I chewed my bottom lip, empty water jug still in hand. How could I move him without causing more pain? With an infection, a carriage ride could kill him. It would take days to get him back to the castle, even if I could find a carriage. And that assumed all the roads were open, which they weren't. I needed to move him quickly, without jarring him, and without being seen. I needed . . .

To fly.

My eyes widened. "Brecken," I breathed, grabbing his arm. "I have a plan. I'll be back tonight."

He'd already fallen into a light, troubled sleep.

Dear Isobel,

Forgive my hasty letter, but I must beg your help on an errand of mercy to save the fading life of a friend.

In the interest of discretion, I need you to help me fly.

Your friend,
Bianca Monroe

My Dearest Bianca,

My wings are yours. Be safe, dear friend.

Isobel

The Volare

I sat on the edge of my bed and stared at the Volare with a mute sense of awe. Isobel's response had appeared with the Volare less than twenty minutes after I'd transported the letter to her.

I'd seen the Volare when I visited Isobel's personal chambers, but I hadn't touched it, so I hadn't fully appreciated the intricate beauty of the woven patterns. It lay sprawled on the ground in front of me just like a normal rug, albeit a magnificent one. A deep plum color ran along the edges, bordering an image of trees and stone. I wondered about the Volare's history: Who made it? Where did it begin? How did Diego find it?

My eyes strayed outside. Darkness had fallen hours before, which meant it was nearly time for me to go. Less than three hours left until midnight. I hadn't dared leave any earlier for fear of being seen, and I hoped that fewer witches would remain near the wounded late at night.

I skimmed Isobel's instructions a third time.

The Volare will return to me at midnight; that is all the time that I can give you. It will not be parted from me for any longer. Be warned: If you are in the middle of a flight, it will still disappear at the appointed time.

The magic is ancient and precise. Only one witch may command it at a time. Be discreet, for I know of no other Volares in use. If anyone saw it, there's no telling what they might do to possess it. The incantations needed are listed below. The Volare will know what you want and need. Except against fire, it can act as a shield to protect its occupants during the ride.

The Volare leapt to life at my magical command, springing to waist height and hovering in the air. I grinned.

"Excellent."

I'd already sent a note to Camille, telling her to go see Tabby for the night and I'd explain later. I hoped she received it. After tucking the instructions in the pocket of the slacks that I'd filched from the laundry, I pressed my hands onto the Volare to test it, delighted when it rippled as fluidly and lightly as silk. It lowered itself so I could scoot on rear first. I slipped across the soft weave, expecting it to feel loose, like sitting on a piece of cloth suspended between two chairs. But the Volare remained sure and firm. I didn't sink, but it conformed to my body—it was neither stiff nor flimsy.

"Be good to me," I said to the Volare, commanding the window of my bedroom to open. "We have a life to save."

I hid myself with an invisibility incantation, ecstatic to see that it extended to the Volare also. A cold draft of air flew into the room from the open window, and I shuddered, pulling my oldest, most threadbare cloak more tightly around me. I sat upright on the rug, and though I hovered above the ground, felt no dizziness or fear.

"This won't be so bad. No. Not so bad." I gripped the sides of the rug in my hand. Holding onto something made me feel better. "Not so bad."

The Volare inched forward but didn't leave the room. It trembled, as if it were impatient to begin. I commanded it with a spell, picturing Brecken's cot in the Southern Covens.

It moved easily out the window and hovered over the castle grounds, which made me dizzy, for with the invisibility incantation I couldn't see the Volare beneath me. While I didn't hate heights, I certainly didn't enjoy them.

Fortunately, the Volare didn't give me long to think but kept moving at impressive speed. We seemed to hover over the sea of Letum Wood. Comforted by the sight of the forest, even from my bird's-eye view, I settled into the ride with a little sigh. The passage of air felt ice cold on my face, but it gave me a heady rush that made me feel alive. I soared over the darkness of the Central Network like a bird.

A very fast bird.

Before I knew it, the empty cotton fields of the Middle Covens bled into the thick forest of Letum Wood again. Before an hour had passed, the fires of Perth appeared on the horizon. It would be half past ten by this point. I had ninety minutes to retrieve him and take him home.

"Let down quietly," I murmured. Although I didn't understand how, I had the distinct impression that the Volare understood me. Perhaps even magic could sense fear and desperation. The most dangerous part of the whole night approached: removing Brecken without making a scene. I didn't know whether he'd get in trouble for being taken away, but I knew I'd be in trouble for taking him.

Mentally, I'd already planned for the worst because my luck usually dictated it. No matter what came to pass, I refused to let the Volare be seen. Doing so would violate the trust of my friend and draw suspicion, and it could lead to the loss of one of the greatest treasures of our day.

Still invisible, the Volare responded to my command to hover in place over the camp until I located Brecken's spot. Someone had erected a tent over the top of him and four other cots, which caused me to waste precious time searching.

The camp of the wounded whispered in the background when the Volare lowered me to the ground next to Brecken. I slipped off it without a sound, and the Volare rested on the earth. The invisibility incantation broke, leaving me exposed. Grateful that I'd shucked the dress and replaced it with the easy freedom of pants, I slipped up to Brecken's side. His forehead furrowed into deep lines of strain, and the red in his cheeks made me nervous. I certainly hadn't come too early.

No Apothecary Assistants hovered nearby when I crouched at his side. "Brecken?" I pressed a hand to his shoulder. "Brecken?"

His eyes fluttered open, appearing drugged and hazy. They must have just given him a tonic for pain. Perfect.

"What?" he croaked, as if his mouth were dry.

"I'm here to take you home."

He blankly stared at me for another moment, then his head dropped back to the pillow, and his even, steady breathing resumed.

"That's for the best, my friend," I murmured, pulling the blanket farther over him. "The less you're aware of, the better for you."

Another glance around the camp verified that no one appeared to be watching, so I used an incantation to shift Brecken onto the Volare. He sank seamlessly, settling onto the fabric with barely a lurch. His forehead creased again, but he didn't wake. The Volare seemed to have widened to accommodate both of us.

"Okay, Breck. Let's take you home."

Just as I began to whisper the invisibility incantation, a booted foot stepped on the Volare right next to Brecken's head. My gaze traveled slowly up a pant leg to a pair of strong shoulders, past folded arms, and stopped on a familiar pair of green eyes.

"Merrick!" I whispered in disbelief, forgetting my panic in relief. "You're alive!"

I launched myself forward and threw my arms around him. He stiffened, then relaxed just enough to put an arm around my back. He felt surprisingly warm, though leaner. Realizing what I'd done, I hastily backed away. My body seemed to burn where he had touched it.

"Sorry. I just . . . I haven't heard from you, you know and . . . jikes. You're a mess."

Several cuts, held together by stitches, marred his face. A bandage was wrapped around the top of his arm, and I couldn't tell if the blood staining the leather of his half-armor came from him or someone else. I hoped the latter.

"I've been busy."

"You couldn't even write or stop in once to let me know you were alive?" I snapped, folding my arms across my chest, feeling exposed. "It's almost been two weeks! I've been worried sick."

His eyes burned with a sudden, surprising intensity. "I didn't realize you would care so much."

"Well we're friends, aren't we?"

"Sure."

"Sure?" I asked, fuming. I pushed him, striking his chest. "Sure? What kind of answer is that? I've been worried about you!"

He grinned in that lazy way that undid all my anger in a moment and then made it flare up again.

"It's a good answer. We *are* friends, Bianca." He hesitated. "Good friends."

I wanted to slap him but didn't know why. "If you didn't already look so hurt, I'd make *sure* you left injured."

"You could use a good fight," he said, studying me with a wrinkled forehead. "You're a mess yourself. Have you been running? I can feel your magic."

"Oh, be quiet," I said, relieved to see him alive and so upset at the same time that I didn't know how act. "I need to go."

He lifted an eyebrow and glanced down at the Volare. "What are you traveling with now, little troublemaker?"

A shot of panic darted through me. What if Merrick told Papa about the Volare? What if Merrick told Papa about *me*?

"I-I know what you're thinking," I said, holding out a shaky hand. "I shouldn't be here. And you're right, I'll give you that. Papa would be livid. It's not safe. The Volare isn't mine. I know. I thought of all those things, but I had to save Brecken. I needed a way to take him home before his fever gets worse. If he dies, Camille will . . . she'll never recover. I can't let that happen. She's just now finding a family to love her."

"You're more protective of your friends than yourself, you know."

"Well, someone has to do it."

"Where did you find a Volare?" he asked with an even tone, gesturing to the rug, which sat innocently on the ground with a restless, fitful Brecken on top. The camp moved on around us without interruption. My eyes strayed to the moon. I needed to leave now.

"It's . . . nothing you need to worry about."

But it was too late. Merrick had seen it, and now I'd have to explain myself in full. Likely not only to him, which would be bad enough, but to Papa, who might lock me in the castle for the rest of the foreseeable future.

"What are you doing here?" I asked, folding my arms across my chest. He motioned to Brecken.

"Checking on my friend. I was there when the accident happened."

"Oh."

"B, don't change the subject. What is—"

"Look, you can scold me, yell at me, or make me train for hours later to *teach me a lesson* on making stupid decisions, but I have to go now. Brecken is getting worse. I won't let him die here in this hellhole, and I refuse to fall from the sky just because you want to get mad at me for taking a risk."

Merrick opened his mouth, but on studying my panicked expression a moment longer, seemed to relent. He held up a finger.

"Fine. But only on one condition. You explain yourself the moment I return." His eyes wandered uneasily to the Volare. "Knowing that you're wandering around here, where diseases and death run rampant, is the last thing your father needs on his mind."

"I know," I whispered, stuffing aside a pang of guilt. "But I still don't regret it. Get off my rug."

He shot me an annoyed glare, then let out a long breath and ran a hand through his hair, drawing my attention to an odd bald spot on the side of his head.

"Promise me you won't leave Chatham Castle again."

But I dug my figurative heels into the field of his stubbornness. He might be angry at me for risking my life, but he wasn't my father and couldn't order me around. Despite his strange surprise, Merrick and I *were* friends. Good friends, if the weightless feeling I got when I was around him meant anything at all.

"No, I won't promise."

"Bianca, I don't want you wandering around at night with West Guards and—"

"Well I don't want you to do something stupid and hurt yourself, but clearly I won't get what I want."

"Of the two of us, I think I'm the one with the shorter history of stupid decisions."

"Fine. Trust yourself, but I'll do what I must to keep my friends safe," I said, stepping back onto the Volare. The invisibility incantation bled back through me, covering Brecken, myself, and the Volare. When I spoke, my voice came from empty air. "That is what I promise. By the way, it's good to see you again."

With that, I commanded the Volare to rise. Merrick let out a heavy sigh.

"Just be careful, *friend*," he said softly, though a tinge of something deeper marked his voice.

"I will."

The Volare flew, soaring into the sky, far from the field of wounded Guardians. I watched Merrick until I could no longer see him, and I felt strangely empty once he disappeared.

True to Isobel's word, the Volare seemed to sense my worry, or Brecken's illness, and the return ride passed with even greater speed. The top of the rug curled over Brecken's head, and the sides moved inward, cocooning both of us in a tube of safety. I stared at the passing stars overhead, losing myself in the whistle of the wind.

Since Camille hadn't sent a response to my letter, I assumed she had obeyed. When Brecken and I landed outside a beautiful two-story house set just inside a little copse of trees, I hoped that my arrival wouldn't seem too strange. I'd never been to Brecken's house before, but based on Camille's many descriptions of the local area and the house, managed to find it.

The Volare deposited Brecken on the porch, then rolled into a cylinder. I stashed it in the trees on a dry patch of ground and rushed back to the porch. Brecken trembled when I rapped on the door, which opened to reveal a squat woman with graying brown curls. Camille stood just behind her.

"Bianca?" Camille asked, mouth agape. "What in the—"

"I brought Brecken home. I found him in Perth today and . . . he's sick. He needs immediate help. I didn't know if he'd make it there, so I brought him back."

Brecken's mother dropped her candlestick with a gasp. I stopped it with an incantation before it crashed to the floor and splattered his face with hot wax.

"He needs to get inside!" I said. "He's burning up with fever. They had to cut off one of his legs at the knee."

"His leg! Oh, my darling son. Paul!" Tabby screeched. "Paul, come here!"

I used a spell to move Brecken into the house, and it spurred them into motion. Camille threw open the door, Tabby toddled out of the way, and I lowered Brecken onto a divan near the fire. The clock above the mantle read five minutes to midnight. Tabby jumped into her work, commanding a wooden box with a spell and flaming the fire higher. Camille turned to me.

"Bianca, I don't know what to say." Her eyes filled with tears. "I can't believe—"

"Go," I said, motioning to Brecken. "I think Tabby will need your help for several days."

"His leg?" Camille whispered, hoarse and strained. "They cut it off?"

I nodded. "Yes. They had to. Now it's infected, and he's not doing well."

"But how did you—"

"Let's just say I grew wings," I whispered, and a wave of understanding passed over her face. "If Tabby asks, tell her you don't know, understood? No one can know, Camille. No one."

"But—" She stared at me, blinked, and seemed to understand. In a rush, she threw her arms around me in a teary hug. "Thank you," she whispered, holding me so tight it hurt. A tear rolled down her cheek and onto my neck. "Thank you for saving him. Tell Isobel thank you."

When I went back outside to find the Volare, it had disappeared. A note from Isobel popped into the air in front of me.

It has returned. Thank you, dear friend, for allowing me to help.

Isobel

Send Him Home

Three more interminable days passed without a word from Papa or Merrick. Even though spring started showing signs of her return, no one seemed to notice. Marten returned to the castle full-time, which removed the worst demands of work from my life and left me with more time to stew over Merrick and Papa. Without Letum Wood to run through, my magic flared in restless spurts. I paced the gardens, but it only made it worse. Standing so close to Letum Wood tortured me.

Camille didn't return to the castle but sent me updates every day. Brecken healed with slower progress than desired, but he did improve. Michelle transported to Cousin Luke's house every evening to visit her family, and Leda worked fourteen hours a day as Jansson's temporary Assistant. When I did see her, she appeared deliriously happy. Priscilla occasionally ventured into the Witchery without Camille but seemed busy enough helping Miss Scarlett.

I slept on the divan every night, hoping I'd wake up if Papa came home. Reeves often covered me with a second blanket or left a cup of tea that never cooled. He puttered around the apartment, cleaning things that had already been cleaned, searching for meaning in a world without Papa to give his job purpose.

"I'm going to visit Stella before I go to work, Reeves," I said early on the third morning. He shot me a murderous look, so I scooped the toast off my plate and chewed a bite. "I'll eat on my way."

Satisfied, he nodded in his usual mute way. I walked through the castle halls, enjoying the early morning quiet before most of the servants started work. A frost had fallen on the gardens below, coating everything in a layer of thin, white frosting. I'd just approached Stella's office when a familiar voice stopped my heart.

"We've pushed the South Guards back into the Southern Network for now," Papa said in a steady drone. "We've been able to remove all the Southern Covens' residents. I've started the evacuation of the wounded out of Perth because Tiberius needs more room for his Guardians. We're sending them here and to Ashleigh House. Donovan's old palace will house most of them."

"What of the roaming West Guards?" Stella asked. "What can we do to stop them? They continue attacking at random across the Network. Stilton, in the Middle Covens, was just burned to the ground by ten West Guards two nights ago. Twenty witches died, including two children."

I hovered just outside the door, barely able to restrain the impulse to throw myself into Papa's arms. He was alive! I forced myself to wait another moment, hoping to hear unfiltered news.

"Zane and I have come up with a few ideas that we've put into motion," Papa said. "A few Protectors are out on missions right now, and I've been on a few."

"You're going to wear yourself out, Derek." Stella's voice lowered with warning. "You'll be no good to us if you don't take care of yourself."

"We don't have the luxury of stopping right now."

Stella sighed. "Please be careful. I don't want to tell Bianca that she's also lost her father. She's having a hard enough time since I made her promise to stay out of Letum Wood. I can feel her magic some days; it's burning strongly. Running through the forest seems to be her only release for agitation and stress."

"The good gods know I worry about her," he muttered, his voice husky. "Has she been doing all right otherwise?"

"She's worried, but she understands."

"I'll owe her a big vacation once this is over."

Stella chuckled. "If you can peel her off of you, that is. What can we do from here to help you?"

"Isadora has anticipated some of the West Guards' most significant attacks but not the smaller ones," he said, resuming his usual businesslike tone. "Marten is sending out an announcement to all villages and cities tomorrow with ways to prepare for and prevent attacks."

"I've met with most of the Coven Leaders and Council Members, so that advice went out through those channels as well. You're my main concern. How are you holding up? You look as if you haven't slept in days."

"I can't justify sleeping when the West Guards are using Almorran magic to slaughter us in the night."

"I know how you feel."

The sound of defeat in Papa's voice made my heart quiver. "I don't know how to fight it, Stella. All we're doing is trying to hold it off. I feel . . . totally useless. These Guardians—many just boys—are dying, waiting for me to end this war, and I don't know how we're going to do that."

I heard a rustle of movement. "Derek, this burden is not yours to bear alone."

"I've been trying to think of a plan to avoid going after Dane myself, but I can't," he said, as if she hadn't spoken. I closed my eyes in disappointment.

A dramatic pause followed his declaration. I held my breath.

"Come in, B," Papa called. "There's no need to eavesdrop."

I pressed into the room, forgetting to be embarrassed that I'd been caught. "Papa," I cried, grateful to see him with my own eyes. "You're back!"

He was leaning against the wall by the window, clad in dirty half-armor torn at the shoulders but still covering his broad chest. Only a remnant of his familiar smile appeared when he saw me. Fatigue and desperation buried the rest. He opened his arms. "Come here, girl."

I rushed into his waiting embrace. When his strong arms encircled me, I fought back the tears I'd been swallowing for days. He smelled like sweat and torch oil and blood. I pulled away only when his grip went slack a minute later.

"Are you hurt?" I asked, glancing him over. "Because we have—"

"I'm fine. Have Reeves draw me up a bath and lay out a fresh pair of clothes. And scrounge up some food, will you? I need to clean up before I come back to work."

He wasn't fine, but I acted like I believed him because Papa was still in High Priest mode. I saw it in the half-glazed look in his eyes. Bruises and blood covered his arms and his face, as if someone had taken a whip and hacked away at him. He needed sleep but telling him that wouldn't do any good. Whatever I said wouldn't matter when he had that expression on his face.

"Yes, Papa. Will I see you at all?"

"Go now," he said gently, softening the command with a squeeze of my shoulder. "I need to finish speaking with Stella, and I'll be right up. You and I can talk while I eat."

Stella gave me a warm, encouraging nod, and I slowly stepped out. The doors closed behind me with a resolute clang.

Within fifteen minutes Reeves readied a hot bath, laid out a new set of clothes, and fluttered around the apartment cleaning silver in his strange way of expressing excitement until I sent him to the kitchen to get Papa's food. I was standing at the bay window, staring at Letum Wood, when Papa came back. He sent me a crooked smile, smelled his own shirt, and grimaced.

"Let me bathe," he said. "You don't want to talk to me like this."

I would have talked to him if he smelled like a pile of dung. "You do smell pretty ripe."

He set a sneezing hex on me and disappeared into his room. Reeves materialized with a silver platter of bread, a few slices of cheese, and some dipping broth. Meager fare considering he'd once brought Papa an entire rotisserie chicken and a slice of birthday cake—even though Papa had forgotten it was his own birthday—for dinner when meetings had run until midnight last fall.

"It's not much," Reeves said, his nose wrinkled as if he took personal offense at the portion size. "But it'll fill his stomach."

"I'm sure he'll enjoy it."

Reeves puttered toward Papa's room. While his gait couldn't be described as sprightly, because nothing about Reeves could ever be anything but sedate, he walked with a much more determined stride than usual. No doubt it felt good for him to feel useful again. I could empathize.

I sank back into my thoughts at the window until Papa returned, his hair brushed back, wearing a fresh pair of clothes. A bruise that had previously been hidden by grime circled his right eye.

"Thank you, Reeves," Papa said as he sat at the table. "This smells like a feast."

Reeves faded into the background, leaving us in privacy. Papa's chocolate eyes looked almost hazel in the bright morning light. I hardly recognized him for the weary fatigue in his movements. Keeping him closest to the warm fire, I sat in the chair next to him and picked half-heartedly at a piece of cheese.

"I'm sorry I couldn't contact you more, B," he said, leaning back once he'd eaten everything on the platter, including the broth. "I know how worried you've been. Stella keeps me updated."

"It's all right, Papa," I said with a quiet smile. "I understand. Sounds like you have the Southern Network under control for now."

"A little bit." His eyes narrowed in thought. He ran his tongue around the inside of his mouth, then shook his head. "It's the West Guards that have me worried."

"Think they'll try to come after Chatham Castle?"

"They'd be fools not to."

My heart pounded faster. Being at war was bad enough. It tilted the world upside down and disoriented any sense of what was real and what wasn't. But at least the fighting remained far removed from Chatham.

For now.

"We've learned a lot," Papa said, as if weighing the pros and cons. "That'll help us plan in the future."

"Oh?" I inquired with a lifted eyebrow.

He gave a weak, rueful smile and stacked his hands behind his head. "Nothing you'd be interested in, B."

His dismissal split a chasm in my heart. I wanted to beg him to tell me, to include me in his life and plans again, but refrained. Putting it into words made it seem too real. I'd lost Papa to his career and this war, and I missed him desperately. But asking him to remember me while he tried to save the Central Network felt selfish. I could only hope we'd have time to be a family again after it ended, that he wouldn't be taken from me.

"So now what?" I asked, brushing aside my thoughts. "We just keep fighting?"

"Until we can find Angelina, or until I can kill Dane, we do the best we can to keep them from invading further into our land. The first flurry of attacks is over. It's all stealth and maintenance at this point. On which, thanks to the Brotherhood, we have an advantage over the West Guards. They're talented, with brute strength on their side—"

"Not to mention Almorran magic."

"That too," he said. "But they don't possess an organized, dedicated force like the Protectors. And we started to prepare last summer, so our supplies will last for some time. At least until I get rid of Dane."

The ice in his voice sent a shiver through me. *Until I get rid of Dane.* I recalled Dane's broad strength and fury, standing on top of the Southern Network wall before the invasion. Papa straightened.

"I need to go to my office for a few hours to settle some issues. Thanks for eating with me, B."

"Already? I've only seen you for fifteen minutes."

"It'll only be for a few hours," he said, grabbing my arm and tucking me into his side with a kiss on top of my head. "I'll come back before you go to bed, I promise."

I squeezed him, but felt like a little girl losing her father all over again. Moments later, he stood, tugged affectionately on my hair, and disappeared in the whisper of a transportation spell as if he'd never been there. I stared at the wall with tears in my eyes.

"I miss you, Papa," I whispered, and the empty room returned my lonely echo.

"I wish I could say something to make this all better," Camille whispered, tears in her eyes. "Death is so awful."

Leda, Camille, Priscilla, and I stood in a semi-circle behind Michelle and Nicolas. None of us had said much since Michelle burst into the Witchery the day before, sobbing into her hands to announce the death of her older brother, Rian. The cold, branching network of Letum Wood stretched over our heads, hiding the blustery spring sky far above. A few tufts of snow still lived here, far from the reach of the warming spring sun.

"You can't make this better," I said.

"I know," Camille whispered, tears in her eyes. "That's the worst part of all."

Priscilla said nothing, but stared at the empty hole with a haunted expression. Michelle hovered close to her family, keeping her hand folded safely in Nicolas's. Even though she held onto him, she constantly checked to make sure he still stood next to her. He would smile, squeeze her hand, give her a reassuring nod. She seemed to draw strength from him and would take a breath and steel herself for the next interminable minute.

Rian lay in a fresh casket stacked on two piles of stones. A fresh hole in the soggy earth awaited him, dug by Michelle's oldest brother Ted and youngest brother Mace, while her ill father watched with blank eyes. A mournful voice chanted a blessing of farewell that stretched over the hallowed cemetery, kept safe by a protective incantation that not even the West Guards would break. They were monsters, but honorable monsters. Unlike the South Guards, who left their dead where they lay, the West Guards returned to claim them all. Papa, a witch of honor himself, allowed it in exchange for our own.

"So many," Leda whispered, looking around. "I didn't . . . I never realized how many."

"This is so few of them, too."

We were not the only witches burying a lost friend. Many families moved by like ghosts in the background. Mounds of dirt, new caskets, and fresh headstones littered the cemetery. The clear air meant that Papa had stopped the fires that had clogged the sky, holding the Southern Network back while the Southern Covens' residents escaped to safety. I felt uneasy, as if war could travel on the wind.

"It's done, Father," Ted said, sticking his spade into the mound of earth.

Michelle's family stared ahead, eyes blank, mouths pulled into frowns, as if they operated from one mind. They all wore torn clothes and had dirt under their fingernails from volunteering to help build shelters in which the Apothecaries could do surgery. Michelle was the only one who expressed any real sense of grief.

"Let's send him home," Michelle's father said, speaking so low I barely understood him. "Then he can be with Mother again."

The four living brothers stepped forward as one. Michelle lingered behind, swaying until Nicolas put an arm around her shoulders to steady her. Tears rose in her small eyes but didn't fall. I doubted she'd release them in front of her family. They used three ropes to lower the casket into the ground. Once the casket settled on the bottom, they dropped in a handful of petals mixed with dirt. Her father struggled forward at the very last. He grabbed a handful of moist black earth, hesitated, and let it fall.

"Go on to greater adventures, son."

He turned and walked away without another word. No one stopped him, and no one followed.

Two of the groundskeepers lurked in the background, ready to fill in the hole. In an instant my mind leapt back to Mama's funeral. The site of her grave. The flowers. The gnawing hollowness inside my body. It all happened so fast that for a moment I couldn't tell if it was real or not. Had Mama just died? A familiar rush of power born from grief darted through my chest, nearly seizing control of my whole body. I froze. Papa's face flashed through my mind with the lightest whisper from my nightmares.

You shall lose many more, Bianca Monroe, unless you let my daughter go.

Never, I replied with determination, feeling a surge of rage. *We'll never bow to your demands.*

We shall see.

Her voice drifted away on a damp spring breeze. I remained behind, stuck in a pulse of rage and magic so strong it took my breath away. Leda glanced at me in confusion, no doubt detecting something without even realizing it.

Never, I promised again.

Your War

The glistening white walls of Magnolia Castle glowed when Marten and I walked up its stairs the next day.

"Figure out what he's going to do," Papa had instructed us just before transporting back to the Letum Wood Covens. "The Mansfeld Pact is over. He doesn't have to fear an alliance anymore."

Papa had woken up at five that morning, after returning just after two, and the fatigue showed in his eyes. I had stopped trying to wait up for him, and instead listened to him shuffle around his room from the privacy of my own bed.

The fighting in the Southern Covens had fallen into a lull in an early spring blizzard. Both sides retreated to gather their strength. Zane told Stella that Tiberius prowled around like a panther, yelling at the Southern Network, cursing their children's children, and waving a fist. He refused to leave, even though Zane had tried everything short of force. The West Guards continued their brutal attacks, but our witches were more prepared, and their effectiveness decreased.

"You may be tempted to share your own opinion in this meeting, but I don't want you to say a word," Marten said. Like Papa, new lines of stress had popped up on his face, and he seemed old and tired.

"I won't," I said just before we transported. "I have no desire to speak with Diego."

Marten had responded with a strained smile. Getting a second audience with Diego after the attack hadn't been easy. And not just because Marten and I were busy trying to hold off the anarchy of Factios attacks in Chatham City—Diego didn't want anything to do with anyone. Whether he was nursing his wounded pride or just scared no one could decide.

Ariana steered us to the Sword Room without a word. The air had warmed, and a salty breeze drifted through the room. If I hadn't seen so many dead Guardians, the beauty of this Network could have almost convinced me that no war or tragedy raged outside it.

Diego stood when we walked into the Sword Room. I glanced discreetly around, seeing no one except servants, and wondered where Niko was and what he thought of the war. I'd secretly hoped that Isobel would be with Diego and felt disappointed when her beautiful brown eyes weren't waiting for us.

"Marten, Bianca, good to see you again," Diego said.

His succinct greeting was a far cry from the warm welcome that he had received us with a month before. Marten responded with a nod of diplomatic indifference. Neither made a move to sit down.

"I think neither of us have time to waste, least of all you," Marten began, "so let's get right to the point. What are you going to do now that war has begun?"

And we were right, I wanted to add.

Diego leaned onto his fists on the desk, met Marten straight in the eye, and said, "You aren't going to like what I have to say, Marten."

I tensed, but Marten didn't.

"The Eastern Network is not as strong as the Central Network on land," Diego said. "We are a sea people and sea fighters. Our population isn't so vast as yours either. To assist you in your war would run contrary to the best interests of my witches. We are fishermen and artists, not warriors. We will not fight."

"I see," Marten said when Diego stopped. "And if the Central Network doesn't win against the power of the Western Network and the Southern Network?"

"You will."

I clenched my fists, wanting to ask Diego if he'd lost his mind. Stubborn, foolish witch! He hoped that the Central Network would deal with the war so he didn't have to. He wanted our witches to die so they could live.

"If the worst should happen, and the Southern Network attacks your land?" Marten asked.

"They won't get through my defenses," Diego said. "I am not worried. The Southern Network cannot use magic because they broke the Pact. They would have to invade on foot, and the passable parts of the border between us are very small."

"Clavas don't travel by foot and neither do West Guards," Marten said in a cold tone. Diego stared at him as if deciding whether or not he should respond.

"Have Clavas attacked you during this war?"

"Not yet. But the West Guards have transported in and killed our innocent witches."

"Perhaps the West Guards could transport here," Diego agreed in an offhand way. "But the West Guards will be busy dealing with Derek, will they not? He is the greatest threat in Antebellum. Not the Eastern Network. We sit here quietly, minding our own business. The West will not care about us."

"The Southern and Western Networks have ports," Marten said. "They may not limit themselves to a land attack. Only a fool would underestimate them right now."

Diego scoffed. "Our ports are secure. Let them try to attack us. The Southern Network fairs no better than mortals now, and the West cannot defeat us on the sea."

"The West is strong. They've started to support the South now that the Pact is broken and a little time has passed. Dane could have sent ships out months ago. They may be ready to attack, and you don't even know it."

Diego paused for a moment. I held my breath. "Then let Dane come." He slammed a fist onto the table. "We will be ready."

The fateful words fell like the crash of a gong, and I could tell that our time to leave drew near. Diego's blindness would destroy the beautiful witches of the Eastern Network. My eyes flickered to the doorway. I had to exhaust every option.

"Without your help, this war could go on for years. You'll get caught up in it eventually. If we work together, we can stop it now before they attack y—"

"Excuse me," I said, touching Marten's sleeve. "May I use the bathroom?"

Diego gestured out the door with a scowl and an impatient wave of his hand. "On the right."

I ducked out, avoiding Marten's gaze, and slipped into the hall. Luckily, no servants waited outside. Because I'd committed the layout of the castle to memory when Niko escorted me on my tour, I knew I could find the path to Isobel's chambers on the lower floors. Ensuring no one saw me, I used an invisibility incantation and tiptoed away.

Two young maids passed me in the hall, but I pressed my back to the wall and narrowly avoided their elbows. They spoke in the smooth dialect of the Eastern Network instead of the common tongue, so I didn't understand their words. When I arrived at Isobel's, one of the two doors sat propped open. With a whisper, I removed the invisibility incantation and tapped my knuckle against the wood.

Isobel glanced up. Her face shifted from narrowed confusion to wide-eyed surprise.

"Bianca! Whatever are you doing here?"

I pressed my fingers to my lips and shook my head. The approach of feet from the hallway frightened me, so I stepped behind the door and held my breath. A pair of East Guards marched by, their polished boots echoing on the tiled floor until they stopped in the doorway. The leather of their coats creaked when they bowed to Isobel.

"Your Highness," one of them said in a deep, rich timbre. "We just detected an unfamiliar magic. Have you seen anything?"

My heart pounded beneath my ribs. Isobel straightened. "No, I haven't seen anything suspicious, but I thank you for the warning. I shall keep my eyes open and will lock my door behind you."

Their feet echoed on the ground as they marched away. Isobel and I waited in strained silence for several moments before her doors swung closed and locked. Only when their footsteps faded completely did she turn to me with a long exhale.

"Something must be wrong for you to visit me without permission," she said in the calm, controlled tone of a mother who recognized panic in her child. "Come in, come in. You likely don't have much time. Tell me quickly."

"Thank you, Your Highness. You're right, I don't have very long."

I recounted the conversation with Diego and watched her eyes droop in concern. She turned away and stared out at the ocean's swelling and ebbing waves. When she swallowed, the muscles in her neck contracted with tension.

"Diego is a very stubborn man," she said with a heavy sigh. "He feels he's making the best decision for the Network, although he's just sticking his head in the sand."

"Isobel, I've seen what the West can do," I whispered, swallowing back my emotion. "They're using Almorran magic. It's . . . it's literally consuming our witches. Burning them alive. The South Guards are burning and raping and looting. So many are dead."

She slipped a hand over mine. Her sorrowful gaze nearly broke my tenuous restraint. "Bianca, I'm so sorry for your Network. You seem genuinely scared."

"Not for myself but for everyone else, for my friends."

She smiled gently. "You're very self-sacrificing."

"They mean so much to me."

Her lips puckered in a sudden frown. "Are your friends safe? Are they at the castle with you?"

"Yes, they're fine. Leda is busier than ever helping Jansson in Chatham City. The others are . . . getting by."

She relaxed a little. "War is so hard on the young."

"I don't want the same to happen here. That's why I came to warn you. Has Diego mentioned anything to you?"

"No, of course not. My only information comes from you. Bianca, please trust me. My husband is not a bad witch. He simply can't comprehend an attack after a century of peace under the Mansfeld Pact. His grandfather was instrumental in forming the Pact, and he holds so very tightly to it."

"Rules can't protect us against those that don't play by the rules. And trust me," I said. "The South and the West aren't playing by any rules."

"What is your father's plan? Perhaps if I can tell Diego, I may convince him to help."

"I think he's going to try to go after Dane."

"Kill Dane?" she whispered, pressing a hand to her chest. "My goodness. Can it be done?"

"I don't know."

Isobel sat in troubled thought for a moment. "Perhaps, if Derek succeeds, Diego might join the cause. I can't guarantee it. But if Dane were gone, the risk to our Network would be less severe. Diego will only act in the best interest of our witches."

She squeezed my hand.

"I will talk to Diego about it as soon as you leave. I promise. We shall do everything we can."

"Thank you, Isobel. I don't ask for my own Network alone, but for all the innocent witches in yours."

A scuffle of voices outside the room caught our attention, reminding me that I needed to return. I'd already been gone far too long. Diego didn't seem like the type to forgive or forget such a suspicious absence.

"I'll take you back to Diego," Isobel said, straightening her skirt and putting a hand up to check her hair. "He'll be suspicious, and I don't want him to ban you from Magnolia Castle. Take the handles behind me. You can wheel me to the Sword Room."

I obeyed, and we wheeled into the hallway as soon as it lay empty. By the time we returned, Diego and Marten stood several paces apart in the doorway.

"Hello Marten," Isobel sang, lifting a hand and smiling wide. "It is so good to see you again. Good morning, my love," she said to Diego, taking his hand with obvious adoration. "You know it's always a delight to see you as well."

Diego's rigid expression melted when he smiled down at her, but his dark eyes flickered to me in a narrow question. I didn't flinch away.

"Always good to see you, High Priestess Isobel," Marten said, bowing over her hand but sending a sharp glance to me. "Did you find my Assistant wandering the halls?"

"No, actually," Isobel said with an easy laugh. "Bianca had just stepped out of the washroom when I stopped her and pulled her into a quick conversation. I tried to convince her to take tea with me again, but she insisted she had to return at once. If you've been waiting, you must accept my apology, for I had her wheel me here to see you, Marten. I missed you last time."

Marten met my eyes over Isobel's head, and the quick flash of curiosity in them said he didn't buy it for a moment. Diego had relaxed however, detecting no guile in his wife's story.

Well done, Isobel, I thought with relief.

"As much as I would love to take tea with you myself," Marten said, motioning for me to join him at his side. "We must be going back. It was wonderful to see you again. You're looking as lovely as ever."

Isobel beamed at him and threaded her fingers through Diego's hand.

"Come again soon for a longer visit next time," she admonished, as if she had no idea that a war raged beyond the borders. "I'm sure we can arrange an Ambassador's dinner."

"Anything for you, High Priestess. Thank you for your time, Diego. Best of luck."

A hint of tension flared between Diego and Marten. Marten steered me down the hallway to the patio we'd arrived on. A pair of Guardians appeared from a doorway and followed us down the hall. Marten and I didn't speak, and I didn't care, wanting nothing more than to get away.

I glanced over my shoulder to see Diego and Isobel in deep discussion at the far end of the hall, hands clasped. Isobel's forehead had wrinkled with concern. The Guardians stepped to the right, obscuring my view with their scowling faces. I studied their uniforms indifferently, then followed Marten's example and transported home.

Weakest of All

"No," I said in exasperation, fighting not to roll my eyes. "If you see a witch trying to cross the Central Network border into the Eastern Network, you may paralyze them with an incantation long enough to restrain them for interrogation later, but you cannot leave the spell on for more than half an hour. Have you ever been stuck in the same position for hours? It will cause harm, and you will lose your job."

The disappointed Border Guard, Todd, scuffed his foot in the dirt. "Fine. But I'm not afraid to stop them with a paralyzing spell! I've done it before, you know."

"Good. Because that's your job."

The small border town of Lockwood, south of Newberry, lay sprawled on the rolling foothills below me like the sleepy stretch of a cat. I stood on top of a small hill that marked the boundary between the Eastern and Central Networks. Houses and chimneys dotted the landscape. Letum Wood abutted Lockwood, providing a dark backdrop to the single road that cut straight through the village. The end of the first month of spring neared, bringing the first hint of grass blades in the field.

"So what's going on down there?" Todd asked, motioning south with his head. "Anything new? We haven't seen Marten in a while, just you."

"New is relative. What's the last thing you heard?"

"That we were invaded."

I blinked in disbelief. "That's the last thing you heard?"

"We keep track of some scattered details from witches like you, but I've never been to the Southern Covens so it's hard to really know what's going on."

Except for the hundreds of articles the Chatham Chatterer pours out every day, of course, I wanted to point out. The war consumed life at Chatham Castle. When I wasn't dealing with its side effects, like the increase in black market trading, witches pouring across the borders, and the Factios terrorizing Chatham City, I was worrying it would kill my father. Such a cozy little village, so untouched by the horror, seemed both novel and annoying. I wanted to protect them from it while also shaking them into reality.

We're at war. Don't you get it?

"The invasion happened over a month ago. A lot is going on."

He shrugged. "So something must have happened since then. What is it?"

I sighed. "The South Guards are spread out along the border, and they keep trying to push back into the Southern Covens. The West Guards attack villages and settlements at random, but we've been able to hold off some of those as well. That's the main gist of it."

"So we aren't losing?"

"Everyone loses in war," I snapped, thinking of all the dying Guardians I'd seen. He took the news in with little change in expression.

"Hmm."

Perturbed that someone could appear so apathetic to the change that this war brought to our world, I released the bottom of my open scroll so it rolled shut with a slam.

"Well, Todd, that's all I have to say. I wanted to check and see how things were going here. Looks fine. No more paralyzing witches for over an hour, okay? You've been warned. Marten will fire you. Let me know if you have any questions."

He grunted. "Sure. I'll keep these other guys in line. Don't worry about us up here. Sounds like you have bigger problems."

You have no idea.

I transported back to Marten's office, the bottoms of my feet aching from walking all day. Marten sat at his desk when I appeared. He spent half his time in the Southern Covens, advising Papa and working with the Protectors—though he wouldn't say what he was doing—and the other half at Chatham.

"Marten," I said in surprise. "Lovely to see you again. How was your vacation in the south?"

"Enchanting. How is Todd?" he asked.

"As clueless as ever." I tossed the report onto my desk. "He let a Border Guard paralyze a fleeing witch for two hours. I threatened his job, so if he does it again, I'll need you to fire him."

"Fair enough."

"How are things down there?"

"The same. We're holding them off, and they keep trying."

"The West Guards' attacks have slowed," I said, forehead ruffled. "I read the reports. There's only been one in the last week. What's that about?"

He frowned. "We don't know."

"Is Papa still planning on going after Dane?"

Marten's eyes flickered up to mine in surprise. "I don't know. I can't stay for too long today, just wanted to look things over. You're doing a beautiful job here, Bianca. I'm very proud of you."

"As delightful as it is to chastise witches twice my age, I'd rather be running through the forest."

"Well, thank you for all you're doing. It frees me up to help your father and participate in the fighting where I can be of more use."

I didn't want to tell him I resented being stuck at the castle when I could fight better than half the Guardians, because that wasn't his fault. I smiled instead. "Sure, Marten. I'm glad to help any way I can."

"Can you go to the border towns near the Western Network tomorrow? I have a message for them—a few more tips to help them protect themselves. Derek thinks the South Guards will abandon the Southern Covens to try to work their way northward and claim the Borderlands."

"Toward Chatham City?"

He nodded. "I want our border towns ready but not panicking."

He sent a rolled parchment to my desk, and I used an incantation to duplicate it thirty times. Visiting each border town meant I'd travel to thirty different places tomorrow. I'd need an early start. I yawned just thinking about it.

"Sure," I said. "Anything else?"

He ticked off another list of things for me to accomplish, promised to be back in two days, and left again. In his absence, the silence of the office nearly lulled me to sleep. I glanced at the clock. Six-thirty. My stomach growled in protest. I'd forgotten to eat lunch again.

"Tomorrow. This can all wait until tomorrow."

When I transported back to the apartment, a note sticking to the door by an arrow arrested my attention. Recognizing the design of the flange, a flutter of surprise overtook my belly. *Merrick.* It had been two weeks since I'd last heard from him, when I'd escaped with Brecken. I tugged the arrow away from the door and took the piece of paper between my fingers.

Meet me on the Wall.

—M

Merrick stood right where I thought he'd be: leaning against the top of the Wall near the Gatehouse. The gardens below had become a spongy field of grass. I welcomed the warming spring air with a deep breath and wondered why he wanted to meet here, of all places.

"Hey," I said, standing next to him, my heart flip-flopping.

"Hey."

He smiled when I leaned against the wall next to him. His hair sat loose on his shoulders today, and his eyes shone bright but tired. We sat in the quiet for several long moments.

"How long are you back at Chatham for?" I asked. Ever since the second week of fighting, Protectors had been circulating out of the Southern Covens two at a time to stay in Chatham City and fight the rising Factios. The gypsies put up a good defense but couldn't work alone. And with the war, Tiberius had to scale back the Guardians in Chatham City by a full contingent, leaving a skeleton crew behind.

The two Protectors here were more necessary than ever to keep the gypsies from leaving. I hadn't heard from Jackie since she left and wondered if they'd made it to their homeland.

Merrick's face darkened. "I'm here for a while."

"What?"

"Zane sent me back permanently to deal with the Factios. Probably because I'm the youngest Protector in the Brotherhood, or they think I'm the weakest. He's still going to send at least one Protector back to work with me every week. Tobias is here now."

"So you aren't going back to the Southern Covens?"

He chucked a rock off the Wall and watched it fall into the trees. "Not unless the Factios and the gypsies decide to start holding hands and stop killing each other."

Relief swept through me. Merrick wouldn't be in the fighting. At least not in the Southern Covens, though the argument could be made that Chatham City was a far more dangerous battleground. Perhaps I'd always be on the verge of losing my best friend.

"You, uh, don't seem happy about it," I said, clearing my throat and steering my thoughts away from my uncertain friendship—or was it something else?—with Merrick and back toward safer ground. Merrick looked down at the ground.

"I'm happy to serve my Network."

"But not when the Brotherhood serves it somewhere else," I said, glancing at him from the corner of my eye.

"Yes," he said, tossing another rock. "Exactly."

Despite the twisted logic, I understood his frustration. Every Protector toiled and sacrificed to be part of the Brotherhood; forcible separation from their most active, difficult battles would hurt. Papa had always been the same way. Although Merrick would be closer to me—though likely just as busy—I felt sad for him.

"You've always been strongest working with the Factios, Merrick. You're one of the only Protectors that really gets results in the slums. At least that's what Zane and Papa have said. So I doubt Zane sent you here because you have less experience. I'm sure it's more to do with the need for results."

He appeared to think it over, although it was almost impossible to interpret Merrick's emotions from his stoic expression. Moments later he straightened up, and his stormy eyes calmed.

"You owe me an explanation," he said, taking me by surprise. His cool eyes slid to mine. "Where did you find that Volare?"

I sighed. He never forgot. "A friend."

"You mean Isobel."

I stared at him. "How did you know?"

"I pay attention," he said vaguely, scowling. "And I don't trust Niko."

"You followed us, didn't you? You followed Niko and I around Magnolia Castle, you creep!"

A hint of a smile played around the edges of his lips. "I knew you weren't a fan of etiquette, but taking off your shoes with the High Priestess? You're either brave or clueless. Sometimes I tend to think the latter."

I slugged him on the shoulder, and he ducked away, laughing. "Hey! You were spying on me. And she *invited* me to remove my shoes, thank you very much. We're practically soul sisters. Thanks to her, Brecken is still alive."

He sobered. "No, I wasn't spying. I was protecting you, as Derek assigned me. That's all. I don't spy on you for enjoyment. I protected you. Understand?"

For some reason, my acknowledgment seemed important to him. "Okay. I get it."

His shoulders relaxed.

"Why didn't you say something earlier?" I asked. "It would be nice to know when you're lurking around my life."

"Your father makes sure it's not that often anymore," he said. "Look, the less you know, the better. How good of friends did you and Isobel become, exactly? She must think a lot of you to lend you a Volare."

I glared at him but couldn't stay angry at those emerald eyes for long and gave in with a resigned sigh. "We've written a few letters, that's all. She reminds me of my grandmother."

The deep furrows in his brow meant he didn't feel as inclined to the friendship as I did.

"Just be careful, okay? She may seem nice, but she's still a ruling member of the Eastern Network. Who knows if she's using you for something, like information."

I rolled my eyes. "Seriously, Merrick? Isobel? She's so weak she can't walk. Her husband doesn't even want her to know there's a war going on. She spends all day alone in her room, not even the maids can give her information. She's *dying*."

He scowled, and I found the intensity of his expression both attractive and reassuring. Whatever Merrick was to me, best friend or assigned protection or . . . whatever, I was just glad he was on my side.

"Exactly. Sometimes the ones we perceive as weakest are just hiding their strength. Never underestimate your opponent. You already know that rule."

"Isobel isn't my opponent. Angelina is."

He didn't disagree.

"Let's go for a run," I suggested, brightening. "Please? Oh, Merrick, I need to hit the trails, but Stella made me promise not to go on my own because of the West Guard hysteria. I think it's safe because of the dragons, but whatever. Will you go with me? Please?"

He studied me, hesitating. When he turned away, the muscles in his jaw ticked.

"I can't."

"Why not?" I asked, floundering in desperation. "Can't you feel it? Can't you feel my magic? It's getting out of control again."

"Because I made a promise to your father to keep you safe, and Letum Wood isn't safe."

I grabbed his arm. My skin burned where his touched mine, the sensation almost as strong as the disappointment of my crashing hopes. "It's just a run, Merrick. Please?"

His eyes met mine. "I can't, Bianca. I want to, believe me. I miss our runs. But I can't."

"Why?"

"Trust me," he muttered, turning away. "You don't want to know."

The Book of Light

E ver since the Southern Network's invasion five weeks before, I hadn't seen Isadora once.

She spent most of her time with my father, helping coordinate attacks and responses. Her presence at his side didn't guarantee success, but it certainly gave us an advantage that we desperately needed against the Almorran magic. So when I walked into the apartment one evening after being cooped up in Marten's office all day to see Isadora sitting on our divan chatting with Reeves, I stopped in my tracks.

"Isadora?"

Her bent, old back curled around a cup of tea. Until that moment I had forgotten that she'd agreed to look into a way to prevent Angelina from taking over the world.

"Merry meet, Bianca," Isadora called, as if she made social calls like this every day. "I'm glad you've returned. I'll wait while you clean up."

Reeves eyes drifted to my muddy, bare feet and the messy hem of my dress. He cleared his throat and lifted an eyebrow.

"Sorry, Reeves," I said, grabbing a towel he kept folded near the door for just this event. He lifted his eyebrows but said nothing as I wiped down my feet and cleared the mud particles with a collection incantation. They soared to the window and flew outside when it opened. Reeves had a warm basin of water waiting in my bedroom, so I stripped off my muddy clothes and scrubbed down in a quick bath before changing into a fresh dress. Sitting by herself in front of the low fire when I returned, Isadora motioned to the chair across from her.

"Eat while I explain what I've seen."

"I'd forgotten that you were going to look into something to combat the *Book of Spells,*" I said when I sat down. "What did you find?"

Reeves had set out a few slices of bread and a crock of butter for my dinner. Tough find these days, when most butter was sent to the Guardians or kept for the sick. Of course, anything would have tasted better than an empty stomach.

"Most witches know about the Almorran *Book of Spells* because it's the reason we fear so much from history," Isadora began. "Despite Esmelda's many attempts to find and destroy the book after the settling of the Networks, it was lost. Most believe it was destroyed in the final battle that brought down the Almorran race, but there's no historical confirmation of that."

"The *Book of Spells* obviously wasn't destroyed," I said with confidence. "How else would Miss Mabel have called Clavas last summer? Or do the lesser scrolls really exist the way Miss Mabel said?"

"There are rumors a few scrolls survived with some spells on them, yes. But whether or not the scrolls exist doesn't really matter anymore. I realized when we were last speaking that I've overlooked a very important detail: Every black magic has a counter."

The slice of bread halted halfway to my mouth. "A counter?"

"Every black magic has a counter," she repeated. "It's the nature of magic, of life. It's the law of opposition. You cannot form a truly great, powerful magic without some way of controlling it, and the Almorrans were no exception, no matter how hard they tried. Opposition lies in all things, Bianca, even magic."

"So what's the counter?"

"In Almorran circles, it was referred to as the *Book of Secrets* because they didn't want anyone to know the spells inside," she said with greater enthusiasm. "The rest of the world knew it as the *Book of Light* because it fights off the Almorran darkness. It isn't well known, and is less believed in than the *Book of Spells,* but I believe that it may have also survived. We must hope it did. For if it didn't, Antebellum cannot fight back against Angelina and Mabel. But if it can be found, we have the smallest glimmer of hope."

My mind flew back to my conversation with Miss Mabel. Hadn't she said they weren't looking for the *Book of Spells* all along? And I vaguely remembered her once saying the words *Book of Secrets*. Perhaps Angelina had tasked Miss Mabel with finding the *Book of Light* to prevent any other witch from stopping their ascent to power.

"Where is it?" I asked, my heart fluttering. "The *Book of Light*, I mean."

Isadora swallowed hard. "I don't know. I've been studying and searching, but I can't see very much. I'm worried that something big needs to happen for the future possibilities to shift enough for me to see a path that ends with us finding the *Book of Light*. As it stands, none of our paths show anything very encouraging."

I couldn't fathom the power and concentration it must take for Isadora to predict future possibilities for an entire Network. Leda managed it for one or two witches at a time and occasionally for a group, but that gave her a headache that took total silence and a potion to recover from.

"So my suspicion is true," I concluded. "Marten and I have been looking for the wrong book all this time."

"I don't think you'd find either of them in a library," Isadora replied with a smile. "If the *Book of Light* does exist still, which is unlikely, it must be very well hidden, I would imagine."

"The *Book of Spells* was found in a farmhouse."

"If the story is true, yes. I suppose either of them could be anywhere."

"Do you know the last person to have it?"

Isadora shook her head. "No. There's even less information on the *Book of Light* than on the *Book of Spells*."

"What if we do find it? What then? Are we able to just defeat Angelina?"

"I'm sure it will take a very powerful witch to wield the magic appropriately. Even good magic can be used for foul purposes."

"Did Mildred know about the *Book of Light*?"

"I doubt it. If Marten hasn't said anything, I don't know that she knew either."

I felt weak. "Do you think Angelina or Miss Mabel have the *Book of Light* already? If they have both books, we have no chance. Perhaps that's why Angelina is stirring up the Factios and the other Networks."

"If so, I doubt they've had it for long, or I think they would have acted before now. I believe now more than ever that my earlier suspicions were correct: Mabel—and Angelina, for that matter—didn't act sooner because of Mildred."

"What are we going to do, Isadora?"

She blinked several times, eventually pulling herself from what must have been a tangled web of thought.

"I'm going to tell your father and Marten," she said, stacking her hands on top of each other on her lap. "And then I'll continue searching the future."

"I suppose there's nothing more we can do?" I asked with a glimmer of hope. "What if I started searching libraries? Or the ancient scrolls in the Chatham Castle library? Maybe there's something about the *Book of Light*."

"In all your research on the *Book of Spells*, have you ever seen the *Book of Light* mentioned?"

"No," I whispered, dismayed. "I suppose not."

"You could try, but I'm afraid it would lead to dead ends. I feel the best course is to wait. Let me continue searching. Sometimes we need to let fate decide her own course. It's amazing what possibilities can open in just a few minutes. For now, we must press forward and see what the future brings."

"Do we have that luxury?" I asked. "Witches are dying."

"We don't have a choice."

Whatever It Takes

Later that week I fell into an uneasy sleep on the divan while waiting for Papa to come home from a visit to the Borderlands. I hadn't seen him in over a week, and the only letters he managed to send were updates that went right to Stella.

Another nightmare held me back, bands of darkness tightening around me. I resisted at first, but remembering that I'd be able to face Angelina again, finally gave in. Once I stopped fighting it, I found myself standing in Letum Wood on a foggy spring day, surrounded by wispy clouds. The flash of a pair of familiar, different-colored eyes startled me in the swirling darkness.

Leda.

I reached out, but she disappeared in a flash of white, then blue, and white again. Someone screamed. An unexpected blaze of blue light nearly blinded me. I whirled away from it, and when I looked up again, Leda stood only a few paces away, her face twisted in horror.

Let my daughter go.

No. I watched Leda fade from my sight. *We'll never release Miss Mabel.*

Shadows danced in the distance, moving in the vague form of a womanly figure walking toward me. My heart sped up, but I felt no fear, only anger.

Aren't you afraid of me, Bianca?

No.

You should be. I'll destroy you.

Fine. You can try. My father will break you first.

Angelina laughed, but it wasn't like Miss Mabel's sultry, low tones. It sounded hard and unamused.

I hold your Network in my hands. Not even war scares you?

No.

Leda appeared again, reaching out to me, fear etched in her expression.

Then I shall have to hit closer to home until you give me what I want. I'll do whatever it takes to get my daughter back.

Leda flickered before my eyes again, then disappeared. I realized that the fog wasn't fog; it was smoke. An acrid, bitter smell burned my nostrils. The ground beneath my feet billowed in clouds of the noxious smoke, wrapping around my ankles and reaching up my legs in long tongues of gray.

I jerked awake with a strangled scream.

My neck ached from the cricked position I lay in, so I rolled onto the floor with a groan. A low fire crackled in the hearth, casting a little warmth on the open space of our apartment. Outside, a brand new sun brightened the sky. I must have slept in.

Angelina's voice whispered through my mind, distant, fading as the last clutches of sleep left me.

Whatever it takes.

I shoved thick locks of my dark hair from my face. They clung to my damp skin like seaweed. The touch of my cool palm on my cheek brought me back closer to reality.

"How's the view down there?" a deep voice asked. I shot off the floor, grabbed Viveet from her place at my side, and whirled around to find Papa sitting in the chair across from me.

"Papa!" I cried, straightening. "Please help me! I have to go find Leda right now."

He stood, alerted by the fear in my voice. "What?"

"I had a dream," I said, stumbling over the words while I sheathed Viveet again. "We have to go find her!"

"She'll be with Jansson, right?" he asked, moving toward me without hesitation.

"I-I think. I don't know!"

He grabbed my arm above the elbow and before I knew what had happened, both of us were transporting. I found myself standing next to him in Jansson's empty office.

"Not here," I whispered. Papa transported us to Stella's office.

"Stella, have you seen Jansson anywhere?" he asked the moment we arrived. "We're looking for him and Leda."

Stella glanced up from where she sat behind the massive High Priestess's desk, looking swamped by its enormous size. Mildred had never seemed small behind it, even though she had been short and compact. Stella's more fragile look made her seem petite.

"I think he's in Chatham City for meetings with Clive and a few High Witches," she said. "Why?"

"Papa," I whispered, a dark feeling growing in my chest. "I—"

"Check the Witchery. I'll go to Clive's office."

"Derek, what's—"

The door to Stella's office slammed open. A witch that looked a little like Merrick—it must be Merrick under a transformation spell, I realized a moment later—

burst into Stella's office carrying a large bundle draped in a cloak. A patch of white hair rested on his shoulder.

"Stella! We need help."

Tobias strode in behind him, Jansson slung over his shoulder. A rivulet of blood ran down Jansson's face and over his mouth. His nose looked badly broken. One eyebrow bled, and his arm bent at an unnatural, grotesque angle. An odious smell trailed in with them, so faint I barely recognized it as the scent from my dream.

"What happened?" Papa demanded, carefully pulling Jansson from Tobias's shoulder. They guided him into a chair, where he groaned.

"Another Factios attack in Chatham City. We levitated them with a spell and ran back as fast as we could," Merrick panted. "Chatham City is in chaos again. I didn't want to try going to an apothecary there."

"Get my healing herbs and oils," Stella said to Dyana, her Assistant, as she calmly rose to her feet. Dyana transported away while I rushed to Merrick.

"Leda! Put her here on the couch."

Merrick—with red hair and a long nose—carried Leda to the divan and set her down. A rush of darkness overwhelmed my mind.

Whatever it takes.

"What happened?" I asked, banishing Angelina's voice. Leda's eyes fluttered open, her mouth tugging down in a grimace.

"Oh, just a friendly little attack," she muttered, pressing a hand to her head. "That's all."

"Are you all right? You're alive?"

"I'm fine," she said, frantically pushing herself up to seek out Jansson. "Is Council Member Jansson all right? Will he make it?"

"He'll make it," Merrick said, turning to Papa. The reddish strands of his hair started to deepen back into his normal sandy blonde. "The Factios attacked Council Member Jansson when he walked into Clive's office for a meeting."

"You were there?" I asked. Merrick nodded once. The chocolate color of his eyes faded, giving way to emerald green.

Stella pressed a cool cloth to the side of Jansson's face. "Hush," she crooned. "Don't try to speak, Jansson. Just relax for a minute."

"They used a series of explosions," Tobias said to Papa, stepping out of Stella's way. Blood stained the white sleeves of his shirt. "I've never seen it before, brother. It was just like the Southern Covens, only in the streets of the Chatham City, and far worse."

"Burning ash?" Papa asked.

Tobias shook his head. "No. The smoke it gave off choked any witch that breathed it in. Once they took a deep breath of it, they didn't breathe again. We removed every witch we could, but . . ."

"Were the explosions white and blue?" I asked, whirling around. Tobias peered at me with a queer expression.

"Yes."

"Get back to Chatham City," Papa ordered Tobias and Merrick. "Get it under control. Take a contingent of Guardians from the castle if you have to."

"Be careful," I whispered to Merrick.

"No worries, little troublemaker," he murmured under his breath, and the sudden warmth in his voice sent a rush of heat through my skin.

"There are already a few Guardians there," Tobias said, but Merrick had already left. "At least ten bystanders are dead already I would guess, twenty more injured. Jansson would have died if it wasn't for that pale little girl."

He motioned to Leda with his head.

"What happened?" Papa asked.

He shrugged. "Don't know, but someone saw her run out of the crowd and shove Jansson into the building right before the explosion went off. She moved him just in time. Both of them fell to the ground, which saved them from the strangling smoke."

The back of Leda's neck turned bright red, but she boldly met Papa's questioning gaze. My stomach turned with sudden nervousness on her behalf. She'd have to explain how she knew Jansson would need saving, which meant she'd have to explain her curse. Jansson, meanwhile, moaned from his spot at the chair while Stella worked.

"I'd like to talk to both of you once all this has settled," Papa said to Leda and me. "Tobias, you may go."

The door slammed, and a bevy of witches filled the room: High Witches, Coven Leaders, and other influential business witches from Chatham City. They spoke in a mad flurry of voices I couldn't—and didn't try—to understand. Amidst the scramble of arms and voices, I caught a familiar glimpse of wide ears. Clive. He stood in the midst of all of them, bellowing in rage, exacerbating the chaos instead of soothing it. I scowled, wondering if he didn't have something to do with the whole mess.

"Out!" Papa bellowed, herding them all back into the hall. "Now!"

The sudden onslaught departed as quickly as it had arrived, taking their chattering madness into the hall for Papa to deal with. Two Apothecaries arrived and hovered over Jansson with incantations, bandages, and several potion bottles that bobbed in the air.

"How do you feel?" I asked Leda, studying a bruise forming on her forehead.

"Like dancing," she retorted, but a hint of a smile lingered at the corner of her lips. I grinned.

"You've basically guaranteed yourself a position as Assistant somewhere in the Network after such a heroic move."

"That's not why I did it, Bianca," she said imperiously. "But that wouldn't be unwelcome, by any means, I suppose."

"Were you frightened?"

She hesitated, then nodded. "Yes but everything happened so fast that I didn't have a lot of time to think about what I was doing. I just . . . reacted."

"Are you hurting anywhere, Leda?" Stella asked, slipping up to my side. I scooted back to make room for her. She sat on the very edge of the divan near Leda's legs. "How are you feeling?"

Leda dropped the attitude for Stella. "I'm all right, High Priestess." She wiggled her shoulders with a wince. "Just a bit sore, with a slight headache."

Stella pressed her gentle fingers to the swollen area around Leda's forehead. "You have a little bit of a bump but nothing concerning. Do you hurt anywhere else?"

"Not too much."

"I'll get you a potion for the headache," Stella said, squeezing her arm with a warm smile. "You saved Council Member Jansson, you know, and by doing that, maybe Chatham City. Had he died, the chaos would be unmanageable right now. Thank you."

"It was . . . I mean . . . Thank you, High Priestess."

"Do you mind if I ask you how you saved Council Member Jansson?"

Leda froze, her mouth half-open. She remained that way for several long seconds before admitting the truth.

"A witch cursed me when I was a baby with the Foresight Curse. I saw it was a possibility a few seconds before it happened."

Stella reared back in surprise. "That's rare and complicated magic."

Leda sighed. "I know. Poor luck, isn't it?"

"And you still have it?"

"Isadora says I will always have it. The witch who cursed me was more powerful than we thought."

"You've worked with Isadora?"

Leda nodded. "She's taught me how to control my thoughts enough to make sense of what I see. I'm not *very* strong with it.

Sometimes I can see for other witches, sometimes I can't. I don't have anywhere near the ability that Isadora has and never will."

Stella's lips pressed together. She made a little noise of surprise in the back of her throat. "Well," she said, "that was certainly an unexpected response. Have you told Jansson?"

"No!" Leda said emphatically, shaking her head. She grimaced and stopped, putting a hand to her forehead. "Forgive me, Your Highness. I mean no, I haven't. I . . . I don't know how he'd respond. It makes some witches uneasy and downright awkward."

"I can imagine. Take my advice, Leda, and come clean to Jansson about it. I believe his reaction won't be as strong as you believe."

Leda nodded meekly. "Yes, High Priestess."

Stella looked over at me with a heavy sigh. "You and your friends, Bianca," she murmured, turning away. "If one of you isn't getting into trouble, the other is."

I smiled half-heartedly. "We take turns, High Priestess, so one doesn't bear the brunt of the burden."

To my relief, Stella smiled. "Give me just a minute, girls, and I'll have that headache potion for you. Then you can go to your Witchery for the rest of the day. Just take it easy, will you? No more jumping to the rescue will be needed, I hope."

"Go ahead," Papa said later that night as he walked into the apartment and sank into a chair. "I just spoke with Leda about her Foresight Curse, and now you owe me an explanation of your clairvoyance."

I set aside the book on archery that Merrick had loaned me. The corners of Papa's eyes tugged down in exhaustion, like usual. But he wore a new intensity that I knew came from this strange mystery of my dream.

"Is everything settled in Chatham City?" I asked. He scowled.

"As settled as it can be. Thirty dead in all. Ten seriously injured, on the brink of death, and a handful of others that will make it but need continued attention."

My stomach churned. It seemed that the Central Network was attacked on all fronts.

"How many were gypsies?"

"None, thank heavens. Jansson was the target. A Head Witch died and a Coven Leader is seriously injured, but it wasn't targeting the gypsies."

"Was it Angelina?"

"If the red *A* painted on the door to Clive's office means anything."

I drew in a shaky breath at the confirmation, even more frightened to admit the truth to Papa now. What would he say when he learned about my strange connection?

"This is just one example of why I need you to be more careful, B," Papa said, rubbing a hand over his face. "There's no telling where danger lurks. That's why Stella made you promise not to run in Letum Wood. Danger can, and will, spring up anywhere but especially in a dark, dangerous forest."

"Yes Papa," I murmured, wounded at the reminder.

"I have a meeting in a few minutes, so I just stopped by briefly. You were dreaming about something just before you woke up," Papa said, straightening. He leaned forward, resting his elbows on his knees. "What's going on, B?"

I hesitated. Papa and I hadn't spoken in private for weeks. This certainly wasn't the conversation I would have picked. Although I understood the reasons that kept him away, I couldn't help resenting his absence.

Magic swirled in my chest like an agitated dragon, but I forced it down. "Yes, Papa. I was dreaming. I was . . . I was dreaming about Angelina."

He motioned for me to continue with a wordless nod of his head.

"I dream with her every now and then."

As I expected, my choice of wording wasn't lost on him. "With her?" he asked. "What exactly does that mean? And what are you dreaming?"

"Well, it's not just a dream," I admitted, tucking my feet up underneath me. "It's more like a conversation."

He leaned forward. "What?"

"She wants me to let Miss Mabel go," I said, frightened by the sudden intensity in his expression. "She tells me to do it all the time, but I always refuse. Sometimes . . . sometimes after the dreams something terrible happens. I told Isadora about it a while ago, and she thinks Angelina is communicating with me through Almorran magic."

"You didn't think to tell your father? Jikes, Bianca! How can I protect you if you won't talk to me?"

"How could I tell you? You're never here. The Network is at war. Why would I burden you with more? Nothing happens to me in the conversations, except sometimes they foretell awful events."

"Like today?"

"Yes."

"Start with the first dream." He stood up to pace, dragging a hand through his hair. "Tell me everything you've seen, everything she's said."

And so I told Papa everything. How they started, when I had them, and what I'd seen. He listened without interruption, but the more I spoke, the deeper the lines in his face grew.

"I see," he murmured when I finished.

"I don't know why she's speaking to me!" I cried, feeling responsible for the communication even though I had nothing to do with it. "I've never even met her."

"She's using you to get to me."

"I don't think so, Papa," I said. "She's never once brought you into it, never once mentioned you. I think she's using me *instead* of you. Because I'm not as strong or something? I don't know."

He sent me a sharp look of reprimand that stung. "No more secrets, B."

"It was never a secret, Papa," I whispered. "It was a burden."

"That's what I'm for," he snapped. "You're supposed to share all your worries and burdens with me."

"Am I?" I shot back before I could stop myself, regretting it when he recoiled. His voice sharpened.

"What does that mean?"

It means I miss you. It means we don't know each other anymore. It means I'm angry and scared and frustrated, and I need to run through Letum Wood, but I can't.

My heart ached. I couldn't share everything with him because I didn't want him to know the strain his job put on me. The sleepless nights when I feared he'd die just like Mama. The empty days when I wondered if Stella would tell me he was gone.

"Nothing," I said, dismissing it. I didn't have the heart to tell him. "I'm sorry, Papa. I'll tell you whenever I have a dream now."

His eyes darkened. He opened his mouth but eventually closed it without saying anything. Everything we left unsaid lingered in the air, as choking as the cloud of death Angelina had released on Chatham City.

"I need to talk to Stella about this and think it over," he said, his voice tight with tension. "We're going to have to figure out a way to keep you safe from these dreams. Don't wait up for me tonight. I have to return to the Southern Covens in an hour."

"Papa, are you mad at me?"

"Yes." He strode to the door, pulled on the handle, and stopped with a heavy exhale. His voice dropped low, as if he carried all the weight of the Central Network.

"I love you, B. That's why I'm upset. You kept a secret from me again, and that makes me very . . . sad."

You keep secrets from me all the time, I wanted to say, but I bit my bottom lip, not trusting my voice. *I don't want protection. I want you.*

"I love you too, Papa," I said, and the door closed resolutely behind him. A long tear slid down my cheek, and I didn't bother to wipe it away.

Troublemaker

The second month of spring brought a strange lull in the fighting. Thanks to whatever the Protectors did behind the scenes—Papa wouldn't give specifics—the West Guards halted their attacks on our cities.

The Southern Network stopped attacking the border, and everything lay still, as if Antebellum held its breath. Even in the calm, Papa rarely returned to the apartment, and when he did, he paced, spoke to himself, or brooded over plans. Jansson healed from his injuries and didn't seem to mind Leda's curse at all. She started predicting when Coven Leaders would arrive late to meetings, which greatly increased his productivity. Camille spent half her time with Brecken while he healed, and the rest of it helping Michelle plan her wedding.

"Marten, I think Angelina's getting desperate."

He looked over at me in surprise. We stood on the edge of the Central Network and the Borderlands, staring out at the strange fields of sand that stretched to the distant horizon. A few lizards scuttled by. The sun felt so warm it seemed as if winter had never been. I wondered if it would be hot on my feet if I ran across the sand. Surely it couldn't burn as hot as the magic broiling inside me, more temperamental than ever since my disagreement with Papa.

"Your father told me about your dreams," he said, returning his gaze to the setting sun in the distance.

I quirked an eyebrow. "Do you think I'm crazy?" I asked.

He chortled. "I thought you were crazy long before that."

"Angelina must be getting desperate," I said, continuing my thought with restless energy. "Why else would she have tried to kill

Jansson or Leda? She's trying to get to me so that I'll release her daughter. It's the only conclusion I can come to."

"You might be right. With Derek's blood in you, you might be able to release Miss Mabel."

I mulled the thought over, uncertain whether I could set Miss Mabel free, even if the magic allowed it.

"If I am right, we need to act while she's desperate because it makes her vulnerable. We need to do something. I feel like this war rests on my shoulders, but no one knows it. Can't we do something?" I asked. "Can't we stop Angelina?"

"You talk as if we haven't been trying. We can't even find her. Derek has pulled Protectors from the fighting to look for her to no avail. We just don't know enough about her."

"I know, I know. I didn't mean it like that. I'm just . . . there must be something I can do."

"Are you willing to give Mabel to her?"

I watched a lizard slide up a sun-baked rock and perch on the top, head cocked to the side. I'd already asked myself that question a hundred times.

"I don't know. I don't think I could."

"This war will happen regardless of whether Angelina communicates with you through dreams. It has nothing to do with you, Bianca."

"She tried to kill one of my best friends four days ago," I said, finally giving vent to the thoughts that I'd trapped inside. It felt good to let them out, releasing the building pressure in my chest. "She's going to go after Papa next. I can feel it."

Marten's eyes snapped to mine. "Did she show you that?"

"No." I shifted uneasily. "But it makes the most sense. It's what I would do if I were her. I wish . . . I wish I could talk to Isadora about it, but every time I go to her cottage it's empty. She said there's another book, but she doesn't know much about it. I've looked but—"

"The *Book of Light*," he said. I pulled my eyes away from the red glare of the sunset off the hot sand.

"Yes. How did you know?"

"I spoke with her a few days ago."

"Is there anyone you don't talk to?"

"No."

I snorted. "Well, with the war, I doubt she's had any time to look for the *Book of Light*. But what if Bartie Stacey knew something about it? What if I went to talk to him?"

Marten's brow furrowed. "Why would Bartie know? Not even I had heard of it."

"I think his story about the *Book of Spells* is the most credible we've found. He knew more than I thought he would. It's worth a shot, don't you think?"

"Would it make you feel better?" Marten asked in his quiet way.

"Yes. I think so."

"Then go, but be careful. The Southern Covens are no place for witches right now. If you were any less trained, I wouldn't allow it, but considering how stubborn you are, I might as well. You'd likely just go on your own."

He smirked, and I thanked him with a smile.

"I'll visit the rest of the border towns here," he said, nudging me. "Go see if you can find him now. I'd rather you go during the day when attacks are less likely. But keep in mind that the Southern Covens have fallen apart; most witches have fled. You may not be able to find him."

Which was exactly what I feared most.

I decided to start with the easiest plan: going to Bartie's dilapidated farmhouse to see if, by some miracle, he'd stayed.

I transported from the Borderlands, leaving Marten to troop through the sparse, dusty villages alone. Bartie's quiet farmhouse showed no signs of life. Not even the fresh grass poking from the ground seemed to stir. The eerie sense of stillness honed my senses. I held my breath and listened but heard nothing except the occasional flutter of a bird nearby.

"Hello? Bartie? Are you here?"

The front porch felt strangely empty without his dog to growl in warning. The aged boards seemed to groan on their own, telling me he wasn't here. It was so empty that I wondered for a brief moment if I hadn't imagined Bartie Stacy.

"Get out of here!"

I collapsed to the ground under a paralyzing incantation, smacking the back of my head on a rock. Although I could still breathe and see, I couldn't blink, grimace, or respond to my surroundings. I'd been paralyzed before—plenty of times during training with Papa or Merrick—but still couldn't get used to the inability to command my own limbs.

A gruff, old man with thick, reddened skin moved into my line of sight, scowling. He kicked me onto my back and leered over me, white hair hanging off his head through a hat made of straw.

"What do you want here, troublemaker?"

Using silent magic that Merrick had taught me, I overpowered the paralyzing incantation by putting a powerful, invisible protective shield around myself. Luckily, the farmer wasn't strong with magic, so it was easy enough to do.

"I want to talk to Bartie," I said, and the old man reared back, nearly stumbling over his own feet.

"Hey!" he cried. "You can't move! I paralyzed you."

He tried another spell that my shield absorbed. I sat up, holding my hands in the air in a gesture of surrender.

"It's all right. I'm not here to hurt anyone. I'm Bartie's friend."

The old man's heavy forehead wrinkled over his suspicious eyes. He swallowed. "Who are you?" he barked. "I've known Bartie all my life. He didn't have any friends except for me."

"My name is Bianca Monroe. I visited him this winter and came back to see if he made it through the attack."

The old man stepped back again, eyebrows knitted together, but as he hadn't attempted another spell, I took heart. Just to set him at ease, I waited for him without moving.

"He's not here," he finally said, wheezing. He leaned against the wall. "Bartie died."

I choked on my own surprise.

"What? He died?"

"You would have known if you were really a friend of his, wouldn't you? So maybe you're just snooping around here to get in trouble or something."

I rolled my eyes. "Because Bartie has such secret treasure around this old farmhouse? He didn't even have enough currency for tea."

He growled. "Well . . . maybe you . . . that is—"

"How did he die?"

"West Guards," he said in a hoarse whisper. "Came in the night and cut his throat."

"Did they do the same to anyone else around here?"

"Not that I know of. Maybe, but I doubt it. I would have heard."

Despite the atrocities of war, nothing could convince me that Bartie's murder was happenstance. I felt sure it was linked to Angelina and the stolen *Book of Spells*. I felt bad for Bartie, caught in a war that was never his, a victim of a greedy witch.

But then, weren't we all?

My last potential link to the strange *Book of Light*—outside Isadora, of course—was gone. Not that uneducated Bartie, who chugged hot water like it was ipsum and had probably never ventured far outside this farmhouse, would have known anything about it. Still, I felt more disheartened than ever.

"Get out of here," the old man snarled. "Leave so I can get back to my life."

"Why are you still in the Southern Covens, sir?" I asked. "It's not safe. The South Guards are still pillaging villages and homes for supplies."

He grunted. "It's my home. No South Guard or half-naked West Guard is going to scare me away from it. I can protect myself *and* my cow, thank you very much! Now leave!"

"I don't doubt that," I said ruefully. Any witch that wanted to mess with him surely deserved whatever they got in response. "Thank you for answering my questions. I appreciate your help."

The old man hesitated. "That's it? You're really going to leave?"

"That's it," I said, lowering my hands. "I wanted to see if Bartie was still alive, that's all. I'm sad to hear he's not."

His shaggy brows furrowed like a long, white caterpillar. "Then get out of here."

"Gladly."

I transported back to Marten's office, grateful to find he hadn't yet returned. The quiet room gave my thoughts space to swell and shrink while I sat in the chair. I truly did feel sad that Bartie had died, another innocent casualty in the war.

And the elusive mystery remained: Did the *Book of Light* exist?

The next weekend I walked into the Witchery to find a most unexpected sight: Priscilla and Leda sitting across from each other at the table. Their heads were bent, and they were clearly interacting.

On purpose.

The pile of firewood I had carried—to keep myself strong per Merrick's orders—flew from my arms and stacked itself by the fireplace with a spell.

"Merry meet, Bianca," Camille chirped from where she sat on top of her bed, a gown spread over her knees. She held a needle in one hand and a spool of thread in the other. "How was work?"

"Fine." I motioned to Leda and Priscilla with a questioning jerk of my head. Camille grinned, her eyes sparkling. Even Michelle, who sat in a chair next to Camille's bed perusing old cookbooks, smiled.

"I'm just working on my new summer dress, thanks for asking," Camille said as if our conversation had never waned. "I think it will be just lovely. I've chosen a light pink muslin because it will be nice and cool and isn't that expensive. Not that material is easy to find right now anyway. Tabby helped me with the pattern because Henrietta is busy making extra bandages and shirts for the wounded."

Despite Brecken's insistence that he come back to the castle to work out of the Gatehouse—although he hadn't fully healed—I hadn't seen Camille in days. I dropped my bag on the table, but neither Priscilla nor Leda looked up. Priscilla had taken a backseat in the Witchery and said very little, even when Leda wasn't around. Either she'd outgrown the need for a constant following, or Camille's willingness to prattle on and on kept Priscilla quiet, like it did most of us.

"Remember," Priscilla said quietly to Leda, pointing to a line on the page, "Coven Leaders are invited to the Esbat to report, so this format is required of all attendees."

"Oh," Leda whispered. "I see. I didn't realize that. So what about—"

"What's going on?" I asked Camille and Michelle under my breath, my eyes still glued on the strange couple at the table. "Has the world truly come to an end now? Are Leda and Priscilla . . . *friends?*"

Camille flounced her hair over her shoulder with a giggle. "Leda finally climbed off her high horse when she realized Priscilla was a good resource."

"They started studying together last week," Michelle said, writing on a scroll that had been lying on the floor. "Now Priscilla tutors her every day."

From the patient, even cadence of Priscilla's tone, she seemed to be a willing teacher. I shook my head, unable to imagine the two girls together.

"How did it happen?" I asked, leaning back on my hands.

Camille grinned. "I passed my transformation class with highest marks thanks to Priscilla. Leda said if Priscilla can do that, she must be a miracle worker, and she decided to ask for help."

Michelle guffawed. "You should have seen Priscilla's face when Leda walked up to her. I think Priscilla thought Leda was going to curse her or yell at her at first."

"What?" I screeched, eyes wide. "You received highest marks in transformation, Camille?"

"I know!" she beamed, blushing. "It was the second-best moment of my life. I never thought I'd pass highest marks on anything except embroidery, but Miss Scarlett won't let me take that class. She says I'm too good already and need to learn something useful."

I glanced skeptically at the flag hanging above the fireplace that read *The Wits* instead of *The Witchery.* It had been Camille's first project when she moved to the castle the year before. "Uh, embroidery, sure. If passing transformation was the second-best moment of your life, what was the first?"

Camille's smile deepened with a wispy sigh. "The moment Brecken first kissed me."

I rolled my eyes and collapsed back on her bed. A flash of Merrick's face floated through my mind, but I banished it.

"Ugh. Can we talk about something else?"

"Nicolas and I decided to go ahead with the hand fasting ceremony instead of waiting for the war to end," Michelle said. "We're going to do it in Letum Wood on the first day of the first month of summer. Fina even offered to cook for it. There isn't much we can have for refreshments, so I'm trying to find simple recipes."

"I wish you could decorate with all the tulips blooming in the gardens," Camille said with a dramatic sigh, yelping when she pricked her finger. "But I suppose they'll be gone by summer. It's almost the third month of spring now."

"We can use tulips," Michelle said with a quiet smile. "You and Priscilla could just transform some of the other flowers. That was on your final, remember?"

Priscilla glanced up from the table at the sound of her name. Camille beamed at her. "I forgot! We have an expert on transformation in our midst now! Priscilla can transform anything. Priscilla, will you transform flowers into tulips for Michelle's hand fasting ceremony?"

"Of course." Priscilla smiled, appearing pleased at Camille's praise.

"How is work, Priscilla?" I asked, calling across the room. She blinked, as if startled by my attention, but rallied herself again.

"Good," she said. "It's settled back into the usual education work, I suppose. Although Miss Scarlett and I have been helping with a few orphanages that had to be moved from the Southern Covens."

I thought back to my etiquette lesson when Miss Scarlett had admitted her own orphan heritage, and I wasn't surprised she would be the one to take them under her wing.

"Sounds great."

Priscilla hesitated, staring at the three of us before turning back to

Leda. A knock on the door below startled all of us, and for a second everyone looked at each other in question.

"I'll get it," I said, transporting to the bottom of the stairs. When I pulled it open, Brecken stood on the other side.

"Brecken! Merry meet!"

He half-grinned in a lopsided way, although a permanent edge of pain showed in his eyes. Attached to his right leg was a wooden peg, carved with the names of his Guardians and enchanted with a spell that left the end of the wood soft and cushioned for the stump at his knee. He still appeared thin and pale.

"Merry meet, Bianca. I'm glad you answered. I never had a chance to thank you for everything you did."

I waved it off. "Don't worry about it."

"Well, I've actually wanted to ask. How *did* you get me home? I was so delirious with fever that I don't really remember much. My mom and Camille said you just sort of showed up with me. How did you do it? I know I didn't transport."

My grin felt strained. "Oh, just a few tricks up my sleeve."

"I swear I remember being in the air, almost like I was flying. There was wind and . . . stars?" He looked at me in question. "Were there stars?"

"Stars? Uh . . . why would there be stars?"

"Maybe it was the pain potion that made me remember funny things, like wind. And you next to me."

"Uh . . . it was just a . . . not a big . . ." I stopped stammering to look him straight in the eye. "Do you trust me, Brecken?"

He snorted in amusement. "With my life."

"Good. Let's leave it at that?"

He hesitated, but must have seen something in my face that stopped him because he nodded.

"Okay."

"Great! How are you feeling?"

"Better." He lifted a carved cane. "Just moved off crutches, and I'm trying this out now. Once the war ends, Tiberius says he knows an apothecary that specializes in fake legs. He could use some kind of magic to make it so I wouldn't need a cane or anything."

"Sounds great."

He shrugged. "It would have been better to never have lost it, of course."

"Hey Breck," Camille said, coming down the stairs with a warm smile. She kissed him gently on the lips and took his hand. "How is it feeling today? You look a bit more stable."

"Not bad."

"Hurting?"

"I'm okay."

She frowned. "That means it's hurting. I brought some extra potion with me just in case." She pulled a purple vial from her pocket and dangled it between her thumb and forefinger. "Why don't you take some before the date? Just one dose."

Brecken sent a discreet glance at me. "Camille, we'll talk about this later."

She rolled her eyes. "It's just Bianca. You don't have to be brave for her. Please take some? You'll have a better time. Remember last time you went out without it?"

Her voice took on a long drawl. Brecken let out a sigh before giving in. "Fine, Camille. You're right."

Camille winked at me. "I normally am." Brecken swigged a bit of the bottle, then stopped it up again and gave it back to her. Despite the tinge of annoyance in his voice, I saw nothing but love in his eyes. Losing his leg had done nothing for Camille's adoration of him. If anything, their relationship had suddenly taken on a deeper significance. I smiled at both of them.

"Have a great time tonight."

"Priscilla is on her way down," Camille said, straightening Brecken's skewed shirt. "She just had to grab her cloak."

"Garth just arrived." He motioned to another witch striding down the hallway toward the Witchery door.

"We're going on a double date tonight," Camille said to me. "Garth found us some opera tickets."

Garth stopped at Brecken's side. I smiled, but my heart sank a little. Two friends down. If Leda and Michelle had plans, it would be another empty Witchery night for me.

"I'll go check on Priscilla," I offered. "I hope you guys have fun."

I transported back to the top to find Priscilla trying to back away from the desk, but Leda holding her captive with questions.

"Let her go, Leda," I said. "They're waiting."

Priscilla straightened her dress and calmly ran her fingers through her hair. Despite the lacking ministrations, she still looked exquisite and vibrant, with a waterfall of red hair over one shoulder. I thought back to our conversation alone, when Priscilla had admitted she hated courting, and sent her a secret, understanding smile. To my surprise, she returned it before disappearing down the turret stairs.

Leda, apparently deeming it pointless to study the Esbat without Priscilla, sent three books to her sheeted-off area of the Witchery with a spell. Her forehead bruise was almost gone.

"Rupert and I are going to go over last quarter's taxes together tonight," she announced, though no one had asked. "He promised to explain how he manages the ledger."

"Riveting," I said, sprawling across Camille's bed again. Michelle's lips twitched, but her focus remained intent on the recipe book. Leda shot me a sharp, suspicious look.

"I'm excited about it."

"I see that you and Priscilla are friends now," I said nonchalantly, drawing a smile from Michelle. "Anything spur this change of heart?"

"Acquaintances," Leda said, checking her hair in one of Camille's many mirrors. She wore a new burgundy dress with long sleeves, and her hair fell down around her shoulders in soft strands of pale blonde. "She has more skill as a teacher than I expected, I'll admit."

"You're acquaintances with a girl who was once your mortal enemy. Well done, Leda. If I didn't know any better, I'd say you may even become friends with Priscilla soon." I *tsked*. "So unlike you."

Leda rolled her eyes. "I don't like anyone, Bianca. Least of all you right now."

Michelle and I both laughed, drawing a reluctant smile from Leda. An envelope fluttered into the room from the stairwell and stopped in front of Michelle.

"Oh, good. It's Nicolas. He must be ready for me. We're going to work with the red dragon again this evening. She's finally warming up."

My throat tightened, but I forced out a strangled, "Have fun," to Michelle's back when she stood and transported away. The disquieted powers in my chest jumped, making it difficult to breathe. I closed my eyes and forced myself to concentrate, but felt the sudden flare of heat when the fire grew in the hearth.

Leda stood near the door, hands on her hips. "What's wrong with you? You seem upset."

"Me?" I asked, forcing the words out with subdued ease. "What do you mean? I've been perfectly pleasant tonight."

"Exactly. You're never pleasant when all of us have plans. So what's up?"

"Nothing. Just go."

"If you're bored, you could go see Fina. I think she needs some help moving bags of grain. Sounds like something you would like."

"It's fine," I insisted, feeling the familiar coil of magic about to spring free. I reined it back in desperately. "Go have fun with Rupert."

"Bianca—"

"Go!" The torches popped with a bright white light. She startled back, protecting her face from the wall of heat.

"Oh," she whispered once it had dissipated, her eyes wide. "Is it that bad?"

I swallowed. "Sometimes."

"What if you found a Guardian to sword fight with? Beating them always makes you feel better. Merrick is around, isn't he?"

The compassion in her tone nearly undid me. I rolled my eyes and straightened my back. "I'll figure something out. Have fun with Rupert."

She lingered for a moment, her face elongating with worry the longer she studied me.

"Seriously, Bianca. Are you okay?"

I stared at the ceiling to avoid her gaze, breathless with magic and power and fear. "No. No, I'm not."

She swallowed. "I'm sorry about your papa. I know this has been really hard on you."

"Thanks."

When I gave no further indication of conversing, Leda disappeared. I pressed a hand to my forehead. My magic, having found a short-lived release, felt edgier than ever.

This would be a very long night.

Can't You Feel It?

"Where are all your friends?"

Merrick walked up behind me just before I disappeared back into the Witchery after scrounging up dinner. I jumped, nearly dropping the pile of dried apples I'd carried up from the kitchen. A new set of stitches held his left eyebrow together. I hadn't seen him for almost three days, despite his residence at Chatham Castle. Although I'd harbored a secret hope I'd be able to spend time with him tonight, I hadn't actually thought it would happen. Night represented a prime opportunity for action for Factios members.

"Merry meet to you too," I muttered, flashing him an annoyed look. "And all my friends are . . . out tonight. Don't you have to work?"

"I have a few hours before I need to be anywhere. Why aren't you out with them?"

I cleared my throat. "Oh . . . well, they're all out with . . . you know . . . uh . . . interested parties."

He grinned. "Dates, you mean."

"Yes." I sighed. "Dates."

His expression turned serious. "And why aren't you?"

Because you didn't ask me, I thought with a flurry of butterflies. "Are you kidding? Who would ask me out? They're all scared of my father."

He agreed with a tilt of his head. "With good reason. He's more protective than a mama bear."

"Well, to be fair, they're probably afraid of me too."

My victory against Miss Mabel in a magical fight last summer put a damper on interested male prospects. I wasn't exactly a simpering, submissive female.

"Definitely afraid of you," Merrick said with a lazy grin.

"Why aren't *you* out courting a girl?" I asked, scowling. "I've never seen you take a girl to the opera before."

His eyes flickered. "Let's just say it's complicated."

"Oh?" I asked, forcing disinterest into my tone.

"Besides, my idea of courting doesn't have anything to do with the opera."

"What do you mean?"

"An awkward dinner and the opera? No thanks. I'll pass. There are plenty of other things I'd rather do."

"What else is there?" I asked. "Courting is doing stuff like dinner and the opera. Camille and Brecken sometimes switch it up by visiting new places or eating dinner with his family, but, you know. That's basically it."

He laughed in a deep, rolling wave that made his eyes crinkle. My stomach curled in a nervous little ball. Why did he have to be so attractive?

"Courting doesn't have to be what everyone else says it is," he said. "Since when do you go by popular definitions anyway?"

I opened my mouth to respond but didn't know what to say. While I had never defined my life by what everyone else did—I'd never had the luxury—it hadn't occurred to me that my attitude could extend to courting.

"I don't . . . I mean . . . I don't understand what you mean by all this."

He grinned, enjoying my confusion. "All I mean is that I'm not interested in courting if it means I have to do it by someone else's rules. I'd rather do my own thing. And finding a girl who is up for it is challenge enough."

"Like what, hunting a bear with your bare hands?"

"If I thought the girl would join me, sure. Sounds like a good time."

My eyes widened in disbelief before I saw hints of a mocking smile. I glared at him, and he laughed.

"Don't you want to get married?" I asked, thinking of Papa's admonition not to ruin Merrick's career by distracting him. But what if Merrick wanted a marriage? What if courting him was an option? "Or are you holding off because you want to become Head of Protectors?"

He paused to think it over. "That would depend on what kind of girl I meet."

My breath caught in my throat. *What about me?* Hints of a beard stubbled his face in a sandy golden shimmer. I wanted to run my fingertips across it.

"I think there must be a witch out there worth giving up such a high position for," he said, his eyes focused intently on mine. "If I found her, I'd give up the idea of serving as Head of Protectors. She'd have to be brave enough to pass a test first, of course."

"Oh? And what exactly is this test you've conjured up?"

"She'd have to run with me."

My heart thudded double time. "No girl would be crazy enough to run with you."

He grinned, and suddenly we weren't standing all that far apart. The wall grazed my back, trapping me close to Merrick's broad chest. He braced his hands on either side of my head and leaned in close. His masculine pine scent filled my lungs. I could feel the warm caress of his breath on my cheek.

"You run with me."

"Yes," I whispered. "I guess I do."

If my heart had been pounding before, it was nothing in comparison to the way I felt now. I studied him, my breath coming fast and uncertain. His jaw tightened while he stared at me with an uneasy blend of amusement and challenge. I wasn't used to a look so open, as if I were less Derek's daughter and more . . . an actual *girl*. My powers flared, and a torch nearby brightened.

"I have a feeling your father wouldn't appreciate my showing interest in you."

"No, he wouldn't. But I'm not sure I care."

He smiled softly and touched my cheek with the back of his knuckle. His eyes darkened, like a green cloud roiling with thunder.

"I won't betray your father, B. I can't do this. I promised him."

My throat thickened. So Papa had spoken to Merrick about his concerns. A storm of emotions grew in my chest, and I feared my magic wasn't stable.

"But you need to know that I would if I could," he continued. "Oh, how I would."

But he couldn't because Papa had forbidden it. Papa who wanted to protect me but didn't even write. Papa who'd been gone trying to save the world on his own. The injustice burned deep in my chest. The torch next to us sparked. Magic surged through me, stirring my blood in frustration.

"Will you take me on a run in Letum Wood?" I asked. "Please?"

A moment of confusion flickered in his eyes. "A run?"

"I haven't been in weeks, and my powers are getting out of control. Especially now. Especially . . . please?"

If I could just run and let it out, I could deal with Papa's long absences, the war, my sudden, frustrating attraction to Merrick that I could do nothing about. Letum Wood called to me.

"I . . . I can't."

"Merrick, I have to do this," I said, pleading. Magic swirled in painful agony through my chest. Pictures of Papa's weary face whipped through my mind. Mama dying. The torches blazed again and again. "If I don't, I won't be able to keep it under control, and we both know what happens then."

I saw the slow crumbling in his eyes. "Is it that bad?"

"Can't you feel it?"

He scowled and shoved away from the wall. The absence of his warm body left me feeling cold. "Fine. Let's go now before it gets too dark. Don't worry about changing. You'll just have to run in that."

Fifteen minutes later, spirals of budding green leaves coated the trees around us as we sped through Letum Wood. The ground, warm on my bare feet, felt soft and pliable from spring rain, absorbing every footfall. My heart soared, and the magic released. Flowers bloomed on the trail behind me as I ran, faster and faster, addicted to the rush I felt in my newfound freedom. My pulse reverberated through my legs and bones in a rhythmic pattern. *Boom. Boom boom. Boom.* I could leave it all behind out here. All the frustration, all the angst, all the attraction I couldn't act on.

"Slow down!" Merrick called from behind me. "There's still mud on the trail. You're going to fall again."

Ha! I wanted to laugh. *Slow down? Never.*

I soared through the forest, leaping over boulders and ducking branches. It felt wonderful to leave my breath far behind and take in a fresh, new gasp of air. I never wanted to go back to the castle, to my entrapped life within its walls. I hadn't felt this good since before the war started.

Something to my left caught my eye, stopping me. A skinny brown trail snuck off to the side. It could hardly be called a trail—more like a footpath worn into the ground by who-knew-what kind of creature.

"Let's go this way." I motioned to the path with a nod, bracing my hands on my hips to catch my breath.

Merrick's brow furrowed. "Is that a new trail?" he asked, peering into the trees. "I've never seen it before."

Neither had I. Nighttime had started to fall, leaving long shadows to cover the spongy ground, green with fresh growth. But even so, this trail was definitely new. Papa would never allow me to take a new trail at a time like this.

"Let's try."

He hesitated, but I felt an undeniable pull drawing me closer to the path.

"I don't know, B. We shouldn't even be out here."

"It heads back to Chatham Castle, see? I'm sure it probably just cuts back to a different part of the gardens."

"Fine," he said, looking relieved at the prospect of cutting short our adventure. "You have five minutes. If it's not clearly going back to the castle, we transport."

I stepped onto the trail and the pull strengthened. The closer I moved toward it, the stronger I felt it. The path ran between a thick cluster of trees. Their branches trembled when I looked at them. A sweet breeze towed me closer. The odd suspicion that Letum Wood was trying to communicate with me crept through my mind. Almost like the day I escaped the West Guards by finding a path in the forest that didn't exist, leading me and the little girl to safety.

I shook the thoughts away. Absurd. Forests didn't communicate. Besides, I recognized magic when I saw it, and this strange feeling had magic written all over it. Forests didn't have magic. At least, I didn't think they did.

I ventured forward, taking the lead. The skinny dirt trail disappeared just through the cluster of trees, but branches and deadwood moved aside to let us through as soon as we approached. I obeyed the haphazard trail that opened as we came upon it, just wide enough for us to pass.

"At least it's taking us back to the castle," Merrick said, eyes on the canopy. Still, he didn't relax.

The branches around me rattled, so I held up a hand to silence him. "Just a little bit more," I mouthed, though I didn't understand why. Merrick shot me a strange glance but followed without question. "Something is different," I mouthed, gesturing around. "Can't you feel it?"

He shook his head. "Nothing is different," he mouthed back. "I can't sense any magic."

I brushed him off as I started forward again. It wasn't someone—or something—using magic that I could see. An uneasiness filled me, sending me onward again. Merrick moved closer, only a breath away from me.

Just when I'd started to worry we were on a dangerous magical path set by an unknown creature native to Letum Wood, the trail disappeared, ending at a wall of branches that didn't move out of our way like the others had. I skidded to a stop with my heart in my throat. On the other side of the tangled mat of sticks stood four burly men. Merrick halted just behind me, standing so close his chest touched my back. Both of us stared between the branches without uttering a word.

The broad, strong witches wore familiar linen pants and robes over bare chests that I'd seen when Miss Mabel transported me to the

Western Network. The synchronous clicking of their words, though spoken in hushed tones, confirmed my suspicions.

West Guards.

Merrick and I crouched down until our knees rested in the dirt. Through the deadfall above, the turrets and spires of Chatham Castle could be seen, partially obscured by trees. We'd followed the trail so far we'd nearly circled back to the castle.

The West Guards crouched over what appeared to be a map, gesturing to the castle and then motioning to the rolled parchment. I couldn't see any signs of magic, which meant they likely knew they couldn't use it without drawing the attention of the dragons or patrolling Guardians. My eyes darted around the forest to find another group of them to the left, hidden near a clump of trees. I could hear three far to the right. At least ten had come.

The West Guards in front of us ripped a few branches off a nearby tree, creating a symbol with them on the ground to mark the spot. Another cold breeze trickled by, brushing against the back of my neck.

The West Guards were staking out Chatham Castle.

Merrick squeezed my arm just above the elbow, and I glanced over at him warily. He motioned back with his head, and I nodded. We'd have to walk back or the West Guards would sense the magic we used to transport away.

Just as we were about to move, one of the West Guards flipped around to stare right in our direction. We froze. Another burst of wind swelled up, stirring leaves and bits of bark into the air in front of us. The West Guard ran his eyes across the thick brambles surrounding Merrick and I, seeming to stop right on me. After he stared at me for a moment or two, his eyes continued to the left in a studious sweep. I held my breath in disbelief.

He didn't see us.

Vines and dead leaves had sprung up on the sustained gust of wind, obscuring the branches we already hid behind. Merrick squeezed my arm again, and we hurried away, crouched low. Once we were far enough they couldn't see us, Merrick stopped.

"I'm going to tell Zane," he whispered. "We need to stop them right now, and try to take a few prisoners if we can. Go for Sanna."

My eyes widened. "Sanna?"

"Tell her the dragons have a few visitors to deal with. They'll know what to do. And Bianca, whatever you do, do *not* come back here."

"Sanna!" I cried. "Sanna!"

I landed a few paces away from the brook trickling past her little cottage in the woods. Without a moment's hesitation, I sprang over the small bridge and ran up to her dilapidated house. Sanna sat on the porch, holding a silver flask—likely filled with one of the strongest ipsums in the Central Network. I went to step onto her porch, but a sudden burst of heat and a roar stopped me.

"Wouldn't move if I were you," she said jovially, wiping her lips with the back of a hand. "The red is out, and she's surly."

The red. I'd forgotten. Michelle had mentioned that she and Nicolas meant to work with her tonight.

I slowly spun around to see Nicolas standing in front of the fierce red dragon that had wanted to eat me since the first time I stumbled onto her in the forest. She gnashed her teeth in my direction, sending a second spurt of fire toward me that would have burned me if I hadn't recoiled from it.

"Oy!" Nicolas yelled from where he stood below. He hollered something else in a language I didn't understand, and the red backed away. She retreated a few steps but kept her slivered yellow eyes on me. Fire glowed in her nostrils whenever she released a sultry breath. The blue slunk through the tree line. His trust for me, while much greater than the red's, remained limited. No doubt my still-agitated magic influenced their snappish behaviors.

"Sanna, we need you right away!" I said, stepping away from her porch. The red snorted once I put space between myself and Sanna but kept her vigilant observation of me.

"What for? Can't you see I'm busy?"

No doubt sensing Sanna's annoyance, the blue slipped out of the trees to stand next to the house, his nostrils flaring. I stumbled back.

The red let out another high screech, lowering her head to the ground like a slithering snake.

"West Guards are in Letum Wood, near the castle."

She perked up. The dragons followed suit. "What?" she barked. "West Guards in Letum Wood?"

Nicolas swung around to stare at me. Michelle, who stood off to the side, moved forward.

"What do you mean, Bianca?" Michelle asked in her usual calm voice. The red, seeing her, let out a low purr but kept her angry eyes on me. Michelle calmed the giant beasts, while I riled them into a frenzy. Seemed about right.

"I just saw them! Merrick and I were on a run. There's at least ten. They have a map and are in the forest near Chatham Castle. I—"

"Impossible," Sanna said. "The green is patrolling and would have detected them by now."

"They aren't using magic. They must have snuck in on foot somehow. They hardly even spoke. Merrick didn't even sense them."

Sanna thought it over for a moment. "Bloody monster West Guards," she yelled, raising a fist in a way that reminded me a bit of Tiberius. "We'll teach them a lesson for coming onto our land to attack *our* castle!"

Nicolas stepped forward, moving between the red and me. His heavy forehead creased. The red swayed behind him, her eyes narrowed on me again. "Are you sure, Bianca?"

"Without a doubt. Merrick sent me here. They want to take a few prisoners, so don't kill them all. I think he went to get more Protectors, but I'm not sure. Look, we don't have a lot of time and—"

"Sounds like we might need to take care of a problem, Sanna," Nicolas said, grinning.

"Oh ho!" Sanna cried. The silver flask fell to the ground when she stood, and liquid glugged onto her porch, smoking as it poured between the slats. "A little evening snack for my babies, eh? Nicolas, you take the red this time. She's starting to trust you. I'll take the blue. The red's going to be excited once she gets there, so keep her under control. But let her have a little fun."

"Keep at least one of the West Guards alive!"

"Dragons make no promises," Sanna snapped. "Now let us do our business."

By the time Sanna made it to the edge of the porch, the blue awaited her, his body pressed close to the ground and wings twitching in anticipation. I had to stumble back to avoid being smacked by his long, supple neck. Sanna used magic to lift herself onto his back, then settled astride, her skinny old legs suddenly strong. Nicolas murmured something to the red, who still stared at me in suspicion. Apparently deciding the prospect of a snack sounded better than dealing with me, the red used her head to bop Nicolas onto her back. Sanna called out an order in a different language and cackled.

"They've got their noses on now," she cried when the dragons lifted their heads to the sky, their massive nostrils flaring wide. "Let's go kick some West Guards out of our Network, eh?"

The two dragons pushed off from the ground with their mighty legs and took to the sky, expansive wings unfurled. I watched them go for only a few seconds before transporting away myself. This was one fight I wouldn't miss.

Dragon Fury

Whether due to the intensity of my excitement or just good luck, I transported to the exact spot I wanted: the top branches of the forest.

The West Guards would be less likely to detect my magic so high. Based on the pristine view of Chatham Castle from my spot, I imagined myself to be right above the intruders and slipped down the tree like I was a ten-year-old girl again. The branches supported me without moving or creaking, which seemed odd considering how thin they were at this height.

When the heads of the West Guards appeared below, I stopped. All ten had converged into a small group, as soundless as a dark winter day. Their robes blended in with the forest floor, but that wouldn't matter to the dragons. They knew what to look for. Evening had replaced daylight, leaving the forest particularly dark. The strange pull that brought me to this spot had faded.

I lay on my stomach on a thick branch, straddling it with my legs to keep from falling. Moments after I'd settled in, I thought I detected something move above me but glanced up to see only a patch of bare sky. Despite their big, scaly bodies, the dragons moved through Letum Wood with more finesse than robins. No doubt they had just arrived.

If I hadn't been looking down when the dragons attacked, I might have missed it, for they moved with such sudden, relentless force.

A plume of fire erupted below, illuminating the West Guards in their crouched positions. The distinct scream of the red followed. One of the West Guards transported away, another scrambled for what appeared to be the map, and the rest bellowed in surprise, drawing their swords. The glittering ebony and sapphire scales of the blue appeared from the depths of Letum Wood, and moments later four Protectors—Merrick included—sprang from nowhere, converging on the remaining West Guards with perfect synchronicity.

A terrific clash of swords came next. I paralyzed a West Guard just before he attacked Merrick from behind. The red dragon pinned two West Guards against a massive tree with her long talons. Nicolas sat astride her back, his lips moving. Based on the bright flare of the red's nostrils, and the sweat pouring down the West Guards' faces, only Nicolas's impressive control over the beast kept the dragon from devouring her prey.

The raucous ambush ended in less than three minutes. The blue tracked a fleeing West Guard—too frightened to transport, I supposed—while smoke billowing from the red partially obscured my vision. I saw enough to curse a West Guard headed for Tobias, sending him to the ground under a tripping curse.

When it all settled, two West Guards lay lifeless near Zane, two remained pinned by the red, and the blue held one under his massive talons. The other West Guards must have transported away. I couldn't see Merrick, which meant he had likely tried to follow them.

"Take that, scumbags!" Sanna screamed, waving a triumphant hand in the air. "No one challenges my Network!"

"Take them to the dungeons," Zane commanded, motioning to the West Guards trapped by the dragons. Tobias grabbed them by their throats. A special kind of rope coiled around their wrists that could only be undone by a certain incantation. The strength of the magic would overpower any other magic the West Guards could attempt and prevent them from transporting away. The red dragon let out a disappointed moan and reluctantly backed away on Nicolas's command.

"Fast response, Sanna," Zane called. "We appreciate the backup. Well done, old lady."

"Anything to rid the earth of these violent West Guard scum," she sang back.

One of the West Guards shot her a glare, but the blue snapped at him, and he cringed. Sanna cackled and turned the blue in another direction.

"Not tonight, my beautiful baby," she crooned, stroking its scales. "Not tonight."

Although discreet, the blue's eyes flickered up to me in the tree-tops. I met his shiny yellow gaze in a moment of fear, but he looked away, keeping my secret. Luckily the red had been too distracted to notice me.

"We'll question them tonight," Zane said. "Seems like they might have a few plans in mind."

The Protectors shoved the West Guards into the thick brush of Letum Wood, forcing them to stumble back toward Chatham Castle. I sat up as everyone faded away, leaving me alone in the quiet stillness of Letum Wood. When I pulled in a deep breath, I could smell the sharp tang of wet earth and pine. I listened but heard and felt nothing unusual.

Letum Wood had always been dangerous. Unknown creatures lurked amongst its thick, tall trees, and the forest floor rarely saw full sunlight. But I'd never imagined Letum Wood had power.

The forest had fallen silent again. For a moment, I wondered if I had just imagined it.

An Explicit Command

Meet me in my office now. We need to talk.

I folded Papa's unexpected note and set it on the side table the next night, excited at the prospect of seeing him again. Getting a personal note was rare enough these days. After the fiasco with the dragons the night before, I hadn't seen Merrick, though I'd searched for him. He must have been sent on a mission.

"Sounds like Papa is home," I said to Reeves. "I need to meet with him in his office over the whole West Guard thing."

"I shall preserve your dinner until you return," Reeves promised.

"Thanks."

Word about the West Guards staking out Chatham Castle had exploded across Chatham City overnight; most witches demanded the blood of the captured in retribution. Others fled to the country, saying the war had finally come too close. Clive staged yet another protest against Papa's handling of the war, saying that Papa had proven he didn't have control and none of us were safe. The Factios took advantage of the fear and doubled their efforts against the gypsies. Outside the walls of the castle, Chatham City burned in endless war.

Chatham Castle itself had exploded with nervous preparations and a frightening new energy. Boards went up over windows. Guardians patrolled deep into Letum Wood. A cloud of dragons circled overhead. Mrs. L commanded her army of butlers and witches with determined force, storing food, training maids, and keeping the fireboys busy finding and cleaning old weapons from the deepest basements.

When I arrived at Papa's office, Merrick stood just inside, hands folded behind his back and legs braced as if he expected a blow to the midsection.

"Hey," I said, but he didn't respond or look at me. His clenched jaw and flared nostrils told me something wasn't right; Papa's irritable expression confirmed it. Papa stood behind his desk, drawn and haggard. Soot and sweat streaked his face, and a smear of blood covered the back of his right hand. He must have transported back from the Southern Covens just for this.

This wasn't going to be good.

An awkward silence hovered in the air once I arrived. "Merry meet, Papa," I said, testing it. He didn't respond.

Nope, I thought. *Definitely not my imagination.*

Stella and Zane both entered the room, looking as solemn as a funeral. My stomach clenched. Something was very wrong if Stella and Zane looked so stressed.

"Thank you for waiting, Derek," Stella said when the door closed behind them. "You may begin whenever you like."

Stella moved farther into the room until she stood next to me without her usual, reassuring smile. Zane stopped next to Merrick, his hands folded in front of him. The two didn't make any motion to acknowledge the other, but Merrick's jaw relaxed just a bit. It felt like Stella and Zane had subtly taken sides, or felt they needed to stand near us for support.

"Thank you for coming," Papa said, leaning on his desk wearily. "Bianca, I asked you to come so I can hear from your point of view what happened in Letum Wood yesterday evening. Begin."

I hesitated. Was Papa angry with me? He rarely called me Bianca and never spoke in such a formal tone. Merrick continued to stare at the floor.

"O-okay. We were out for a run," I began, purposefully avoiding the unnecessary details of the conversation I'd had with Merrick. "I found a new trail and decided to take it. We ended up stumbling on the West Guards. Sanna and Zane told you the rest."

Neither of them knew I'd been sitting in the treetops watching the attack, thank the good gods. This angry confrontation with Papa would be a breeze compared to what he would do if he knew I'd hovered just above a dragon battle.

"And you went with her?" Papa asked, turning to Merrick. His low, gravelly voice set my instincts on fire.

"Papa," I said, stepping forward. "I—"

"I didn't ask you," he snapped, keeping his unwavering gaze on Merrick. "I asked Merrick."

Stella reached over and put a cool, soothing hand on my arm, but it didn't calm the flare of magic that rose with my panic. Merrick met Papa's intense gaze with an expression that remained as stoic as ever, though his breath sped up just a little.

"We went out for a run, sir. Just as Bianca said."

"Even though I ordered you to stay away from my daughter."

"Yes, sir."

"You *ordered* him to stay away from me?" I burst out. "Papa!"

"This doesn't concern you, Bianca. Stay out of it."

"It most certainly does concern me," I said, stepping forward again. "Merrick and I went on a run. That's it. He was doing me a favor. It's not like we kissed or—"

"You are not part of this!" Papa said, slamming his fist on the desk and leaning into it. He leveled a dangerous warning glare at me that I ignored. How dare he act so upset! How dare he act like I had no part in this!

"Yes I am! I'm the reason we were out there! I talked Merrick into taking me for a run. He didn't want me to go, but I had to. We were only out there for fifteen minutes."

"You promised Stella you wouldn't go into Letum Wood. You knew it was dangerous."

"I promised I wouldn't go in alone!" I shot back. "And I wasn't alone. Merrick went with me. I never broke my promise."

"Bianca," Stella murmured, pulling me back. "This isn't helping. Take a deep breath. We'll work this out, okay?"

"There's a bloody war going on out there, Bianca, and hundreds of witches are dying every day! You are the High Priest's daughter. That means any one of those West Guards would do just about anything to kidnap you and hold you hostage," Papa bellowed. "Now go to the apartment. I'll deal with you later."

"We didn't know the West Guards were in Letum Wood.

Shouldn't we be glad that Merrick and I found them and weren't harmed?"

"No!" Papa roared. "I told both of you how I felt, and both of you went against my wishes."

Zane stepped forward, putting himself in front of Merrick. "Your Highness," he said, "I believe Merrick was trying his best to keep your daughter safe."

"Stay out of this, Zane."

"I'm seventeen, Papa," I cried, rushing closer before Stella could pull me back. "You can't protect me forever."

"I bloody well can."

"I'm always in danger, Papa. Always! I've faced West Guards twice now. But you didn't even know about the first time, did you? No! Because you're too busy working to even remember that *I'm still here.*"

"What?" His eyes narrowed. "When did you face the West Guards before last night?"

"I've faced dragons before too, but nothing happened to me last night. The forest protected me. Merrick protected me. *I* protected me! I'm not a helpless child. I won against Miss Mabel, or have you forgotten?"

"The forest protected you?" Papa repeated. "What in the good gods are you talking about?"

I hesitated. I hadn't actually worked that part out myself, so I didn't know how to explain it.

"It's just . . . well . . . I don't know entirely," I admitted. "At least not yet. I'll figure it out at some point. But we would never have seen those West Guards if I hadn't felt compelled to go on the trail. There was magic in it, Papa. It guided us. Merrick didn't want to go and even tried to convince me otherwise. He tried to keep us on the main trail. He didn't do anything wrong. I'll take responsibility, Papa. This is all my fault. Punish me, not him."

Merrick closed his eyes and hung his head. Papa's eyes widened.

"You damn well better believe you're going to take responsibility for disobeying me. You followed a magical impulse into a part of Letum Wood you'd never been?" He pivoted toward Merrick. "And you *let* her?"

Oh, no, I thought in panic. This was rapidly falling apart.

"It wasn't like that!" I cried, frantic. "The magic was Letum Wood. It wanted us to see the West Guards. It was protecting us and the Central Network! It's done it before. Merrick didn't know I felt it."

Stella held onto my arm with both hands now, keeping me back. Even her calming incantations weren't working; my powers bubbled up like a pot of boiling water. The torches blazed. Zane eyed me warily.

"Letum Wood can't communicate with witches, Bianca. You willingly went into the forest during a time of war when you know that West Guards are springing up everywhere. You followed an unknown trail that could have been enchanted with Almorran magic and ended up face to face with ten West Guards intent on harm. Do you understand why I'm angry?"

His eyes bored into mine, leaving me hurt and breathless and afraid. Papa had never spoken to me with such unrestrained fury before. I'd never seen him so livid. He always maintained control. Either this testified to the strain he felt as High Priest, or something else was going on. My reply stuck in my throat. Papa didn't understand. He didn't know what it was like staying behind at the castle, waiting every day to see if he had died. And to take Letum Wood—my only reprieve, my only safety—away from me?

"We didn't do anything wrong," I whispered, forcing my voice to a calmer cadence when all I wanted to do was shout, grab his shoulders, and beg him to understand. "I needed to run. I have no other outlet, and my powers are becoming dangerous again. Running in Letum Wood is all I have."

"I wanted you safe at home! I can't protect you if you're off doing crazy things."

"Well, this isn't home!" I shouted, tears filling my eyes. The fire popped in a hot flare of sparks. "This isn't home, and it never will be. Home is with Mama."

"Marie is gone," he said coldly.

"So are you!"

He stared at me with a stunned, stark gaze, as if I'd slapped him.

"You're gone fighting a war. You never write. When you are home, you're in meetings or you work or you're thinking about work. I might as well not exist for you anymore. I'm stuck in the castle with friends who are always too busy with their own lives, and then I'm banned from going to the one place that gives me any peace. What was I supposed to do to control my magic, Papa? What was I supposed to do? Let my powers fly out of control? I'm afraid every single moment of every single day that you're going to die. That you'll leave just like Mama. What if I hurt someone again?"

I turned away, unable to bear his pained eyes. A sob stuck in my throat.

"It was just a run," I said to Stella in a haunted whisper when she put a hand on my shoulder. "Letum Wood protected me."

"Derek," Stella said, pushing me behind her. "I know you're scared for Bianca, but perhaps we should talk about this after you've had some time to think it out. Both of you are under an incredible amount of stress, especially now."

Papa had turned away to stare out the window, jaw tight, arms folded across his chest.

"Go to the apartment Bianca," he said quietly.

I opened my mouth to speak but didn't know what to say. All my emotions had converged into a jumble of hot, teeming worms in my chest far more powerful than they'd been before last night. Papa didn't look back, as if he couldn't even bear seeing me. Merrick kept his gaze on the floor.

"Go, Bianca. Let him cool off," Stella whispered, squeezing my arm. "Trust me."

I'd never felt so alone or frightened in my life, like Mama had died all over again. Where could I turn? I felt betrayed, forsaken by Papa, the very witch who had always had my back. I felt as if I didn't even know him, and that was the most frightening thing of all.

The room fell quiet as I departed without another word. I didn't even try to listen to what they said after I left. I just transported to my room, sank to my bed, and stared at the wall.

Papa didn't come back to the apartment that night.

You've Come to Fight

Merrick disappeared. I couldn't find him the next morning and hadn't heard from him after sending repeated letters through the night. I asked every Guardian and Protector I could find, but no one knew.

"Reeves," I called late that afternoon, feeling restless and cagey. I'd paced back and forth for so long that Reeves had finally removed the rug, afraid I'd wear a hole in it. "Have you seen or heard from Papa?"

"No, Miss Bianca."

I swore under my breath, ignored his silent reprimand, and transported to the hall just outside Stella's office. Warm sunshine poured through pointed windows lining the hallway. A few of them were cracked open, admitting a fresh spring breeze.

"Have you heard from him, Stella?" I asked, peeking into her office from the doorway. She looked up from her desk with a sigh.

"Come in, Bianca. I'm glad you've come. I've been wanting to talk to you since last night but couldn't break away until very late. How are you?"

She closed the door behind me with a spell while I lowered my body into a chair across from her desk.

"Not good. He's never done this before," I whispered, tears filling my eyes. "We always make up after an argument. And I've never seen him that upset. He's . . . it's like I don't know him anymore."

Stella walked around the desk. A chair scooted next to mine for her to sit in, and she put a warm hand on mine.

"Can I be frank with you, Bianca?"

"Of course."

She studied my teary eyes for a breathless moment.

"Your father is under an incredible amount of stress right now. More than I've ever seen a witch bear, even Mildred. The Central Network isn't doing well in the war. The Protectors have been counter-attacking the Western Network for the past three weeks, but nothing seems to make enough of a difference to give us an advantage. We're holding the Southern Network back but still losing witches. It's weakening us. And just this morning Isadora saw a few very frightening things that your father can't control or change unless . . ." She trailed away, swallowing.

"Unless what?"

She paused. "Unless he faces Dane on his own tonight."

"What?"

"He didn't have time to speak with you the way he wanted. He had to leave right away—on Isadora's urgent recommendation—for us to have a chance."

My heart stopped. "He's going to face Dane?" I asked, breathless.

"Yes."

"But Dane!" I cried. "He's a Watcher and a High Priest. Papa is strong, but surely Dane is at least as strong and is able to see future possibilities on top of it. He'll see Papa coming!"

"It's possible," Stella said. "Dane is a very powerful witch. But your father feels this is the only way we can stop them and save more lives. We don't know if the West Guards will attack the castle tonight or not. Several of them returned back to the West."

"What if something happens? What if Dane wins and I never see Papa again? The last things we would have said to each other would have been—"

I broke off, unable to finish. Stella squeezed my hand.

"He doesn't plan on losing, Bianca. Isadora says there's a chance it will work out, that unexpected circumstances could fall into place that would enable us to pull ahead. She didn't say what those circumstances were, of course, but we must trust that she would not lead us astray."

Even Isadora's blessing brought me no comfort. I stared at the floor in stunned disbelief.

"Our Protectors that spy on the West report that at least five contingents of West Guards have disappeared," Stella continued, rubbing a hand over her weary eyes. "As there have been no new attacks, we can only assume something is in the works."

The word *Protector* stirred my mind back to Merrick. "Did he kick Merrick out of the Protectors?"

She shook her head. "No. Derek was upset with Merrick, but he thanked him for keeping you safe. Merrick is still in the Brotherhood."

"Where is he?"

"I don't know. Reassigned away from here, I believe."

"Why would Papa care so much about Merrick and I?"

Stella pushed her lips to one side with a hint of a smile. "I think *that* had something more to do with your father's fear of losing his daughter to a handsome young witch."

"Jikes," I whispered, for so many reasons.

"I'm not privy to all the details, but I believe that Derek was nothing more than a protective Papa last night and not a High Priest. Go easy on him. He bears the weight of a Network of witches on his shoulders. He's terrified he'll lose you, or somehow fail you. Your fight with Mabel really scared him last summer."

I stared at her. In all the years being a Protector's daughter, of never knowing if he'd come back, I'd never felt this kind of blood-curling fright in my life. The stakes hadn't been this high before.

"It's never been this scary," I said.

"You've never been the High Priest's daughter before. And, for the record, neither has anyone else in all our history."

"I'm beginning to see why Esmelda pioneered the tradition," I said ruefully, and Stella agreed with a humorless chuckle.

"Yes. It would seem she understood a great deal about the world of magic and politics."

A heavy bank of black clouds hovered on the horizon. Lightning streaked across the sky, and I heard a distant roll of thunder. Wondering if I'd ever talk to Merrick or Papa again, I fell into a restless swirl of thoughts, not having felt so helpless since Mama fell into my arms.

"Stella," I whispered. "I'm not going to lose Papa, am I?"
She sighed. "I don't know, Bianca. I don't know."

My friends eluded the Witchery, and the castle bustled with preparations, so I lay on the divan alone to sort through my heavy thoughts. Reeves had been puttering around the apartment, cleaning everything twice, so the gentle smell of lavender lulled me into an uneasy nap under a churning afternoon thunderstorm.

Another nightmare captured me as soon as I slipped out of consciousness.

I stood at the mouth of a watery, musty cavern. The air seemed wet when I reached out to touch the glistening cave wall, unable to feel the cool, slimy texture with my fingertips. Water covered my bare feet, lapping around my ankles. Darkness oozed out of the stalactites dripping from the ceiling, and the gentle hiss of waves rolled in from behind me. My hand went for Viveet but found nothing.

A flicker of bright torchlight around a corner caught my gaze. When I ventured forward, a familiar heaviness pressed into me like an oncoming wall of wind. I struggled to breathe.

It all felt so real, and yet . . .

I gave you plenty of opportunities to avoid my wrath, Bianca Monroe. Tonight you shall see what happens when you don't obey my will.

Angelina's voice sent a shudder down my spine. The weight of her power threatened to push the very marrow from my bones. It seemed stronger than it had ever been.

There's nothing you can say that would change my mind, I replied, surprised when I didn't hear my own voice echo off the cave walls, as if I wasn't even there. But I was. Wasn't I?

Oh, I think there is something that will change your mind. Your own weakness is clear.

"You've come to fight me, Derek," a thick, accented voice said, startling me with the way it rolled around the empty space. "Just as I had always hoped."

I peered around the turn to see a man standing within a circle of torchlight in an open area. Cords of muscle rippled through his bare chest and arms. A pair of thin linen pants rolled halfway up the calves covered his legs. The rhythmic sway of a braid hanging down his back swung back and forth. My heart seized. I choked over my own fear. *Dane.*

"I came to destroy you, Dane," Papa responded easily.

"You came to die."

"I don't start fights I can't win."

"You won't win this one because it's not me you'll be fighting."

Papa! I called, but it faded in my own mind, a wisp of a dream. I wasn't really there, just as I wasn't sleeping back at Chatham Castle.

You made your weakness very clear.

Through the darkness of the cave, I could just make out Papa's face. He stood back in the shadows, not showing the same arrogance as Dane by flaunting his power in the light. The torchlight gleamed off Papa's half-armor, stained with dirt and streaks of blood. Despite the situation, Papa certainly appeared confident.

Dane smiled, his perfect teeth glowing. "You may think that killing me will help your cause, but you're wrong. The Western Network doesn't fall or thrive on my life. My orders do not move it forward. In fact, I'm not the true leader of the West after all."

Papa's eyes flickered in a second of uncertainty. Out of the shadows glided another witch with a familiar hourglass figure and dark ebony hair. I knew her by the darkness that accompanied her and the even keel of her unwavering voice. The voice I'd heard in the Western Network. The voice that plagued my nightmares.

The voice that threatened to take everything away.

"Derek Black," Angelina said, stepping closer to the circle of light but hovering in the shadows. "You've come to save your Network, have you?"

Papa said nothing, keeping his eyes and attention split between Angelina and Dane, who stood on opposite sides of the circle. Papa reached back to make sure nothing but the wall remained behind him.

"Angelina," he drawled. "I expected to see you here."

"Did you?" she asked, though her voice betrayed no inflection. "Yet you came anyway."

I sloshed through the water to the other side of the cave where I could see Papa more clearly, but my movements made no ripples.

"Aren't you going to try to transport away now that you've seen me?" Angelina asked. "I expected your instincts to be faster than this."

Papa's grip on his sword tightened. "Not my courage. I never leave a fight."

Angelina sashayed into full view. A beam of light fell across her raven black hair and fine-boned facial features under pale white skin. She had a slight build like Mabel but stood shorter. My heart stuttered in my chest when I noticed the familiar blue eyes peering out of her face. Unlike Miss Mabel, who moved with a sultry attitude and seemed to find sarcastic amusement in everything, Angelina appeared quiet and composed. Monotonous in the most frightening way.

My eyes narrowed on her beautiful, familiar face. If the eyes were dark brown, and the skin more wrinkled around the eyes, she'd look exactly like . . .

I gasped. *Isobel.*

My horror multiplied exponentially. Isobel. The powerful, aged High Priestess of the Eastern Network. My new friend. She'd been Angelina all along. My trusted companion that helped me save Brecken, that loaned me her Volare. I grabbed the wall to keep from falling. It wouldn't have mattered. I wasn't really there; she'd trapped me in an ominous in-between.

You made your weakness clear. Angelina's voice sounded amused, and for a second, her blue eyes flickered to where I stood.

A thousand questions spun through my mind. What of Niko? Did Diego know? Had she killed them already in her bid to take over the world? Why had she posed as my friend? Where did Miss Mabel fit into all this?

"No, Derek," Angelina said, pulling me from my frantic thoughts. "You never have left a fight, have you? You've proven a formidable foe, which Mildred must have suspected about you. My daughter had good reason to fear your innate strength. If it weren't for you and that vile witch Mildred, I'd already be the most powerful witch in Antebellum."

"Forgive me for not apologizing," he retorted.

Angelina didn't smile the way Miss Mabel would have. She regarded him through tempered eyes.

"I don't like it when witches stand in my way," she continued as if he hadn't spoken. "Fortunately, you won't stall me anymore. I have you right where I want you."

Papa kept a wary eye on both of them. *Transport!* I screamed in my head, but I knew he wouldn't. Papa would never back down. Not even at the expense of his life. Is this what Isadora had seen? Is this what she said must take place so that the Network could be saved?

"I don't fear you the way Dane does," Papa said. "I fight my own wars."

"You may try battling me with curses or a silly Mactos, but Almorran magic is infinitely stronger than yours. It will absorb any puny attempt at harming me. Almorran magic is a power unto itself, you understand, and draws all spells into its own strength. Use magic against me, and I'll crush you with it."

Papa seemed unimpressed. "Let's end this war on my Network, shall we?"

Angelina's expression didn't waver. "You're so certain you can? If you don't fear me yet, perhaps I simply haven't given you a reason."

Papa's sword fell. He dropped to his knees with a shout. His knuckles and hands tensed until the skin blanched. His head dropped back on his shoulders as he silently screamed; his arms and legs writhed. Both Angelina and Dane stared at Papa as he fell into the water, his body contorting.

No! I screamed into the nothing of the space from which I watched. *Papa, no!*

My heart cramped in incomprehensible pain. What if Isobel—Angelina—had brought me here to watch Papa's death? Mama's gray eyes flickered through my mind again and again. No, I couldn't bear losing Papa. Not this way. Not ever.

"What do you think now, Derek?" Angelina asked when the awful tremors ceased. His body spasmed. He tucked his head into his chest with a groan. "That's what I thought. Your pathetic magic renders you nothing against my power. You might as well be a mortal for all you can do against the Almorran Master, you fool."

Almorran Master. Just as Isadora had speculated. Papa pushed a hand against a rock and slowly, one breath at a time, straightened up, out of the water. Under Angelina's scrutiny he rose, nostrils flaring, face contorted, to stand on his own two feet. Rivulets of water dripped off his armor when he held out a trembling hand, and his sword leapt back to his grip.

"It's going to take more than that," he muttered, voice hoarse. Angelina sighed.

"Very well."

Papa fell again, dropping his sword a second time. His body splashed in the water, writhing. This time he yelled through clenched teeth, his eyes shut in agony. It went on and on until the moments felt like hours.

"You'll kill him," Dane whispered. Angelina's eyes glowed a fanatical red. Magic exploded through my chest, tripling my power in an instant.

"What a pleasure that would be."

"At the expense of your other plans?" Dane asked.

Power ran through me in long, desperate rivulets. "Angelina!" I roared, putting all the force of my building magic behind the words. This time my voice reverberated through the cave, through whatever strange spell she had over me. Dane glanced up in surprise, though his darting eyes didn't see me. "If you kill him, I swear on my life that your daughter will never leave the dungeons."

The vile magic infusing pain into Papa's body paused. He went limp, head falling back against a rock. His eyes rolled back in his head, and for a moment he looked so pale I thought I was too late.

"Go on, Bianca," Angelina said, her eyes falling right on me. "Explain yourself."

"I'm the only one with enough of Papa's blood in my veins to let Miss Mabel go," I continued, projecting my voice from the in-between where her Almorran powers entrapped me. "If Papa dies, I'll transport into the middle of the ocean with a rock tied to my legs so that no one can ever release the magic. Your daughter will rot in the dungeons, bound there until she dies."

Dane stepped back against the wall, unsure of where my voice came from. My wrath echoed through the cave in great swells. Angelina closed her eyes and then opened them right onto me.

What exactly did you have in mind? she asked, her voice rippling again. This time she spoke into my mind, and I answered in the same way, drenching the cave in an unnatural quiet.

Miss Mabel for Papa, I said, giving no thought to what it would mean for the Central Network or the war. No thought to what it would mean for me. No thought to how I'd do it.

Interesting. I'm not inclined to let Derek live. Perhaps I'll just compel you to release my daughter.

It doesn't work like that. The magic of the dungeon will only work if I do it willingly. You know that though, don't you? That's why you haven't tried compelling me to do it before. That's why we're both here, isn't it?

Angelina's lips pursed in thought. I waited, fists clenched. Papa still hadn't moved. The gentle rise and fall of his chest gave me a weak reassurance that he still lived for now. Angelina turned to Dane. "Bind Derek," she commanded.

"Your Greatness, I—"

"Bind him!"

Dane fell to his knees with a grunt, displaying a subdued version of the same painful jerking motions that had overcome Papa. Dane's agony ended within moments. He regained his footing, his face pale, though resigned, as if this happened often enough. "Yes, Your Greatness."

Why are you doing this? I asked. *Why do you want to destroy Antebellum?*

Because I can.

We stared at each other for so long the edges of my vision began to blur, forming a halo around her.

You'll never win, I said. *Not ever. We won't let you.*

She smiled, and a cold chill ran through my bones. *With Mabel on my side, I have already won,* she replied. *Together my daughter and I shall finally have what we've worked for so long for. If you had a* little less spunk and a little more intelligence, I might have invited you along. Mabel certainly thought you'd come in handy one day, and she was right.

The dream blurred, until I no longer saw the scene in the cave. Instead, I flashed back to my visit to Magnolia Castle after the invasion. I watched it unfold again, as if I were there. Isobel sat in her chair, concern on her kind, aged face.

"Bianca, I'm so sorry for your Network," she had said. *"You seem genuinely scared."*

I saw myself responding, my voice echoing in a dreamlike state. *"Not for me but for everyone else, for my friends."*

"You're very self-sacrificing."

"They mean so much to me."

"Are your friends safe? Are they at the castle with you?"

"Yes, they're fine. Leda is busier than ever helping Jansson in Chatham City. The others are . . . getting by."

My stomach clenched with disbelief when I saw Leda throwing Jansson out of the way while blue and white light exploded around them. *I* had done it. Angelina had gone after Leda because I'd mentioned her.

Knowing how much your friends meant to you proved quite helpful, Angelina said, and the scene wafted away like receding smoke. *You were an open book, even if you were too stupid and stubborn to listen to me after I almost killed your friend Leda.*

But you didn't kill her, I said. *Leda saw what was about to happen. She saved Jansson.*

My response didn't provoke Angelina, the way it would have Miss Mabel. She blinked, not caring.

You're right. You and your friends ended up being resourceful.

I heard myself say, *I travel with Marten to the border towns quite often.* My stomach twisted in horror and disbelief. I'd told her that when we had first met over hot chocolate and cookies. I'd played into her hand like a little kitten.

Knowing that you travelled with Marten so much made it only too convenient, Angelina continued as soon as my voice faded away, *to have the Southern Network attack when I knew you and Marten would* be there. *I encouraged Niko to push Diego to complain about the black market trading, which drew you down there just before the invasion. I had plans for you to be taken hostage in the chaos, but somehow you escaped the West Guards waiting for you.*

A hazy image of two West Guards chasing me resurfaced from my memory. I recalled the heady beating of my heart in my ears, the way Letum Wood saved me from such a horrible fate.

And then the best part of all was when you confirmed my suspicions, Angelina said, conjuring up another memory from our second visit. I saw it happen with a heavy sense of shame.

What is your father's plan? Isobel had asked me. *Perhaps if I can tell Diego, I may convince him to help.*

The urge to vomit curled up in my stomach. If I'd had a body in that trancelike state, I would have fallen to my knees.

I think he's going to try to go after Dane, I had told my friend, Isobel, in confidence.

It seemed likely that was Derek's next move, but the confirmation did help me move a few final pieces into place. Now, she gestured to Papa's prostrate form on the ground, *I have you and your father right where I want you. You have two hours to release my daughter. Mabel will know where to find me. Bring her to me, and I'll have your father for you. What happens after that is entirely up to you.*

The shame burned so hot in my throat I almost couldn't breathe. I forced myself to calm, to stay in the moment. I never thought I'd face a witch more cunning and infuriating than Miss Mabel.

But I had been wrong oh-so-many times.

Sign a binding right now, I said, fist clenched. *Or I won't do a damn thing for you.*

Angelina conjured a parchment out of vapors.

It will be in your bedroom when you awake, she said in her strange, calm manner. *Two hours.*

Will You Help Me?

I shot awake with a gasp.

Chilly air embraced me. Evening shadows filled the apartment, the setting sun covered by thick storm clouds churning in the sky. I sat upright so fast my head whirled. A rolled piece of parchment waited next to me on the table. I yanked it open to find a damning witness to the greatest of all my nightmares.

I bind myself in agreement to keep Derek Black alive until such time as my daughter is safely delivered into my care and no longer in the dungeons.

Her signature swooped across the bottom. *Angelina.*

The letter caused a wash of shame to spill over me. Angelina wasn't Angelina, not really. She was Isobel. She was death and darkness and betrayal. I'd been duped. I closed my fist around the binding. I had to make this right. I had to have my revenge.

One way or another.

I pushed off the couch, grateful that I remembered every event without the strange haze of a dream to get in the way. I needed help. The moment I showed up with Miss Mabel, I had to get Papa out of there, or both of us would die. Just as I shoved my hair out of my eyes and settled on a haphazard new plan, a letter fluttered in front of my face and unfolded itself.

I'm with Jansson saving Chatham City, Leda's handwriting said. *I'll find you when I'm safe again. Don't worry about me, but I'm seeing only darkness for you. Be safe.*

"Saving Chatham City?" I muttered in confusion. "What?"

A loud noise reverberated through the room. I crinkled Leda's letter in my fist and tossed it into the cold bank of coals, wondering where Reeves had gone.

"Bianca!" Merrick yelled, banging on the door. "Open up!"

The door slammed open against the wall on my command. Merrick barreled inside, a bloody split down the middle of his bottom lip. Once his eyes fell on me, he let out a breath of relief.

"Good. You're all right. The Western Network is attacking," he said, rushing to the window and glancing outside. "They've broken through the Borderlands and are moving through the Western Covens toward Chatham City. Zane sent me to take you to Newberry, where it should be safest."

"What?"

"The West Guards are pushing through the Western Covens as we speak, moving across the land to invade Chatham City," he repeated impatiently. "But the Factios will probably take over long before they arrive. I need to get you out of here."

I hurried to the window to find fire spreading through pockets of Chatham City. A strange popping sound came from the distance. If the Factios controlled Chatham City and the West Guards were on their way, Chatham Castle would be at the mercy of invaders.

Of Angelina.

"The gypsies," I whispered, whirling around to face him. "Are the gypsies fighting? Can they hold the city?"

"I think they're fighting, but whether they're able to hold the city or not I don't know. It doesn't look good. Jansson just removed Clive as Coven Leader and took over the entire thing. Jansson has a fast mind, so there might be a chance. Tiberius is occupied with a new wave of attacks from the Southern Network and can't help."

Leda's letter suddenly made more sense.

"He has Leda," I said. "She can help more than you think."

"We can't spare many Guardians to help Chatham City because they're trying to stop the South and West Guards." Merrick painted a bleak picture. How bleak he didn't even know.

So this was Angelina's final push. Her attempt to take over the world would culminate tonight. Papa captured. Her daughter set free.

The Central Network attacked on three fronts. I pushed all the news away. The Network could take care of itself. It had to. In the meantime, I had to save Papa or die trying.

"Have you seen Papa?" I asked.

"What?"

"Where's Papa?"

Merrick's jaw tightened, and his nostrils flared. "He's on a mission."

"Do you know where?"

"No," he lied, as he was supposed to.

"Does Zane?"

"Yes."

"Tell Zane that he has to go to Papa now. We might not be too late. Maybe Zane can save him."

Merrick's eyes narrowed. "Bianca, what's—"

"Just do it!" I cried. The binding in my hand was proof enough that everything I'd witnessed was real, but I had to be sure. What if Angelina was trying to trick me? What if none of that had actually happened, but I thought it had, and I let Miss Mabel go free? I couldn't underestimate Angelina in any regard. "Trust me! Angelina . . . she's . . . just go!"

Merrick hesitated. "I'm supposed to take you to Stella's old estate in Newberry. It's not safe here. It was a direct order from the Head of Protectors."

"Angelina has Papa. Zane might be able to help. Maybe he can find him, I don't know. But not if you're wasting time. *Go!*"

I shoved him toward the door. His eyes held just enough panic to reassure me that he'd do what I said and ask questions later. He paused in the doorway, swallowing.

"Don't do anything stupid, Bianca."

"*Go!*"

After shooting me one last murderous look of frustration, he disappeared. I summoned Viveet with an incantation. The clock on the wall taunted me with every tick of its hand.

You have two hours.

Only one witch would know how to help me break into the dungeons and get Papa home. If Isadora had really been convinced this was the only way to end the war, she'd be waiting for me.

"I hope you're home, Isadora," I murmured, transporting into the night.

The trees of Letum Wood whipped past my face as I ran for Isadora's cottage alone, promise to Stella forgotten. What did it matter now? Angelina didn't have to hunt for me. She had me right in her hideous claws.

I'd transported close to Isadora's cottage but not right to it, giving myself a stretch of trail to let my legs fly free. The dragon that had lived in my heart resurfaced with a vengeful fury. My fingertips tingled with power, so much stronger than I had ever been before. If I wanted to make it through the night, I needed an outlet for the rampant energy stirred by the image of Papa screaming in pain. My feet had numbed to the discomfort of stepping on rocks and roots, and I flew with the speed of a bird of prey.

Isadora's cottage came sooner than I expected, or maybe I'd run faster than I thought. The worst flares of rage had calmed when I stormed up her porch and threw myself into her cottage.

"Isadora!" I cried, my chest heaving. "I need to—"

"I know, Bianca," she said, lifting a hand to stop me. She stood in the middle of her cottage, as if she had known I was coming after all. "Sanna and I have been waiting for you."

I doubled over, my ribs aching, my sides cramped. Sanna and Isadora exchanged a knowing look—never mind that Sanna was supposed to be blind—and waited for me to catch my breath.

"I need—"

"I've seen what you need already."

"Great. Will you . . . help me?"

"I cannot go with you to save your father, but I can aid you now."

"With releasing Miss Mabel? Can you help me break her free?" The sudden worry that my deal with the Almorran Master had been too hasty overcame me. Perhaps I had promised something that could not be. Releasing Miss Mabel might unleash a far greater evil power. But to forfeit Papa's life on a chance?

To just let Angelina win?

Isadora and Sanna exchanged another cryptic glance, as if they didn't need sight to really see each other. "Are you ready?" Isadora asked her sister. Sanna nodded.

"So is the blue."

"Then get going. You'll need all the time you can get. Go with speed and safety."

Sanna hesitated, throwing her blind eyes in my direction. "Be safe, sister," she said in a raspy voice. "Our lives are tied together. Nicolas still hasn't bonded with the purple, and I don't fancy it will happen without me there to help."

Sanna disappeared with a soft sigh of moving air. I opened my mouth to ask Isadora what their strange conversation meant, but she cut me off.

"There is no other way to save Antebellum than to release Miss Mabel." Her confidence gave me a boost of strength I desperately needed. "You must go forward with your plan even though I sense much doubt and frustration on your part. You're doing exactly what needs to be done."

I sensed an undercurrent in her words, something that went deeper than saving my father. A heavy knot in my chest formed where my heart used to be.

"What do you mean?"

"Angelina will take over Chatham City tonight unless we stop her. The moment Chatham City falls, so does the castle, and then the Central Network. This is her final plan. She wants her daughter at her side to share the victory."

I swallowed. As if the cards weren't stacked enough against us tonight, adding one more dimension to the already complicated fight made me nervous. But at least it meant Angelina needed Papa or me to release Miss Mabel. Which meant I still had a chance.

"How do we stop Angelina?"

"*We* don't. We aren't powerful enough, not against such dark magic."

My heart plummeted. "Then who? This can't be all for nothing."

"Mabel. She's the only one who can."

"What?" I fell to my knees, unable to take one more surprise. "Miss Mabel will fight her mother? But Angelina said they are going to rule together."

Isadora grimaced. "Mabel will gladly destroy Angelina, if my interpretation is right, anyway, and I've never been wrong."

"If she defeats Angelina, we're just delaying the war," I said. "Miss Mabel will try to take over, just as Angelina is now."

Isadora agreed with a low hum. "Yes, but it gives us a chance to fight. Freedom is earned, Bianca. Not given. No witch is infallible. Angelina can fall, and so can Mabel. Let us hope on that. Releasing Miss Mabel will change the future in a way that may enable us to find the *Book of Light*."

"But you don't know for sure that it will."

"No. Nothing is certain."

The mention of the book granted me a moment of courage. At least Isadora hadn't given up on it. "Angelina is Isobel," I added bitterly. Isadora nodded once but betrayed nothing with her expression. "I . . . I fell into her hands. I enabled all of this to happen. Isadora, this is all my fault!"

"No," she said. "It's not. You were too trusting, yes, but that says more about her than about you. This outcome would likely have come eventually, if not by some other way. You can make it right tonight, Bianca."

"Have you already seen what's going to happen?" I asked. "Can I save Papa by setting Miss Mabel free? Will that stop Angelina?"

"It's hard to say," Isadora said with great reluctance. "Without the *Book of Light*, we cannot prevent Angelina from conducting Almorran magic, which puts us at a heavy disadvantage. I don't know if we can stop Angelina or save your father."

"Is there even a small possibility that I could bring Papa back before Angelina kills him or both of us?"

She paused, and I let it ride, knowing she was looking into future possibilities. Whatever she saw must not have been good because the creases in her forehead deepened.

"You cannot," she concluded, "but Mabel can."

My eyes narrowed in disbelief. Miss Mabel would never save my father. The madness of this night just kept deepening.

"Time is counting down, my girl. Let us act now, or you'll run out of it completely. What do you know about the magic holding Miss Mabel in her cell?"

"I know it opens only to Papa's blood."

Isadora appraised me with narrowed eyes. "You're so much like Derek, this should work. It may cost a lot of power, for you are not Derek, but the lock should still open. The familiarity of your blood will be diluted. It's as simple as an incantation and a blood sacrifice."

"That's it?"

"Reversing complicated magic isn't as difficult as implementing it," she said, waving a book down from a high shelf. "I have the incantation here."

"How did you get a hold of the incantation? I thought it was only allowed to the Highest Witch."

Her eyes twinkled with dimmed pleasure. "Because your father trusts me without question." She rifled through the pages and glanced up at me once she found what she wanted. "Are you ready?"

"Yes."

"Good. Let's free Mabel and save our Network."

"There's no way this is going to work," I muttered, shaking my head. The door to Mrs. L's private chambers loomed in front of me, almost as foreboding as the task of releasing Miss Mabel. "Isadora is off her rocker if she thinks Mrs. L will help me do anything except walk into a cave of snakes."

Except for the dragons, no one hated my presence more than Mrs. L, the Head Housekeeper of Chatham Castle. My penchant for running around in bare feet and wreaking havoc with all my adventures meant she didn't trust me not to ruin the control she held over the castle. She'd been running Chatham for ages, some rumors said even before she turned twenty-five. Putting age on a woman like Mrs. L was unnatural. She was an eternal creature that belonged to the castle and somehow knew everything.

Seconds after I rapped on her door, it creaked open, revealing her pinched face. Dim candlelight flowed from her bedroom out to the hall, illuminating her from behind. To my relief, she still wore her uniform. Of course she did. The world could end tonight. No doubt she'd be busy making sure the castle remained clean while it fell.

"Merry meet, Mrs. L," I said, swallowing. "I came to request a favor."

If possible her thin face elongated even further. She said nothing.

"Well, Isadora sent me, actually. I need help."

"Isadora told me you'd be coming," she said, straightening. "I've been waiting for you, which is very kind of me considering all there is to do tonight. Wait right here."

She slammed the door in my face and returned moments later, a shawl around her shoulders.

"That's it?" I asked incredulously. "You're going to help me?"

She rolled her eyes. "Believe it or not, Bianca Monroe, I was once a young witch like you." I certainly didn't believe it, but I kept my mouth shut. She continued. "I lived in days that were dark and frightening as well. When a witch like Isadora asks a favor, I do it without wanting or needing an explanation. Now follow me," she finished with a snap. "I haven't got all night."

Not daring to protest, I did as she instructed.

We wound through the castle with impressive speed, seeing no one else along the way. She stopped unexpectedly on a deserted stretch of stone hall and pressed her hand to a wall on my left. A flash of light formed at the tip of her fingers and transferred into the stones. They moaned, shuddered, and a small portion of the wall, just large enough for me to duck through, peeled away. A wave of frigid, musty air billowed out of the space.

"It worked," she said in relief while stepping back. "I haven't used that spell in some time. Follow the stairs down. Make two rights. When you come upon a dead end, press your hand to it, and it will let you in. You won't get back through that way unless you have the right incantation, which you don't and never will," she added with a haughty tilt of her chin. "So don't mess up."

"Where does it end?"

"The dungeons."

I should have been surprised that she had a mental map of the dungeons of all places, but I wasn't.

"Thank you," I said. I didn't know the dungeons well enough to transport there, and using that magic would draw the Guardians, who would ask questions I wasn't prepared to answer. Sneaking through the castle without being seen would be infinitely easier through the secret passageways.

"I won't presume to understand why you're doing whatever it is you are doing," Mrs. L said as if I hadn't thanked her, "nor do I want to even know what it is, but I can understand that desperate times call for desperate measures. Whatever you do, don't mess it up."

On that note, Mrs. L spun on her heel and departed. I stared at the open passageway with a moment's hesitation before plunging inside.

Infinitely More

The dungeons were filthy and disgusting when I wasn't trying to slink through them, but all my heightened senses made their raunchy stink far worse.

Because the Guardians used magic to prevent the escape of criminals, only a few Guardians worked in the dungeons now. They were more needed in the war. I heard steps only once, and I ducked into an empty cell until they passed. After that, all I could hear was the drip of water in the background, the occasional scream of someone driven mad with boredom, and the restless clink of metal on stone.

I didn't know where I was at first, so it took me at least twenty minutes to orient myself in the darkness. When I finally found the door leading into Miss Mabel's personal prison, a cold rush of dread gripped my heart like a fist.

Here I was, facing Miss Mabel yet again.

"For Papa," I whispered, opening the door with the spell that I'd overheard him use before. The heavy wooden door creaked on old hinges, admitting a single sliver of light. One lone torch burned in the close cell, barely illuminating the bars that held Miss Mabel prisoner.

"Merry meet, Bianca, darling. I had a feeling you'd be back."

I stepped into the room, fists clenched, paying wary attention to the building magic in my chest. Just being near her made me want to rake my fingernails across her face.

"Miss Mabel."

"Oh, you are quite angry, aren't you? Angelina must have found your nerve, did she? She always does."

Miss Mabel moved into the dim light, wrapping a bumpy white

hand around the bars. Something of her original beauty still lingered in her bright eyes and cold smile, though I hardly recognized it behind the wrinkled old face she'd always hidden from the world. I let a blip of power slip away from my heart and pressed it all into her. Miss Mabel flew back, slamming into the wall behind her with a trickle of stone and dust in her hair.

"Cut the jokes. We need to make an agreement."

Her eyes gleamed with a maniacal enjoyment I'd seen before. "Are you here to set me free after all? How delightful. I thought this day would come."

I stared at her with equal parts loathing, equal parts hope. She could help me save Papa, perhaps the Central Network—for a while—though she'd want to destroy both herself later.

"Come, Bianca, don't look so murderous. Although the hatred I feel from you is delightful." She shuddered with pleasure.

"You're nothing like your mother," I said, unsure of which was worse: Miss Mabel's cynical amusement or Angelina's vapid indifference.

Miss Mabel tilted her head back and laughed, her scraggly, uneven hair falling onto bony shoulders. "Thank you for the compliment. I worked hard to avoid becoming like Mother dearest."

I reached out to touch the prison bars, feeling faint in my heart for just a moment. Release the murderer who killed my mother and the High Priestess? Who also threatened to destroy all I loved? A deep breath, and a renewed vision of Papa screaming, increased my courage. Isadora had told me what I needed to do to release the magic.

"I'm here to set you free."

Miss Mabel withdrew, slinking back to the shadows.

"Now that I think about it, I don't believe I want to leave," she said in a bored, singsong voice. "I find the confinement relaxing after so many years in a school full of noisy, emotional teenage girls."

"Right," I muttered. "Because *you* had so much interaction with the students."

"I appreciate what you're doing, Bianca, but I'd rather stay here."

Her rotting smile still shone in the deep darkness. She was playing her cards. She wanted me to beg, to plead, to put the power in her hands. Two could play that game. Miss Mabel had no idea what was going on in the outside world, which meant she had no idea how much she stood to lose tonight. If her hatred for Angelina ran as deep as Isadora suspected, I could use it against her.

"Fine," I said, pulling away. "I'll leave you to rot in prison while Angelina takes over the castle tonight."

She sucked in a breath, fighting between her interest and her desire to prove I had nothing important to say. Her curiosity won out. "Oh really?"

I met her sharp gaze. "Really. *Mother dearest* is moving forward without you. The West Guards are attempting to cross the Western Covens as we speak, and the Factios are tearing apart Chatham City. Even the Southern Network is attacking. Chatham City will fall soon enough, which means so will the castle and the Central Network. Apparently she doesn't need you around. She'll be the greatest witch in all of Antebellum without your aid."

Miss Mabel's eyes flashed. "The West Guards have pushed into the Central Network without my command, have they?" she murmured, her eyes brewing a hot, blue storm. "Poor little Dane has been a naughty boy."

She stepped back into the dim light of the torch flickering lazily behind me, as if it, too, were weary of its imprisonment beneath the earth. She studied me for one breathless moment, the cogs behind her eyes whirring. "What do you want from me, Bianca?"

"I want you to kill your mother."

Miss Mabel's thin gray eyebrows rose. "Is this the first time we've wanted the same thing?"

"And I want you to save my father," I added.

Her face fell, but a smile still lingered in the corners of her eyes. "No, I suppose we don't want the same thing. For a moment there I thought you and I could fight together, you know. A real dynamic duo we'd make. Just *how* dynamic you have no idea, for there's much I suspect you still don't know about yourself. The offer still stands."

"I'll die before I fight alongside you."

"Now that can be arranged. What trouble has Derek gotten himself into?"

"Angelina is holding him hostage in exchange for you."

"Ah!" she cried. "So Mother does want to see me. She adores me, you know. She doesn't even realize how much I loathe her for abandoning me on the doorstep of Grandmother's school. I suppose now is as good a time as any to defeat her."

She spoke idly, more to herself than me.

"How convenient that you want her dead as much as I do."

"No," she hissed, her eyes flaring. "I want it infinitely more."

"I'll only set you free on one condition," I said, venturing closer until I stood within reach of her nasty hands. The wrinkles around her eyes cast deep shadows.

"You're starting to sound more like me, Bianca. I'd be proud except I really don't care about you."

"I'll release you from prison and go with you to meet Angelina if you vow to transport Papa back here before Angelina kills him."

"You'll set me free whether I make the vow or not. If you don't, Angelina will kill him and take over the world, and you and all your friends will burn in the painful fires of Almorran magic."

I leaned into the bars, separating our faces by a mere breath.

"And you'll die watching your mother achieve what you weren't good enough for. She's taking over Antebellum without you, and she'll rule it without you as well. Are you ready, after an entire lifetime of living under her thumb, to watch her achieve greatness as the ruler of Antebellum? She will gain everything she wants, while you remain in this cold prison cell. Make the vow, or I'll leave you here to rot in your own failure for the rest of your life."

Miss Mabel snarled, but I didn't retreat. We met each other fury for fury.

"Fine," she spat. "I'll make the vow to save Derek, but I can't say that I'll be able to save you. No doubt Angelina wants to rip all the hair from your scalp piece by piece." She smiled coyly. "She's done that to witches before, you know."

She held out her arm through the bars of the dungeon cell. I stared at her skinny wrist, the bones and blood beneath it. Her veins appeared a bright blue-green underneath her translucent skin. I took her cold arm in my grasp and suppressed the urge to release it.

Sensing my imminent use, power curled again in my chest, warm and reassuring. I was the one in control here.

"I vow to take you to Angelina. In return, you must transport my father back to his personal apartment here at Chatham Castle and away from harm the moment we arrive."

I would have added an addendum *and you may not kill me*, but a vow didn't work on multiple lines. I could only specify one promise on each side, which meant I'd throw myself at the mercy of fate.

"Oh, you've learned your lesson, haven't you? I'm glad I could teach you something. Very good, specific details to include, or I would have sent sweet Derek into the hands of the Factios leaders." She smiled. "I accept."

Instead of the usual warmth spiraling from my fingertips and through my arm, a telltale cold slipped into my veins. It wound through my arm and ended at my chest, blossoming in a chilly explosion. Nothing good could come from Miss Mabel. Our hands broke apart when the magic faded.

"What about you?" Miss Mabel asked with false levity, one eyebrow raised. "If Derek escapes, you can be sure Angelina won't let you get away."

I ground my teeth together, pulled Viveet half out of her sheath, and slipped the pad of my little finger along the sharp blade. A bubble of blood popped up from under the skin.

"That's something I'll deal with later," I said, grabbing the lock in my hand, ensuring the bloody tip of my finger rested on the top.

Miss Mabel grinned. "You and your family have always been so self-sacrificing, you silly witch," she murmured, her eyes alight. "Saving your own life is something you'll need to figure out. Angelina doesn't take kindly to being preempted."

I used silent magic to activate the incantation Isadora had shown me from the ancient grimoire dating back to the Mortal Wars. My blood dripped down the lock's face. The air vibrated around us, pulsing in long waves that hurt my ears. A wall of air moved from my feet and up, stirring our hair. The incantation pulled the magic it required from me like it removed part of my soul. Once I finished, the lock broke apart in my hand, disintegrating into dust. I pulled the door open, trying to hide the wave of weakness that overcame my body.

"You're free," I croaked.

Miss Mabel smiled and stepped through the door. I moved back to avoid touching her. "Indulge me for a moment," she said. "It's not classy to defeat one's enemy looking like this. Oh, magic. How delightful. I've missed it!"

Within seconds her skin glowed with bubbles and pockets of light that broke out across her arms and face. The wrinkles tightened. The crow's feet disappeared. Her lips became plump and lush and cherry red again. Rays of light slipped down her hair and shot out the ends until it lay in full, silky blonde splendor. Her bony shoulders disappeared, as did the limp rag she'd worn. A beautiful sapphire brocade dress replaced it, slipping all the way down to her dainty feet clad with new sandals.

When she turned to face me again, I saw the same sultry Miss Mabel I'd always known. Seeing her in her full, lustrous glory made her seem like an illusion, not a real witch.

"Now I'm ready, Bianca," she said with a contented sigh. "Shall we go meet Mother dearest? I know right where she'll be."

I braced myself for the worst. "I'm ready. Transport me with you since you have so much power."

She grinned. "I do. Isn't it wonderful? Hold your breath. It's a long ride over."

I landed on a soft beach of sand.

The sharp tang of salty air made my eyes water as it burned my nostrils. My finger still stung from the cut, but a healing incantation had stopped the bleeding.

"This way," Miss Mabel said, motioning with a tilt of her head to the right. Magnolia Castle loomed off to the left, its many floors illuminated with torchlight. Shadows shifted inside, servants moving about their business, I assumed. I wondered if they knew who Isobel really was, if her betrayal extended to the family she had once seemed to love. For some reason, knowing she'd betrayed them as well as me softened my shame. I wasn't her only victim.

Waves lapped at my ankles, soaking the hem of my dress. The soft spray of stars in the midnight sky would have reassured me if it had been any other night. Tonight, they felt vast and cold.

We started walking toward the high cliffs whose sheer rock faces plunged into the depths of the ocean. The waves broke in explosions of salty white spray. A familiar foreboding shrank my pounding heart in my chest. Miss Mabel stopped at the mouth of a cave hidden in the many crevices of rock jutting out from the cliff. The sand lay undisturbed, as if a foot had never trodden it.

She sent me a sidelong glance. "Are you ready?"

"Are you?"

She smiled. "I've been ready for this moment my whole life," she replied easily, moving into the cave. "Follow me. Hopefully you don't mind wet feet. The tide will be moving into this cave soon, so it will only get deeper."

The darkness swallowed us in moments. I couldn't see and shuffled through the ankle-deep water under only a vague impression of where Miss Mabel moved in front of me. The brush of a cold, wet wall against my left shoulder startled me at first, but I put my hand out as a guide and followed it. The curve of the cave steered us to the right, and I paused, sucking in a deep breath. Light bled around a familiar corner.

I'd been here before.

"A little further," she murmured happily, and I forced my feet to follow. Around the corner came a familiar open arena illuminated by torchlight. It made me feel like I was drowning in rocks and earth. Papa lay on the floor, his right eye swollen shut, and his dark hair mussed. I held my breath, watching as his chest lifted slowly and fell again. I could see neither Dane nor Angelina, but I knew she lurked somewhere in the shadow.

"Ah! He's alive," Miss Mabel said. "What a disappointment."

She didn't stop me when I rushed forward and fell to my knees at Papa's side. He'd been lying in the rising ocean water, hands bound behind his back.

"Papa? Can you hear me?" He didn't answer. I quickly checked over him with my hands, my eyes roving over everything I could see. One bound arm was broken. His nose appeared crooked, and a bluish bruise had formed under his right eye. I murmured a few healing incantations, but they didn't soothe the gash on his arm or even out his raspy breathing. Why wasn't my magic working?

"Wonderful to see both of you here."

A wall of oppressive evil announced Angelina, and I struggled to take in a breath. My gaze caught movement on the far side of the cave. Angelina stepped away from a dark wall and into the light, her gleaming eyes resting on me. I stopped, heart in my throat.

Now, Miss Mabel, I thought. *Transport him now!*

"Mother," Miss Mabel said, inclining her head. "How nice to see you again." Her once maniacal eyes had grown cool, if not bored, but she acutely assessed the situation. Her gaze flickered from shadow to shadow, as if she were trying to take in every single detail, right down to the last torch.

Angelina surveyed her daughter with an open, affectionate gaze. "You as well, dearest girl. Are you all right? I am relieved to see you again. I've been quite worried."

"As well as can be expected after so long in the dungeons. Couldn't break through Derek's defenses?"

A blaze of indignation showed in Angelina's gaze but faded. "Something like that," she murmured, turning back to me. "You have him, Bianca. I fulfilled my part of the binding. But you won't get far before I take my revenge on both of you."

Miss Mabel stepped forward. *Do it!* I willed her, keeping my eyes on Angelina. *You made a vow!*

"Forgive me," Miss Mabel said with a sarcastic smile, "but I have a vow to fulfill."

Papa disappeared, as if he had never been there. A breath of relief escaped me, and I gave into the momentary weakness and leaned my palms into the cool sand. Angelina's nostrils flared with rage, and her skin turned white in a rare display of emotion. Miss Mabel had never looked more pleased.

"You think you're smarter than me, Bianca Monroe?" Angelina

hissed, stepping toward me. I rose, unwilling to die on my knees. "Perhaps I shall just have to show you how smart I can be about punishing annoying brats."

I didn't have time to respond. A violent tug on my navel jerked me backward into the wall. My head and shoulders slammed into a jutting stone, and the telltale warmth of blood dripped down my scalp within moments. Bright spots popped into my blurry vision. I kicked my legs to find that I hung suspended from the wall, stunned as a rag doll. Fire shot underneath my skin in long bursts of pain. It started at my fingertips, raged past my elbows, and zipped into my shoulders. I screamed.

Do you feel the pain, Bianca?

Angelina's voice stirred up memories. Grandmother's grave. Papa leaving. Mama dying in my arms. I relived every exquisite, agonizing moment. I heard screams again and again, only to realize they weren't echoes from my mind but came from my own throat.

This is nothing compared to what your father endured, Angelina said. *Shall I turn it up a notch?*

The red-hot flames crawled from my shoulders to my collarbones, dancing around my neck with threatening force. My muscles burned like smoldering coals. There was no escape, no end. My heart bucked in agony in my chest, unable to bear it.

"Angelina, that's enough!"

The pain disappeared, and I fell into the water. A small body appeared in between Angelina and me with a flash of blinding light. All three of us recoiled from the unexpected brightness. When I glanced up, Isadora's curved, old back stood just a breath away from me. An indescribable light lingered around her. Angelina stepped back, her lips curling in disgust.

"Isadora, you meddling old witch."

"You shall not harm this child," Isadora said, her voice ringing out clear and firm. "She is under my protection."

"By what power?" Angelina snarled.

"My power." Isadora's voice boomed with authority. "Rooted in goodness and light."

"Not even goodness can defeat Almorran magic, foolish hag."

"Perhaps it cannot banish the evil of Almorran magic alone, but it can fight, and it will, through me. You overestimate your own ability, Angelina, and underestimate the power of courage and loyalty, just like your mother did."

The palpable evil in the air around Angelina faded when Isadora stood close to me, her presence repelling the darkness. I sucked in a deep breath, grateful to feel my lungs expand and the sharp shooting pains subside. The air didn't weigh so heavily on my shoulders.

Miss Mabel grinned with one side of her lips, then clapped. "Oh, how delightful to see you here, Isadora. Isn't this wonderful, Mother? There's no one my family loves more than a powerful Watcher."

Angelina's knuckles clenched so tightly they turned white, but her face remained calm and in control. "Why have you come?" she asked Isadora. "You never meddle in things unless you have an angle. Isn't that some code for your kind?"

"My reasons are my own."

"Are they?" Angelina asked, an eyebrow rising.

Isadora stared at her without flinching. I held my breath, so grateful to see Isadora that I nearly sank back to my knees again. Even under Isadora's protection, I could still feel Angelina's burning rage.

"Perhaps she's here to be a witness," Miss Mabel suggested. Her eyes had latched onto Angelina. Angelina pulled her eyes from Isadora to look at her daughter.

"Witness to what, my darling?"

"My ascension to power."

"Your what?"

"I should think it's fairly obvious to a witch of your intelligence and power, Almorran Master." Miss Mabel spread her hands in an innocent gesture. "I'm going to take over now."

We rode in a long pause until Angelina tilted her head back in haughty appraisal. Something flickered in the depths of her eyes, though her inscrutable expression gave me little idea what it meant. "Take over?"

Miss Mabel smiled. Not even the comforting crash of the waves broke the monotonous silence. Nothing sounded but the echo of my pounding heart. The rigid tension expanded to fill the cave, as if they were trying to force each other out.

"Isadora," I whispered. "We must go. We'll never survive if they fight with Almorran—"

"Do you trust me, Bianca?" she asked so quietly I almost didn't hear. I hesitated.

"Yes."

"We must stay."

"But—"

"I've seen it all," she whispered, her voice wavering. The edges of her eyes had begun to droop, and I wondered if protecting me drained her. "Trust me. If you want to defeat Miss Mabel in the end, we must stay. I will protect you from Angelina."

Can you protect me from Miss Mabel? I wanted to ask, but I bit my bottom lip instead. "I thought you couldn't help me."

"I couldn't come with you," she said softly. "Angelina would have detected me. But I can help you, and I'm here to do so."

"You want to betray me?" Angelina finally asked Miss Mabel, her eyes widening.

"In payment for leaving me on the doorstep of May's house and forcing me to endure the horror of living under her controlling, manipulative hand. In payment for the years of your control, your greed, your misplaced affection, your demands. You controlled me just like May. You left me!"

"I did what was best for you, darling. I . . ."

"You left me with her!"

Miss Mabel's shriek echoed off the walls. She calmed herself with a deep breath and lifted her chin. "I've been dreaming about it for over nine months now. I will kill you and take over Antebellum myself. This is the day of my revenge!"

Her words echoed through the cave. *My revenge.* Angelina blinked, as if she couldn't believe what she'd heard.

"Mabel, I left you with her because I loved you. I couldn't give you any kind of life, you know that. I was a vagabond! Homeless!" Her voice climbed a notch in desperation. "I wandered into the Eastern Network on the verge of death after giving birth to you. Until I married Diego, I had no one and nothing. I couldn't tell him the truth. He would never have married me if he'd known I had a living daughter. I watched you from a distance nearly every week until the day I met you in Letum Wood when you were ten."

Miss Mabel tilted her head back in a maniacal cackle. "You think you helped me by forcing me to live with May? You think I ever wanted your visits, your time?"

Angelina reared back as if she'd been struck. "Mabel . . . if you want to become the Almorran Master, you'll have to kill me first. Would you do that?"

Miss Mabel bowed. "Gladly."

The cave fell into complete darkness.

In Her Darkness

The bony ridge of Isadora's spine pressed into my chest when she forced me back into the cave wall, putting as much distance between Angelina, Miss Mabel, and ourselves as we could get in the confined area. Not even Isadora's power could shield me from the sudden, overwhelming terror of the damp darkness. After what felt like an eternity, the torches sprang back to life.

Shadows had descended, swamping Angelina in a flying cyclone of black magic. She didn't make a sound, but a sudden rush of surprise passed through her eyes. Moments later, the whirling windstorm around her faded, overpowered by a second rush of wind so strong it nearly tore me from the wall when it swept away Miss Mabel's cyclone. I held onto Isadora's shoulder to keep her from pitching forward.

"I left you because I loved you, Mabel," Angelina cried. "I had nothing and nowhere to go."

"You loved controlling me, just like May," Miss Mabel hissed. A pair of Clavas swept into the cave, shoving Angelina against the wall with a heavy *crack* of her body against stone. They hissed and howled, frothing at the mouth. Angelina winced, pinned in place by the half-living shadows, but didn't fight back. Whether she was stunned from Mabel's betrayal or slamming her head into the wall, I couldn't tell.

"How long have you planned this?" Angelina asked. "Why would you betray me?"

Miss Mabel rolled her eyes. "Since the beginning. I allowed Bianca to defeat me so I could hide in the dungeons, hoping you would get rid of Derek, but you couldn't even do that. I suppose I can dispatch him myself now." Miss Mabel's eyes flickered over to Isadora and me. "I have just what I need to defeat him."

Angelina's nostrils flared. "I did everything for you that I could," she whispered. Had she even heard Miss Mabel's explanation? "Everything. I shared the *Book of Spells* hoping we could rule together. I waited for you to learn it. I—"

"Was a fool," Mabel said. Her cold face, so emotionless and careless in the face of Angelina's pain, frightened me. "I never loved you, Mother dearest. Never."

Miss Mabel's face twisted with hate, Angelina's with something close to the awful agony of love and uncertainty. They remained locked in each other's gaze for so long that I felt as if Isadora had somehow paused time.

"I could never bring harm to you," Angelina whispered. "It is against my nature, against my instincts as your mother. I shall not fight you for my life. If you will not be at my side, I have no reason to live."

"So mote it be," Miss Mabel whispered. The Clavas released Angelina. She fell into the water with a splash. Mabel stepped forward and pressed her foot to Angelina's throat.

"This is how you will end it," Angelina whispered, choking. Water lapped at the side of her face, threatening to cover her mouth and nose. Black ropes sprung from the sand and anchored her down, arms and legs spread wide. "You'll get rid of me just as you got rid of May."

Miss Mabel paused, hovering over Angelina's prostrate body.

"Yes, I will. Just as I planned. Merry part, Mother dearest."

A cloud of black, ghoulish bats descended on Angelina, wrapping around her head and body until she lay in a cocoon of the blackest night. Miss Mabel stepped back with casual indifference, watching the bats draw the life from Angelina's struggling form. Her body twisted against the anchors, shrieking. Miss Mabel watched, her eyes on fire with delight and fury.

I ducked away, unable to watch.

The assault continued until I had to look out to see if it had ended. The evil in the room seemed to have sucked the very air from the cave. I sputtered and coughed, fighting against the unseen power that reigned so strong not even Isadora could battle it now. She stumbled, her strength waning.

"Merry part, Mother dearest," Miss Mabel sang as the life bled from Angelina's frame. As Angelina dimmed, Miss Mabel grew more sinister, as if she pulled the life from her mother and took it into herself. "It feels so good to finally achieve my long-awaited goal."

I blinked, peering through watery eyes to find the bats had disappeared. Angelina's skin shone an unearthly white, so pale not even the bite marks showed. The irises of her eyes and the flesh beneath her fingernails had turned white. In death, Angelina looked more like my friend Isobel than the evil Almorran Master.

Angelina's chest lifted up and down in weak spasms. Her lips moved, forming the word *Mabel,* but no sound came out. She died with her face twisted in a silent scream. The luscious appearance of her body faded, her beauty replaced with deep wrinkles, thin lips, and missing teeth. Her hair blew away on the wind, disintegrating into mere strands. The pale field of skin left on her body started to wear away, crumbling into the water until she was nothing but a pile of sand.

A circle of black fire wrapped around Miss Mabel. She tilted her head back, lifted her arms, and surrendered her body into it. The flames consumed her, swathing her in a coat of darkness. Silver danced in the heart of the fire, a color so cold I would have expected it to freeze anything it touched. Screeches rang in the background, like the demons of hell chanting for their new master. I covered my ears but could still hear it. The evil felt so hot I screamed in pain. Blisters formed on the backs of my arms when I lifted my hand to protect my face.

"This is it," Isadora whispered, turning away. "She's becoming the Almorran Master."

"Can't we stop it?"

"No."

My heart stalled when the curtain of ebony flames dropped to the floor, dissolving into a noxious cloud that hovered around Miss Mabel's feet. She turned to face us, and my breath disappeared.

Her once bright blue irises now smoldered red-hot, and her blue brocade had been replaced with a lacy dress the color of darkest night, simple in design but exquisite. The neckline plunged between her breasts, revealing milky-white skin. Her hair fluttered around her face in perfect blonde curls.

"How fitting that you of all witches should witness my triumphant rise to power, Bianca," Miss Mabel said, her powerful voice echoing through the cave. It seemed to break through my skin like hot talons. I grimaced. Every moment in her presence felt unbearable.

"You won, Mabel," Isadora said, as though not surprised. "Now you're the Almorran Master. What is your plan now?"

"Funny you should even ask," Miss Mabel said, the red centers of her eyes blazing. "You already know, don't you?"

"I see much."

"Yes," Miss Mabel murmured, "you do, don't you? You're the most powerful Watcher in Antebellum. You see my plan. You know that I will take you and Bianca back to the Western Network with me, don't you old lady? That's what you're getting at here."

My chest lurched. "It won't work," I said quietly. "You can kidnap and torture me and flaunt it to my father, but it will only make him more determined to destroy you."

Miss Mabel peered at me curiously, then closed her eyes. When she opened them again, the red had faded back to piercing blue. The moment our gazes met, I felt as if a knife had cleaved my brain into two pieces. I grabbed my head.

Merry meet, she crooned in my mind. *I've wanted to get inside your head for ages now, strange girl. Just when I think I have you figured out, you do something to surprise me. Are you really so foolish to think your father can win against me now that I'm the Almorran Master? He may have been stronger than me before now, but he isn't anymore.*

Get out! I wanted to scream, but I couldn't even think. Miss Mabel had invaded my mind with the same black presence Angelina once had. Unlike Angelina, however, I could feel Miss Mabel rooting through my head and I fell to my knees.

You are very brave, aren't you? But still hurting so much. So much worry for your father. So much . . . affection. It makes me sick. How can you live while worrying so much about someone else? Not caring is the true path, Bianca. It's very freeing.

Go away! I commanded, managing to think around the blackness taking up space in my mind. *You can't do this!*

Oh, but I can. You see, I'm very curious how a girl from such an intelligent, powerful family line would do such stupid things. The pain of losing your mother still lingers, I can feel it. But then, agony will always remain, no matter the source. It's what I love about it the most: Pain remains forever. An eternal fountain of power.

Her trespass into my mind—she filled all the crevices, read every single thought, saw every memory, imprinted herself on the good and bad alike—drove me mad.

I still think I could use a girl like you, you know, she continued as if we were having a lazy conversation on a beach. Her presence doubled with stifling power. *Now that Angelina is dead, I shall finalize my revenge and take over all of Antebellum on my own. And I will, you know. I've been successful so far, haven't I? Even—*

Something shifted with a discernible click. Her voice disappeared. My horror vanished with a burst of hot fire that ripped through my mind. I felt suddenly separated from myself, as if I had been scooped out of my own brain and deposited somewhere else. Somewhere dark, filled with blackness. A whisper sang in the background of the new place. It reminded me of an underground tunnel. Cold, haunted by images and the vague shapes of witches who had come before.

Wherever I was, I was not alone. Voices spoke in the background, moving around me like currents of wind.

She left me there with her. She left me.

I loved you, Mabel, from the moment I first saw you. But I couldn't keep you, so I left you with her. She could give you what I could not. Security. Food. Shelter. A chance at life. I was a wandering nomad after she kicked me out. I barely survived the pregnancy.

Mabel. I was inside Miss Mabel's head, listening to her thoughts, her memories, her wounds. I tried to leave the awful place, frightened beyond comprehension, but as I felt no real body, I could do nothing. The pain in the black space loomed so great it pressed upon me with dizzying power.

I loved your father, you know. Loved him with all my heart. Then he left us. He left me pregnant and poor, and I had no choice. I had to give you to May.

She left me . . .

The agony of the blackness pulsed and throbbed, sometimes humming, sometimes shrieking, until I couldn't tell pain from pleasure. Then pain was pleasure, and I was sinking into it. Crimson, sadness, despair. They all surrounded me, became me. I didn't know my own name. All I knew was the pain, and the endless voice inside.

She left me.

He left us.

You'll never be anything, Mabel. You may have looks, but that's it. Your stubbornness is annoying and pathetic. I'd feel bad for you except you don't deserve it. Get out of my sight. You're a greater disappointment than your mother.

She left me.

The alternating voices didn't make sense at first, but I had no choice but to listen. I couldn't leave. They replayed and replayed until I began to understand, until I began to see that the pain I swam in, that encompassed me, was connected to those soft whispers.

You'll never be anything. I'll achieve my means through Evelyn because you're worthless.

Just like your mother.

I love you, Mabel, but it makes me weak. I hope one day you'll see past my weakness. That's all love is. You'd be best not to love another soul, you know, than suffer the way I do. I suffer, but still I love you. It's the strangest feeling.

She left me.

A new feeling arose. Strong, fresh, powerful. With the new emotion, I banished the suffocating pain. I hated those voices. I hated what they said, what they didn't say. I hated their words, their tone, their secret lies. I curled into the enmity, hiding there because it felt safe. The more I sank into it, the more relief I felt. The pain still lingered, but at least it didn't see me. The darkness of my loathing hid me. It buffeted me. It made the whispers stop until only one remained, like a pulse that kept me strong.

She left me.

Just as I forgot that I existed apart from the pain, that the agony had nothing to do with my existence, a rending came. A shot of fire. Tearing, shrieking, panic, and madness. I'd existed an eternity in that darkness, so the strange sensation of having a body again came with tingles and shock and a gasp of air. A burst of light pulled me from the tendrils of pain and shoved me back into my own mind again.

I saw a flicker of light, heard Isadora's voice, and blacked out.

The not-so-subtle shock of a hand slapping my face repeatedly stung my cheek. I welcomed the sensation, for it was superficial pain. It was mortality. It had nothing to do with the bone-deep weariness of the eternal suffering I'd just escaped. No blackness, no suffocating darkness and evil.

Just friendly, smarting pain.

"Wake up you daft idiot! We don't have time for this!"

The rough sound of Sanna's voice accompanied each slap. I groggily opened my eyes, trying to fight her off with a weak wave of my hand.

"S-stop," I whispered. "Stop!"

"Finally!"

I opened my blurry eyes to find myself back in the wet, black cave. A fresh pile of sand lay in the midst of it. No Miss Mabel. No Isadora.

"No!" I screamed, sitting upright. "No!"

"Stop it!" Sanna slapped me again, this time so hard I fell back into the cave wall with a splash. Water surrounded my body up to my waist, lapping against me in salty waves. "Wake up! We have to go!"

I put a hand to my head and forced myself to concentrate. My eyes swam. The room spun. Focusing on the rough edges of the stone wall and the tang of salt in my mouth reoriented me away from the whispers that still taunted my mind.

She left me.

"Miss Mabel," I said, pressing a hand to my flushed face. "She—"

"I know." Sanna grabbed me by the arm and hauled me to my feet.

"We have to get out of here before she comes back for you. Isadora transported her back to the Western Network before Mabel could take you with them. Let's go or you're dead, because I'm not going to wait around to save you!"

I stumbled with a cry of pain, the same pain that had racked Miss Mabel's mind with constant torment. I couldn't pull away from it so fast. Death would surely be more comfortable.

She left me.

"Let me go!" I cried, unable to bear the touch. "Let me go!"

Sanna obeyed immediately, and I fell to my knees. My whole body ached, right down to my fingernails and eyelids. A dull *thud* moved through my head with even, relentless force. The darkness still clung to my memories.

She left me.

"Jikes, girl. You're a sopping wet disaster. Why does Isadora always leave me with the mess? Can't she deal with it once or twice?"

"Isadora. Where is she?"

"I already told you. She's gone with Mabel to the West so I can get you home safe. Can you walk?"

"I—I don't know."

"Well figure it out!" Sanna snapped. "The tide is coming in, and you're in no shape to transport. If we wait any longer we won't get back out. I'm not going to drown for you, that's for sure. And you can bet the blue isn't going to come in here."

She shoved me forward. I stumbled into the waist-high cave water. She was right, I had no presence of mind to do magic. The darkness and pain and confusion wrapped me in a spiderweb of uncertainty and fog.

Saltwater rubbed against the raw flesh of my blistered skin. It kept me awake, kept the darkness around the edges of my vision at bay, so I dragged my arms through the frigid water with every forward movement. Pain. More pain. After sharing Miss Mabel's mind, I felt like I had an infinite tolerance for suffering. Hadn't I already lived an eternity in torment?

Slowly I crept into the darkness. It seemed as if I only moved an inch at a time. My breaths came in long gasps. Sand changed to rock.

I grappled over the sharp points, crying out with every stab, every painful jab of their weatherworn faces.

"Sanna." My legs buckled. Spots moved across my vision. "I-I can't."

"Go!" she yelled. Water covered my head when I stepped off an outcropping. A wave of weakness overcame me, and I paddled with pathetic bats of my hand for the surface. A shot of magic slammed into my back, propelling me through the water. Suddenly I was coughing on the beach, the sand at my back and a sky of bright stars above me. The air was clear and calm here. No evil. No Miss Mabel.

I saw a glimmer and a flash of a bright blue wing and collapsed onto the sandy beach.

Safety

The next hour or so passed in snatches of a velvet sky and stars. I felt the warmth of the blue dragon's scales beneath me. Sanna's mumbling voice. Occasionally I could open my eyes just enough to see the familiar treetops of Letum Wood below. In the background, the dull pulse of Miss Mabel's hatred beat.

She left me.

I passed out just when Chatham Castle came into view through a haze of smoke lingering above Chatham City. I woke up screaming.

A firm hand grabbed my flailing wrists and pinned them to my sides. My eyes flew open to stare at a familiar ceiling marked by dark stones and a thick wooden beam. Beneath my other hand lay a soft, velvety texture. My racing heart slowed. Our apartment at Chatham Castle. I lay on my back on the divan. Reeves crouched next to me, bottles of Stella's healing oils littering the table. I pressed my palm to my forehead to find a bandage covering my arm.

Safety.

"You're quite safe now, Miss Bianca." Reeves' face swam into my blurry vision. I stared at him in disbelief. Was this finally real? Not another nightmare? I feared Angelina would spring from the shadows before I remembered she was gone. Disintegrated.

"Reeves?"

"Are you in pain, Miss?"

I blinked, taking a mental inventory of my body. Pain, my new friend. Yes. I hurt everywhere. I straightened but instantly regretted it when my tired body protested, feeling like I'd swum through a pool of metal. Reeves put a hand behind my shoulders and helped me sit up.

"How did I get back?" I asked, snatches of my memory returning. The answer came from the other side of the room.

"The blue," Sanna said in her raspy voice. "We flew you back."

"Isadora?"

"Gone." Sanna sat near the hearth, hunched over. Her silver flask glowed, reflecting the light of the fire when she tossed back a swig.

"Papa? Where is he? Did he make it?"

Marten stepped out of the shadows, a worried expression on his face as he sat next to me on the edge of the divan. He motioned to Papa's room. "Stella is in with him now. He's very injured and very angry."

"But he's alive?"

Marten smiled softly and patted my hand. His strained eyes seemed almost frightened. "Yes, of course he's alive. And it's good to see that you are too. You gave us . . . quite a scare."

"Bianca?"

A deep, raspy voice caught my attention. Papa stood in the doorway to his room. He looked gaunt, with one eye still swollen closed, and his arm wrapped in a sling. He leaned to one side, as if both feet couldn't bear all his weight.

"Derek!" Stella admonished from behind him. "Derek, you must lay back down!"

He ignored her and limped forward. Marten stood, giving my shoulder one last affectionate squeeze.

"You're alive," said Papa.

"Like you could rule the Central Network without me," I whispered, forcing a faltering, teary smile.

A strangled sound burst from his throat when he sank to the couch next to me and pulled me in his arms. A tear fell from his cheek. He ran a hand over my head, the hair still matted with blood, and held me so tight with his good arm I could barely breathe. I closed my eyes, inhaled his woodsy smell, and let the past few days melt away.

"I'm so sorry! Papa, I'm so sorry!"

"No, B. The fault is mine. In trying to protect you, I nearly forgot everything else important. I'm so sorry, girl."

Papa was alive. Against all odds we'd saved him and destroyed

Angelina. I sank into him, ready to sleep for days. The relief was overpowering. A knock sounded on the door before it swung open. Tiberius swaggered into the room, beard thin and patchy. His once full face now drooped with long lines and loose skin.

"Tiberius." I pulled away from Papa. "Is everything all right? Chatham City? The West Guards? The Southern Covens? What's happening? What time is it?"

The words tumbled off my lips so fast they jumbled together.

"The Central Network is fine. Well, as fine as it can be, I suppose. Calm down, reckless girl. Who are you anyway? Thinking you're a man trying to save the world?" he snapped, but his gaze softened with a grudging admission. "Well . . . you did do damn good tonight getting our High Priest back."

You don't even know the horrible thing I've done.

"What happened?" Papa asked, putting a comforting hand on the back of my neck the way he used to. He searched my eyes. "Tell me why Isadora is with Mabel. How did you get me out of there? Why did you stay behind with Angelina?"

The burning pain I'd endured shot through my arms again. Like an echo, Miss Mabel's haunted words bounced off the inner parts of my skull.

She left me.

"I don't know why Isadora is with Mabel. It has something to do with Mabel's plans or saving me or . . . I . . . I wasn't really conscious for that part. I made a deal with Miss Mabel to have her transport you back and . . ."

I stumbled to a stop, tears filling my weary eyes. I wanted to sleep. I wanted to forget the agony of Miss Mabel's mind. "Do I have to tell you everything now?"

"Yes," Papa said, tucking a strand of hair away from my face. "We need to know now."

Zane shuffled out of the shadows where he'd been standing, though I hadn't seen him. Stella sat on a chair near Marten. They all stared at me, waiting.

A cup of tea rose from the tray and hovered in front of me. I glanced up to find Reeves nod from the corner. "A special tonic to help you, Miss Bianca," he drawled. I gave him a half-hearted smile and accepted the cup. To my surprise, the tea did help. A wave of calm passed through me at once, and I allowed it to soothe my aching insides. Tiberius sat down and leaned his forearms on his knees.

With the tea to help, I did explain. I recounted every single thing I could remember, from when Angelina pulled me into the nightmare, to Isadora's cottage, to Angelina's defeat, but I left out the part when I glimpsed Miss Mabel's mind. I still hadn't processed it myself and didn't know if I could bear to live through it again.

They listened with quiet, stoic attention. The skin behind my left ear burned every time I mentioned the Almorran magic, and I idly put a hand to it to make it stop. Once I finished, Papa leaned back in his chair and stared at the ceiling. Tiberius grunted. Sanna took another drink from her flask, and Zane kept his deadpan gaze on the floor.

"Did I ruin everything?" I asked, trembling. "Have I brought destruction down on all of Antebellum by releasing Miss Mabel?"

I'd been afraid to ask it, afraid to even say the words, but they poured out in terrified hysteria.

"No," Sanna said, tossing her empty flask onto the table.

"But your sister—"

"Knew what she was doing. She knew all along what was going to happen. How do you think I knew where to be with the blue, eh?"

Sanna's declaration still didn't comfort me because it didn't change the fact that Isadora was with the most dangerous, powerful witch in the world and likely wouldn't make it back alive. Losing Isadora would cripple our ability to predict the West Guards.

"And Chatham City?" I asked.

"The Protectors and the gypsies managed to keep the Factios from taking over, thanks to Leda," Stella said with a smile. "She saved the city yet again."

"Leda?"

"She put her foresight to good use. Without her, we wouldn't have been able to keep up with the Almorran magic. She predicted many attacks, which we were then able to preempt."

"She'll be impossible to live with after this."

Marten laughed under his breath. "I believe she's earned her place as an Assistant somewhere. Maybe we should give her your job, Bianca."

I smirked but didn't take the bait.

"It wasn't until a few hours ago that the tide turned in our favor," Zane said. "We were just about to lose everything when the Factios seemed to fall apart."

I swallowed. "When Angelina died. It's likely she was controlling them with Almorran magic, giving them power and strength. Without her, all of that would have left them."

"The West Guards pushed halfway through the Western Covens before the Guardians intercepted them. We drove them back, then held them a short distance from the Borderlands," Tiberius said with an annoyed huff. "Half-naked savages. You come into my Network?" he bellowed at the wall, fist raised.

"The Southern Network attacked, but without the West Guards to help, we held them at bay with magic without too much loss in the Southern Covens," Stella said, anticipating my next question. She put a hand on my shoulder, and warmth passed through my body.

"So all is not lost?"

"Not yet," Papa concluded grimly. "Not yet."

Stella looked at Zane, Tiberius, Marten, and Sanna as she rose. "I think it's time we give the two of you a minute to catch your breaths. The Network is under control for now. Derek, you need to sleep. I'll take over from here."

He grunted. "Fine."

Stella squeezed my shoulder. "Thank you, Bianca," she whispered. "For being so brave. Make sure he takes the potion on the table, will you?"

"If I don't, Reeves will," I said, taking another sip of the tea he'd provided. Reeves straightened with pride.

They shuffled out slowly, and Reeves moved into his own quarters. In their absence, only the silence of the apartment remained.

"I'm sorry about the situation with Merrick," Papa said, rubbing his good hand over his stubbled chin. "After watching you fight Mabel last summer, I couldn't handle the thought of you growing up. Of losing you."

"Losing me to Merrick?" I asked.

He met my eyes. "To Merrick."

"And now?" I asked, my heart speeding up to double time. "What do you think now?"

Papa scowled. "I think I don't like the idea of any witch trying to win my daughter's affections. But if it has to happen eventually, you can't do any better than Merrick. Are you sure you want to court a Protector?"

I grinned ruefully. "Are you sure you're not just afraid that Merrick is too much like you?"

"Oh, he's definitely too much like me."

I squeezed his good hand. "Which is just what I want. Thank you, Papa, for understanding. Where is Merrick now?"

Papa's expression darkened. "I tried to send him on a special mission. Not to get rid of him, although there is that, but because he's the only one that could do it."

His words gave me pause. Merrick the only one? He was the youngest Protector. The least experienced. What kind of mission could it have been? "What do you mean you *tried* to send him on a mission?"

"He wouldn't go until he knew you were safe."

I smiled. "Really?"

Papa shoved my face gently with the palm of his good hand. "Don't start getting all girly and romantic on me now. But, yes, really. He waited until you showed up with Sanna, then he left. He left this for you."

He extracted a letter from his vest. I took it with an acute feeling of anticipation and disappointment, wanting nothing more than to see Merrick's bright green eyes. I set the letter aside to read in private.

"What now, Papa? What happens to the Central Network now?"

"Now?" He brushed a strand of hair away from my eyes. "Now we fight Mabel. We try to save Isadora before it's too late."

"How will we know it's too late?"

"Her life is tied to Sanna's. If Sanna dies, Isadora has as well."

"How are you going to save her?"

He sighed and leaned his head back on the divan. "If we can save her? I don't know."

Exhausted, I leaned back against the divan and closed my eyes. All the rest of it didn't matter, not right then. Not for a while.

Because Papa was alive and so was I.

B,

I'm glad you're alive, little troublemaker. Save time for a run when I return.

—M

Friends Forever

Tulips decorated every part of the field outside Sanna's cottage. I had taken Leda—with much coaxing—into Letum Wood to gather summer flowers for Michelle's hand fasting early in the morning on the first day of the first month of summer. Priscilla and Camille had transformed the summer flowers into a variegated display of tulips, filling the field outside Sanna's house with fresh, vibrant colors. Camille had decorated the little bridge over the brook with large yellow bows for the ceremony, tucking bouquets of flowers around them.

"A perfect way to celebrate the first day of summer," Camille said, inhaling the sweet scent with a sigh. "Tulips and a hand fasting ceremony. You can tell which tulips Priscilla did because they actually smell like tulips. I'm still not that talented at transformation."

"They're lovely, Camille," I said, touching the delicate skin of a petal. "I'm very proud of you."

Camille smiled. "Thanks."

The difficult experiences she'd endured in the past year had served Camille well; she'd lost some of her frantic, panicked energy. It almost made me want the other Camille back, but when I remembered all the mindless prattling, I banned the thought immediately.

"I'm going to go check on Michelle," she said with a contented sigh, glancing at her work. "I'll see you after the hand fasting."

"Here," Leda said, nudging me to the left. "Rupert saved us the last two seats. Jikes, this is a full ceremony."

We settled into the back row. Shadows and shapes moved in the distant forest, accompanied by the occasional crash of a sapling falling or snort of smoke. Several visitors kept worried eyes on the forest, though we couldn't actually see the dragons.

"What do you think?" Leda asked, leaning over in a whisper. She looked politically perfect with her hair in a bun and a modest dress that stretched all the way to her wrists. "Is Nicolas going to pass out?"

Nicolas fidgeted at the front, shifting his weight from foot to foot, tugging at a tight collar that nearly choked him. The rest of the crowd murmured while waiting for Michelle to appear out of Sanna's cottage. Because she had no mother to help her get ready, Camille and Priscilla saw to her ministrations inside.

I laughed. "If he sweats any more, he's going to pass out from dehydration."

Leda smirked and leaned back in her seat. Rupert sat at her side, hands as twitchy as a spider leg. I held my breath when he reached over and pressed his hand on top of Leda's. She froze, eyes wide. I stared at their hands, and then her face, in disbelief. Even Rupert seemed to be holding his breath. After an interminable ten seconds, she relaxed but didn't pull away. Rupert let out a long breath, the corner of his mouth curling up.

"Don't read into it," she hissed to me. "He's just a friend."

I rolled my eyes. "Give him some hope, Leda. Look how hard he's worked to get your favor. He's been fighting for you for almost a year."

Leda eyed me in suspicion. "How come you sound so okay with it? I thought you didn't want any of us to grow up."

"I don't." I fidgeted with the elbow-length sleeve of my olive green dress. "I don't want anything to change. At least, I didn't for a long time."

"Well, here you are at Michelle's hand fasting ceremony, which means you must be okay with it at least a little."

Things must move on, I thought. *Or else I'll become just like Miss Mabel.*

"Miss Mabel held onto the past. She never really let it go, did she? Which means she was afraid to move forward. I don't want to be like her."

Leda quirked an eyebrow. "There are a lot of reasons you won't be like her. The least of which is the fact that you aren't trying to murder the entire world."

I laughed, grateful for a moment of levity to break up the sudden string of dark thoughts in my mind. I still hadn't told my friends about my encounter with Miss Mabel's mind. It felt too personal to share, too raw to make real. The only witch I felt I could really tell was Merrick, and he still wasn't back from his mission. How could I explain a pain of such depth to anyone who hadn't experienced it? Could such an agony be overstated?

Looking back, it felt as if seeing that glimpse of Miss Mabel's mind meant everything had changed, and yet nothing had changed, really.

"Don't worry, Bianca," Leda said, misinterpreting the sudden darkness in my expression. "I understand your hesitation about all these changes. I've felt it myself. But just because we're moving on doesn't mean we're moving apart. Camille will still be at the castle until she graduates. Michelle won't be very far away and still plans on working in the kitchens twice a week. You and I are both stuck at Chatham Castle for now. Me? Forever. You? Until you find some other heathen job to work at for the rest of your life."

I grinned. It was so good to have her condescension again that I wouldn't have minded if she told me I looked like a toad. Besides, she was right. Moving on wasn't the same as moving apart.

Rupert cleared his throat before I came up with a proper retort and motioned to the small stage Nicolas stood on. A few quieting *hisses* moved through the crowd, and a respectful silence followed as the hand fasting began.

Nicolas's father, a High Witch for an obscure village in the Eastern Covens, hand fasted them. He stood as tall and thick as his son with the same shy, sweet disposition. When he stood on the platform, the crowd rose. Michelle appeared at the end of the walkway that stretched between the chairs. She faced Nicolas with a sparkling smile and started a slow walk down the aisle.

Instead of the elaborate gown Camille had chattered about making for weeks, Michelle chose a simple dress of pale yellow linen. She beamed every moment, her small eyes shining with happy tears when she looked out at the gathered crowd. Cousin Luke, her father, her brothers, and half her old town had turned up, not to mention the entire Chatham Castle kitchen staff. Despite the glimmer of pain that crossed her face whenever she glanced at her family and noticed her missing brother, she'd never looked more beautiful.

"It's wonderful, isn't it?" Rupert asked Leda and me with a content little smile that spread his red goatee into a thin line. "Ta see something so good happen in a time so dark."

"Doesn't mean the darkness has left," Leda muttered. I smirked and studied his response, but Rupert didn't seem bothered by her callous reply. In fact, he didn't even try to change his opinion to suit her, the way I expected.

"No, but for a moment, it seems like life is still going on," he said.

Perhaps he's not as spineless as I thought, I mused, wondering if there was just a slender chance that Rupert could eventually win Leda over. She'd already removed her hand from his, but any physical contact with Leda was a win.

"Perhaps in one small regard it feels as if life continues," Leda said with a kinder tone. "For us, anyway. Michelle's just about to strap herself down into the unending nightmare of marriage and babies."

Rupert's eyes flashed with disappointment. Ah, not *so* invincible to her charms. I felt a moment of pity for him. Courting Leda would be like trying to cuddle a porcupine. One had to have strong motivation to complete the deed.

Nicolas's father raised his hand as Michelle arrived, sliding her hand into Nicolas's awaiting grip.

"Gentle witches," he called. "Let us begin the ceremony to hand fast my son to his beautiful bride, Michelle. I am most proud to be part of this day. First we shall observe a moment of silence for those of us who have given all to our Network, and who still fight for our protection and safety."

A sober silence stretched over the crowd. No matter how bright things seemed to be here, the world still waged war. Perhaps more than we ever had since the last rise of the Almorran powers.

"Any word from Merrick?" Leda asked under her breath. My heart tugged.

"Not yet."

"Do you miss him?"

I hesitated. "Yes, I do."

The ceremony began.

When Michelle echoed Nicolas's own sentiments by saying, "My wish is to be one with Nicolas," Camille, who sat on the front row with Brecken, burst into tears and had to use Priscilla's handkerchief. Leda snorted. I grinned.

"You are now hand fasted together for as long as the love between you shall last," the High Witch declared. "Be happy and prosper together. So mote it be."

When Michelle and Nicolas sealed the ceremony with a kiss, Camille burst into a fresh round of tears, Leda tilted her head back and laughed, and I applauded and whistled in a most inappropriate fashion. Michelle blushed, grinning at us from the platform.

Maybe we weren't destined to live in the Witchery together for the rest of our lives, but we were meant to be friends forever. And we would.

I knew we would.

Epilogue

I stopped halfway through the doorway to my bedroom, still laughing over a joke Papa had told me. My mirth ceased immediately, interrupted by a gasp of surprise that stuck in my throat.

A familiar, exquisite rug lay surreptitiously on the ground, as if it had always been there.

The Volare.

A rolled-up parchment lay on top. I closed the door behind me and picked up the parchment without touching the intricate weave of the rug.

Dear Witch Who Finds This Note,

This rug is a Volare.

It was formed in the hot sands of the Western Network during the Time of the Weaver. Its roots lie deep in my heart. Creating it was no easy process. The magic the Volare works by is deep, born of love and sacrifice and my own blood. As its original weaver, I've enchanted this note to appear to the new owner of the Volare, should it find itself without an heir to pass on to. In such a case as this, the Volare chooses its next owner.

The magic is loyal; it will serve you well. Do not take this gift lightly. Be good to it, and it shall be good to you. In this way my legacy shall live on.

Wishing you many happy flights under the stars,

Tuffer, the Weaver of Magic

Epilogue

I folded the note in my palm, looked at the Volare, and commanded it to rise. It sprang from the floor and hovered at my waist.

I tilted my head back and laughed.

About the Author

Magic captivated me the moment I held my first book. I lived many lives as I scoured story after story. Now, I write fantasy books so you can seize the light, hold magic in your fingertips, and forget the shadows of real life to live your wildest adventure.

Lightning Source UK Ltd.
Milton Keynes UK
UKHW011030260720
367199UK00001B/154